PRAISE FOR
FOOL ME TWICE

"A warning: don't start reading *Fool Me Twice* at bedtime unless your reading mantra is 'Just one more chapter . . . just one more chapter!'" —*New York Journal of Books*

"Watching Wolfe plan and execute his daring caper is pure pleasure." —Adam Woog, *The Seattle Times*

"This frequently funny, always inventive, often quite dark thriller will delight fans of Lindsay's bestselling Dexter series and the hit TV show it inspired." —*BookPage*

"Readers looking for a page-turner won't be disappointed." —*Publishers Weekly*

"A rousing caper novel." —*Booklist*

"A well-written, complex, tension-filled yarn." —Bruce DeSilva, Associated Press

"A nearly breathless rush involving perhaps the most ingenious heist ever conceived . . . some of the most fun I had reading this entire year. As much as I want Jeff Lindsay to resurrect Dexter Morgan, I just love Riley Wolfe and cannot wait to spend more time with him. For those readers who are about to pick up *Fool Me Twice*, I envy the thrill ride you will be going on!" —*Bookreporter*

ALSO BY JEFF LINDSAY

The Riley Wolfe Series

JUST WATCH ME

The Dexter Series

DARKLY DREAMING DEXTER

DEARLY DEVOTED DEXTER

DEXTER IN THE DARK

DEXTER BY DESIGN

DEXTER IS DELICIOUS

DOUBLE DEXTER

DEXTER'S FINAL CUT

DEXTER IS DEAD

FOOL ME TWICE

A NOVEL

JEFF LINDSAY

DUTTON

DUTTON

An imprint of Penguin Random House LLC
penguinrandomhouse.com

Previously published as a Dutton hardcover in December 2020

First Dutton premium mass market printing: December 2021

Copyright © 2020 by Jeff Lindsay

DUTTON and the D colophon are registered trademarks of
Penguin Random House LLC.

ISBN: 9780593186381

Printed in the United States of America
1 3 5 7 9 10 8 6 4 2

For Hilary. And for Bear, Pookie, and Tink,
with all my love.

PART 1

CHAPTER 1

Arkady Kuznetsov was tired. It had been a long day on the job, a day with extra strain beyond the usual annoyance of dealing with tourists. He didn't like tourists. But he had learned to put up with them. He had to. Thousands of them came to St. Petersburg to see the art treasures here at the Hermitage Museum. None of them spoke Russian, of course. Most of them just spoke their own language louder, as if shouting would make foreign words turn themselves into Russian. Arkady was polite to all of them, no matter how loud and stupid. It was part of his job. But a busy day left him very tired.

Not often as tired as he was right now. There had of course been the usual tourists. It was summer, the season when they came here in great flocks from all over the world. But today there was even more to deal with than annoying foreign visitors. Today there had been a "credible threat"—that's what his supervisor called it— that someone would try to steal one of the paintings Arkady and his colleagues spent their days guarding. Someone would try to steal a Van Gogh called *Ladies of Arles*. Arkady could not imagine why. He didn't like that painting. To him it looked smeared. He preferred a picture to look like a *picture*. It should look like what it was, not all scrambled like this one. But that didn't matter. The important thing was that somebody meant to take it—take it from the Hermitage, while he was watching it! As a matter of national and professional pride, Arkady would not let that happen.

So he answered the usual shouted and pantomimed questions as he stood at the door to Room 413, General Staff Building. And on top of that, he had added an extra layer of vigilance. It was a skill he had acquired in his twenty years in the Army, a very high percentage of it spent on guard duty. He had never been strong or smart or skillful enough for anything but regular infantry, and it had taken him fifteen years to rise to the rank of corporal. But he knew how to stand watch and stay alert. And when he had retired six years ago, his service had been just the right ticket to land him this comfortable job, security guard at the Hermitage in St. Petersburg.

But Arkady was feeling his years, and to be honest, he had put on a few pounds since leaving the Army. His back hurt, and his feet were killing him. The flow of ordinary tourists had not slowed down at all. If anything, there were more of the annoying kind today than usual.

Like this one now, the fat Frenchman, standing in his face and lecturing. He had approached Arkady in a reasonable way. The man smelled of garlic and stale wine. His appearance was messy, too. He wore a rumpled off-white suit, which did not hide the bulge of his belly. And it accented the man's shaggy gray hair and disordered beard. Still, for a Frenchman, he had been polite at first, pointing to himself and loudly mouthing his name, Hervé Thierry. That was all Arkady understood. Arkady spoke no more than a dozen words of French. But he made the mistake of answering, "Plaisir," which he thought was the right thing to say. Mr. Thierry took this as a sign and had immediately asked a series of questions in rapid French.

Arkady could not stop the flow and Mr. Thierry became more heated when no answers came. His voice got louder, and his fat, sweaty face got sweatier and redder, and that did not increase Arkady's understanding of the man's pointed speech at all—which of course increased Mr. Thierry's frustration. He seemed to grow larger and redder all the time. He began to gesture at the paintings, and the word "France" came with frequency. Arkady figured that it had become a matter of national interest for Mr. Thierry. Probably because most of the paintings here were by French artists or had been taken from collectors who had taken them from France.

Finally, just when Arkady had started to think he

would have to encourage the Frenchman to move along, Mr. Thierry raised an index finger in Arkady's face, as if to scold him. For a moment, Arkady thought he saw a puff of smoke.

When they woke him much later, that was all Arkady remembered.

Ludmila Ukhtomsky was hungover. This was not truly an unusual condition for her, nor for many in her social circle. Normally a few cups of tea would set her right. Not today. She was halfway through her eighth cup of strong black tea for the day, and her head still ached. The rhythmic pounding in her skull still thumped in tandem with her heartbeat, and she had not yet decided if she wanted to live another day.

And then the alarm began to ring.

For a moment Ludmila thought it was another symptom of her hangover. She clutched at her temples, willing the sound to go away. But it didn't, and then the call came from the security station. A guard was on the floor, unresponsive, either unconscious or dead. That did not matter to Ludmila. What mattered was the location—Room 413. As an assistant curator, she was of course aware that a threat had been made to one of the paintings in that room. She swallowed her rising bile, put her tea on the desk, and hurried out of her office.

When she got to Room 413, the alarm was still ringing, an unreasonably loud and discordant sound.

Ludmila pushed through the crowd of gawkers in the doorway and peered anxiously into the room. She was relieved to see that the Van Gogh was still on the wall where it belonged. A ring of guards spread across the room, watching doors and windows. Ludmila turned her attention to the men at the doorway standing above the body of the fallen guard. One of them was Security Chief Loskutnikhov.

"He appears to be merely unconscious," the chief told her, nodding at the man on the floor.

"Unconscious? In what sense of the word?" she asked. She was aware that her words were phrased oddly, but the alarm made thought nearly impossible.

At least her meaning seemed clear to Chief Loskutnikhov. He shrugged and said, "It is my guess that he was drugged."

"But the painting is untouched?"

"It appears to be," Loskutnikhov said. "Certainly it is still in its place and has suffered no apparent harm."

"Then can it—Why is—Damn it, Chief, can we not turn off the *chertovskiy* alarm?"

Loskutnikhov raised an eyebrow fractionally. He seemed amused at her irritation, as if he knew she was hungover and he himself was above such things. "Of course," he said. He removed the radio from his belt and spoke into it. "This is Loskutnikhov. Turn off the alarm for Room 413." There was a pause, and then a reply crackled from the radio. Ludmila couldn't hear the words, and the chief seemed uncertain, too. "Say again?" he demanded. The reply came again.

The chief frowned but didn't speak. Then he looked at Ludmila. "They say the alarm is off," he said.

"But it isn't off—I can still hear it!" Ludmila said.

"Yes," Loskutnikhov said. "But not for this room."

It did not take long to trace the second alarm. The signal was coming from just below them, in Room 302. When Ludmila and Chief Loskutnikhov arrived, two security guards already stood in the doorway, holding back the curious tourists. One of the guards stepped forward. "Chief," he said. He motioned at a dark-haired young woman, who stepped up beside him. "This is Anna Sokolov. A tour guide."

Chief Loskutnikhov raised an eyebrow. "Fascinating. Is there more?"

Flustered, the guard cleared his throat. "Yes, of course. Anna is a witness."

"Ah," Loskutnikhov said. "And what exactly did you witness, miss?"

"I was bringing my group in," she said. "I stopped in the doorway—to introduce the exhibits in this room? And I heard a crash?"

Loskutnikhov nodded encouragingly. "And then?" he said.

"I look in. And there is a man—he has broken open the window. And he leaps out the window!"

Loskutnikhov frowned. "Surely he has a rope in hand? Or does he simply fall to his death?"

"No, not at all—he goes up!" she said.

"Up," Loskutnikhov said. "You are certain?"

"I saw his feet disappear—at the top of the window. And then he was gone," Anna said. "Gone *up*."

"Thank you, miss," Loskutnikhov said. He stepped around her and into Room 302, toward the window, where a drape was blowing in the breeze. He could smell the salt air—the Neva River, flowing to the nearby Baltic, was very close, just across the square and on the other side of the Winter Palace.

"Chief!" Ludmila called. "I need to see if anything is missing or damaged."

"Yes, of course," the chief said, and Ludmila scurried past him and into the room.

Chief Loskutnikhov followed in her wake. But halfway to the now-open window he paused. A pile of rumpled clothing lay scattered on the floor. It was a dingy, off-white color but seemed to be of decent make. "What is this?" Loskutnikhov said over his shoulder.

One of the guards hurried to his side. "It is a suit, Chief," he said. "It was here when we arrived—we have not touched it."

"Hmp," Loskutnikhov muttered. He nudged the clothing with his foot, revealing some kind of padding buried in the heap, the kind an actor might wear to look fatter. The surveillance cameras would reveal how it had come to be there, but he was quite sure what it meant. "A disguise," he said. He shook his head and continued on to the window.

There was nothing to see there. Large shards of glass littered the floor below it, but the window frame itself was free of them. Someone could easily have made an exit here, without risk of a cut from the broken glass. But then what? Loskutnikhov stuck his head out. He looked down. No broken body lay beneath the window. Only the usual colorful summer crowd moving across the Palace Square.

He looked up. There was nothing to see there, either. There were no hanging ropes, no sign of anything that might aid someone climbing to the roof. If the man had truly gone up, as the tour guide claimed, he had to be part spider.

"Chief!" Ludmila called from inside the room. He turned and saw her standing beside an empty display case, a look of shock on her face. "It is gone," she said. "The Rothschild Fabergé Egg is gone."

CHAPTER

2

I don't get political. I've got enough problems, and honestly? Politics is just too dirty, mean, and corrupt. Give me nice, clean thievery with an occasional hit on some overprivileged asshole who gets in my way. It's a whole lot more honest, even the hit. Which is mostly on the kind of asshat who thinks a pile of inherited money makes him immune to the shit the rest of us have to slog through every day. I admit it, I like showing them just how wrong they are. And that's me, anyhow—Riley Hood. Steal from the rotten rich and give to the formerly poor, meaning Me. Politics doesn't fit in that picture, and so it doesn't matter.

But every now and then something breaks through my wall of I-don't-give-a-shit and gets my attention. Like recently; I usually don't watch the news, but when the level of public hysteria starts to hit all the high notes for a long enough time so it's all anybody is talking about, I figure I better tune in. It could mean money—losing it—if I don't know what's up, or making some if I can figure an angle.

So when the noise on something specific hits a certain level of manic frenzy, I pay attention. I mean, I walk into a bakery and hear the same shit I heard at the hardware store. I go to the cleaner's and they're talking the same smack I heard at the barber's. If every jukebox is playing the same song everywhere I go, I have to figure it's a number one hit and I need to learn the words.

And that's what had happened for the past six months. Everywhere I went, same angry crap. Everybody talking, arguing, even fighting about the same thing.

So I paid attention, I did a little research, and let's just say I was pissed off at Russia right now. If you know me at all, you know I'm a firm believer in the old saying—I think it's from Shakespeare? Maybe the Bible? It's the one that says, "Don't get mad. Get even."

Since I was bored anyway, I went to St. Petersburg, and I got even. With an absolute eye-knocker of an old Russian bauble. They were proud of it, too—like on the national-treasure level—which made it even more ideal. And to be honest, a lot more fun. *Po'shyol 'na hui,* Ivan. Fuck you.

I spent a week coming up with a plan. It looked like a very nice scheme, practically a cakewalk all the way through. I even had a private buyer lined up, which sweetened the deal. I usually take short money and sell back to the insurance company. It's safer, more certain, and for me it's not about the money—I mean, as long as there's enough to keep me in beans and beer. But this time, if I sold the egg to the insurance company, that meant the Russians would get it back, and like I said, I was pissed off at them. I wanted to sting them, make them *lose* their pretty little treasure.

So I had a private buyer, and I'll just say that if it had been about the money, this guy would have been my new best friend. It's amazing how much somebody will pay for one of those eggs. I mean, sure, they're gorgeous, covered with jewels, have a cool history, all that. And let's face it, a true collector gets a hard-on when he has something that special—especially when his other collector buddies can never have it.

This guy was a true collector. What he was paying me was enough to buy two of these Fabergé eggs at auction. And I barely worked up a sweat. It went like a Swiss watch all the way through, which was only a little ironic, since this particular Fabergé egg was partly a clock. Anyway, it was all good. That worried me a little; when things go well, that always means something really bad is sneaking up behind you. But it kept unrolling perfectly, so I took a deep breath and shut out the nagging little voice that said something terrible was going to happen.

I should've listened.

No problem at all putting the guard on his ass and setting off the first alarm, which would distract the

Russians and cover the second alarm when I took the egg. It was an old trick, but the Russians went for it. I got the egg and made it up to the roof without a hitch.

So I was feeling pretty good about myself when I slid down from the rooftop of the Winter Palace and out onto the pier that's across the street. I had a boat waiting. It was a forty-footer, built for the hideous weather they get up there in the Baltic. The engines were running, and there was a guy at the wheel, Arvid, who knew his stuff. And I knew him. I'd used him on a couple of jobs before this one. Arvid was Swedish. His father, grandfather, great-grandfather, and who the hell knows how many more great-greats had all been fishermen in the Baltic and North Atlantic. They knew the waters and the weather the way only old-world craftsmen can know their turf. And it turns out that part of the turf when you're a Swedish fisherman can also mean being a smuggler now and then.

Totally understandable. Fishing for a living is very dicey. The fish come and go, the weather works over-time to screw you, and market prices are never in your favor. So for more generations than I can count, Arvid's family had been bringing things across the Baltic without paying a whole lot of attention to technical formalities like import duties and taxes. Wine, brandy, silk, English wool, whatever people wanted and thought they paid too much for. It was all supply and demand, a pure lesson in market economics. And for the last two generations, that meant drugs, too. The money was too good to ignore.

It also made the enforcement get more serious. And that meant Arvid's family boat was fast. It had to be to outrun the assorted national and international patrols. The boat looked like a beat-up old trawler—grease stains, fish blood, nets hanging off the side, old-fashioned round portholes—but Arvid had put a couple of great big brutish diesel engines in it and modified the hull, and he could outrun just about anything the cops had.

Arvid could practically fly if he had to. Which smugglers have to do every now and then. And times being what they were, he didn't mind making a few off the record trips for me. I paid him really well, too—like, two years of fishing income for a couple of days of shut-the-fuck-up-and-drive-the-boat.

I prefer to work alone. It's a whole hell of a lot safer, which counts for a lot. But if I need somebody—like to fly a chopper or whatever—I always pay well. Riley's Fourteenth Law: If you have to have help, pay them too much and promise them more later.

In the past five or six years, Arvid had made a shit-load of money off me, and he figured to make more in the future. And I'm talking early-retirement-in-Tahiti money. I never mind spending too much if it gets the job done right. Arvid did just that. Anytime I needed a boat in that part of the world, he was my go-to guy. He knew what he was doing, which is rare enough. Plus he had always been reliable—and kept his mouth shut—and he always came through for me. So when I got on board his boat and he steered us down the river toward the Baltic, I relaxed.

Stupid. I mean, I *know* that. But in spite of the fact that I really do know better, I kind of trusted Arvid.

Hindsight is always 20/20. But in retrospect, I should have remembered Riley's Eleventh Law: Trust is what you're doing when the knife comes down. Maybe I should have that tattooed on my hand, where I can look at it anytime I'm feeling stupid. In my line of work, stupid is always the lead-in for the fat lady singing. And sure as shit, that's what happened.

Arvid didn't use a knife. And he waited for me to pay him, which shows he had a whole lot more sense than I do. He just counted his cash, looked up with this goofy grin, and pointed a pistol at me. Before I could even say, "What the fuck," he pulled the trigger. I heard a loud *PPFFFUTTT!* and felt something sharp jab into my chest. I took one step toward Arvid—I was definitely going to heave him over the side and let him swim home—and then . . .

Nothing. No lights or music or dreams—just deep, dark nothing.

CHAPTER
3

Until suddenly my eyes opened. My mouth was dry and tasted like ancient sewer. I had a headache, and the bright light coming in through the porthole didn't help. There was no way to know how long I'd been out. I was still on the boat. I didn't smell the usual fish and diesel stink of Arvid's boat, but I could feel the strong and steady *thrum thrum thrum* of the boat's engine and the slow pitch and roll as we plowed through some big waves. So we had to be out in the open sea now. The Baltic is mostly smaller, sloppy chop, but it can roll big when it wants to. It wanted to now, and it did. And it was cold, a lot colder than it should have been for July.

I closed my eyes again. On top of the headache, I was feeling like I might vomit. I don't get seasick, so it had to be because of, of . . . What? I couldn't remember what had happened, and that worried the shit out of me. I had been on Arvid's boat, right? And we were headed out to sea and—

And Arvid shot me.

I opened my eyes. I couldn't see any holes in my shirt. So had I imagined it? I touched my chest and found a tender place. I pulled up my shirt and looked. There was a purple circle on my chest. It had a small red spot in the middle, a puncture, like a bad nurse would leave when she gives you a shot.

So Arvid really did shoot me, but obviously not with a bullet—a dart? Like they use to put animals to sleep? Yeah, had to be. And that explained the headache and nausea, too. Aftereffects of the tranquilizer.

Okay. Arvid knocked me out with a tranquilizer dart. Why?

I frowned. That made my head hurt even more, so I stopped. I mean, I can think without frowning, right? Except at the moment, I couldn't think at all.

I took a big breath to clear my head. That turned out to be a mistake. I barely managed to turn my head to one side and then I was vomiting violently. That lasted for a minute, but when I was done I felt a little better, and my brain seemed to be working a little. Plus, Arvid was going to have some puke to clean up, and that cheered me up. So I put my brain back to work.

Question One: What the fuck was going on?

It seemed like a safe bet that Arvid had shivved me. Why?

Obvious Answer: Money.

Arvid liked money. I mean, who doesn't? I always paid him well. It was supposed to keep him tame. Could somebody pay him more to go wild on me? Sure, why not? It would have to be a lot, but it could be done.

But wait—even with a lot of extra money, Arvid would know he had to stay cool with the deal he made with me. Word gets out, and if it got out that he'd betrayed me, he'd be fucked. Plus, he had to know I would match the offer. If not straight out, then with future work.

So there was another reason, something that would overrule all that shit, and that was an easy guess, too.

Fear. Fear of somebody who was scarier than me and had enough money to throw around that it took the sting out of losing his lucrative side job. And somebody who could combine fear and money would be very tough to turn down.

So, okay; who would do that? Well, that was a little tougher to nail down. There was a long list of people who would part with very big dollars to get their hands on me. And a lot of them had the kind of operational profile you don't put on Facebook.

So now the question was, which one of them? It had to be somebody who had the resources to track me all the way to Russia, find Arvid, and convince him to flip on me. Besides a lot of money, that meant an organization with a lot of high-skill people—and it also meant somebody who could bring a lot of pressure. The kind of pressure that Arvid would believe would change his life—or end it.

Who fit that description? When you make a living like I do, the easy answer would be somebody like Interpol or the FBI. And a very big percentage of my enemies were cops, too. It's only natural. But they didn't work this way, not by getting another crim to boink me with a tranquilizer dart. They would bring a team, surround me, holler through a bullhorn to put my hands up, all that by-the-book bullshit you've seen on TV a million times. And anyway, all their money was in resources like boats, planes, people. Not cash. They couldn't outspend me with Arvid. And they wouldn't trust him to put me out with a dart. No way.

So, not the cops. That still left a pretty healthy number of people who would love to dance at my funeral. But most of them would probably want me killed, not doped. I know it's all over the movies and TV that the bad guy wants to take the hero alive and make him squeal for a long-ass time, and *then* kill him. But it doesn't work that way in real life. Not in the big leagues, where I play. If somebody wants you dead, they do it the quick, no-chances way. That's what my enemies would do. And the same for my business rivals—they'd all pull the trigger with a big smile on their face—the bigger the bullet, the bigger their smile. But knock me out and take me on a long boat ride? I didn't think so.

So, okay; not cops, not enemies, not rivals. Probably

revenge, then. Who did that leave? It was still a long list, but none of the names made sense.

I went all over my life for the past fifteen years, and I dug up a lot of names with reasons to pursue an active dislike of me. None of them really made any more sense than the others. Either they were out of commission— prison, graveyard, like that—or they wouldn't know how to organize something like this.

So finally, I figured, okay. I give up. I'll ask Arvid. He owes me that much. And if he doesn't see it that way, what the hell, the worst he can do is not tell me. So I figured I'd go up on deck and ask him. Or if the cabin door was locked, which seemed pretty likely, I'd pound on it until he came down to talk to me.

I stood up and took a step toward the door. Anyway, I tried to.

It turns out you can't step anywhere when there's a great big fucking chain locked to your ankle with the other end bolted to the hull.

I had been too woozy until now to do anything but lie there. So I hadn't noticed it before. I sure as shit noticed it now. One step and it yanked me straight back. And now my ankle hurt worse than my head.

I reached for the door. Even leaning and stretching as far as I could, I was about four feet away. So I sat back down and checked out the chain. It was a solid professional job. I could probably get it off—if I had an hour and a couple of tools. Which I didn't. So that kind of narrowed down my options. Mostly to sit and wait.

I sat. I waited.

It was around an hour before anything happened. Then I heard footsteps on the deck above my head. They clumped down a flight of stairs to my door. Arvid was coming down at last. I stood up and watched the door swing open. Which it finally did, but—

It wasn't Arvid.

I'd never seen this guy before. Whoever he was, he was big, nasty-looking, and dirty. He had a face like an Army surplus combat boot. It was covered with stubble that wasn't long enough to be a beard but was too long to be anything but who-gives-a-fuck. He had a big hooked nose that looked like it had been broken more than once, and the kind of angry sneer that made you want to break it again. He stood there in the doorway and poured the sneer on me.

"You are awake," he said. A weird high voice and a French accent.

"Not me," I said. "I'm sound asleep."

His face didn't change at all. Like either he didn't understand me or he just didn't give a shit about anything I might say or do. I was pretty sure he understood me.

But he just nodded and said, "Soon we are there."

"Good to know. Where exactly?"

His face twitched into a small smile. It was the kind of smile a psycho gets watching puppies drown. "I will show you," he said.

He stepped forward, and while I was looking for some kind of opening—some way to make a move on him—he launched a kick at my crotch. I barely saw it coming—but I sure as shit felt it.

If you have ever been kicked in the balls, you will know that there's not a whole lot you can do for a couple of minutes. To say it hurts a lot doesn't come close to covering it. So let's just say that I was busy moaning, retching, and wishing I was unconscious again.

By the time I could stand up straight and see things again, my new best friend had the chain off my leg and my hands handcuffed behind my back. He reached behind me and grabbed the cuffs, yanking up until I thought he was going to pull my arms off. Then he frog-marched me out of the little cabin and up onto the deck. It wasn't Arvid's boat, either. From the little I could see of it, it was a lot newer, sleeker, and cleaner, in spite of Frenchy's personal filthiness.

It was also obviously a working boat. There was a heavy crane mounted on the gunwale, with a big hook on the end of a steel cable. It stuck up ten feet above the deck. The cable was wound all the way up so the hook wouldn't swing with the motion of the boat, which was smart. Aside from being heavy, the hook looked kind of sharp. On the deck below the crane, lashed to a series of cleats, were some large shipping crates. So I wasn't the only cargo, wherever we were headed.

I didn't get a whole lot of time to admire the boat. Frenchy yanked me up the ladder to the pilot's station on the flybridge. There was a bench at the back of the bridge where a passenger or two could sit. I didn't get to use it. Frenchy jerked me over beside the wheel and dropped the chain on my cuffs over a big steel hook screwed into the wall. The hook was almost shoulder height, which put all my weight on it and meant I couldn't unhook myself.

But at least I could see ahead, presumably to wherever we were headed. "Look," he said.

I looked. Big surprise: I was pretty sure this wasn't the Baltic, either.

Straight ahead of us, maybe a mile away, an island loomed up. Calling it an island was being polite. It looked like a big chunk of dark rock. There was some green showing on it, but it didn't look like happy, let's-have-a-picnic green. More like some kind of unhealthy mold that would give you a wasting disease if you touched it. And no trees or beaches or anything like that. Just jagged black rock that rose up out of the water, and big waves crashing into it, and no way I could see to land on it without smashing the boat. And just to make an absolutely perfect picture, there was a crust of ice on top of the whole thing.

"Île des Choux." The voice startled me. Not just because it was so high and raspy and weird sounding but because I'd been kind of lost, staring at the rock we were steering toward. And I was startled enough that I whipped my head around and looked at Frenchy and just blinked for a minute without a clue about what he'd said, before I remembered that I speak French. I knew what Île des Choux meant. I just didn't get why.

"Cabbage Island?" I said.

He gave me one of those whole-body shrugs that only the French can do.

"We're going there?" I asked him.

He went back to his default expression, the sneer. "Your new 'ome," he said.

I had a lot of questions about that. I mean, "home" sounded better than "grave," even with the French accent leaving off the *h*. On the other hand, from what I could see of the island, if I was stuck there it would turn into my grave in about two weeks. So was that why he was bringing me here? Just so I could die on a cold and empty rock? Or was there more to Cabbage Island than you could see from a mile away on a boat?

That last question was answered pretty quickly. As we passed a bright orange buoy, a shrill beeping started up from the control panel, and a red light began to blink. Frenchy leaned over the red light and stuck a key into a panel below it. He twisted the key and the face of the panel swung down, revealing a keypad. He punched in a string of numbers, at least ten digits long. Maybe more; he worked fast and I wasn't really counting. Whatever, the beeping cut out and the light stopped blinking.

Frenchy straightened and looked at me. "Put the wrong number, put no number—BOOM!" He smiled, really happy, and flipped his hands up to show me what "BOOM" looked like in French.

"Boom?" I said. "From something named Cabbage Island?"

He nodded and made the hand signal again. "Boom," he said. "The cabbage has many teeth."

He seemed pretty pleased with that, and he turned back to the wheel, smiling. I let him have his happy moment and just watched the island as we got closer. A cabbage with teeth. I wondered if it had fingernails, toes, maybe even an elbow or two. I was pretty sure I would find out soon enough.

Keeping us about a half mile off, Frenchy circled the boat around to the far side of the island. I wondered if that was to avoid more teeth. In any case, when we got to the far side, he spun the wheel and pointed our bow straight at a huge and jagged outcropping of black rock. And then he held us steady, aimed right for the biggest, sharpest spot.

I was pretty sure he wasn't going to run us onto the rocks. Why would he bring me all this way just to kill himself with me watching? But as we got closer it occurred to me that I didn't know a thing about this guy except he was ugly. I mean, he might not even be French—what if he was Belgian? So maybe he was some kind of sick twitch who didn't mind dying if he took me with him. Because he wasn't turning, he wasn't slowing down—and as we got even closer he gave me that nasty smile again, like he knew I was worried and that made him happy.

Just a few seconds before we would definitely smash into the rocks, he turned the wheel sharply to the left. The nose of the boat swung around, Frenchy throttled back—and we were pointed into a gap in the rocks that was invisible from anywhere but right here. Built into the rocks right above was something that looked like a missile battery. Cabbage teeth. We went right under it and into a channel between two walls of rock. It was wide enough for our boat to get through with a couple of feet to spare on each side. The channel made two quick turns, and then we headed into a cave. Or maybe it was a tunnel. The deeper into it we went, the more you could see that the walls had been carved away by human hands. There were dim lights hung at intervals of around thirty feet.

We cruised slowly along the tunnel for three or four minutes, the sound of the engine burbling back at us from the walls. Then we swung through one last sharp turn to the right, and ahead of us the lights got brighter. Up against a back wall a concrete pier stuck out into the water. And standing on the pier was a group of six men wearing black paramilitary clothing and carrying automatic weapons; my welcome wagon.

There was something about the way these guys stood that told me all I needed to know. I don't know how to explain it. But if you have ever seen a group of elite professional soldiers, you will know what I mean. Just the way they stood there, like they were ready for anything and expected to kick its ass when it came, whatever it was. And the way they cradled their weapons, like a short-order cook holding a spatula. It just said an automatic weapon was no big deal, just a utensil they used every day.

More than that, and maybe more important—at least to me, which was all that mattered right now—it said that I was in a world of trouble. Any tiny hope I had that I might get out of whatever this was flickered out. I tried to fan it back up. I repeated my mantra, *There's always a way.* And I would keep looking for some small opening, some tiny little advantage, that would give me a way out. I told myself I'd always found that way, and I'd been in some pretty deep shit. But myself talked back. It said I'd never before been inside a black, cold rock in the middle of an unknown ocean surrounded by missiles and highly trained professional killers and who the fuck knew what else. At the moment that sounded a lot more convincing than blind optimism.

Frenchy backed the engines and eased us close. Two of the men in black stepped forward and snagged the boat, bow and stern, and secured it to cleats on the pier. There was a final growl as the engines raced in reverse. The boat slowed to a stop and kissed the pier, and the engines died.

CHAPTER
4

I was right about the guys in black.

I have been dragged into a lot of cells in my time, from backcountry lockups to maximum-security prisons. So when I say these guys knew what they were doing, you can take my word for it. There's a number of tells an amateur might show that can give you a chance. Like, if they're needlessly cruel or kind of sloppy, or if they talk a lot or try to show you how tough they are. Just little things, but they leave a lot of holes for somebody like me to crawl through. Maybe you wouldn't see it, but to me they're definite signs. When the guy holding the gun shows you one of these, it means he's not a pro, and you have a chance.

These guys didn't show any of the tells. They didn't say or do anything they didn't have to do to get the job done. They moved efficiently, on the balls of their feet, eyes on everything at the same time. When they spoke at all, it was terse orders in French. There didn't seem to be any point in pretending I didn't understand them. I did what they said.

They pulled me off the dock as a couple of other guys in black unloaded the big crates from the boat. Frenchy stood on the bridge and worked the crane from a set of controls, beside the wheel swinging the crates up and onto the dock. Before the first crate made it onto the pier, I was steered into a dimly lit passage carved out of the rock of the island. The walls were smooth and unpainted and radiated the kind of permanent coolness you feel from cave walls. We went down a long, circular stairway, maybe as far as forty feet down. It dumped us out into another hallway, the twin of the one we'd taken from the pier. After walking along this passage for a couple of minutes, we took a right-hand passage, and we were in a short hallway. It had six steel doors, three on each side, set into rock walls. The doors had small, high-set windows, covered by thick steel grills. Below that was a slot just big enough for a food tray.

I knew the look. Maximum-security lockup.

I was pretty sure we'd gotten to my new 'ome.

One of the men in black opened the last door down on the left. They led me through and into a small cell. I'd seen worse, but only in comic books. The room was about eight feet by eight feet, bare stone walls, bare stone floor and ceiling. One dim light hung from the ceiling inside a steel-mesh cage. Opposite the door there was a shelf carved out of the stone. It was just big enough to lie down on. Just so I didn't have to figure it out by myself, there was a thin blanket folded on the foot of the "bed." And hanging from the wall above it there were two chains. On the floor below were two more. I didn't have to guess what they were for.

In two minutes my hands and feet were locked into the chains and I was sitting on the stone bed.

That's pretty much all I did for a truly long-ass time. I think it had to be three days, but it's impossible to be sure. The one light in the ceiling never flickered. It was always the same dim no-time in the cell. There were no sounds, no smells, nothing. Six times the door opened and two guards came in. They stood at either side of the door, weapons at the ready, while a third guard dropped a tray on the floor where I could just reach it if I stretched out all the way. Then they left.

Each tray held a bottle of water and a paper plate. On the plate it was always the same—a gray-green glop that looked like something they'd scraped off the walls. I ate it anyway. It wasn't awful. I mean, compared to eating dog shit or rotten squid it was sort of tasty. But I figured they weren't planning to kill me with the food, so I had to stay alive and as healthy as I could, just in case. I ate it all.

So like I said, I was pretty sure it was three days. I knew the whole arrangement was all set up to fuck with my head, make me unsure about time and everything else—steady dim light, no external sight or sound, all that. It's a popular old-time technique. Stick you in a cell with light always on, no way to tell if it's night or day. They change the feeding intervals, keep you isolated from absolutely everything, and make you just sit there. There's no way at all to tell how much time is going by, or anything else. Nobody to talk to, nothing to listen to, no way to move more than a few inches. After a while your brain short-circuits. Two minutes seems like an hour—or three hours can feel like a couple of minutes. Like I said, it fucks with your head. And if it goes on long enough you can even start to hallucinate.

I could take it. I'd been there before. My head has gotten pretty hard to fuck. And I actually started getting optimistic. The longer it went on, the more certain I got that they were softening me up for something. Sure, that probably meant something heinous was coming at me. But it also meant there was going to be some way out, even if it was tiny. There's no reason to soften up somebody to kill them. You do it to get them to jump at some truly stupid, lethal idea that looks like a great way out when you're softened enough. But if they really wanted me dead, I would be already.

So I stayed cool. I didn't talk to myself, hallucinate angels, or flip a finger on my lips and go, *buh-bee, buh-bee*. I sat and waited. I was going to get through this. Somehow, some way, I was going to survive. They might make it hard, but I was used to that, and I always find a way.

I kept that thought with me all the time. I would

make it. And as long as I was alive, there would be some way, somehow, some time, to get out of here. I hung on to that, and it kept me calm.

I mean, I'm not Batman. Nobody can keep focus 24/7. So there were plenty of times when I wondered if I was kidding myself. I didn't really know that somebody wanted me alive for some reason. After all, I didn't even know why I was here—or even where here was. I could be the Count of Monte Cristo, and I'd be out in a few days. But I might be the Man in the Iron Mask and I was here until I died. Why? Who knows? There could be some weird irrational reasons I couldn't imagine. Maybe it was a cult and they were just keeping me until the full moon, and then they'd sacrifice me to a goat god or something.

And every now and then I thought about being forty or fifty feet below sea level, chained to a stone wall. Floods happen all the time. And it wouldn't take much of a flood to put me plenty far enough underwater to drown. Or just as likely, think about the fact that I was guarded by a bunch of paramilitary dudes. The fact that they were here meant whoever was in charge had enemies. So what happens if the enemies invade this rock, kill all the guys in black? And they don't know about me—why would they? So they kill everybody and go home, and now I'm left to slowly starve to death. Maybe the flood was better. At least drowning is quick.

I thought up lots of other really cool ways I might

die, with lots of time to get the details right. So there was plenty to keep me entertained, in between fits of stupid optimism.

On what I figured was the third day, the optimism got a little stupider. And a whole lot harder to call up.

I had just finished a delightful, sumptuous meal of slimy green glop, accompanied by a full bottle of a superb vintage of water. I'd tossed the empty plate on the floor and settled back on my luxurious stone bed when I heard footsteps. The sound was different—like, the feet making them were smaller, lighter, and not wearing boots. I didn't know what that meant, but it was different, so I figured I better pay attention.

I sat up. The door swung open. Slowly. And then a woman came in. She had blond hair that showed dark roots, and it was pulled back into a tight bun, like ballet dancers wear. She moved like a ballet dancer, too, and she had a body to match, except that there was a whole lot of muscle showing that looked more MMA than ballet. She stared at me like I was a piece of furniture, probably a worn footstool, and turned slowly, surveying the entire cell. That gave me a good opportunity to look again and check her out. She was no footstool. Her face had probably started out as beautiful as the rest of her. In profile, the right side was close to perfect. Classic high cheekbones, a cute little button nose, and those dark green eyes. True beauty—on the right side. But the left side . . .

Once upon a time it had probably been just as perfect as the right side. But somebody had hacked the left side of her face with something big and sharp, probably a large knife. Just for the hell of it, they'd hacked a couple more times. Okay, maybe a whole bunch of times. That side of her face was a mess. It looked like a raised-relief map of the Grand Tetons. It was dominated by a couple of parallel scars that looked like the cheek had fallen off and a drunk tailor had sewed it back on. Those two scars ran all the way down her cheek, from the eyebrow to the chin.

I would have felt sorry for her, until she turned her eyes back on me and just stared.

I'd been wondering why anyone would come here alone, way down in the dungeon with a dangerous thug like me. But then she came soundlessly across the stone floor to me and stood close. She looked right into my face, and I didn't wonder anymore.

She put two green eyes on me that were colder than the bottom shelf of the deep freeze. Green eyes do not generally do cold very well. I don't know if you've noticed this, but if you haven't, take my word for it. Blue eyes can be North Pole cold, brown eyes can fry your ass, but green eyes are always warm, welcoming. Always.

Until this woman came along. These green eyes were way beyond what blue can do. Cold, but way past that; they were dead, but at the same time filled with something that looked like endless pain and a burning need to share it. She made me squirm, just by looking. I mean, I have stared down some hard cases. Most of the time it's either you know what they'll do and you're ready, or you can see they're not taking it any further than a stare-down. With this woman, I stared back for fifteen seconds, and it opened up a deep, dark pit underneath me. I couldn't tell what the fuck she might do, or why, but I knew it would be a small slice of hell.

And it wasn't smart and it wasn't something I planned, but I looked down real quick and stared at my feet. I could still feel her eyes on me, but she didn't do anything, didn't say anything. We did this for a really long minute. She still didn't talk or do anything else. Just stood there. It was enough. She was scaring the shit out of me without doing a goddamned thing. Something seemed to come off her, maybe pheromones or something, I don't know. All I know is I was more scared than I'd been for a truly long time. I told myself it was because I was chained to the wall, but it wasn't. It was her.

It never entered my mind to try anything. I didn't even want to look up at her. But I did. And when I did, she smiled. It was worse than the stare. If her eyes had been an invitation to Hell, the smile said never mind, Hell was right here already. It actually made my stomach turn over. And while I was still swallowing bile, she reached down, took my left hand, and held it in hers.

It was such a weird thing for her to do, I just let her, and gaped at her. She turned my hand over, looking at it like she was checking for fleas or something. And then she turned it palm down, grabbed my little finger, and locked those terrible green eyes on mine. She watched me like she was looking for something, nothing really amazing or important. Just more like she was going to turn over a stone and wondered what might come out. And while I was still trying to figure out which end was up, she gripped my little finger tighter— and pulled it savagely backward.

The world went dark. Somewhere in the distance I heard a snapping sound. Then a wave of pain crashed into me and I came back into my body just in time for it to take me over.

It hurt. I mean, a *lot*. It was so sudden and so painful that I couldn't even scream. I just sort of squeaked and then, just barely in time, turned my head to the side and threw up, a big wet fountain of secondhand green goop.

She didn't let go of my broken finger. She waited for me to stop barfing and turn back to her. Then her smile got a little wider and she pulled the finger even farther back, until I thought I was going to faint. She held it there for a minute, and then, just when I thought the lights would go out again, she let go. She took a step back, nodded like she'd just finished a minor chore, and turned away.

In the doorway she paused. She turned around and looked at me for a moment with the kind of smile you get from a cat standing over a half-dead mouse. Then she turned and walked out of the cell with that same weird ballet-dancer grace. And I was left sitting in a puddle of green puke, cradling a busted finger, and wondering what the fuck had just happened.

Another day went by, maybe a day and a half. It was

hard to think about things like that, because the pain in my broken finger didn't get any better. It swelled up, and it throbbed like an evil metronome. But you get used to that kind of thing. I mean, it hadn't killed me, and it sort of confirmed that they were keeping me alive, softening me up for something.

So I kept breathing, which was usually a good idea. And like I said, it wasn't too long before we moved on to the third act of Softening Riley.

I was sitting on my bed, listening to my stomach growl and thinking it had to be time for a meal. And I was kind of looking forward to it. I know it sounds stupid, weird, considering what that meal was going to be, but it was the only thing I had to look forward to, and I did.

I heard footsteps in the hall, nice heavy combat boots, for which I was grateful. Not just because it meant food but also because it meant that the Queen of Evil wasn't coming for another finger.

I was wrong about both things.

The door opened, and the two guards took their stations beside the door. But this time the third guy didn't bring in a tray. Instead, he carried in a chair and set it down, just out of reach of the farthest I could possibly stretch my chains. Then he went out. The other two guards stayed.

Nothing happened. I looked at the chair. It was very nice. If it was real, it was a Louis XVI and worth a couple of grand. It was probably something I was not supposed to put my ragged ass into. It was way too nice to stick in a stone cell with a reprehensible reprobate like me. Especially since there was no way I could stretch my ass far enough to sit in it. So I figured I was about to find out why I was here, straight from somebody important. Maybe Mr. Big himself. I wondered if I should brush my teeth.

I was right. Not about brushing my teeth; about Mr. Big. A couple of minutes after the chair ceremony, I heard feet in the hallway. Then two more guards came in and stood against the walls on either side of me. All four guards stood up straight, kind of at attention but still focused on me. No more than half a minute after that, my dear friend Our Lady of the Finger came through the door.

She glanced around the cell one more time, then turned to the guard on the right side of the door. She murmured something to him I couldn't hear, and he practically fell over agreeing with her. The woman nodded and went out, and I went back to waiting. Compared to looking at the woman with the scar, it was a real vacation.

A couple of minutes after that, two more guards appeared in the hall and took position beside the door outside my cell. And then a man strolled into my room and sat in the very nice chair. Scarface came back in and stood behind him, hands behind her back.

He just looked at me for a couple of minutes, so I looked back. Maybe it was too soon for another stare-down, after the nightmare I'd had with his girlfriend. But this guy was relaxed, smooth. He had a kind of bland look on his face, and I could see he thought he was king shit, and that always gets me going. So I met his eyes. No biggie. I mean, I've run into a lot of people who think they're important. Most of the time, they're the easiest to take down. I've done plenty of them. I'm hard to impress. If this guy was trying to make me tremble with awe, he should have left it to the woman. I studied him back like he was just another dork with a Napoleon complex.

He was in his midforties, with dark hair and light brown eyes that seemed a little too big for his face. He didn't blink, which can get on your nerves pretty quick. He was thin, with cheekbones that stuck out and thick black eyebrows. He wore a suit that was so perfect it almost made me dizzy. I mean, I've got a bunch of Savile Row suits, custom tailored for me, that go for almost as much as a new Chevrolet. This one made them look like somebody parked a new Bugatti Divo next to your Chevy.

The shirt and tie were in the same class, and his shoes, too. What he spent on his outfit would feed a family of eight for fifty years, and pay for their gas, too.

But I kept coming back to his eyes. Aside from being big and brown, there was just something about them that made you want to scurry under a rock and hide. Or if you couldn't hide, stand at attention and say "sir" a lot.

That pissed me off. I don't bow down to anybody, and the more they expect me to, the more I don't. So

I kept my eyes on him, daring him to show me something that would impress me and betting he couldn't.

"Mr. Wolfe," he said at last. His voice was measured, commanding, and he had no accent I could hear—but it was the kind of no-accent that comes from practice, from getting rid of an old accent. It told me nothing. Neither did the tiny little smile. But then he said, "I am Patrick Boniface."

Okay, I was wrong. He impressed me. I knew that name, and I knew what it meant.

I was fucked.

CHAPTER
5

In this mean and dirty world there are many dangerous people. Drug lords get the most publicity. I think it's because of the so-called War on Drugs. The badder we make the cartels and kingpins, the worse we all think drugs are. And as a side benefit, if we think they are all really and truly terrifying evil boogeymen, it's a lot easier to understand why we can't put them out of business and win the so-called war once and for all.

Which means nobody has to think about the real reason we can't put drug dealers out of business. Sure, they're bad. Bad to the bone, mean, ruthless, violent, all of that. But the fact is, they don't really need to be to stay in business. They just have to keep providing dope. Because people want drugs. And as long as people want to get high, get mellow, get a fix, and don't even mind getting addicted—and that means forever—

there's going to be drugs, and drug dealers. It's pure supply and demand. People will always want it, so other people will always supply it.

There's one other thing people will always want. Weapons. And not just pissant toys like pistols and rifles. I mean big-time stuff that can take out a city block, wipe out a few hundred people at a pop, turn a band of guerrilla fighters into an army of resistance.

Drug dealers really are plenty bad. But a big-time arms dealer makes them look like kids playing Power Rangers. It just stands to reason. Drug dealers sell to people who want to make money or people who want to get high. But arms dealers sell to violent people who want to be even more violent, and efficient about it. These customers would not hesitate to keep the money and kill the dealer, just take the weapons, and the only reason they don't is that they can't. Because the arms dealer scares the crap out of them, too.

And of course the scary arms dealers would just as soon be the biggest weapons seller on the block. They wouldn't hesitate to knock off all their competitors and corner the market and make ten times as much money. Which they try to do every now and then, because when you are a violent, amoral person who is all about making money, it just makes sense to kill a few dozen people so you can make more. So if you are one of the big, badass weapons sellers, you are always looking over your shoulder. You sleep with one eye open, and you surround yourself with people who don't mind killing anybody you tell them to. Because sooner or later, one of your peers is coming for you, and he has a bunch of hired killers just as good as yours. He wants what you have, all of it, and to get it, he's very happy to kill you and a few hundred of your closest friends. The thought of all that extra cash makes you an irresistible target. Sooner or later, one of your competitors will take a shot.

Unless, of course, you are an arms dealer who scares the crap out of the other arms dealers, who scare the crap out of everybody else. There are two or three of those top-dog dealers I know about, guys who nobody would dream of fucking with. And there was one guy so far above all of them that even those kingpins would be scared to fuck with him. One guy who was so big, bad, rich, ruthless, and powerful that he was totally untouchable. One guy who had clawed his way to the top of the heap with ruthlessness and violence so extreme that it absolutely terrified everybody else. A guy who showed time after time that he didn't negotiate, didn't back down, didn't mind killing anybody or everybody, and he was happy to wipe out twenty people just to get the one he was after.

His name was Patrick Boniface.

Yeah. The guy looking me in the eye and sitting in the Louis XVI chair. Which I now figured, by the way, was probably real. Boniface had a reputation as a guy who demanded truly fine things. He was just as ruthless latching on to artworks, too.

I did not actually say, "Oh shit I'm dead and fucked." But I must have thought it so loud that he heard me anyway. He gave me two millimeters of smile and one small shake of the head. "You are in no danger, Mr. Wolfe," he said. "For the time being."

I tried to swallow. It didn't work. "I'm happy to hear it," I said. "So grabbing me like that, and the chains and the guards, four goddamn days chained to a rock—that was just for practice?"

"Three days, actually," he said. He glanced behind him at Scarface. "Bernadette thought it would soften you up." He cocked his head slightly to the left. "I don't think it has, though."

"No," I said. "I don't soften."

"Forgive me if I disagree," Boniface said. "I can assure you that a few days with Bernadette would work wonders. I'm quite sure she could persuade you of almost anything. And she would love to have a chance."

Bernadette put her hands on the back of the chair and leaned forward with a smile that could short-circuit a pacemaker. Ridges of hard muscle popped out on her arms.

"Thanks," I said. "I already got her warm-up." I held up my left hand, which by now was purple and about the size of a basketball. Bernadette smiled, just a girl remembering one special dance at the prom.

"We'll have that looked at," Boniface said. He raised one eyebrow. "Unless you'd like to get better acquainted with Bernadette?"

"I think I know her too well already," I said. "And I don't think she's my type."

"Nor anyone else's type, I think," he said. He

reached back and patted her hand, and she straightened back up.

"Well, a date to go dancing is out," I said. "So why all the spy-movie bullshit?"

His smile went way the hell up to three millimeters. "I find that negotiations go much easier if I strengthen my position." He raised an eyebrow. "I think I have done so?"

He looked so fucking cool and smug that for just a second I was mad enough to forget who he was. "I don't call it negotiating if I'm chained to a fucking wall with automatic weapons pointed at me, with Bernadette waiting for a chance to pull out my intestines," I said.

"Oh, but it is," Boniface said. "I am a businessman, Mr. Wolfe. A good businessman should always try to gain every possible advantage before negotiating. Don't you think?"

I thought about that. Just for a few seconds, because that's all it took. He definitely had all the cards. Oh, sure, I could've thought up a couple of cutesy things he'd skipped if I felt like a smart-ass. Or maybe gone with some tired, barf-inducing pablum like, "Where there's life, there's hope" or some kind of New Age bullshit about Positating My Image Reality into a New Nexus of Tangible Affirmation. But I never did go for that crap, and the truth was, I was chained to a stone wall in the basement of a huge rock that was in the middle of some unknown body of water, surrounded by heavily armed mercenaries, every possible kind of

lethal security, and a sadistic bitch who loved to "persuade" people held in reserve. And one hand was temporarily out of commission. Yeah, he had the high
ground. Boniface was in charge, and that was all there
was to it. So I did what anybody with a three-digit IQ
would've done.

I smiled. "How can I help you?" I said.

Bernadette looked disappointed, but Boniface nod-
ded, to show this was pretty much what he'd expected.
"I would like you to steal something for me," he said.
"Something rather . . . *special*."

My first thought was relief, because I was back on
familiar turf. Stealing I can do. And if it was something
so hard to get at he had to get me to get it, well, that
was exactly the kind of challenge I live for.

But my second thought was that the way he said that
word, "special," was exactly the way I thought Bernadette would say a word like "scalpel." A little too eager,
like, "Here comes something that will hurt a lot and I
am going to totally love watching you scream and
bleed." Like I said, I love a challenge, but there are
limits. I mean, I am the best there is, but I'm not Superman. I'm not even Deadpool. There's plenty of
things that are just flat-out impossible. Sometimes
there's just no fucking way, even for me, and I'm man
enough to admit it. I mean, I haven't found anything
like that yet, but I'm a realist. I know damn well that
sooner or later something will come along that's just
flat-out no-fucking-way impossible. And I had a nasty
little feeling that Boniface was about to hand it to me.

Because if he'd gone to all this trouble to get me to steal it, it had to be a total motherfucker.

On the other hand, it didn't look like I had a whole lot of options here. And if it was something completely impossible, trying to do it was still better than a date with Bernadette.

"Let's hear it," I said.

Boniface studied me for a few seconds, like I was a horse he was thinking of buying and he wanted to find any flaws. Finally, with no change of expression, he said, "I wonder how much you may have heard about me." He waited, so I would know I was supposed to tell him.

"You are the biggest, baddest, most successful arms dealer in the world," I said. And just to show I wasn't blowing smoke up his ass, I added, "On top of making a profit by helping to kill large numbers of people, you don't seem to mind getting your own hands dirty, taking out anybody—everybody—who pisses you off."

Boniface frowned.

"What?" I said. "What'd I miss?"

"Almost everything," he said. And he actually sighed, which was kind of like hearing Dracula say, "Can't we just be friends?" "Perhaps I should hire a— what do they call them? Image consultant?" He shook his head, and he looked thoughtful, maybe a little sad, which was just as weird. "People think a man like me is without finer feelings."

"Maybe they don't know about your Louis XVI chair," I said.

The two-millimeter smile again. It lasted about half a second, and then he went on. "Some would even say I have no soul. The very fact that I sell weapons, that I promote and even indulge in such massive and brutal violence, makes me . . . immune to finer human sentiments. And so they assume I am coarse, unfeeling, unable to experience spiritual joy or beauty." He pursed his lips slightly. "They are wrong."

"Of course they are," I murmured.

Boniface ignored me. "As I said, I am a businessman." He shrugged. "The object of commerce is to make as much money as possible, to maximize your profit. Selling weapons was the surest way to do that. But," he said, holding up a hand to stop an objection I wasn't going to make, "to me, it has always been a means to an end." He paused, glanced at his fingernails. They looked fine to me. "The true measure is how a man uses his wealth, whether he chooses to regard money as an end in itself—or as a tool to accomplish something else. For me—?"

Boniface frowned, like he'd found a bad spot on his fingernails. "I'm a collector, Mr. Wolfe," he said. "I love beautiful things, and I love to own them, to look at them and touch them."

I tried as hard as I could not to look up at Bernadette, but I couldn't help myself. I looked up—and she was looking right back at me, waiting for me to say something, make some joke about "beautiful things." I didn't say anything. I just looked away. I didn't fall off a cabbage truck, like Mom used to say.

Boniface didn't seem to notice. He just flicked his glance up off his nails and back at me. "In some ways, it's rather amazing that our paths haven't crossed before now. You have quite a reputation among a small circle of people who don't mind going outside the law to acquire a treasure. Of course that includes me." The two-millimeter smile. "But for the most part, making sure I was the high bidder has been enough. When it isn't, I have one or two other means of persuading buyers." I couldn't help it; I looked at Bernadette again. She smiled. "One way or the other, I usually get what I go after," Boniface continued. Three-millimeter frown. "Until now."

Here it comes, I thought. "Which is why I am here," I said. Just like I'd thought. He wanted something nobody else could get for him, because even the thought of stealing it was impossible. And so, like any intelligent, thoughtful man of the world, he'd said to himself, *This looks like a job for Riley Wolfe!* I wished I'd brought my cape.

"Exactly so," he said. "One of the keys to my success is that I know my limits." He glanced behind him. "When I fail to recognize one, Bernadette is quite adept at pointing out my inadequacies."

"I'll bet," I said.

"I have conceived a passion for something of unearthly beauty," Boniface said, turning back toward me. "Even more, it feeds my soul." One shake of his head. "The soul that so many think I lack." He turned one hand over, palm up. "Perhaps my acquisition of this treasure will persuade them otherwise. If not—"

He shrugged. "That doesn't matter. What matters is that I must have it, and I believe you are the only man on earth who can get it for me."

"You're probably right," I said. I mean, not cocky or anything. It's just a fact. I do stuff that everybody else thinks is impossible. "What is it?"

"I understand that you are well versed in the art world?"

"Yup," I said. "You have to know what something is if you're going to take it." He frowned a little, which didn't seem healthy for me, so I added, "And I love beautiful things, too."

He nodded. "Exactly. Then I hope you will appreciate this work, which is widely regarded as one of the greatest of its kind. I assume you're familiar with the works of Raphael?"

I just nodded. Of course I know Raphael—who doesn't? Some ways, I thought he was better than either Leonardo or Michelangelo. They just had better publicists.

Boniface nodded back. "Then you will know *The Liberation of St. Peter.*"

I nodded again. It was a fresco—a truly awesome fresco, one of the best ever. I wondered why he mentioned it, though. Was it related somehow to the thing he wanted me to steal? He didn't give me any clues. He didn't say anything—just kept looking at me like he expected me to say something smart. Like what? I mean, I could tell him all about Raphael, or frescoes, or—

Or hold on just one fucking minute. Was he trying to tell me that—I mean, it was totally not possible, but that was what we had started with, and it would certainly fit that description if—I mean, it wasn't even impossible; it was unthinkable! But was he really suggesting that—

"Stop the clock, Slim," I said. "Is that it? You want me to steal a fucking *fresco*?"

"I want you to steal *the* fucking fresco," he said. "I want you to steal Raphael's *Liberation of St. Peter* and bring it to me."

"Jesus fucking Christ," I said.

"No, just Saint Peter," he said—the first little touch of humor he'd shown.

"You do understand what a fresco is? I mean, it's a painting that is literally part of a fucking *wall*! Like painted right *into* the fucking wall."

"You don't need to steal the entire wall, Mr. Wolfe. Just the fresco."

"Wonderful. Just the fresco, not the wall—which conveniently ignores the fact that the fresco is actually part of the actual wall."

"So I have been led to believe," he said.

"And you know that on top of asking me to steal a fucking wall, this particular fucking wall is in the *Vatican*?! Which has like the tightest security in the world?"

"So we are told," he said.

"I mean, the fucking Vatican—with twenty thousand visitors every fucking day—and if I steal a fucking wall from the fucking Vatican, don't you think somebody is going to notice?!"

"I suppose that depends on how you do it," he said. Totally calm, relaxed, like he'd just said, "Hey, let's take a walk in the fucking park."

"No," I said. "That's crazy. No. It can't be done. No fucking way."

He cocked his head to the left, just a little. "You're sure?"

"Absolutely positive," I said.

"Perhaps you could think of some way? If, perhaps, you brainstorm with Bernadette?"

"On the other hand," I said, "there are a couple of things I could try."

Four millimeters of smile this time. "I'm delighted to hear it," he said.

CHAPTER
6

The call came on her unsecured cell phone. But Betty Dougherty recognized the area code. It said the call came from Iasi, Romania. She was pretty sure it didn't. She didn't know anybody in Romania. She had no idea where Iasi was. But that area code was used by one of her special clients. All his calls went through dozens of servers around the world before they got to her. She was fairly sure he was nowhere near Romania. That was just routine caution. And she had no idea where the calls really came from. She didn't need to know, and the rules of her profession were clear. The less everybody knew, the better. All that mattered was that the wire transfers went through, and this client's always did. Where he sent them from was none of Betty's concern.

Even so, Betty was alarmed. None of her clients ever

called her at this personal, unsecured number. In theory, they shouldn't even know this number existed. Anyone getting in touch to request Betty's professional services sent a note to a PO box in Newark. The box was not in the name of Betty Dougherty, of course. It was registered to an extra identity, one she would never use for anything except that PO box. When the time came to abandon the box, that identity would die, too. No big deal. IDs were cheap, and the box was important. She went across the river from her modest Manhattan apartment once a week to check it and collect any messages waiting there.

This private phone number ringing now had no apparent connection to the box, or to her working identity. This phone was for her "real" life, the day-to-day normal existence she lived as a cover for her true occupation.

But Betty was not really surprised that this particular client knew her cell phone number. He had enough money and raw power to get whatever he wanted. Betty knew that better than most; she had gotten it for him often enough. Until now, he had always played by the rules, too. As far as she knew, he had always been content to use her professional services and had never tried to track her down. That's how it was supposed to work.

Something had changed that. It probably wasn't good.

Still, she was sure it was him, so she answered cautiously. "What," she said.

A voice with a slight British accent on the other end

said four words. "You have a letter." And then the connection broke.

Betty thought for a moment. Obviously, this client had a job for her, and he regarded it as urgent enough to break normal protocol. Normally she would simply pick up the information about the job at her PO box. She had checked the box only two days ago. Normally she would not check again for several more days. The client knew that. So he had to have a job for her so pressing he was willing to run the risk of using an unsecured number. Even more, to take a much larger risk by revealing that he knew her private number—and therefore that he knew who she really was. That was troubling. The fact that the caller had been cautious with his words was a very small relief.

She put all that out of her mind for the moment. Whatever the implications for the long run, the message meant the details of the job had gone to her PO box; they had not been conveyed in the open over the phone. And the call itself had given away nothing at all. Even though anybody could access her call register and see that the call had come in, there was no way to trace it back to the caller. Betty could say it had been a wrong number, and no one could prove otherwise. After all, the call came from Romania, for God's sake. Who even knew where that was?

More important at the moment was the job itself. It was much riskier this way, being notified by phone. It could even mean that somebody was setting her up, sending her to the PO box so they could tail her, and either get a warrant for the contents or catch her with something incriminating planted in the box. It was a large risk to attempt a pickup after an unsecured call. Would it be worth it?

She thought about this client. He paid well and promptly. Beyond that, he had a vast network of connections in the world that her clients came from. If she made him mad, he could poison her name with all those people. More, if he was angry enough, he could easily have her killed—especially since he had shown her that he knew how to find her.

The smart thing was to pick up the "letter." At least that. Once she knew what the job was, she could make a decision.

That settled, Betty headed for her PO box. She always assumed she was under surveillance—this time even more so. She worked the shady side of the street, and there were plenty of organizations and individuals who would be very interested in what she did. It wasn't important if it was someone from law enforcement or from the darker side. She knew too much, and that made her a target. If anybody broke her cover, it didn't matter if they wore a white hat or a black hat, she was out of business—and possibly dead.

Betty had to assume the call had been monitored and that somebody would be watching to see what she did. When she left her apartment she behaved as if surveillance was a certainty. She walked across town to East 68th and went down the stairs to the subway platform. It wasn't very busy at this time of day, and nobody seemed interested in one doughy middle-aged woman wearing cheap clothing and sensible shoes. She took the train downtown and changed to another. She repeated this several times, changing trains and watching without seeming to do so.

A few hours later, Betty finally came up at Grand Central Terminal. She went to the dining concourse, sat on a bench, and looked "casually" all around. She meant it to look fake, like somebody who wanted to be sure they were not observed without looking suspicious. Then she reached under the bench and pulled out a manila envelope taped to the underside. If she was watched, they might grab her now and open the manila envelope. They would find three brochures for the Hard Rock Cafe, nothing else.

But nobody approached her. Betty stuffed the envelope into her purse and hurried out of the station.

Betty took a bus downtown, got out at Washington Square Park. She went through the arch and sat on a bench. For fifteen minutes she just sat, watching the fountain, the children, the tourists. Then, acting "casually" again, she carefully eased the manila envelope out of her purse and slid it behind her, through the slatted seat back, and onto the ground. She glanced at her wristwatch, got to her feet, and walked back through the arch and away.

This was part of the act, too. What Betty had just performed was a perfect reproduction of a classic intelligence operation: the drop, a maneuver to pass information, undetected, to the next link in the chain. Anyone watching her would recognize the pattern. They would be distracted by the bench at Grand Central, the envelope, and the apparent drop. They would have to check out all those leads. If it was a team of watchers, she had just split them several ways. One to Grand Central, one or two to watch the envelope, see who picked it up. That would leave fewer to follow her, which was important.

Especially because now Betty dropped all the acts. First, she went down to the subway and flipped the switch on a small box in her purse. This turned on an electronic field that would surround her, out to a distance of fifty feet, and blank out electronic surveillance—even if someone had somehow planted a tracking chip on her purse or her person. Then she went back up to the street and slipped into a boutique. A minute later she was out the back door and into the alley.

For the next forty-five minutes, Betty went into stores and out the back, onto subway cars and off again, into large crowds, through the Metropolitan Museum of Art—she used all the tradecraft she had until she was quite certain she had lost any possible surveillance, human or electronic. Only then did she take a train across the river to Newark.

Betty spent another hour in Newark being elusive, just to be safe. When she finally went to her PO box, she was as certain as she could be that no one had eyes on her. With her electronic suppressor still on, even any cameras the post office had would show only a distorted image, a cloud of fuzz. Betty quickly opened her box, retrieved the single letter-size envelope waiting there, and left.

It was late afternoon by the time Betty got back to her apartment. She sat in her easy chair and took off her shoes, wiggling her toes with relief. She'd done a lot of walking today and her feet hurt, even with her sensible shoes. She closed her eyes, breathing deeply and clearing her mind. Then she got up and poured a glass of Chardonnay from the box in the refrigerator. She took a gulp, sat back down, and opened the envelope she'd retrieved in Newark.

There was a single sheet of folded paper. Betty opened it up. There was nothing but a name, an address, and the words "standard plus portrait." Under that was written, "24 hr return. Triple rates."

Frowning, Betty shredded the note and burned the shreds. Two things stood out as unusual: "portrait" and "triple rates." Not that it would be a problem. But no one ever wanted a photograph that might be used as a portrait. So it was odd—but the reasons were not any of her concern. If the client wanted a portrait, Betty would take a portrait. Difficult to do covertly, but she'd manage.

"Triple rates" was much more interesting. This was a good and steady client who paid well, and this job was extra important to the client. And Betty was going to need a little extra cash when this job was done. Because as soon as she finished, "Betty Dougherty" would vanish, the cell phone would go in the river, and the PO box in Newark would expire when the rent stopped coming.

If anyone knew this much about her, even a steady client like this one, Betty Dougherty would have to "die." If she was fast enough, and smart, she could finish the job, disappear, and revive herself in one of the new identities she had prepared for a day like this one.

In the meantime, there was work to do. With a heartfelt sigh, Betty finished her wine and struggled back into her shoes.

Monique wasn't really worried. It was true that Riley had said he'd be back in a week, and two and a half weeks had now passed with no sign of him. But when Riley was working, there were a million things that might happen to delay him. It was even possible that he had been caught. It wasn't likely, and Monique didn't really believe it had happened. It was far more likely that he had just hit some snag and needed more time. Maybe, she thought, he'd run into some woman worth spending a little time with. That seemed almost as unlikely, but the thought came to her, and Monique was not at all sure how she felt about that.

Either way, she told herself it didn't really concern her. He was just a client, and maybe, sometimes, some weird kind of friend. Nothing more, no matter what he wanted to think, and no matter what the little voice in the back of her head whispered to her from time to time. It was business, pure and simple, and every now and then a few moments of friendship; casual talk, a few drinks, some laughs, just like you would have with any business acquaintance. Just that simple.

But of course it wasn't simple at all. Monique had a long history with Riley. Most of it actually was business. But there had been one night when they were celebrating a spectacular success, and things had gone way beyond business—all the way into bed. It had been surprisingly good—for both of them, she was sure. And still, it had been a mistake. Even if it was a wonderful, memorable mistake that still made her shiver when she remembered.

But it was impossible, out of the question, ridiculous, even to think about repeating it. Riley was the most arrogant, conceited, self-centered man she'd ever met. She had to admit that some of the arrogance was justified. He really was the best in the world at what he did. Even so; if he ran into more than he could handle, it would probably be because he thought he was so freaking good nobody could touch him. And when they did—well, in a way it served him right.

But Monique wasn't worried. Not really. Riley was the proverbial bad penny. He'd always come back. If he was late? No big deal.

Still, a small and nagging worry stayed with her. And the longer it nagged, the more irritating it was. Finally, Monique did what any sane Manhattan woman with money to burn would do under the circumstances. She went shopping.

For several hours, Monique drifted from one high-end boutique to another. Money was certainly not a problem. She had plenty—partly thanks to Riley and the work he'd brought her. More so because she was probably the best art forger in the world. Riley certainly thought so. He'd backed up that belief, too, getting some of her best work and paying her exorbitantly for it. A big chunk of the money in her offshore account came from him, and she knew she should be grateful. The problem was, Riley seemed to think so, too. And he had very definite ideas about how she ought to express her gratitude.

When that popped into her head, she found herself grinding her teeth in frustration. And as a result, she found herself buying a pair of handmade glove-leather boots that cost nearly as much as a new car.

Of course, the thoughts of Riley stayed with her, part worry and part something else Monique would rather not define. So she was very much lost in her own thoughts as she hurried along the crowded sidewalk carrying the new boots. So much so that she didn't notice the woman who began carefully tailing her as she left Marina Rinaldi. The follower was very skillful, but it wouldn't have mattered if she was a rank novice. Monique was from an upper-middle-class background. And art forgers don't generally do a lot of fieldwork. Street skills were not in her armory.

Even if she had been more savvy, she still might not

have noticed. The woman following her looked so ordinary, no New Yorker would see her even if they were looking right at her. And even if Monique had noticed her tracker, she would not have seen the camera the woman used. It was well hidden in a Louis Vuitton handbag, and at the end of the day, Monique still had no idea that she'd been followed and photographed during her entire shopping trip.

CHAPTER 7

Whatever else you could say about Patrick Boniface—and I could think of plenty—he was a good host. I mean, once you put aside the whole chain-you-to-a-stone-wall-and-threaten-you thing. And the polite, nonstop reminder of limitless suffering that Bernadette represented. All that stuff aside, Boniface kept me entertained. I stayed for three more weeks, and he gave me a real-life bed in a beautifully furnished room. And he kept me entertained, too. He knew I have a thing for music, like he seemed to know everything else. He had a library of the best—some really rare recordings, too.

And Boniface showed me his art collection. It knocked my socks off. I mean, I've seen the very best, all over the world, everywhere from the Louvre to MoMA. But in a cave on a nowhere chunk of rock called Cabbage Island, Boniface had a collection that ranked with the most famous. He had stuff I'd never heard of, and he had pieces that had been "missing" for years, and other things that were theoretically still in museums somewhere but clearly were not. He didn't just have name-brand stuff, either. What he collected was exactly what he'd told me: *beauty*. There were paintings and sculptures by artists I'd never heard of, and they were not in any museum catalog I'd ever seen, but they were beautiful, no question about it.

So maybe he was right. Maybe he really did have a soul. He just didn't carry it with him when he did business.

The only downside was the food. It turned out that the green glop they'd been feeding me while I was chained up in the cell was standard fare. Boniface had started out as a vegan, stirred that up with massive paranoia and unlimited funds, and come up with an entirely synthetic blend of algae and who-the-fuck-knows. It was all grown and concocted right here on Île des Choux so he didn't need to import any food. He said it contained all the vitamins and trace minerals needed to promote health. But one thing it didn't contain was flavor. The stuff tasted just like it looked—like it had been made from synthetic algae.

Happily for us all, it turns out vegans can drink alcohol—even the vegans who only eat green slime. Boniface was generous with his drinks, and he let me browse through his library of rare and amazing whiskeys, cognacs, Armagnacs, marcs—all the stuff I like, plus bottles of legendary brews I'd heard about but never even seen before. His wine library was every bit as good, stocked with classic vintages from all the world's great domains. The only downside was deciding which one to pair with the slime. I mean, what goes best with algae? Red or white? You'd have to think a really big white—but why not a Beaujolais? And there were so many other great reds in the rack. Boniface pulled out a 1965 Château Lafite that—well, that isn't important. What matters is that with just a few belts of the good stuff I could almost believe the green slime was food.

So we had a jolly old time of it, swilling hooch and yakking about art, and under other circumstances good old Patrick Boniface and I would have become brand-new besties. Of course, that was sort of tough to do under the present conditions. I mean, when somebody is going to kill you unless you do something that can't be done, it's a real strain on a budding bromance. And with Bernadette hovering in the background and watching me with a stare like a deranged hungry tiger, it wasn't something I had any luck forgetting about.

It did begin to wear a little, too, especially after the first week. But there was no help for it. Boniface hadn't intended to keep me for three whole weeks. I mean, Riley says yes and gets to work, or he says no and goes in the ocean. After Bernadette had her quality time, of course. But apparently it was storm season out there in this part of the world, and no boats could get through right now, so I was stuck until the weather cleared.

Still, it was just about as much fun as you could have

under the circumstances. I mean, if you've never taken
a bottle of truly great Armagnac and sat with a collection of mind-bendingly great art—just *sat* with it. Sip,
stare, ponder, sip some more. And the whole time
you're listening to something like Christian Tetzlaff's
recording of Sibelius' string quartets—it doesn't get
much better than that, unless you throw in a hot
woman with really low self-esteem. Sadly, Boniface
didn't stock those, and Bernadette was definitely not a
replacement option.

I even got to know the guy, Boniface himself, a little
bit, and like I said, all things considered, he made a
pretty good companion. I know it sounds like I'm kind
of stretching it a little? But when you take two art lov-
ers, a ton of amazing art, and an open bar stocked with
the very best booze in the world—I mean, that Armagnac was *incredible*—well, shit. Of course tongues loosen
up. You get to talking. You get over your hesitation about
chatting with one of the scariest guys in the known universe, outside of Thanos.

So one night, when we had polished off a bottle or
two and were looking through an amazing collection
of Japanese ukiyo-e prints, I felt mellow enough to ask
him something that had been bugging me. And probably more important, he looked mellow enough to answer.

"Patrick," I said. Yeah, first names; like I said, mellow.

"Yes?" he said.

"Why *The Liberation of St. Peter*?" He didn't say
anything. "I mean, out of all the art in the world—and

you know I could get you just about anything." I couldn't help it—the Armagnac. And anyway, it was true. "So why this?"

He looked at me without blinking, for just about long enough that I thought I'd made a mistake and maybe misjudged things. Then he got up and walked over to the bar. And God bless him, he opened another bottle and brought it back with him. He topped off my glass, poured himself some, and sat. He sipped. So did I. I figured maybe I really had crossed the line and I should just wait and see what happened.

That was a good move. When he'd whet his whistle, he gave me one of his tiny little smiles. "I have been a bad man for most of my life," he said. I thought I could hear just a little bit of a French accent creeping into his voice. He kept it neutral all the time, so nobody could have guessed where he was from originally, but now— either the drinks or the memories colored his words just a little bit. "I have told myself, so, I have no choice, but I know this is not true. I chose it. And I have been . . . very bad." He looked at me and raised an eyebrow. I didn't contradict him.

He shrugged. "So. I have been bad, and sometimes, I have paid the price." He sipped. "Prison, hm? Not unknown to you, Riley?"

I shook my head. "Not unknown," I admitted.

"Of course. It is the life we chose." He frowned. "But the second time . . . *Merde* . . ." He drained his glass and refilled it. "La Santé," he said. It wasn't a toast. It was the name of one of the toughest prisons in

France. I knew La Santé by reputation. It was supposed to be a very hard place.

"I was in solitary confinement. Because I was so very dangerous." He smiled slightly. "Difficult, hm? But I had made plans—you must do the same? Plans?" I nodded again, but he was already going on. "Yes. But the plans were not for solitary, which is much more challenging. I did not know if my . . . *instruments* could adapt."

I assumed that when he said "instruments" he meant his "people," and not that he had planned a rescue led by the Tower of Power horn section.

"I had already been there too long, hm?" he said. "And I thought perhaps, this time, the plans would not work. And the days went on. And the months . . ."

He sipped again, and he smiled, which I thought was an odd thing to do when you're remembering solitary in a very hard prison. "They let me have a book. *Art of the Italian Renaissance*. And in that book . . . No. I will show you."

He got up again and went over to the bookshelf. He returned with a large but very battered book. It was dirty, smudged, and dog-eared. He opened it to an illustration. "Here. This is the book itself. There. You see?" He held it out to me, and there it was. *The Liberation of St. Peter*. I knew it, but I looked anyway, until Boniface began to speak again.

"There you see it all," he said. "The entire story. I became fascinated with this work. Perhaps even obsessed, hm? I stared at it for hours, and I began to really *see* it and hear what it said. Its true message. Which is what, Riley?"

It startled me so I almost dropped the book. But I took a stab at it. "Uh—faith, of course. The power of faith opens all, um, doors?"

He beamed at me. A huge, nearly human smile. "Exactly. That is precisely right. Faith opens all doors. And I let that knowledge . . . *sustain* me. I had faith. And—I was delivered. My doors were opened. My instruments adapted." He smiled again, but this time it was not quite as pleasant. "And my enemies paid the price," he said.

He leaned over and pointed to the picture in the battered old book.

"You see it? You see the angel—she comes to him as he sleeps, and she leads him past the guards and out to freedom." He smiled. "Just as it happened to me. Although my angel was perhaps not so . . . angelic? And the guards were not dazed by glory." Shrug. "They were dead, of course. By the hand of my angel."

"Bernadette," I said.

He nodded. "Of course. Bernadette."

Boniface smiled, like a proud parent remembering how their kid scored the winning goal for the state championship. "Bernadette," he said again, softer, and he looked down. Not really looking at the book that rested on his knee, just pointing his eyes down, away from me, so he could remember better. "You must understand that Bernadette has always been different," he said.

I thought that was probably an understatement, but it didn't seem really smart to say so.

"Always. She was *born* with . . . *gifts*," he said, and the smile was gone now. "Talents that are . . . what? Perhaps I should say, *challenging*, for a woman." He took a large sip from his glass. "She is freakishly strong, stronger than most men. More physically gifted than any other human I have ever seen. And her reflexes, her movements. She is so fast—" He shook his head. "As I say, these things are not truly appreciated in a woman. I'm sure she had a quite unhappy childhood. Which may have—"

Boniface shook his head again. "Feh. We all had unhappy childhoods, eh? Why do so many fools seem to think childhood is a wonderful, magical time? If true, it is a very dark magic, *mon ami*. And even without early trauma, Bernadette was always—She has a . . . a what— a flair? She truly enjoys to—she actually *craves* . . ."

Boniface paused, still looking down. He seemed to see his glass for the first time, and drained it. He poured it half full again, sipped. "This is perhaps Bernadette's greatest gift," he said. He locked eyes with me. "I think the two of us, we have sometimes had to cause pain to other people? And even death?"

He waited for me to answer. So I did. "I guess that's part of the life we live," I said. Really clever answer, cribbed straight from *The Godfather*. Like I said, that Armagnac was good.

It seemed to satisfy Boniface. He nodded. "Just so. But it is not pleasant, hm? It leaves a bad taste. Most people find it difficult, even impossible."

"Not Bernadette," I said. I couldn't help it.

"Not Bernadette," he repeated. "I called her my angel? In truth, she is Azrael, the angel of death. Killing people is like the food her spirit needs. And if she can, she kills them slowly. With great imagination. Very useful in my business, but . . ."

Boniface made a slight hissing sound and took a large sip. He took a long breath and shrugged. "It doesn't matter. Whatever she is, she is mine. For what she is, useful, yes—but more, for what she did. For when she came for me in prison," he said, "of course there were guards. She went through them as though they were papier-mâché. She set me free. And so I will never abandon her."

That answered at least one question. And the next one—what the hell happened to her face—I was not about to ask. That kind of brass balls would take a lot more than a couple of bottles of Armagnac.

"In any case," Boniface said. "*The Liberation of St. Peter* sustained me through a difficult time. It taught me an important course of lessons. It became my . . . my *talisman*, if you will. And so?" He shrugged, using both hands, the very first extremely French gesture I'd seen from him. "I vowed that someday, if ever I had the means, I would own that fresco. As a monument to my faith." He sipped and looked at me over the rim of his glass. "And then you came to my attention, and I thought, *eh bien*, why not? What do you think?"

I don't remember what I said. I assume it was something agreeable. Because the story as Boniface told it was just plain nuts, filled with megalomania, murder, and madness, and all kinds of other words that start with *M*. He really should have been under a doctor's care—except for one thing. He was making it all come true.

Or anyway, I was. And I didn't have his faith.

Other than that, it was a great vacation. I made it through three weeks without major trauma. My finger even healed up. Boniface had some kind of doctor there, a guy who'd obviously had experience with what to do in an ER on a Saturday night in Detroit. He set the finger, splinted it, got the swelling down, and altogether set me right.

And at the start of the fourth week, Boniface called me into his office. He sat behind a massive desk, and Bernadette stood behind him, like before. I sat across from him, and her, and waited for the shoe to drop.

"I hope you have enjoyed your visit," Boniface said as I settled into my chair.

Which meant it was coming to an end. "Delightful," I said.

"I have not pressed you for your plan to get my fresco," he said. A good thing, since I didn't have a plan. I was still pretty sure there wasn't one. "I am trusting you to do the job, in your own way."

"That's how I work," I said.

"And I will not stoop to reminding you of the consequences for failure," he said. Which was, of course, a truly classy way of reminding me of the consequences for failure.

"Thanks," I said, glancing at Bernadette. She glanced back.

"So," he said, putting both hands on the desktop, palms down, "I expect to hear from you soon—if not to report success, then to inform me of your progress." He gave me the tiny smile. "Just so we both know there is, in fact, progress."

"I'm sure there will be," I said, even though I wasn't sure at all.

He looked at me without blinking. "Good," he said at last. He pushed a fat manila envelope across the desk for me. "This will help you in your travels." Then he gave a kind of see-you-go-away-now wave. "Étienne has arrived with the boat to take you back. Good luck, Mr. Wolfe." The tiny smile again. "Riley."

I stood up, took the envelope, and left. I know when I've been dismissed.

A guard took me down to the dock. Just one guard this time. I was one of the gang now. "Étienne" turned out to be the same cheerful French guy who'd delivered me. He was behind the wheel of what looked like the same boat. He watched me climb on board without a word. Just that same happy sneer. I sneered back and sat on the bench to the right of the pilot's seat. I had no gear to stow. I had the clothes I was wearing, and no more. They'd given me a jacket against the cold, and the envelope, but that was it.

Boniface had anticipated that I'd at least need some new clothes. He'd put some cash in that envelope— around ten grand; I didn't count it. And he had told me that I hadn't had anything on my person when Arvid had delivered me. That gave me one more small item to think about.

In the meantime, I was off to sea on a great adventure. And I had no seabag, no sextant, no official Royal Navy midshipman's dirk—nothing at all to carry. No luggage, no clean undies, nothing. At least I wasn't in chains this time. After all, I was on the payroll now. And to be fair to Boniface, which I thought was a really smart idea, it was going to be one hell of a payday. He'd even agreed to pay expenses off the top. Agreed, hell, he'd suggested it. It was a very good deal, a ton of money, and it would have made me happy, except for one small detail.

It couldn't be done. No fucking way.

Steal an entire *wall*? From the *Vatican*?

Come on, Riley. You can do that, right? Sure, why not? Just because it was totally fucking impossible, so what? That's what I do! And while I was there, maybe I could snatch the dome of the basilica, too. I could stuff it right into my imaginary dimension-bending backpack, along with the wall. It would fit right next to Schrödinger's cat. And hell, why not just take the entire Vatican City while I was at it? I could shrink it and put it in a bottle, like the city of Kandor in *Superman*.

Except I really had to get that fresco, and I was pretty sure a fictional solution wasn't going to work. At least not one from an old Superman comic—Marvel, maybe, but old-time Superman? No way. But I had to find an answer somewhere. Boniface hadn't made any threats. He didn't have to. One of the big advantages of having a reputation like his was that he never had to use the corny lines the bad guys used in James Bond movies. He didn't have to tell me what would happen if I didn't get him his fresco. I knew. It would be lights-out for Riley Wolfe. And that is something I generally try to avoid.

This time, I could not see a way to do that.

So I had a lot to think about, and I was just as glad that my dear friend Frenchy didn't talk. He kept his lip zipped all the way through the tunnel, out the channel, and away from the island. He didn't speak until we were out into open sea, heading away from the island.

"I will now take you to the airplane," he said.

I looked out the windscreen. I didn't see anything but water. "Really?" I said. "Is it a seaplane?"

"No." He shook his head. "There is a small airport. Monsieur keeps his jet there."

"Of course," I said. "And, uh—where exactly is *there*?"

He curled his lip at me. "Les Îles de la Désolation," he said. Then he added, like he was accusing me of something heinous, "You would say, Kerguelen Islands."

"Would I?" I said. I was pretty sure I wouldn't say that, since I'd never heard of it, by either name. But there was time to Google it later. "So where does Mon-sewer's jet take me?"

"Perth," he said. He made it sound like he was spitting. His sneer got sneerier. "Zat is een *Australia,*" he added. And then he went silent again and turned away to look out the windscreen.

Fine by me. I couldn't really come to an appreciation of his conversational skills anyway. And now I kind of knew what part of the world I was in. That didn't cheer me up a lot. If the closest chunk of civilization was Perth, I was way the fuck out in the middle of nothing at all. The South Pole was closer than Rome. And Perth was just about the last civilized stop before you started to run into icebergs. And I wasn't all that sure about the "civilized" part. I didn't know much about Perth.

But at least it would have an airport. I mean, I was pretty sure it did. That would be a very good thing, especially since a plane with me on board was going to land there. Landing is a lot harder where there's no airport.

Perth. Shit. It was at least a full day to get back to the States, to the place in the Ozarks where I was stay-ing at the moment. I had Mom in a good extended-care facility in Fayetteville, about ninety minutes' drive from my hidey-hole in the mountains. The flight from Perth would probably take me to L.A. Then a flight to Fayetteville—or probably more than one; you can't go direct to anywhere nowadays.

So add in a couple of stopovers, and call it two days, maybe two and a half, to get from Perth to Fayetteville, check on Mom, and head back to my snug little bed in the mountains. And nothing to do the whole trip except try to figure some unlikely way to keep breathing long term.

Double shit.

It was around five hours before we came in sight of a large island. Frenchy aimed the boat right at it, so I figured it had to be where we were going. It had been a very quiet trip. Frenchy concentrated on sneering out the windshield, and I spent my time chewing my teeth and swearing. I have never been the kind of guy who pouts, but I have to admit I was pretty close to it this time.

We pulled in at a rough concrete dock and I climbed off. I don't think I would have said any fond farewells to Frenchy, but I didn't get a chance. He was already backing the boat out while I still had only one foot on land. I scrambled up the rest of the way and looked around. Not much to see, but at the far end of the dock an ATV was waiting, with a uniformed man standing beside it. It was the same black uniform Boniface's mercs wore, so I figured it was my ride.

I was right. With only a few necessary words, he drove me across the island, about fifteen minutes of bumping over mossy rocks, circling around big holes, until we finally came to the airstrip. Mon-sewer's jet was waiting. It was a very pleasant little aircraft, a Cessna Citation X that went for around twenty-five mil, plus whatever personal comforts Boniface might have required. I decided it wasn't really beneath me to be seen on such a modest conveyance, and I would let it carry me to Perth.

A uniformed flight attendant was waiting at the foot of the boarding stairs. She was a woman in her thirties, good-looking in that kind of tight, buttoned-up way that a top executive secretary has. The look that says, "Yeah, I'm decorative as hell—but lay one finger on me and if the frostbite doesn't kill you, my TigerLady knife will."

"Bonjour, m'sieur," she said. "I am Danielle. It will be my pleasure to serve you today." She smiled and beckoned me up the stairs, and I boarded.

The interior did nothing that might have endangered my social standing. It was furnished like somebody had decided to decorate the world's most exclusive whorehouse in quiet good taste. I buckled myself into a seat that would have looked okay in the penthouse suite of a luxury hotel, and three minutes later we were in the air.

CHAPTER
8

The trip to Perth took around four hours. I wasn't watching the clock. But I wasn't suffering, either. At least, not physically. Danielle plied me with food and drink, top-quality stuff that did not disgrace the plane's luxurious interior. And real food this time; the Day of the Algae was over at last. Good fluids, too. I limited myself to a couple of glasses of wine—a really terrific Domaine de Chevalier—and a light meal of snails in butter and garlic, Caesar salad (with anchovies, of course), fresh lamb shank in a blackberry-mint sauce, new potatoes with rosemary, grilled asparagus, and a nice crème brûlée that I watched Danielle set on fire, and then a very modest two or three glasses of Châteauneuf marc.

When I was finished I leaned back with a cup of coffee—I would swear it was *kopi luwak,* but it's possible to be wrong. After the wine and the marc, it was hard to say whether the beans had actually gone all the way through a civet's digestive system. They could have gone through a common house cat, and I wouldn't have known the difference.

It didn't much matter. The coffee was good, as good as the rest of the meal. I sipped and pondered just how deep the shit was that I'd been dumped into. Somehow, the rich décor of the cabin and the mellow afterglow of the meal made it seem a little less terrifying. Or at least, a little easier to ponder without ripping out my hair and screeching. Because I was still in very deep shit, no doubt about it. And after an hour of figuring, it still looked pretty deep. I was going to steal a wall. From the Vatican. Or else I was going to be dead. Probably after a long visit with Bernadette. Taking it all into consideration, *dead* looked most likely.

Yup. That covered it. Very deep shit. Exceptionally deep.

I was still looking for a way out, and not finding one, when we landed. It turns out Perth does have an airport. So the landing was uneventful, which is always nice. When we stopped moving, Danielle beckoned me to the door and opened it. A blast of warm air hit me as the port swung open. Just another lovely day in Oz. But after the cold and damp in Boniface's fortress of solitude, it seemed hot. The stairs were already in place, so I climbed off the jet. I was soaked with sweat by the time I got down onto the tarmac.

I stopped at the foot of the stairs and scanned the

horizon. We'd landed at the private flight terminal, where all the billionaires land their jets. What looked to be the main commercial terminal was about a mile away. More shit. But what the hell, a nice stroll across pavement might clear my head. And it's always nice to stroll while inhaling jet fuel fumes.

"M'sieur?" Danielle said from the bottom step. I turned to her. She gave me one last professional smile and handed me a large manila envelope before heading back up the steps. I opened the envelope. Inside was a passport with my picture in it. It was French, in the name of Hervé Thierry. The name I'd used in Russia. I stuck it in a pocket and reached back into the envelope to find a first-class ticket in the same name.

All the way through to Little Rock, Arkansas. The closest major airport to Fayetteville.

The sonofabitch knew everything. It shouldn't have been a surprise. He had the money, the connections, and the squeeze to find out whatever he wanted, pretty much anywhere in the world. Still, it was a nasty shock. And it meant I was going to be moving me and Mom as soon as I got home. Which was not going to be as soon as Boniface thought, so he didn't know everything after all.

I closed the envelope and watched Danielle sashay up the stairway into the jet. As she pulled the door closed I turned and looked at the distant terminal. We come into this world to suffer, Mom used to say. She was always right about that sort of thing. I started to walk, and behind me Boniface's jet taxied away.

I hadn't gotten more than fifty yards when I heard the whisper of tires behind me and turned.

A large black Escalade came to a stop and a guy in a chauffeur's suit hopped out. "Mr. Wolfe?" he said. He had a cheery Aussie accent, and he spoke really politely and carefully, like he thought I might kick him in the balls if he was rude.

I just nodded, and he smiled and opened the back door of the car. "The main terminal is quite far, sir. I am instructed to give you a ride."

It was just the kind of thoughtful detail I should have expected from my new best friend, and even though I'd been sort of looking forward to delightful stroll and accompanying sweat bath, I didn't want Boniface to think I had spurned his thoughtful gesture. So I nodded and climbed into the Escalade back seat.

We were rolling as soon as I buckled in. The door locks clicked, like they usually do when a car gets moving. I didn't think anything of it—until I saw we were headed in the opposite direction from the main terminal. Okay, so maybe we had to get onto an access road and circle around? Sure, that was it. You can't drive a car across the runway. Not even an Escalade. Nothing to worry about.

But we hit the access road, and we turned away from the airport.

"Hey," I said to the driver. "The terminal's over there."

He looked up and caught my eye in the rearview mirror. He winked.

And he leaned forward and hit a switch I couldn't see, and a pane of thick glass, almost certainly bullet-proof, shot up between us.

I tried the car's door. It stayed locked. I tried to undo my seat belt. It wouldn't undo.

So it was definite. I was in some brand-new shit. And this time I didn't even know what it was.

I got no clues over the next forty minutes. We rolled smoothly through Perth and out into an area with no buildings, just scrubby trees. We turned onto a small road. There was a big sign that read, "PRIVATE ROAD—NO TRESPASSING." And under that, in red letters, "ARMED RESPONSE."

That was the final touch. I'd been kidnapped from my kidnapper by someone who lived in the Australian fucking outback with armed responders. It was totally clear to me now. God really did hate me.

The private road wound up a hill through more of the scrub for a couple of miles and then up to a massive iron gate. The driver stuck a plastic card into a slot on the gatepost, the gate swung open, and we went through, following the road for another mile, until we came to a large circular driveway in front of a big stone house. The circle had a large patch of manicured lawn in the center, and there was a fountain in the middle of it, squirting water twenty feet into the air. A little ostentatious for the outback, but you can't buy good taste.

The car rolled to a stop at the front door, a massive, beautifully carved thing that looked like mahogany. Hard to tell; my view was partially blocked by six guys in gray paramilitary uniforms, holding automatic weapons. My driver hopped out, opened my door, and held it for me.

I didn't move, except to undo my seat belt. It opened fine now. So I unbuckled—and then I just sat there. I had no idea why I'd been brought here, or whose idea it was, or what was supposed to happen next. But nothing that had happened so far had given me an irresistible urge to cooperate. I figured I would just wait and see what the next move would be. Whatever it was, there wasn't a whole lot I could do about it. But if somebody was going to kill me, I wasn't going to make it easy for them. So I just sat there, waiting to see what would happen.

For a minute, nothing did. The guards stood at attention; the driver held the car's door open; the mahogany front door stayed carved. Finally, the driver leaned in. He had a kind of anxious expression on his face. "Mr. Wolfe?" he said. "Please step out, sir."

"No," I said.

The driver looked nervously at the big front door, then back to me. He lowered his voice and said, "Come on, mate, why not? You'll piss him off. You don't want to do that, do you?"

"Sure I do," I said.

"No, mate, you absolutely do not," he said, very serious, like he really, truly meant it. "My word you don't."

I just shrugged.

"Aw, jumping Jesus, please, come on out," he said.

"First," I said, "who is 'him,' why am I here, and in general, what the fuck is going on?"

He swallowed. He blinked. He opened his mouth, but nothing came out.

"Okay, I'll stay here," I said. "Could you please close that door? You're letting out the air-conditioning."

He swallowed again, and then he stood up. He said something I couldn't hear to one of the guards. The guard nodded and hurried through the mahogany door and into the house. And I took a big breath and relaxed a little. Because I was pretty sure now that I had at least one foot out of the cesspool. If I was here to be killed or roughed up, the move would have been for a couple of the guards to grab me and drag me out of the car and smack me around, then pull me into the house by the hair.

That didn't happen. That meant that, whatever the reason I was here, somebody didn't want me roughed up. At least, not yet. So far, that was the most encouraging thing that had happened to me since I stepped onto Arvid's boat in St. Petersburg.

So I sat and waited. There wasn't much to go on, but I tried to figure the angle anyway. Somebody had grabbed me. Whoever they were, they had picked me up at Boniface's plane. So the odds were very good that the reason I was here was connected to my delightful holiday on Boniface's little Eden. But since good old Patrick was my new best friend, it had to be without his knowledge, or he would have said something. And that probably meant that they did not enjoy a really close friendship with Boniface.

Of course, a man like Boniface didn't have very many friends. They were a weakness, a luxury that added too many elements of risk and too few of reward. What he did have was a long list of clients, business associates—and enemies. Someone doing business with Boniface would know the cost of crossing him. They'd stay away from anything he had an interest in. That left enemies.

An enemy who was really worth his salt would know that taking me hostage would not give him any leverage with Boniface. I mean, "Do what I say or Riley Wolfe is dead" would be a total shrug for Boniface. Like, "Okay, sure, kill him, sorry, Riley—Bernadette, who's the next-best thief in the world?" So that was out.

But one thing I might provide is information. I had been to the Fortress of Solitude. So the most likely flavor of enemy would be somebody looking to find out about any weakness the place might have. Nobody would care about that unless they wanted in. The only reason anybody would want in to Cabbage Island was to get Boniface. I mean, unless they wanted the recipe for the Green Slime. Not likely; so it had to mean a rival, probably another arms dealer. The huge fenced-off estate, the big house, the armed guards, and the brass balls of just grabbing me in public all went with that profile.

As it happens, I knew a little about most of the big

dealers. Not that I bought large quantities of military-grade weapons. It's just that they swam in the same murky waters I lived in. And one or two of them got the collecting bug, like Boniface, and became customers.

So I knew the names. As far as I knew, there was only one living in Australia.

His name was Bailey Stone. He'd started life as an American Southern redneck—trailer trash, just like me. But he'd gone into the gun trade and clawed his way up the heap until he was close to the top. Close—he wasn't in the same league as Patrick Boniface; nobody was. But Stone would just naturally want to be top dog. If you have what it takes to go into that line of work, you also have to have something eating at you, pushing you to be the kingpin. Boniface was, and Stone wasn't. He was just a wannabe. Anybody in that position would naturally find some way to keep tabs on whatever the current number one guy, Boniface, was up to. Stone would have a source, human intel. It could be one of the mercenaries on Île des Choux, or somebody at the airport, or even Bernadette the Impaler. I didn't think it was her, but the point is, it was somebody. Stone had to have a set of eyes on Boniface. And whoever that was, he or she had seen me when I showed up on the radar screen, reported the new blip to Stone—and he'd grabbed me.

Why? Curiosity? Probably something more. I mean, he'd want to know what Boniface wanted from me, but that would be secondary. He had seen that there might be a way to use me to get a leg up on Boniface. If it turned out to be no more than a few tips on the defenses at Île des Choux, fine. Stone was still one move further ahead than he had been. And it might be a hell of a lot more than that. No way to know without asking Riley a few friendly questions.

The one thing that really twisted my nuts was that he knew me now. I work my ass off to keep my looks a secret. Boniface had obviously put in a shitload of time and money to track me down. It sucked that he'd been successful, but with his kind of power it was kind of inevitable.

But this guy, Stone—assuming it was him—he knew what I looked like, too. And that sucked way more.

The huge front door of the house swung open, and the same guard who had run in doubled back out. He said a few words to the driver, and the driver opened the door and bent inside.

"Never mind," I said before he could speak. "Tell Mr. Stone I'll be glad to answer a few questions."

The look on the driver's face was almost worth getting kidnapped a second time. He hung there, bent over, with his mouth open, blinking like I'd thrown itching powder into his eyes. If I'd had my phone, I would have snapped a picture and stuck it in "Favorites." And aside from being a true hoot, it told me I was right. I was here to see Bailey Stone.

Good to know. I mean, I was still neck-deep in a pool of flaming shit, but at least I knew who owned it.

CHAPTER
9

Bailey Stone was waiting for me in a room he probably called the Library. He had it fitted out like that, like it was a room in an old-fashioned Southern gentleman's estate. The back wall was floor-to-ceiling books on lacquered teak shelving. The books were all leather-bound classics and I'd bet anybody five bucks he hadn't read even one of them. The other walls, a dark green, were hung with British hunting prints. You know the kind I mean—guys in red coats on horseback, hounds prancing around, some asshole blowing a horn; that kind of ugly dumb-ass pointless crap. The best picture of the whole bunch would probably bring $250 at auction. If they could find somebody drunk or stupid enough to bid.

Bailey himself was pretty much what you'd expect from seeing the room. Stocky, forties, medium-length sandy hair parted on the left. He wore olive-green wool pants and a tan shooting shirt—the kind with a leather patch on the shoulder where you'd rest the stock of your Beretta over-and-under shotgun. He sat in a large, overstuffed chair beside a fireplace. No fire in it—I mean, it was kind of warm outside. Beside him, on an antique end table, was a silver platter holding a decanter and a couple of glasses. And beside the decanter was a photograph in a silver frame. It was a very nice photo, obviously taken candidly. The woman in the picture was smiling at something off to one side. I knew the woman, too.

It was Monique.

I don't have friends, and I've never had a partner. Friends just get in the way, a partner slows everything down, and they are both avoidable risks. The closer to you somebody is, the more likely they are to turn on you. Sooner or later they get jealous, or possessive, or start to resent something you said or did. And then they flip you to the cops, or stick a knife in your head, or arrange for a job to go bad on you. Always. Every time.

So I work alone, and I live alone. But the closest I have ever come to somebody who was a partner and a friend at the same time is Monique. She was probably the best art forger in the world, and she had a flair for costumes—she helped dress the characters I turned into when I was working. I used her forgeries and her tips on disguise on nearly all my jobs. And I had to admit that was partly because I would take just about any excuse to hang around with her.

I mean, she was totally the best at what she did, no doubt about that. But more than that, there was something about her that made me want to paw the ground and snort every time I saw her. I have known plenty of women who were just as good-looking, or maybe even better, but Monique had that something special that just plain set me on fire. I wanted to rub my fingertips across her skin, bury my nose in her neck, nibble her earlobes—you know, all the standard shit for when you have the all-out hots for a woman. What made it worse was that we'd actually spent time doing all those things together.

Once. No matter how hard I tried, Monique wouldn't go for a repeat.

I stuck around her anyway. Because against all my instincts and hard-won smarts—against at least three of Riley's Laws, too—I cared about Monique. I mean, aside from knowing that I'd never find an art forger half as good. I had feelings for her, and I thought the world was a better place with her in it.

And Bailey Stone had her photograph.

He didn't have to say anything about the picture. He didn't even have to point it out. He just sat there and smiled at me and waved at a chair on the opposite side of the fireplace. "Sit down, Riley. May I call you Riley?"

He spoke with a Virginia accent and smiled the whole time. Just like the cat that caught the canary, Mom would've said. And why not? He had me just about every way possible. He didn't need to get all threatening and mean-faced; he didn't have to say anything like, "Do as I tell you or the girl gets it." The picture of Monique said it all. He knew who she was, where she was, and that she mattered to me.

Of course, there was no reason I had to kiss his ass. So I didn't. "Sure, Bailey," I said. I moved to the chair he'd pointed at and sat. "Let's pretend we're old buddies, talking over a hunting trip." I nodded at the decanter. "Is that bourbon?"

Still smiling, he raised his eyebrows, like I'd asked if the sky was blue. "Of course it is," he said. "May I offer you a taste?"

"Sure, why not," I said.

Bailey stood and poured two fingers into one of the heavy cut-glass tumblers. He handed it to me and sat back down again. "Your health," he said, raising his glass and sipping.

"Cheers," I said back, and I sipped, too.

"Well," he said. "I trust you enjoyed your stay in the Kerguelen Islands?"

"Why wouldn't I?" I said. I didn't bother to deny where I'd been or pretend I was surprised he knew. I just sipped and said, "Good company, lovely scenery, and a really chic stone cell with designer chains. Five-star vacation." Bailey nodded. I sipped again. It was pretty good bourbon, which surprised me a little. I mean, considering the pictures on the walls, I wouldn't have guessed he had any taste at all. But he knew his bourbons. This stuff was good. I lifted the glass and nodded appreciatively.

"I'm glad you like it," Stone said. "One Southerner to another, it pleases me to see you appreciate a fine example of our national beverage."

"It's good," I said with a shrug. I mean, it was. Why twist his leash?

"It's called Filibuster," he said. "Difficult to get. Even harder now." His smile got a little bigger. "I bought a great deal of it."

"Of course you did," I said, and we both took a sip.

"I hope you'll forgive me if I cut right to the chase," he said, staying with the fake-Southern-charm act. "I have to get you back to the airport in about an hour." He nodded and sipped. "Assuming, of course, that you go back at all."

Well, there it was. He probably thought of it as the iron hand in the velvet glove. Me? I thought of it as a classless asshole acting like a classless asshole. But I didn't have too many moves except to play along for now, so I did. Sort of.

"Oh, lordy," I said. "Please don't throw me back in that briar patch. Anything but that."

Stone just blinked at me, blank-faced. Some Southerner. Apparently Uncle Remus wasn't part of his childhood. I am constantly appalled at the great holes in our educational system. But now wasn't the time to educate Stone. So I just said, "What do you want?"

He frowned for the first time and poured a little more bourbon into his glass. "In the big picture, Riley," he said, swirling the liquor in his glass, "what I want is to take Patrick Boniface out of the game." He sipped. "The man has done me wrong, on numerous occasions."

"I can't help you there," I said. "I'm not an assassin."

"I am aware of that," Stone said. "But I know several very skilled men who are assassins. I employ a whole mess of 'em. It has so far been impossible to get any of them close to Mr. Boniface." He frowned. "I have lost several expensive men trying." He shook it off and nodded at me. "I believe you might be able to help me with that."

"I don't have a house key," I said. "And I didn't see a whole lot of his island. Boniface kept me chained up in the basement. He doesn't trust me."

Stone smirked. "Hard to blame him for that," he said.

"So what exactly is it you think I can do for you?" I said. "And I'll cut to the chase, too. Why the fuck should I do it?"

"I believe the reason for your cooperation should be fairly clear," he said with a mischievous glance at Monique's picture. "As to what I want from you . . ." He drained his glass and poured another inch into it from the decanter. He took a swig, pretended to savor it for a moment, and then looked back at me. "What does Boniface want you to do?"

I swirled my glass, looked at it, took a sip, stalling for a few seconds while I thought about it. Boniface had not specifically told me not to tell anybody. He didn't have to. I mean, why would I? But I was pretty sure he didn't want Bailey Stone knowing his business.

On the other hand, here I was, sitting in Stone's house, sipping his bourbon, watching him smile as he pointed a gun at my head—and at Monique's head, too, if keeping me alive wasn't enough incentive. If I didn't tell him what he wanted to hear, he would pull the trigger, still smiling.

Of course, it was pretty close to the same thing Boniface would do if he knew I was talking about him to a rival. So where did my loyalty really lie here?

Every now and then, life leads you down a one-way road to a cul-de-sac, a place where the only real option you have is to figure out which cliché you would rather use to describe the shit pile you've landed in. I was there right now. And I just couldn't decide if I should go with "Between a rock and a hard place," which seemed accurate and had the advantage of having a pun in it—"rock" for "Stone." Very funny. But Mom would have said, "Between the devil and the deep blue sea," making that the sentimental choice. And personally, I have always favored something simple, direct, and accurate, like, "In deep shit."

So many good choices, so little time. And none of them told me what I should do. So just when I could see Stone was getting impatient, I settled on the most devious thing I could do.

I told him the truth.

"Bullshit," Stone said when I was done.

"God's truth," I said.

"You can't steal a goddamn wall," he pointed out. "Not from the goddamn Vatican." He shook his head. "It can't be done."

"I know that."

He blinked at me a few times. "What're you gonna do?"

"Steal the goddamn wall," I said. "From the goddamn Vatican."

"How you gonna do that?" he demanded.

"Not a fucking clue," I said. "But I'm gonna do it."

"No way," he said. "It can't be done."

I shrugged. "There's always a way."

"You think you can *do* it?"

I shrugged again. "I sort of have to."

"And then, what? Deliver it? To Boniface's island?"

"Yup."

"Huh," he said. He was quiet for a long time, not really looking at anything, just thinking about it. He finished his drink, poured another one, sipped that, just staring into space.

I finished my drink. Stone still didn't say anything. Finally, he drained his glass and stared into it for a moment. Then he nodded. "Perfect," he muttered. He put the glass down and looked at me and said the one thing in all the world I never expected to hear from him. "How can I help?"

I was pretty sure I'd heard him wrong. "I'm sorry," I said. "I guess I had too much of this good whisky. I thought you said, how can you help."

He smiled, and it wasn't a smile that would make anybody happy. "That's just what I said," he said.

"But that's—you don't want me to fail?"

"Nuh-uh," he said. "I want you to succeed."

I didn't get it. I just shook my head and looked at Stone, and he just smiled and looked back. And then, just as I opened my mouth to ask him what the fuck he meant by that—

"Oh," I said. Then the full weight of what he meant hit me. "No. Sorry, but no. No fucking way."

Stone's smile got bigger. "You got the reputation of a man who always finds a way," he said. "When nobody else in the world would even think about trying something, good ole Riley Wolfe comes along and just does it."

"I draw the line at suicide," I said.

He raised an eyebrow, but the smile didn't go away. "But you're okay with killing a friend?" he asked. And the stupid over-obvious low-class son of a bitch actually turned his head and looked at the picture of Monique, just to make sure I'd get what he was talking about.

Yeah, I got it. Just like I got what he wanted me to do. He said he wanted me to succeed, and he did. He wanted me to steal a fresco from the Vatican and deliver it to Boniface. Because he figured that if I did, he could come along for the ride when I made the delivery. I mean, a wall takes up some space, which means a large boat, probably big enough that he could find room on board for himself and a few close friends—the kind of well-armed friends you'd want to invite to the party when you meant to kill Boniface and his little private army.

Really cool plan, right?

Except I saw a few problems with it. First, and the biggest problem, it had me in it, right in the middle, with a giant bull's-eye on my back. If Stone tried and lost, Boniface would kill me. If Stone won, his best bet was to kill me anyway, to keep things tidy, quiet, and secure. And no matter who won, there was a really good chance that I would take a bullet from all the flying lead. Which is just as dead as if it was on purpose.

So any way you cut it, I was more likely to end up The Late Riley Wolfe than anything else. Or if it wasn't me, it would be Monique—or both of us. Plus a whole bunch of poor innocent mercenaries, an arms dealer or two—the body count was getting way too high for my taste. I mean, I've got no objection to the occasional corpse along the way, not if it helps get a job done. But this was starting to look like a massacre, the kind that makes even the cops sit up and take a look. So even if I lived, which didn't seem likely, there would be some very serious long-term heat.

And for what? Just a lousy eight-figure payday!

It was a horrible, useless, lethal bloody mess. And I was stuck with it.

I looked at Stone. He seemed to have a lot of teeth all of a sudden, and he was showing all of them. It was the kind of smile somebody puts on after an all-night poker game when suddenly he somehow ends up with all the chips and everybody else has to walk home. "How 'bout it?" he said through his teeth.

I looked him right in the eye, a truly steely glare, and because I don't let anybody push me into doing something I don't want to do, I said, "Sure. Why not."

And it's maybe a little weird? But right away I felt better. Because after all that shit, what else could go wrong?

I should've remembered Riley's Ninth Law: Don't ask a question if you don't want to know the answer.

CHAPTER

10

The same cheerful Aussie drove me back to the Perth airport. He didn't put the bulletproof glass shield up between us this time. He probably figured that since I wasn't dead I was on his team now. Except he was from Oz, so he probably would have said "side" instead of "team." And I couldn't really say if he was right or wrong about that. I hadn't even settled into the idea of working for Boniface, and Stone had stepped in and stirred up the whole fucking thing.

I had a lot to think about on the drive to the airport. I thought about it. Or I tried to. But when I get pushed, I push back. I can't help it, and I don't really want to. I've got a deep-rooted thing about being bullied into shit I don't want to do—and here I was being bullied from two directions. By really impressive bullies, too. So I didn't like it even more than usual.

So a whole lot of my "thinking about it" was getting mad. That's counterproductive, and mostly I avoid it. But this was stacking up to be a special case in a lot of ways, and getting mad seemed like just about the only sane response right now. It didn't give me any really clear ideas about anything, but it did make me promise myself I wasn't going to just let this slide. And what the hell, that felt good.

The driver took me to the terminal and held the door while I got out. I didn't tip him. I just went in, still fuming. But when I took out my ticket, it reminded me that this was one hoop I wasn't going to jump through. Not just yet.

I went to the ticket counter and changed my ticket. Not just because I was pissed off at being told what to do. I had one important stop to make before I went home, and it couldn't wait. I had two and a half hours before the new flight took off, so I strolled through the terminal, looking into the shops for a few basics. I found a good hard-shell carry-on suitcase, no problem. And all the normal junk like toothbrush, deodorant, and so on. But clothing was a challenge. Apparently, all the passengers who came to Perth International Airport were on their way to go surfing and had left home without any appropriate outfits. I could have bought a terrific wardrobe if I was going surfing, too. I wasn't, so the choices were limited.

Luckily, I found a couple of shirts without embarrassing patterns or cute slogans, and a really warm jacket lined with merino wool. I also bought a good pair of sturdy boots. And what the fuck, why not?—I bought a really cool hat, too, the kind that would have made Mick Dundee jealous.

I changed in the first-class lounge, stuffed everything else into my new suitcase, and sat down with a cup of coffee. It wasn't as good as the one Danielle gave me. It was okay, but it didn't have the same zesty flavor that a civet's ass gives a cup of coffee.

I finished the coffee and stared at the TV for a while. The time dragged by. I tried not to think. It didn't work.

Finally they called my flight. I climbed on board and settled into a window seat in first class. Half an hour later I was in the air and on my way. Ten minutes after that I was asleep.

CHAPTER
11

Thorsang is a small and picturesque fishing village on the east coast of Sweden. Not surprisingly, its population is almost entirely made up of fishermen, tough people who sail out onto the rough waters of the Baltic and the North Atlantic. Very few guidebooks mention Thorsang, and tourists who stumble onto the quaint old hamlet with its one bed-and-breakfast come away with little more than the smell of fish on their shoes and a few pictures of the big bronze statue at the harbor mouth.

The statue isn't really worth a picture, but once you've taken a few shots of the fishing trawlers and a couple of bearded fishermen, it's about all the town offers. Five meters tall and cast from bronze, it's a battered and slightly crude rendition of Njord, the old Viking god of the sea. He stands there on the jetty, covered with bird shit and the cruddy patina salt air leaves on metal, and he glares out at his watery kingdom with his spear upraised, as if commanding the waves to behave themselves and let the poor fishermen of Thorsang make a living in peace.

Njord stands on the end of the jetty that juts out from the small harbor, breaking the rough chop of the Baltic so the fishing boats can lie at easy anchor inside its protection. Just to the left of where the jetty meets the shore is a dock that belongs to the only real business in town, the small factory where the fresh fish is cleaned, frozen, and shipped away to a hungry world. Behind that an old cobbled road leads into the tiny town square, lined with a few shops, and Thorsang's pub, the Gammal Ankare. It's not merely the town's source for life-sustaining beer. It's also the social center of town, the only gathering place for the men and women who live in Thorsang.

Tonight, as on most nights, the pub was about three-quarters full. But tonight—and on most recent nights—it was a little quieter than a fishermen's pub should be. There was not much jolly talk in the dark and smoky main room. In better times there would be plenty of laughter, loud jokes, even singing, and the room would feel snug, secure, and cheerful. Not tonight. Now it felt like pure gloom, and the conversation was dour.

The fishing was very bad lately, and most people who knew about such things said it would just get worse. It was climate change, most likely. Of course they knew about Greta Thunberg. And they believed her; she was

Swedish, after all, from Stockholm. And nobody who lived with the sea could possibly doubt that climate change was real. The high tides were higher—the town square had even flooded at the last spring tide, and nobody could remember when that had happened before. No, things were changing, and not for the better.

Even worse; in spite of more demand and smaller catches, prices were going *down*! How did that even make sense? In the past, when fishing was bad, the price of fish went up. Now, everything was crazy, upside down. Who could tell what might happen next? Whatever it was, it was sure to be bad. Things only got worse, and that was a historical fact. And it was always workingmen who were stuck with the bill.

So the general feeling in the pub was close to unanimous. This was a truly shitty time to be a fisherman.

But in truth, not everybody was completely full of misery. One of the fishermen sitting there in the pub was clearly feeling pretty good about the way life had been treating him lately. Of course, he didn't say so. He knew very well that no one wanted to hear that song tonight. He certainly wasn't going to tell anyone why his face was not as long as the other men's. He just sipped his pint and agreed that he could not remember when times were worse for the men who fished on the Baltic. But he took larger sips than the others—and if someone wanted to notice such things, it was his *third* pint, at that.

Per Hakansson, sitting across the table from the nearly smiling man, *did* notice it. Three pints! Not that it was any of his business, but really; why flaunt your good fortune when everyone else was feeling the pinch? It wasn't decent. Like most of the other men, Per himself had been nursing the same pint all evening, as he could not really afford more than one. And he had watched his friend buy *three* pints with a careless air, as if money meant nothing. So Per finally said, "Well, my friend, it seems you have had better fishing than the rest of us, is that right?"

The man gave a single shake of his head, but he smiled, just a little. "Klaga inte över för lite vind—lär dig segla," he said. It was an old saying, and Per remembered his own father saying it. Freely translated, it meant, *Don't complain about the wind—learn to sail.*

Per was not a fool, and unfortunately, he was not drunk, either. So he didn't ask for any details. He had a pretty good idea what that meant—but it was none of his business, and he did not press for specifics. And in spite of finishing off three entire pints, Per's friend did not loosen up enough to say any more. But he still had that self-satisfied look on his face when he rose from his chair to walk home.

"Well, and good night, then," Per said. "Perhaps the rest of us can leave the fishing to you and make our money taking selfies with tourists by the statue."

"Ya, the tourists," another man with a large red beard chimed in. "*Both* of them."

This did not get the laugh it might have before the current slump. The men just watched the door close behind the three-pint man.

"Huh," Per said sourly. "Well, so, one of us at least has managed to stay off the point of Njord's spear."

"More fish for us," the bearded man said.

"Feh," Per said. "And where are these fish of yours? I can't find them—but if you know where the fish have gone, you may buy me another pint."

Outside the pub, a cold and wet wind blew in from the sea, the kind of wind that feels much colder than the thermometer says it is. But three pints of good Swedish beer make a fine insulation, and the lucky fisherman was still cheerful as he walked home through the square. And why not? Life was good, and if the other fishermen were not able to adapt as well as he did, that was their lookout. He even whistled a little once he was out of hearing of the men in the pub. Like most men who make their living on the sea, he lived inland, away from the water, and his little cottage stood at the edge of town, slightly isolated from the other homes of the village.

He was still whistling when he opened the door of the cottage. He stopped abruptly after one step inside.

The house was a wreck.

He was not an unusually neat man, but this— someone had been here. Someone had come in while he was at the pub and taken the place apart. Someone who was looking for something.

They hadn't found it; of course not. Although almost everything in the house had been dumped in the center of the floor, there didn't appear to be anything missing. There was nothing here worth taking, nothing at all beyond some pots and pans, a few books, some old knickknacks.

He went quickly into the other two rooms, the kitchen and the bedroom. It was the same there—everything tossed into the center of the room, kicked to splinters, sifted through for something that they would never find, whoever had done this, because it wasn't here. He would never keep anything valuable here, in the battered old cottage. Anything really important, he kept in a very safe place, well hidden on—

On his boat.

For a moment he stopped breathing.

And then, as if he had been jolted into action by an electric shock, he lurched into the bedroom. The mattress had been pulled off the springs, but it was intact. He hurriedly flipped it over. There was a seam hidden on the top edge. He had made it himself and closed it with Velcro so it was nearly invisible but within easy reach when he lay in his bed. He opened it now and thrust a trembling hand inside, coming out a moment later with his pistol, a 9mm Husqvarna M40 that had been his father's. He had kept it handy for years. He sometimes dealt with very questionable people, and although there had never been any need of the pistol, he kept it on the theory that it was better to have it and not need it than need it and not have it.

And now, quite clearly, he needed it. He tucked it into the waist of his trousers, pulled his sweater down to hide it, and hurried from his house.

His boat was in a slip at the municipal docks, down

at the end of a row of similar fishing boats and near the jetty. He kept it there, somewhat isolated, except from the statue of Njord, which loomed over it only seven or eight meters away. There were times when a small bit of privacy was called for—those times when he went out for things that were not, strictly speaking, fish.

Nearly running, he went down the dock to his boat. It seemed undisturbed, still buttoned up just as he had left it. But of course, looks are often deceptive. Moving cautiously now, he took his pistol from the waist of his trousers and stepped on board his trawler. In spite of his care, the boat rocked under his weight, just a little. The locks were all in place, undisturbed. He saw no sign that anything had been touched.

Even so—he paused on the deck, holding his breath, waiting for some sign that someone was there.

Nothing.

He took a breath. His palms were sweating, and he wiped them against his trouser legs. With a firm and much drier grip on his pistol, he unlocked the door into the main cabin and slid it open.

He paused again, listening for any sound. He heard only the slow creak of the mooring lines and a gentle gurgle of water against the hull. Slowly, silently, he moved inside the cabin, closing the door behind him. As quiet as a cat, he went down the short stairway to the interior of the boat. Still no sign that anything had been touched. But with so much at stake—he had to be sure.

He crept along a short corridor and down into the hold. It was dark, and the smell of old fish was overpowering. He barely noticed. Pressing himself against the last bulkhead before the bow, he flipped the switch that turned on the dim light in the bow area. Again— empty. No sign that any intruder had been here.

He moved quickly forward to the bow. Below the waterline, just where the boat's prow came to a point, he had installed a hidden compartment. It had been useful many times in the past. His special, non-fishing clients usually had something they wished to hide. He never showed any of them where this compartment was. No one else knew of its location—not even of its existence. It was masterfully disguised at the bottom of a locker that held old anchor line, smelly and crusted with growth. Now it held something even more important than anything he had put into it before. Now it held his future. His safe, comfortable future in a warm place, away from ice and snow and the stink of fish.

Hardly daring to breathe, he looked into the locker.

The old anchor line was undisturbed. Of course it was; it could not be otherwise. No one knew about this compartment, and no one could ever find it. Even when he had been boarded by police, no one had ever found the compartment. Still, just to be sure, he moved the old anchor line aside and opened the compartment.

It was still there. Breathing a sigh of relief, he reached in and brought it out into the light. He didn't know a lot about Fabergé and had no idea why the man had made eggs. And this one—a big pink egg with a clock. Why? It made no sense to him. But that didn't really matter. All that mattered was that it was worth millions—thirty-five or forty million, perhaps. He didn't care. Twenty million was fine; it would make for a quick sale, and just as soon as the heat died down a bit he would find a buyer, some quiet collector, willing to pay him a bargain price for this rare treasure.

And it was very pretty, he had to admit. He turned it slowly, admiring the little chicken on top, covered with gems, and how they took the pink color of the egg itself. It really was quite—

"Beautiful, isn't it?"

The voice was right behind him, impossibly close. He knew the voice, and he knew what it meant. So he didn't try anything stupid, like reaching for his pistol, or spinning around quickly. Instead, he just froze, the egg held in front of him in both hands.

"It's not really my favorite," the voice went on. "I mean, to be honest? I'm not crazy about any of the Fabergé eggs. They're kind of garish, aren't they? Still, if you like that sort of thing—and a lot of people do. Myself? I'm more of a painting guy. Impressionists are my favorite—you know, the palette and the texture that—"

"Make it quick," the fisherman said. "Go on, get it done."

There was a brief chuckle. "Why, Arvid, what on earth are you talking about?" the voice drawled.

"You're here to kill me," Arvid said. "Go ahead. I took a chance, and I lost. Just make it quick."

A sigh. "Arvid, really, what must you think of me? I'm not going to kill you."

A small ripple of hope surged up in Arvid's breast. "What, then?"

"I'm going to take back my property." A hand snaked over Arvid's shoulder and plucked the egg out of his grasp.

"And then?" Arvid said. "You're just going to walk away? I don't believe you!"

"Why wouldn't I?"

"Because," Arvid said. "I betrayed you. I took your prize. You would let that go?"

"Oh, I won't let it go," the voice said with amusement. "But I won't kill you, either."

"You won't?" Arvid said, and his heart was pounding furiously.

"What you did was very bad. But it's not for me to judge you, Arvid."

"But, what—the police?" Arvid stammered.

"No, Arvid," the voice said. "I'm going to leave your fate to the gods."

"What?" Arvid said—and then he felt the shock of a needle plunging into his neck. He reflexively reached for it—but long before his hands got there, Arvid had already swirled down into deep and heavy darkness.

Fishermen are early risers. Those who lived in Thorsang were no exception. But on this morning, it was not their battered alarm clocks that woke them.

It was the screams.

Horrible, throaty screams, guttural and savage sounding, as if they were coming from some deep, prehistoric place in the soul of a man in such terrible agony that he had been transported out of himself and into a primeval realm where supernatural torment ruled.

And the screams would not stop. They went on and on, rising and falling—growing weaker but never going away. They woke Per Hakansson from his sleep, in his cottage at the edge of town. His wife was already awake, standing at the window and staring out in horror. Per staggered out of bed and stood next to her. "It's coming from the harbor," she said.

They listened together for a moment. Then Per turned and pulled on his pants, boots, and jacket. "I will go see," he said.

"Per—" But when he looked at her, she could only shake her head and then turn back to the window.

Per was not the first to arrive at the harbor. It looked to him like half the town was already there, clustered out on the jetty and looking up at the statue of Njord. In the dimness of predawn, Per could not tell what was so goddamn interesting about it, nor what the screaming was about. He squinted; was there something wiggling at the top of the statue? Not possible. Per moved closer to see better.

He came to the knot of people gathered on the jetty and stopped. Their faces—the faces of his neighbors and friends, faces he knew nearly as well as his own—they were all knotted into the same look. It was an expression he had never seen before, and he didn't like it. Shaking his head, he pushed through them, getting closer to Njord, to where he could finally get a clear look—

"Herregud—!" Per blurted as he saw.

Yes, there was something up there. And yes, it was wriggling, jerking about like a hooked cod. And yes, that was what was screaming, too. It was a man—easy enough to be sure of that, since he wore no pants. And he was screaming and wriggling for a very simple reason.

He was impaled on Njord's spear.

Somehow, someone—or something? Surely nothing human could do this—something had raised this man up and jammed him onto the point of the old sea god's spear, straight up his arse, leaving the poor bastard up there—alive somehow, though clearly that was just a matter of time.

And as Per stared in horror, the speared man swung his head from side to side spasmodically, and Per caught a glimpse of his face.

It was Arvid.

PART 2

CHAPTER
12

FBI Special Agent in Charge Dellmore Finn was pissed off. As head of the Task Force for International Arms Regulation and Enforcement, he always had plenty to be pissed off about. Half the job involved making nice to foreign officials, which was enough to give heartburn to a brass monkey. And most of *them* were pissed off because the mighty USA had sent them a black man and put him in charge, and he had to make them like it. The rest of the time he was dealing with the ATF trying to take away all his cases, right when all the legwork was done.

So being pissed off was all part of a normal day's work. But this—this was special. A senior agent who was nominally under his command, and who was supposed to be tracking an arms dealer they believed to be supplying weapons to terrorist groups—the guy had up and vanished. Gone for a week without a word, without a please and thank-you or "SAC, may I"—nothing. This was an agent with a lot of seniority and a big reputation for getting results. But he also had an even bigger reputation for flying solo, chasing one particular bug in his bonnet, over and over, and so far without success. So Finn had to treat the man with a certain amount of respect. But he also had to make him stay with the program. If this guy screwed the pooch, it would splash on Finn.

Because of the reputation and the seniority, Finn had said nothing when this agent vanished. But now he was back, sitting across from Finn's desk with a blank face and a story that made no sense at all. "Sweden," Finn said, letting the disbelief and the pissed-off show in his voice. "You were in *Sweden*."

Special Agent Frank Delgado just nodded.

"Because Husqvarna was having a sale? Maybe you prefer blond women?" Finn asked.

Delgado shrugged. "Not really," he said. "They're always more trouble."

"Uh-huh." Finn studied Delgado. Nearing forty, stocky build; his dark hair was a little too long for a federal agent, his suit was old and rumpled, and his top shirt button was undone. In short, he did not look at all like a special agent of the FBI. Presently he looked more like somebody's longshoreman uncle dressed up for a wedding. But Delgado had flown close to the sun his whole career, and so far he'd gotten away with it, because he got results. So Finn took a deep breath and simply said, "Right. So why, Frank? Why Sweden?"

Delgado opened the manila folder on his lap, removed an eight-by-ten glossy picture, and slid it onto Finn's desk. Finn waited for an explanation. He didn't get one. So he bit down on what he wanted to say and looked at the picture. "Hervé Thierry," he read. "French national." He looked up at Delgado. "Arms dealer?"

Delgado shook his head.

"Terrorist?" Finn said hopefully.

"No," Delgado said.

"Then why do I care?"

"He got off a flight in Dallas," Delgado said.

Finn waited. Delgado said nothing more. "Dallas," Finn said. "Which is why you went to Sweden."

Maddeningly, Delgado nodded again.

Finn sighed heavily. "Because?" he prompted.

"The flight *came* from Stockholm," Delgado said. And apparently trying to be helpful, he added, "That's in Sweden."

Finn hissed a breath between his teeth. His patience was eroding fast. "I know where Stockholm is, Frank. What I don't know is why I give a shit about this guy. Thierry." He flipped the picture back to Delgado. "So why don't you tell me."

Delgado nodded and reached back into the manila folder. This time, he slid an Interpol report across the desk. Finn picked it up. There were several pages stapled together, and Finn flipped through them quickly. "St. Petersburg. In Russia," he said, raising an eyebrow at Delgado. There were several photos, and Finn looked them over. "Security camera, forensics—your guy Thierry was at the Hermitage Museum when their Fabergé egg was stolen." Again Finn looked at Delgado. "You think Thierry stole the egg, Frank?"

"I know it," Delgado said.

Finn opened his mouth to ask why Delgado was so damn sure—and then closed it again. He examined the last page of the report and put it down on his desk. "You do remember we're doing arms enforcement, right? Not robbery from the fucking Russians?"

"I remember," Delgado said, without changing expression.

"So all this is going somewhere connected with arms enforcement, right?"

Delgado nodded.

Finn tapped his fingers on the desk and decided that violence would be counterproductive. "Okay, wonderful," he said, with remarkable but completely fake patience. "So—Thierry went from St. Petersburg to Sweden."

"No," Delgado said. "He came to Sweden from Perth."

Finn ground his teeth, but he kept his cool. "That's in Australia, isn't it?" Delgado nodded again. "Good, that's settled. Thierry went from Perth to Sweden to Dallas, am I getting this? And you knew he was in Dallas but you went to Sweden anyway. Why?"

Again, Delgado took a report from his folder and put it on Finn's desk. This time it was a case file from the Swedish Police Authority. It included several photos of a man who had been impaled on a statue of some kind. "Jesus," Finn said. "That's a bad way to go."

Delgado nodded and said, "Impalement. Incredibly painful. And it can take a couple of days." And to Finn's mild astonishment, he added, "It's known that the Assyrians used it, and the early Romans—and actually, the historical figure that Dracula is based on made impalement famous."

"Good to know," Finn said. He flicked the Swedish report with a finger. "Who's the victim?"

"Arvid Ekstrom," Delgado said. "A fisherman." He shrugged. "Interpol says he did some smuggling on the side."

"Huh," Finn said. He frowned and then made the kind of connection that got him an SAC position by the age of forty. "You think he smuggled Thierry out of Russia after he stole the egg?"

"Yes," Delgado said. "Airline records show Thierry arriving in St. Petersburg but never leaving." He shrugged. "But the records show him leaving Perth a month later."

Finn frowned. "Okay, so, what—the Swedish guy smuggles Thierry out of Russia. And then Thierry goes to Perth for a couple of weeks and flies back to Sweden, kills Ekstrom. Why, Frank? To cover his trail?"

"No," Delgado said. "I believe Ekstrom betrayed Thierry."

"Okay," Finn said, nodding. "And now you want to go after him. After Thierry."

"No," Delgado said. "Thierry doesn't exist."

Finn closed his eyes and counted to ten. It didn't help. He opened his eyes and flung the report across the room. "Goddamn it, Frank!" he said. "What the fuck does that mean, he doesn't exist? Is he a ghost? A video-game character? What?!"

"The security officers at the Hermitage found this," he said. He slid another photo across the desk. "In the room where the Fabergé egg was displayed."

Finn barely glanced at the picture. "A pile of clothes," he said. "So what?"

"That's the suit Thierry was wearing," Delgado said.

"All right, so we have a naked burglar?"

"Probably not," Delgado said. "He usually wears something underneath."

"Thierry wears something underneath?" Finn said, and he could feel that he was on the verge of a major eruption.

"No, Thierry was just the disguise," Delgado said.

"For *who*?"

For the first time ever, as far as Finn knew, Delgado smiled—just a fraction of an inch, but a smile. "Riley Wolfe," he said.

"Motherfuck—No. No way," Finn said. He should have known. This was the bug in Delgado's head, the unicorn he kept chasing, the thing that had nearly de-railed Delgado's career. And Delgado had been warned not to chase it again. "We're not going there, Frank. We're chasing arms dealers and terrorists, not thieves."

Unbelievably, Delgado's smile got slightly bigger. "Perth," he said, "is where Bailey Stone is."

Finn actually felt his jaw drop. "Fuck me dead," he said. Bailey Stone was very high on his task force's wanted list. Stone had recently made an enormous sale to an offshoot of ISIS that the FBI believed planned to target American facilities across the Middle East and Europe. If it would get him Stone, Dellmore Finn would help Delgado chase UFOs. He leaned across the desk, and his face showed that for the first time, he was truly in this conversation. "Talk to me, Frank," he said.

Delgado closed the manila folder. "Bailey Stone wants Riley Wolfe to do something—"

"To do *what*?" Finn interrupted.

Delgado shrugged. "Something impossible."

"But what, Frank?"

"It isn't important what. Impossible, though—that's what Riley Wolfe does. He will do it—and then he'll deliver it to Bailey Stone."

"But you can find out what Stone wants, right? So we can watch it, put a tracer on it, all that?"

Delgado shook his head. "No," he said. "Whatever it is, we won't see it coming." He frowned. "It doesn't matter."

Finn thought for a moment, then leaned back in his chair. "Frank, don't fuck around," he said. "You want Riley Wolfe." Delgado nodded. "But you think catching him will help us get Bailey Stone, so you're willing to go along with the task force mandate."

Ignoring the obvious sarcasm, Delgado just nodded again.

"And you really think we can turn a hard case like Wolfe, and make him give up Stone?"

"Yes," Delgado said, with no trace of doubt in his voice.

Finn thought about it. It didn't take long. If Delgado was right, they'd get Stone. And if they got Riley Wolfe at the same time—shit. He'd probably get a citation for steering Delgado back to normal. "All right," he said. "But if we don't know what he's going after— and we don't really even know what he looks like—how do we catch Riley Wolfe?"

Delgado smiled again. It looked a little odd, like his face might not have done that more than once before. "Same way we turn him," he said. He opened his folder again and took out one last piece of paper. "We catch him," he said, holding up the paper, "when he goes here. And he always does," he said. The smile grew a little. "And," he said, sliding the paper onto Finn's desk, "it will also give us the leverage to flip him."

Finn looked dubiously at Delgado, then glanced at the paper—and then frowned and read it through. For the first time he smiled. "No shit," he said. He looked up and locked eyes with Delgado. "All right," he said softly. "Make it happen, Frank."

CHAPTER

13

The flight home was long and boring. On top of that, I was already tired when I got on the plane. I had been a very busy guy, what with being shot with a tranq gun, kidnapped twice, chained to a wall, getting a finger broken by a psycho, threatened by several different really bad people—it wears on a man. And on top of that, the impalement. Surprising how much that takes out of you. I mean, hoisting all that deadweight up into the air—and without being seen, too. And then putting on the lube—that was just *nasty*. And getting him onto the spear just right—it was hard work, all of it. Of course, it might have been a little harder on Arvid when he woke up, but he didn't have to deal with the airlines afterward, and a really long flight on top of that.

And then, of course, it was not really "*the* long flight" home. It was a bunch of them. I mean, in the first place, try getting a direct flight from Stockholm to Fayetteville, Arkansas. And anyway, even if there was a direct flight, I didn't want it. I didn't think it would help hide me from either Boniface or Stone, but it's always a good idea for somebody like me to leave a messy trail. So I flew to Heathrow, then from there to Atlanta and then to Dallas.

I got rid of good old Hervé Thierry in Dallas. Just threw the passport and all the other stuff into a messy trash can, one in the middle of restaurant row, so there'd be a lot of half-eaten food, leftover coffee, and other nasty slop on top to discourage anybody from fishing it out.

Then I took a DART bus into downtown Dallas. I got off in midtown and walked toward the public library. I found a drugstore on the way and bought a couple of things—a little bit of makeup, a hoodie, hair dye, like that. There was a burger joint a few blocks away, and I used the restroom to change my appearance.

Now I was ready for my real destination—the library. Not just because they have a first folio of Shakespeare, although they do, and I did plan to pay my respects. And who knows, maybe someday I'd come back and see that it had a better home—mine.

For now, though, I had something else in mind. Some people think libraries are dinosaurs, totally useless in the age of the Internet. I disagree. In the first place, I like books—*real* books, printed on paper, and not so-called e-books. And in the second place—

Okay, maybe this sounds two-faced, but libraries have computers, too. And you can use them anonymously, which is pretty handy now and then. So I strolled in, found the row of desktops, and sat down at one. It took me a few minutes to get it to do what I wanted, but I managed. I got onto the dark web, fished around a little, and found what I needed. Some Bitcoins moved over the web, and two hours later I was riding back to the airport in a cab, with a brand new driver's license and credit card in my pocket. They all agreed that I was Gerald Hunt, thirty-two, an investment banker from Arlington.

Back at DFW, I booked a flight to O'Hare, flew to Charlotte from there, and finally to the Bill and Hillary Clinton National Airport at Little Rock. Gerald Hunt disappeared into another sloppy trash can in the terminal, and I headed out to long-term parking. I'd left my truck there, and I had another identity or two stashed in a hidden compartment. I fished around and pulled out a New Me. Now I was B. J. Lambeth, and I had a matching set of papers for the truck. I wasn't ready to lose it yet.

The truck was kind of special. I'd fixed it up just for my Ozark hideaway. It was a dirty and battered-looking ten-year-old Ford pickup, and anybody seeing it in the parking garage, or on the road, would see something that looked just like ten thousand other trucks in Arkansas. But I'd stuck in a bigger gas tank, a more powerful engine, stiffer suspension, all the stuff that made an old pickup faster, nimbler, and more durable. And also, I'd put in a state-of-the-art sound system. Naturally. I've got to have my tunes.

And as I pulled out of the airport and got onto I-40, I had them. I started with Blondie, moved on to REO Speedwagon and then Elvis—Costello, not the corny old one in the purple jumpsuit. That got me charged up enough to make it through the three-hour drive to Fayetteville. It's a college town, so it has more sophisticated stores and services than you might think—including a really good extended-care facility. Probably meant for retired professors, but it had top-notch care, and that's where I'd stashed Mom.

I didn't fart around trying to be sneaky or clever. There was no point to that. After all, Boniface had given me a ticket to Little Rock. He'd know about Mom, too. He knew this place would be my first stop, and he'd have somebody watching it. That pissed me off. A lot. Mom is important, and I hate like hell when anybody gets close to her. She's been in a persistent vegetative state for years, and maybe she comes out of it someday, and maybe she doesn't. That doesn't matter. She's my mother. I'd be nothing without her. She took care of me when I needed it, and I sure as shit meant to do the same for her.

This wasn't the first time some hard-ass shit-pig had tracked her down, and I had to believe it wouldn't be the last, but I wasn't going to pull the plug, not on

Mom. I'd kept her safe a long time, and I tried to keep her where nobody could find her. It cost a ton of money, sure, but fuck that. If there's something better to spend money on, I'm waiting to hear it. So far, I'm hearing crickets.

But yeah, she was a weakness, something unfriendly acquaintances could use to get at me. I get that. So I worked overtime to keep her location private. Like I said, it hadn't worked this time. I don't know where the fail was, but Boniface knew, and I had to assume Stone did, too. Long term, I would have to find some way to deal with both of them, or whichever one of them survived. The squeeze the two of them had put on me was about as bad as any I'd ever had. They both had a clamp on me that was just short of killing. Worse, I knew damn well it wasn't going to *stay* short. It could only end one way, even if I managed to do all the crazy shit they wanted me to do. People like them don't let go once they have a hold on you. They use you until you turn into more of a liability than an asset, and then they put a neat little bullet hole in your skull and lay you to rest in a nice quiet bed of wet concrete.

And they knew about Mom. So on top of stealing a fucking wall from the fucking Vatican, which just plain can't be done, I would have to think of some way to shake free of the weapons-distribution community. Something permanent, which was totally . . . shit. Let's call it challenging. Permanently discouraging a couple of guys who had their own private armies, practically unlimited resources, and more firepower than most countries smaller than Turkey—Yeah. That was a really good word for it. Challenging.

And that was only one small piece of it. When you add in the whole picture, it was just plain fucking stupid. But what the hell. Impossible is what I do. And I do it really well, too. I'm known for it. Of course, that's what got me into this fuckwad mess I was in now, but I had to believe that it would get me out of it, too. How? Fucked if I know. But there's always a way—and I always find it. *Always.*

In the meantime, I had some hard scrambling to do. And first, I had to get Mom and move her someplace safer.

I parked at the facility and went on inside. I spent a few minutes charming the nurses, then told them why I was there. While they collected all the necessary forms, I made a few phone calls and got a bed for Mom in a good place I had scouted out already. I also lined up a couple of medical transports, with security, and arranged for a few blind switches along the way, transferring her to a different transport, with a different guard. At the third transfer spot, I arranged a small surprise, a guy I'd worked with before who knew which end was up and would keep his mouth shut and do the job. Hopefully, better than Arvid had done. He'd do an electronic sweep and get rid of any little gadgets that might have been sneaked onto Mom's person or property to help track her. Then he'd make sure nobody was following—and if somebody was, he'd discourage them. Hard.

After that, he'd escort Mom to another transfer point, where a medevac chopper was waiting. The whole thing would cost two tons of money, but I have plenty, and like I said—what's money for? Riley's Twelfth Law: Money isn't important! The *lack* of it is.

It took a couple more hours to finish the paperwork and see Mom off on the first leg of her trip. I schmoozed the nurses a little more, said good-bye, and then got myself back on the road.

I didn't bother going back to my house on the mountain. It was a nice place, and I like the Ozarks, but it wasn't secure anymore. I didn't need anything so bad it was worth the risk of going back. The stuff I had left there was all replaceable. Clean clothes, books and music, like that. None of it was worth taking the chance to go back and grab it. If it was ever safe to go back there again, the stuff would still be there. If not, it didn't matter. I could get more.

So I put all that out of my head, filled the truck's gas tank, and put on a new license plate, New York State this time. I got behind the wheel and cranked up the driving music—Yo-Yo Ma, Silk Road—and headed north.

Now came the really hard part.

CHAPTER
14

Monique was probably the best art forger in the world. She didn't think of herself that way, of course. She worked hard to be good, and she appreciated being very well paid for what she did, but it was counterproductive to dwell on her place in the hierarchy. Still, plenty of other people thought she was the best, and she always had plenty of good, paying work to do. That was all that really mattered.

Right now the work space in her twenty-fifth-floor Manhattan apartment was crowded with projects. On her easel there was a half-finished copy of a Caravaggio, and across from that, on a workbench, stood an early version of a Sumerian votive figure. Between the two of these projects, and three more she had waiting, she could keep busy for another two months, and get paid well when she was done, too. So she didn't really need to think about Riley Wolfe. Or where he was and what might have happened to him—it had now been *five* weeks, and still no word from him. All she knew was that he had told her he was about to snag something very special. For Riley that could mean a lot of things, but Monique knew him better than most people. Maybe better than anyone else. And the way he'd said "something special" made her think it was an object of rare beauty. For a thief, Riley had great taste, and he truly knew, and cared, about art. But whether that meant extra danger this time, he did not say. Of course, with Riley, the risk was something she took for granted. It was part of why he did these things—they were usually so insanely dangerous that nobody else would even try them. That was Riley's ballpark, and he was the MVP of the whole league.

Riley also said he had a buyer lined up, a guy who would pay top dollar—but he wanted her to make a copy of it before he delivered it. That way he could sell the copy, too, getting two paydays for one job, and not incidentally providing a good one for her. It was a typical Riley stunt, and Monique actually thought it was pretty smart, unlike some of the crazy bullshit Riley pulled.

So Monique had been standing by to make a copy of this something, whatever it was. Naturally, because he was Riley Wolfe, he wouldn't tell her anything about the object. It could be a fifteen-foot bronze statue, a tiny diamond ring, or anything in between. And no matter how many times she pointed out that it would save a lot of time and effort if she knew what to get ready for, he just smiled and shook his head and said she'd find out when it was time. "When it was time," like she was a little girl waiting for her birthday surprise. It pissed her off maybe more than it should have—again, because it was Riley Wolfe, and there was definitely something about him that made Monique want to slap him silly every time he fed her that line, with his superior smirk.

So she was already fuming, and when he was this late, without a single goddamn word of explanation, those fumes were fanning themselves into flames. But there was work to do—real work, well paid, for people who showed up on time, paid on time, and didn't make Monique want to scream and shred them with her fingernails, like Riley did. So fuck Riley Wolfe. Whatever he was up to, it was his problem, and the fact that he didn't bother to call meant nothing to her, except that it would be a stupid waste of time to sit around worrying and wondering if he was all right.

So she didn't. Not very much, anyway. She buried herself in her work, and if stray Riley thoughts pushed unwanted into her head, she pushed them right back out again. Screw him. He was probably shacked up somewhere with some sleazy slut he'd run into along the way, and if he couldn't at least call and say he was okay, Monique hoped the woman gave him an STD. Serve him right, the rotten amoral bastard.

So for the nine millionth time Monique shoved Riley out of her mind, picked up her paintbrush, and stared at the canvas, where a woman's face was taking shape. The forehead was the key here—Caravaggio had a thing about foreheads, and to get the lines just right took a lot of care, intense concentration on the lines and shadows that—

"Saint Catherine?"

The voice came softly, right at her shoulder, and Monique was two feet off the ground before she realized who it was. And when she did realize—she came down swinging.

"Riley, goddamn you!" She connected with the side of his head before he could flinch away, and it felt so good that Monique swung again. Riley managed to duck this time, but his face was already turning red where the first swat had hit him, and that felt just as good. "I told you not to sneak in the window like that!" she said.

"You left it open, and you know—I kind of wanted to climb a little—"

She swung again, just barely clipping his blocking arm. "Fuck you and your fucking parkay—!"

"Parkour," he corrected mildly.

"I don't care what the fuck it's called. How many fucking times have I told you not to do that!" she demanded.

"Um—a lot?" Riley said, still backing away with his hands held up defensively. "I mean, I didn't count or anything? But it seems like—"

"Oh, shut the fuck up! Where have you been, god-damn it?"

"I can't shut up *and* tell you," he pointed out. She swung again, but he dodged it.

"Fuck you, Riley Wolfe! Do you know how long I've been waiting to hear that you—I mean, it would just take one two-minute phone call! Would that have killed you?"

Riley looked serious for the first time. "Actually, it might have," he said.

Monique opened her mouth to tear into him again, and then paused as she realized what he'd said and that he meant it.

"What the fuck does that mean?" she demanded.

"It means," he said, and he was very serious now, "that I was in some seriously deep shit. I still am."

"You mean, besides the deep shit you're in with me?"

Riley looked away, and Monique saw a look on his face she'd never seen before—deep, intense anxiety. Then he looked back at her and tried to smile. He didn't do a very good job. "I would never underestimate the danger of being on your shit list, Monique," he said, rubbing his face where she'd clocked him. "But yeah, this is worse. A lot worse."

She folded her arms across her chest. "Let's hear it."

"Do you know who Patrick Boniface is?" he asked her quietly—much too quietly for Riley.

She turned the name over in her head. It seemed kind of familiar, like she might have read it in the paper, or heard it in passing, but it didn't seem to have any real connection to her. "Is he that French singer?" she asked.

Riley shook his head. "Not hardly. Patrick Boniface is the biggest, richest, most badass top-dog arms dealer in the world."

She stared at him in horror. "Jesus Christ, Riley— you tried to steal something from *him*?!"

"No," he said. "That would be a cakewalk compared to this." And Monique could tell this was not the usual Riley Wolfe line of egotistical bullshit. He was dead serious.

She swallowed. "Tell me," she said.

He did.

He started with finishing a job, getting zapped, waking up on the wrong boat in the wrong ocean. And he ended with the job Boniface had given him, and the clear threat that made it kind of important to pull off successfully.

When he had finished, she stared at him for a long time, before she finally managed to say, "A fresco. He wants you to steal a fucking *fresco*."

He nodded. "From the fucking Vatican," he said, with a small trace of his normal cheer.

"A fresco is embedded in a *wall*, Riley."

"Yup."

"I mean—it's actually a *part* of the fucking wall—!"

"I know it."

"So he wants you to steal a *wall*."

"Uh-huh."

"Steal a fucking wall from the fucking Vatican— with some of the best security in the world."

"Pretty much."

Monique stared a little longer. "It can't be done," she said at last.

"I know," he said.

"I mean, for Christ's fucking sake, this is really simple—it absolutely cannot be fucking *done*, Riley! And I don't want any of your usual cocky dumb-ass look-at-me bullshit about, 'That's why I'm going to do it!' This categorically, positively, no-fucking-doubt-about-it cannot be fucking done! You cannot steal a fucking wall from the fucking Vatican!"

"I know," he said again.

"Well, what the fuck are you going to do about it?" she demanded.

"I guess," he said—and he seemed weirdly deflated, very un-Riley as he spoke—"I guess I'm going to find a way to do it."

"Riley—"

"Monique, I have no choice here. I can't run. This guy can find me wherever I hide. And if I don't do this he will find me, and take me back to his island, and he has a friend there who will make sure it takes me a couple of weeks to die." He actually shuddered, which was something Monique had never seen before. "And she scares the *shit* out of me. You just look at her and you can see the things that she wants to—" He stopped, shrugged, and, with a very small smile, added, "Spending time with that woman? That seems a lot harder than stealing a fresco."

"Shit," she whispered.

"Yup."

"Holy fucking shit, Riley."

He nodded. Then he looked away, and in a voice so very soft, so very not Riley, he said, "There's more." He looked at her, looked away. "It's worse."

"That's just—How can it possibly be worse than that?" she said.

"Because," he said, still looking away, "the shit gets deeper. And—you are in it with me."

Monique stared at him. After a long moment of silence, she realized her hands were clenched so tightly they had begun to ache, and she let them drop to her sides. "I think you better tell me what that means," she said.

So Riley told her.

Fuck a shit-piss, Riley!" Monique stared across the table at me, all righteous horror, and I have to say it looked really good on her. Of course, just about everything looked good on Monique. And *nothing* on her looked even better. So, too bad she was dressed, but I live in hope. And for now, we had heavy shit to talk over. We sat in the little kitchen nook of her apartment, nursing cups of espresso, one of the few things Monique had learned to make well. "Fuck a goddamn shit-piss!"

That had a really nice ring to it, so I nodded encouragement. "True," I said. "But that's the first time I've heard that one, Monique."

"That's because you've never fucked up this big before!" she said.

I know by now I should never be surprised at the
way a woman can turn things around so that no matter
what she did, it turns out it was *my* fault—but even so,
I thought this was pushing the envelope. *I* fucked up?
How? By letting myself get kidnapped?

But I also knew better than to try to use that logic—
especially on someone who was as talented as Monique
at knocking you upside the head. So I just raised an
eyebrow, which naturally pissed her off even more. "Jesus goddamn fucking shit! Don't you *dare* fucking
smirk at me! What the fuck have you done?!"

"Me?" I said. "I didn't do anything, Monique. I'm
the victim here."

"No, goddamn it, *I'm* the fucking victim! You deserve it! I didn't do shit to get sucked into this!"

There was a lot I could have said to that, but again—
there was no point. So I just sighed. "If I wanted to be
an asshole—"

"Which you usually do!"

"I could point out that Stone got your picture because somebody tailed you, probably all day long, and
you didn't notice."

"But how did they know to tail *me*, Riley?" she demanded. Aside from having absolutely no street smarts,
Monique was also surprisingly ignorant of how things
worked on the dark side of the street—the side she had
chosen to work on. In fact, she was pretty clueless
about just about everything except art and how to copy
it perfectly. And so because she obviously hadn't figured out something that should have been obvious to

any career criminal, I bit back the really funny remark I'd been about to say and explained it to her.

"You do know you're really goddamn good at what you do, right?" I said.

"Don't try to soothe my rumpled feathers, Riley, or I am coming across this table at you."

"I am not soothing," I said, in a very soothing voice. "I am stating a fact. There are only a few people in the world who can do what you do, and as far as I can tell, none of them do it as good as you do."

Monique opened her mouth to say something, probably something like "cut the bullshit," but I held up a hand and cut her off. "Monique, you know it's true, quit the false modesty." She frowned, but then she shrugged and waited for me to go on. So I did. "This is something pretty well-known by now. You've got a rep. And we have done some shit together that has gotten a whole lot of attention." I leaned over the table a little so she'd get that I was dead serious. "Monique, guys like Stone? They can add up two plus two. It's not hard to figure out we have a working relationship. And maybe something more than that."

"It's nothing more, and it never will be," she snapped. Like it was an automatic thing she had to stick in there, just in case I was going to try anything again. And of course I was—but not right now.

"But it *looks* like we do," I said. "That's enough for somebody looking for a handle on me."

"How is this always about you?" she snapped— forgetting that two minutes ago she'd been insisting it actually *was* all about me. "Damn it, Riley, I'm the one getting dragged into your lethal bullshit games!"

"They're dragging you in to get at me," I said, still keeping very cool and patient. "Because they think I care what happens to you."

"And you just fucking *proved* it by caving in to Stone!" she snarled.

"Well," I said, "I guess as long as you know I care . . ."

For a minute I thought she was going to come across the table and strangle me. So did she. But she settled for grinding her teeth. "This has nothing to do with me, and I am not going to let you pull me down *your* goddamn wormhole!" she said. "You just let those two assholes know I am not involved!" Very firm and commanding and all that, and it meant about as much as a sparrow fart in a windstorm.

I sighed. She really didn't get it. I mean, she was not stupid—she was probably smarter than me. But this kind of shit, anything to do with life and the way shit actually works—helpless. "Monique, think about this for a minute. Think about it like you're a really badass dude who doesn't mind fragging just about anybody, whenever you think it might help just a little bit. If I told Stone, hey, she's nothing to me—what's he gonna do? Like, instantly?"

Monique frowned, shook her head, and I had to think she must get it, but I said it anyway. "He'll go okay, fine, so you don't mind if I stick a knife in her throat? And he would, Monique. Because either it gets me to say, 'Stop, I'll do it,' or it's totally meaningless, and either way he's still got me by the nut sack. That's how the game is played."

She bit her lip and looked away for a second. "I don't think I like this game," she said.

"We don't get to choose. We just got to play it out to the end. And god-*damn* it, Monique!" I said, and I felt it ripping through me and filling me up to giant size, like one of those Macy's parade balloons. "We will fucking win this game!"

Monique just looked at me. "How?" she said.

Well, there it was. Just one stupid syllable, and I felt all the air go out of me. "How." Fucked if I knew how.

"I don't know," I said. "But I will find a way."

"Because there's always a way?" she said, and it was as close to a sneer as I'd ever seen from Monique.

"Yes, goddamn it," I said. "There *is* always a way." And I tried to sound like I really meant it.

"Not this time," she said. "This time? It just plain can't be done."

I had a feeling she was right. But what the fuck. Riley's Thirteenth Law: You play the cards you're dealt. "We have to try," I said.

"And it's *we* again," she snarled.

I just nodded. "It's we," I said. "But this next part? I think you're gonna like it."

CHAPTER

15

The Vatican gets six million visitors every year. In the summer, as many as twenty thousand people every day crowd through the square and into the various artistic and spiritual attractions. And Vatican City is small—only about two-tenths-of-an-acre square. That's one-eighth the size of Central Park in Manhattan. So for anyone to stand out when the normal crowd is crammed into a small area like that, they have to be truly unusual.

The nice young couple from Canada was not at all out of the ordinary. They seemed like typical tourists and they attracted no notice at all. A few years ago they might have, if only because he was white and she was black. But that's no longer odd enough to make anyone stare. Their looks were nothing unusual, either. She wore her hair in an Angela Davis Afro with a pair of large black-framed glasses perched on her nose. He had a bushy mustache that did not quite hide a scarred upper lip, the apparent remains of a cleft palate. His bright red T-shirt—it read "GO HABS" in large white letters—was a little too small and stretched over a bit of a paunch. They both wore khaki-colored cargo shorts and carried small backpacks; his was red, of course, and hers was a more demure blue.

To all appearances, they were nothing more than ordinary tourists, here to take in the extraordinary sights of Vatican City. So as they strolled through the square and on into the basilica holding hands, they got no more than a passing glance from anybody—not even the ever-vigilant guards of the Gendarmerie, and the occasional hard-eyed man of the Pontifical Swiss Guard.

The couple spent a long time staring at St. Peter's Baldachin before they moved on, crossed the plaza to the Apostolic Palace, and went in. They lingered and looked at most of the spectacular artworks, gazing with rapt expressions. But when they got up to the third floor and started through the Stanze di Raffaello, they slowed down even more.

And who wouldn't? The *stanze* are one of the great wonders of the art world. There are four large rooms that Raphael adorned with his genius. They are truly breathtaking, and anyone with an eye for great art can certainly be forgiven for lingering. The Canadian couple did linger—but they lingered a great deal longer at one particular work in the Room of Heliodorus. They stood in front of it for a very long time, whispering to each other and pointing at different parts and even taking photographs. Lots of photographs. They even used an actual camera, a rare sight in this smartphone age. But again, not so rare as to draw any attention.

Eventually, the man looked up, appearing somewhat startled at how much time had passed. He took the woman by the hand and led her away, and the young couple vanished into the crowd.

Wow," Monique said. At least, that's what I thought she said. She had this dreamy, blown-away look on her face, and "wow" would definitely go with it. But it came out more like "mowf." She frowned and pulled the fake buckteeth out of her mouth. "I mean, 'wow,'" she said. It's always nice to be right. She glared at the fake teeth. "I fucking *hate* these things," she said.

"Necessary," I said. "Nobody will remember what you look like—just that poor girl with the huge fucking teeth." I looked as innocent and serious as I could and added, "Besides, they kept you quiet, and that was kind of—" I stopped talking and ducked, because Monique threw the teeth at me.

"Fuck off, Riley," she said. But she went right back to looking impressed and happy. "But *damn*," she said. "That was *amazing*! I mean, yeah, I know Raphael is great, his frescoes are fabulous, blah blah blah. I got all that from school and the books—but to see it right in

front of you like that—to get right up into the colors
and all, it was just—wow."

I nodded. I was impressed, too. The Stanze di Raffaello were enough to impress anybody, unless they
were a total brick-head. Four rooms strung together,
like pearls on a string, and all four of them festooned
with fresco after mind-blowing fresco. And the best of
them all, in my humble opinion, was my target, *The
Liberation of St. Peter*. I would have stared at it for
hours even if I wasn't trying to figure out how to make
it portable.

Not that the other frescoes were kindergarten finger
painting. They were every bit as beautiful. Just looking
at them up close was maybe one of the best ways to
spend a day ever. Or anyway, a close second to a day in
the sack with Monique. Which she still swore was never
going to happen again, so for now, taking in the frescoes was very all right. And then *Liberation*—when I
saw that from just a few feet away, it was almost enough
to make me sympathize with Boniface. *Almost*. It was
just incredible. But even without the "almost," if I totally agreed with the bastard that the fresco was just
too wonderful to be wasted on the Vatican and really
ought to be on the wall of a cave in the middle of the
Indian fucking Ocean—that still left a small but kind
of important detail. Like, how the fuck did I make that
happen?

But at least the gorgeous spectacle had distracted
Monique. And not just the frescoes; the art treasures

they have in the Vatican are so fucking awesome you just have to stop and stare while your eyes pop out of your head. For somebody like me it was like the best birthday party ever. And Monique was just as crazy about art as I was, maybe more so. For a lot of reasons, it was good to see her light up like that. I mean, I like her and all, but she's a lot easier to be around when she's happy. And she'd been in an all-time shitty mood this whole trip to Rome. I was paying for it and everything, and it was first-class all the way. And all she could do was snarl and smack me. No shit—my arm was purple from where she'd been slugging me. So whatever made her forget how pissed off she was, even if it was just for a little while, it was worth it.

For me, it was impossible to forget. Even strolling through the Apostolic Palace and seeing all the incredible artwork—while half of me was going, "Holy shit, lookit that!" the other half was going, "Holy shit— how the fuck am I going to pull *this* one off?" And coming up with nothing at all. Not even a hint. Not even a clunky idea that I tossed out after one quick look. Nothing. Because it was just plain old-fashioned fuck-me-dead-it-can't-be-done impossible.

It had been a lot easier for me to think about it without Monique battering my arm and snarling at me. Which, to be honest, was the main reason I had given her the buckteeth. I figured that out of all the disguises I could have given her, this one would at least keep her quiet. And it did.

Which she was making up for now. She was still rid-

ing the high of being right up in the grille of some of
the greatest paintings ever, bubbling on like somebody
had put Molly in her water bottle. In fact, she was so
high that she was taking off the rest of her disguise as
she blathered. I mean, right there in front of me, the
T-shirt was off, and we were down to the black, lacy bra
and totally unaware of Riley standing right there casually staring and drooling. And because I would never
interrupt a great mood like the one she was in just to
remind her that I was watching as she peeled off her
clothes, I just smiled and nodded and watched.

Which she of course noticed, right when things were
getting interesting. "Jesus fuck, Riley," she said, and
we were back to snarling. "You are such a sick pig!"
And she snarled off into the bedroom and slammed the
door.

Well, nothing good lasts forever. Only the shitty
stuff. And at least she hadn't hit me again.

I changed out of my costume, too, and thought
about what I'd seen. I mean, at the Vatican. It was as
bad as I'd figured. Even with the place totally flooded
with gawkers, I could see the alarms, sensors, cameras,
guards, and they were absolutely everywhere. And bottom line? *The Liberation of St. Peter* was still a wall, and
the wall was still attached to a really big, heavy building, and the building was about as secure as you can
make a building. And to get really picky-shit about
things, the doors and windows were way too small to
fit the whole stolen wall through. I was pretty sure
Boniface would be a little bit peeved if I delivered the

thing chopped into handy pieces—and peeved meant a date with Bernadette, which was not something I really wanted to fantasize about.

So it had been a great day at the Vatican. Beautiful stuff everywhere. *Hot diggity fucking damn.* Because all I could think of was why I was really here. And it just plain could not be done.

Monique was fuming again. She'd been in such a great mood, and then she'd looked up to see that miserable prick ogling her as she peeled off her shirt. She ground her teeth together and flung a shoe toward the closet. *What an asshole!* she thought, and threw the other shoe in the same general direction. *Riley fucking Wolfe—the only man alive who can kill the buzz of seeing all that great art.* Standing there and watching her undress, smirking like a middle school kid—and the whole time she was babbling on, completely oblivious. She wasn't sure if she was more angry with herself or Riley.

She tossed the shorts after the shoes. *Riley, definitely,* she concluded. *Nobody else can come close.*

Monique pulled the beautiful plush dressing gown from the closet and wrapped it around herself. Just feeling the luxurious touch of the incredibly soft fabric against her skin was soothing, and for a moment the thought of Riley and the way he always managed to get to her was nearly funny. *That sonofabitch,* she thought, sitting in a gorgeous brocade chair by the window. He got under her skin like nobody else ever had.

Of course, it didn't really occur to Monique to wonder why Riley bothered her so much. Because as she saw it, she really and truly had no feelings for the man, none at all. Except negative ones at the moment—she was absolutely off-the-charts pissed off at him for the mess he'd landed them both in. Arms dealers, for the love of God! And even Riley could see that there was no fucking way out this time. Not that he'd ever admit it, the conceited, arrogant, smirking bastard. And on top of everything else, a Peeping Tom! Serve him right if he finally ran into something he couldn't handle. It was a lesson he really needed.

Because it had clearly gone to his head that he was truly the best ever at what he did. And it didn't help that it seemed like he was good at everything else he did, too. In the past couple of years she'd watched him pilot a boat, ride a horse, hang glide, literally turn into totally different people, climb up a wall like an insect— and now he was proving to be an expert tour guide, too. He'd steered them to a perfect boutique hotel, right by the Spanish Steps, and booked them a freaking *penthouse*. The concierge had been waiting for them and bowed them in like they were the king and queen of Spain, too. She got the impression that the whole staff knew Riley, and actually liked him, as hard as that was for Monique to believe right now. And he had greeted each one of them with a kiss on the cheek and what sounded to her like perfect Italian—Monique didn't speak the language—even calling them by name. They'd grabbed up all the luggage and practically carried Monique, too, all the way up to the top floor and into the most shamefully decadent apartment she'd ever seen, with its own kitchen, a beautifully appointed sitting room—maroon velvet furniture with gold trim— and a lovely terrace, where they could look out at Rome while they ate breakfast or sipped wine in the evening.

It was the perfect romantic retreat for billionaires— but it had two bedrooms, too. Monique had expected Riley to pull some kind of bullshit move about sharing a bed, just for the sake of their cover, but he hadn't. Instead, he'd ushered her into a large and impossibly luxurious room of her own, with a to-die-for view of the city.

Under any other circumstances, it would've been just about impossible not to warm up to a guy who could do all the things Riley Wolfe had managed so easily today. But under these circumstances, Monique was not having a lot of trouble staying mad at him. Mostly.

She had just managed to wrestle a convincing scowl back onto her face when a soft knock came at her door.

"Monique?" Riley's voice came through the door. "I got us reservations for dinner, a really nice little place. If you could put on something sort of dressy? Maybe that black dress with the—"

"I can fucking well dress myself!" she snapped.

"Okay, sorry," he said, and he sounded so humble she almost apologized.

Dinner continued Riley's streak of superbly tasteful choices. His "nice little place" was amazing, and so was the meal. And he was as anxiously attentive to Monique as if he were trying to impress the homecoming queen on their first date. He fussed over her choices, making sure she got exactly what she wanted and lecturing the waiter in his perfect Italian about what to serve, how she preferred it cooked, which wine should go with it—everything. He even sent back the first bottle of wine—as far as Monique could tell, he thought it was corked and hadn't even let her take a sip.

When they were finally settled with an appetizer and a glass of wine—duck foie gras with apple and chestnut, and a bottle of Frescobaldi Gorgona—Riley finally relaxed a little, leaning back with his wine and smiling through the candlelight at her. And he almost seemed human for a moment. Then a shadow flicked over his face; he took a long pull on his wine and turned to stare out the window.

The view was worth a stare, a good, long one. The sun had set, and Rome was a beautiful, flickering spectacle of bright lights. The city spread out below them in all directions in a seemingly endless carpet of blinking magic. But Riley didn't look like he was admiring the view.

Monique studied Riley. He was sipping his wine without really tasting it and looking fixedly at the dome of the basilica, looming up huge and brightly lit right in front of them. As she watched he took another sip of wine, again without apparent awareness of what he was doing. A shame—the wine was excellent. Monique was enjoying it a great deal.

And the evening itself was lovely so far. Even the company, to her surprise. Riley looked very dashing in profile, even James Bond–ish, silhouetted against the night lights of Rome. He had on a gorgeous tuxedo—Monique hadn't even known he owned one. And before he had gone off into his brooding silence, he had seemed like the perfect dinner companion. She could almost—

He turned toward her suddenly, as if sensing her gaze. "What?" he said. "Is it this place? It's kind of touristy, I know, but it has a great wine list—and, you know, I mean, the food is pretty good? But if it's too— I mean, if you want to try someplace more—"

"Riley, stop," Monique said. "This place is fine. More than fine. It's amazing, really."

"Uh-huh. Okay," he said. "So . . . what?"

Monique shook her head. "Nothing. Just . . . I've never seen you like this before, that's all."

"Like what? Dressed up?"

She shook her head. "Kind of moody and introspective and thoughtful all at once. Pensive."

One side of his mouth twitched upward in a quarter smile. "Yeah, well. I mean—I guess I am. All that stuff.

Especially pensive," he added, lightly mocking her use of the word.

"Okay. So what are you pensing about?"

He was all serious again, turning back to look out the window. "You don't want to know," he said.

"Yes, I do," she said. Riley shook his head. "Riley, come on."

He sighed and spoke without looking at her. "I'm thinking maybe I should just relax, enjoy myself. Treat this like my last vacation. Because it looks like it might be."

"Jesus, Riley," Monique said. "What happened to 'there's always a way'?"

"Maybe sometimes there isn't," he said, so softly she barely heard him. "Maybe this is that time."

She watched him for a moment in silence. "Riley," she said, when the silence was too much. "You can't just . . ." She trailed off as she realized that he'd come around to what had been bothering her this whole trip, and more, that she didn't know what she wanted to say.

"Yes, I can," he said, forceful and bitter all of a sudden. "I *can* just. And at the moment I don't know what else I can just." He still didn't look at her. "I have always believed that—I mean, you can make fun if you want—but, goddamn it, Monique," he said, turning toward her at last. "I can't see any way in at all—this one time that's more important than ever because—"

He broke off abruptly, looking at her with an intensity that was a little frightening. For a long moment he held her gaze. Then he said, "Shit," and turned to stare out the window again, toward the Vatican.

Monique wondered what he'd been about to say. She thought it might have been something about her—that this time she was in danger, that her life was on the line, too, and that raised the stakes. And she half hoped she was wrong about that—but the other half of her knew she was right and was oddly glad about it.

"I never thought I would ever have to give you a pep talk, Riley," Monique said at last. "The idea is totally crazy—Riley Wolfe, egomaniac, the self-appointed Best Ever, the man who always finds a way—I mean, Jesus, how could I ever pump up somebody who already thinks he can do anything?" She watched him, hoping for a cocky comeback, or at least a hint of a smile. Nothing. "But, Riley . . ."

Monique wanted to say something like, "You haven't really tried," or, "You always think of something." Or even something horrible like, "It's always darkest just before the dawn." She wanted to say *something,* at least. But with the impeccable timing of waiters everywhere in the world, their waiter chose that perfect moment to interrupt. "Signorina," he said to Monique, with a smile and a half bow. And then he rattled off a rapid but melodic speech in Italian. Monique caught a couple of words, but they didn't add up to anything. She looked at Riley, raising an eyebrow.

"The first course," he told her.

"Oh. Of course," Monique said. "Um—what does he recommend?"

Riley and the waiter exchanged a couple of sentences. Riley glanced at her. "How do you feel about seafood? No allergies?"

"I love seafood," Monique said.

Riley nodded and turned back to the waiter. She heard him say, "Sì, sì," and then he was off in another stream of fast and incomprehensible Italian. Incomprehensible to her—the waiter clearly understood and approved. He bowed, smiled at Monique, and scurried away. "What am I having?" she asked.

"Deep-fried zucchini flower with caviar on shellfish and saffron consommé," Riley said. "Arturo says it's very good tonight."

It was good. In fact, it was far beyond merely good, and the rest of the meal was, too. It was one of the best dinners she'd ever eaten. And the food seemed to snap Riley out of his mood of "pensing." He took great delight in steering her through the various following courses and their wine pairings. He kept up a steady flow of cheerful conversation, speaking of what they'd seen that day and art in general, all the way through dessert and coffee, and there was no opening for Monique to attempt her pep talk.

Which was just as well, she thought. Because even if she came up with something to say that didn't sound stupid, Monique wasn't sure she could believe it. It really did seem as hopeless as Riley said.

But for the rest of the meal, and for the slow stroll back to the hotel, they both put it as far out of their minds as they could. Riley pointed out interesting sights along the way, peppered her with stories from history and from his own experience, and by the time they finally got to their room, Monique thought it had been one of the most pleasant evenings she could remember in a long time.

When she had changed out of her fancy dress, Monique returned to the sitting room of the suite, just in time to see Riley, dressed all in black, heading out the door. He saw her and paused in the doorway. "It's probably pointless," he said, "but I'm going to go take a look around." And he turned to go.

"A look around where? What do you—Riley!" she said.

But he was already gone.

CHAPTER
16

Giovanni Romanelli loved his job. The pay was not wonderful, but it was enough for what he needed. He shared an apartment with a friend, Paolo, who worked in a Vespa repair shop. And that had come in handy more than once, because Giovanni's ruling passion was his Ducati Hypermotard. It was a few years old and needed tender loving care, and with Paolo's help, it got just that. And it had to be said that the bike was a very big help with Giovanni's other passion, tourist women. In his job with the Vatican Gendarmerie, he had a chance to meet many of them, and if he could only talk them into a ride on the back of his Ducati, racing through the streets of Rome, the motorcycle throbbing and purring under them—something about it worked on most women like magic.

Life was good for Giovanni Romanelli. Even now,

when he was on night duty, patrolling the square by the Apostolic Palace. Vatican City, the world's smallest independent country, closed its borders every night. Consequently, there were no tourists at all to be seen. In the dark and humid summer night, there was nothing to see at all except the other gendarmes, an occasional priest, perhaps one of the many domestic workers who served His Holiness and the lesser clerics in residence. So Giovanni had nothing much to do except eight hours of walking back and forth in the darkness. But the late duty was only temporary, just for a few weeks. And the women would seem that much sweeter when he returned to his regular hours during the day.

Truth be told, the relative quiet and calm of the night was a welcome change now and then. And it was much easier to be vigilant without all the distractions of thousands of tourists crowding through, any one of whom might be a terrorist. Giovanni really was vigilant, too. He took that part of the job very seriously. He was not a very good Catholic, but even so, protecting the Holy Father was a serious and important matter. So Giovanni kept his eyes open as he patrolled, looking from side to side, up and down, scanning for anything out of the ordinary.

A little after midnight, he found it.

He had just come across the Via Sant'Anna toward the Cortile del Belvedere when something caught his eye—some shadow flicking among the great row of Doric columns in front of the Apostolic Palace. So close to the Pope's apartments—nothing should be there at this time of night. Especially not moving with such quick and shadowy stealth.

Perhaps it was only some trick of the eye. And the Pope was not in residence at the moment, but even so, Giovanni could not permit someone to be so near to the apartments—if he had really seen something.

One way to be certain. Giovanni moved closer. He saw nothing else, no repeat of the rapid shadowy flicker he had seen—or thought he had. Perhaps he should alert the other gendarmes? But if it was nothing—no. Better to be sure before he raised the alarm.

He stepped carefully into the great stone forest of the double row of Doric columns. The breezeway was dimly lit and he paused, letting his eyes adjust. He looked out into the open area beyond and—there; something moved. Beyond the second row of columns, at the base of the Apostolic Palace. Definitely something, some shadowy, man-sized something. But it moved so quickly, so silently—it couldn't possibly *be* a man, could it?

Giovanni felt the hair go up on the back of his neck. There were stories, going back hundreds of years. Various ghosts, apparitions, hauntings. And there were even photographs, of what was clearly a spirit, up in the bell tower. He was no more superstitious than he was religious, but still . . . It was after midnight, dark, and even in the bright sunlight one could feel unseen powers here. What if—

No; Giovanni was a reasonable man, and he did not believe in such things. And he was a policeman, charged with protecting the Holy See. Ghost or not, it was his duty to investigate.

He hurried forward, his hand going to the Glock in the holster on his hip, moving through the breezeway, and for a moment he could not see into the greater darkness beyond the columns. Then he was through, out onto the pavement on the far side. He hesitated, his eyes readjusting to the darker area beyond the breezeway— and for a moment he thought he saw—

But no. There was nothing here. Nothing at all. What could have been here? Unless whatever it was had gone straight up the side of the palace and onto the roof, in less time than it takes to say "Ave Maria." And that was not possible. Unless it was a spirit, which it was not, certainly not.

Still, Giovanni was diligent. He ran the beam of his flashlight up the side of the palace, walked the entire square looking carefully for any sign that someone had been here. There was nothing. Of course not. Human beings don't walk up walls. And Giovanni did not believe in ghosts. Although, to be truthful, he would certainly not want to go down into the catacombs at this hour. But up here? No, he had seen nothing. It had all been his imagination, some trick of light and shadow on a warm summer's eve.

But if it had been a spirit of some kind? *Eh bene,* it was gone now. Let the priests deal with it, the exorcists.

Giovanni Romanelli put away his flashlight, checked that the strap on his Glock was secure, and moved on through his patrol route, toward the basilica and then back again.

* * *

Monique had not really intended to wait up. She knew very well that when Riley went to look things over, he might be hours, or all night, or even longer. He was ridiculously thorough and prone to follow any relevant side trails that came up. She wouldn't worry even if he wasn't back in the morning.

So her plan had been to have a nightcap, read a little, and then go to bed. At the small stocked bar she found a bottle of grappa. Monique had heard of it but never sampled it before. She examined the label, but it told her almost nothing except that it was old and Italian. With a shrug and a wry smile, she thought, *When in Rome,* and poured some in a tumbler. And then, turning to the bookshelves in their suite, she scanned the titles, hoping for something that would hold her interest and lull her to sleep at the same time.

She didn't find anything of the kind. What she found instead was a wonderful old book, bound in leather, that she had heard about but never before seen: Gunther von Goetz's nineteenth-century tome *Stolen Treasures—Heretic Art in the Vatican Archives.* She riffled the pages; the book was chock-full of gorgeous illustrations. With a thrill of excited pleasure, she took the book to a comfortable chair by the window, lifted the tumbler of grappa, and sat. In just a few moments she was completely engrossed.

Time must have passed, but Monique wasn't aware

of it. In fact, she was aware of almost nothing except the beautiful illustrations, the descriptions of the artworks, in German and English—her German was good—and her glass of grappa, which she refilled twice. And then suddenly there was nothing at all.

Monique awoke with a startled jerk. She was still in the comfortable chair with von Goetz's book on her lap. The tumbler had fallen onto the carpet beside her when she fell asleep. There was light coming in the window now, dawn breaking over Rome, and the door to the suite was swinging open.

Before Monique could even register all these varied impressions, Riley came in. He was still dressed all in black, but the cloth had torn over one knee, and there were patches of grime across his face and chest. He looked tired and deflated. He saw her looking and just shook his head, closing the door behind him.

"What?" Monique said, her voice raspy from sleep. She cleared her throat. "What did you find?"

Riley took the grappa bottle from the table beside Monique, pulled out the cork, and took a long pull, straight from the bottle. "Nothing," he said, sinking onto the divan opposite Monique. "There's nothing to find. The security is even tighter than I thought, and the whole place is—It's all just . . . Nothing," he repeated. "I found nothing." He took another swig of grappa. "Not that I expected to see any kind of—Ah, fuck it . . ." He stared at the carpet for a long moment, then looked up again and caught her eye. "Let's go home, Monique," he said.

CHAPTER
17

Time flies when you're having fun, right? I wasn't, so the three days after we got back to New York seemed like three months. Forget jet lag; we had hope lag. Both of us. I mean, it had been great to see all that wonderful stuff, and we'd had some really good meals, and Rome is wonderful, and blah blah blah. As far as the real purpose of the trip was concerned—finding some small, tiny reason to think I could pull this off—forget it.

I hadn't ever worked closely with another person at the planning stage, and I really hoped that Monique might help me see a way through to something workable. No such luck. I mean, she tried, but her brain just doesn't work that way. That's kind of a good thing? It means she's not all dark and twisted on the inside. Like I am. But in this case, it wasn't that good. Because I was coming up empty, and she wasn't even humming along in the same key.

So I spent three whole days sitting around with Monique and beating my brains out for nothing. Even if she couldn't pitch in, I would've thought that hanging with her would get my brain working. Just on the off chance that I'd think of something and she'd be so impressed that we would move on to *the* thing.

No such luck. Nothing. Three days of nothing, every day making it all seem darker and more pointless, until I was ready to just cut to the chase and jump out the window, get it all over with and save everybody a lot of trouble.

Am I making this sound like it's way too big a deal? Like, oh poor Riley, he just can't get it done?

Maybe. But try this for yourself:

Think about a wall.

Not just a crappy, flimsy metal frame with drywall stuck to it, kind of like the wall you have holding up your cheap imitation Impressionist pictures. No: Think of an old wall, really solid, like they used to make them. Think about a *real* wall, made with hundreds of big, heavy stones. Think about how all the stones are held together, not just by their weight—and they weigh a *lot*—but also by concrete that hardened a few hundred years ago and hasn't budged or cracked or weakened in all that time.

Now think about how that big, heavy, solid, permanent wall is not really just a wall standing around all by itself. Nope; it's attached to a couple of other walls, just as big, heavy, and solid. And these walls are all attached to a big, heavy foundation that goes deep into the ground. And then on top of them, they have more walls stacked, because there's more than one floor. And sitting on top of this huge, multilayered stack of heavy shit, kind of tying everything together, there's a big heavy *roof* that's not just stuck on and balancing there. It's held tight with some gigundo beams—basically just great big trees—and a whole lot of hardware, ratcheted down so tight it hasn't come off for hundreds of years of earthquakes, big winds, Visigoths, and who the fuck knows what else.

So you can't really just think about a wall. That doesn't exist. It's a piece of that whole fucking building. It's not a component part. You can't separate it from the rest, not visually, not conceptually—and definitely not practically. That wall is not going anywhere. Not unless you find a way to detach it from the building. Or maybe just take the whole fucking building—Why not? Just as easy.

Starting to sound impossible, right? Yeah, good call. It is impossible. But you know what? It gets worse. Because guess what—you have to find a way to take the wall, or the whole building if you go that way, without anybody noticing. See, that wall is attached to a building that's attached to a bunch of other buildings all bunched up together. And that place is guarded just about as tight as anyplace on earth, because it is called "the Vatican," and it is where this guy called the Pope lives. And for some complicated and mostly stupid reasons, a whole bunch of very serious people might like to hurt this guy. And so a whole bunch of other people, maybe even more serious, spend their lives protecting him—hundreds of guards who use every possible weapon, every high-tech security device, and a budget so huge you might as well call it unlimited.

They spend every waking hour of their entire lives protecting the guy who lives in these buildings, and that means they protect the buildings just as carefully. So if you just sort of casually decide to take something from one of these buildings—even if it's smaller than a wall—you are absolutely going to end up either locked up or dead and probably both.

And by the way, there are tons of things—and I mean that literally; *tons* of things—worth taking from the Vatican. They have a collection of art treasures like no place else in the world—a lot of them confiscated, which means *stolen*—from a bunch of poor jerks who had impure thoughts or some other bullshit. A lot of these hopeless jerks also had real talent, and you could spend a month walking around and drooling at the stolen paintings and you still wouldn't see ten percent of them. Not even *one* percent.

And not just paintings, either. They have stuff stashed away, down in a nearly endless vault, that is so scary-weird and precious it never sees the light of day. And there is stuff down there that's just rumors, legends, things that some people I can think of would pay hundreds of millions of dollars just to hold in their grubby paws and see that they're real. And I'm talking about mind-blowing things, like a collection of alien skulls, proof that Jesus either did or didn't really live, and if that's not enough to whet your appetite—try the Chronovisor! It's a device that lets you see into the past. And because it's the Vatican, they've supposedly used it to take photographs of the Crucifixion, among other things.

And I mean, you don't have to believe any of it—but nobody really knows! What would somebody pay to be sure, one way or the other?

So because of all that stuff, to a guy like me the place is an electromagnet with the power cranked up all the way. I would absolutely *love* to get down into that vault and let my sticky fingers go for a walk—or waltz out of one of the huge galleries with maybe one or two of their amazing paintings rolled up under my coat. And because it's me, I have to think if I really tried, I could probably get away with one or two small pieces of something beautiful. Truly long odds, but yeah, why not? It's what I do. I mean, like I said—it's *me*. I make a shitload of money taking stuff nobody else can get close to, and I am the very best there is. I can steal just about anything. To me "impossible" just means "I dare you." It's just some asshat claiming I can't, and that means I can and I will. I fucking *love* a challenge like that.

But a whole wall?

I mean, to steal a whole fucking wall? From the fucking Vatican?

Forget it.

It doesn't take a genius to add up the columns here. A fresco is actually part of the wall. The wall is a part of a great big building. The building is part of the Vatican. The Vatican is swarming with eager armed guards. One, two, three, four, equals—forget it. I mean, don't even think about it. You can't fucking steal a fucking wall. Not from the fucking Vatican. It can't be done.

Except—if I don't do it, I am dead. So is Monique.

It just keeps ending up there.

Well, okay, but wait a sec—so why does it have to be the whole wall? I mean, if you're not up to speed on the whole fresco thing, that's a fair question. Nobody really does frescoes anymore, and nobody much talks about them—I mean, it's not something you learn about in fourth-grade art class.

So here's the deal: A fresco is a painting, sure. But it lives on a wall—except not just *on* the wall. It actually lives *in* the wall. It's a part of the wall as much as the bricks and mortar. Because when the basic structural wall is up, the artist comes in, and he's got the whole picture planned out. He's made a full-size drawing of it, called a cartoon, so he's ready to dash off the actual picture very freaking fast. I mean, he better be ready. Because what happens next—what makes it a fresco and not a mural—is that they slap on a thick coat of plaster. And while that stuff is still wet, the artist goes to work. Working from the cartoon, he slops on the paint faster than shit. He has to, because it has to be done before the plaster dries. And what that does is that it makes the paint soak into the setting plaster, and then actually dry, set, so it's a part of the actual coat of plaster.

Which means, an actual part of the wall.

See the problem?

Yeah, me, too. See a solution?

Thought not. I sure as shit didn't.

And I tried. I beat my brains to death. I went up one side and down the other, turned the fucker inside out, everything. I thought up every dodge, every scam, every disguise or trick, everything I'd ever done or heard about—and I thought up some brand-new shit that was absolutely the True Shit—and none of it would work for this.

And I tried to get revved about it so the extra adrenaline would kick my brain into high gear. Thinking about the *who* and not just the *what*. To me, the Vatican is not a sacred place where a bunch of holy men live. To me, it is a place where a bunch of overprivileged, self-entitled, self-deluded crooks have lived for a thousand years, grabbing everything they could get their oily paws on from people who couldn't afford to lose it.

And that made it ideal turf for me. I mean, this was a perfect example of what I love most in the world—grabbing something impossible from some over-rich asshole—and there is nobody on the face of the earth more over-rich than the Vatican. It would serve the pompous, self-righteous bastards right if I grabbed their precious fucking fresco, and if I trashed a building at the same time—tough shit. They can afford it.

But wait a second, you're saying. The Vatican—that's the Catholic Church, right? You can't steal from them! I mean, it's a fucking *church*—they earned that money doing good stuff for people!

Didn't they?

Uh—no.

And if you think they did, I guess you never read any history. Because what they didn't just grab—I mean "confiscate"—the Catholic Church "earned" over hundreds of years by scaring the shit out of people. I mean, literally the holy living shit. Want an example? Among a lot of other sleazy cons, they pulled a scam that none of the con artists I know would ever have the brass balls to even try—there are limits to what you ought to do to scam somebody out of their money. But the church—to be fair, *most* churches—they don't care about those limits. And their big fund-raising project was a perfect example.

It worked like this. A guy from the Vatican comes around and tells everybody, "Guess what! You are mos def going to Hell." And they've got pictures of Hell, and really scary descriptions, and they make it absolutely *terrifying*. And "everybody" is mostly peasants who don't know shit except how to grow enough food to survive. This wasn't easy at the time. Everybody who wasn't growing food had a sword, supposedly to protect you, and you had to let them take some of your food. And of course, the priests had to have their cut, because they were so busy praying for you all the time they couldn't grow their own. And then some gang of bandits would roll in, and they'd take more. And if there's any left at all, you might—*might*—have enough left to feed yourself and your family.

But now this guy from the Vatican comes around and says, "Yo, you're going to Hell." And it sounds bad, but what is that anyway? The guy says, "Ever burn your finger? So imagine that all over your whole body, inside and out. And if your finger hurts, it's over in a day or so, right? But it doesn't work like that in Hell.

"You always wanted to live forever, right? So now you do. And every single second, from now until the end of time, you are feeling that burn, but a million times worse, all over your body, inside and out, and it never gets any better and it never ends—I mean *forever,* 'cause it's Hell. And all because you're a sinner."

"I am? Really?"

"Sure—you can't help it."

"Well, shit, I don't wanna burn forever."

And the guy from the Vatican gives you a really kind smile. "I can help," he says. "Buy one of these things— it's called a papal indulgence, and it means the Pope himself forgives you for your sin."

"Really? What sin?"

"Doesn't matter—this sucker takes care of *all* of 'em! Isn't that great?"

And so you buy it, because Hell scares the shit out of you. And in those days, if you were a peasant, that means you buy it with food. And if you don't have enough left now to make it through the winter—so what? Dying of starvation is temporary. Heaven is permanent, and you just bought a ticket! Guaranteed!

See what I mean about no self-respecting criminal would touch it? And they did it all over Europe, thousands of times, until they'd raised a fortune—maybe two or three fortunes.

But oh—hang on, you say. That is totally immoral. Those guys couldn't have been from the Vatican—not really. I mean, all those priests and bishops and cardinals are totally holy dudes, and they'd never allow that. These indulgence salesmen couldn't possibly be from the Vatican.

Yeah, they were. Really. Sent by the Pope himself. From the eleventh century and on, all is forgiven, even if you haven't done it yet, for a little cash on the barrelhead. But the scam really got going with Leo X. He was a son of Lorenzo Medici, and you have to know that family was capable of just about anything, as long as there was money in it. Leo was no different.

Pope Leo X wanted to raise money—and not so he could feed the poor or take care of lepers. Nope. He wanted money so they could throw up some more pretty buildings and fill them with pretty art. And that's God's truth.

And another truth? That makes the Vatican just exactly the kind of rich, entitled, self-loving, sleazy, useless entity I truly get off on taking things from. It's what I live for—grabbing stuff from people too rich and privileged to deserve it. If anything could give me the last big boost of inspiration, it was thinking about taking it from the Vatican.

But yeah—one last truth? I wasn't going to take it from them this time. Because it was a *wall*. And that just plain can't be done.

CHAPTER
18

So after three days of no more than grinding my teeth and staring at Monique and trying not to think about what Bernadette was going to do to me, I finally figured out that I had to go somewhere alone. I wanted to stay, be close to Monique. Just in case, you know, she changed her mind? Which, let's face it, women do all the time. But after three days, she hadn't changed her mind about me. In fact, she seemed to get more pissed the longer I went without thinking up something brilliant. I mean, she didn't come up with anything either, but I'm not stupid enough to try to tell her that.

So finally, I'd had enough of coming up empty and suffering with turquoise testicles. I told her I needed some alone time, and she didn't exactly beg me to stay. And I took off for a little place I'd been saving for a rainy day. It was just a cabin, stuck in the middle of thirty-five acres of woods and not much else, right on Lake Erie. I had made a few improvements, of course—stronger walls, doors, windows, and roof, a bunch of electronic and mechanical toys to discourage visitors, that kind of thing. I have a couple of places like it, scattered around in quiet, isolated spots, places where it's hard to find me and even harder to get at me. I can afford them, and when I need a safe and quiet place, it's money well spent. Plus, this place was near the facility where Mom was stashed at the moment, just a couple of hours away, so I could visit once or twice. I like to drop in and hold her hand whenever I can. I mean, she's my mom, and all the family I've got.

I'm pretty sure she can't tell the difference between me sitting there holding her hand and me five thousand miles away. That's what all the doctors say, and I've got no reason to think they're wrong. But I do it anyway. Doctors have been wrong before. And who knows? Things can change. I'm not holding my breath. Mom's been like this an awful long time now. And they've told me the chances that she'll ever come out of it are so close to zero the difference doesn't make any difference, too, and I'm just throwing away my money. But they don't object very much when I pay them, either.

So anyway, I left Monique in Manhattan and drove west to my cabin. It's around 570 miles, and I pulled through the gate a little after dark and stopped at what looks like some kind of power-company box. It isn't.

It's my security monitor. It's covered by a hidden camera, one of many on my perimeter. I used my pass code and opened the box to see if I'd had any visitors. I hadn't had any. The state of mind I was in, that actually seemed depressing. Of course it isn't. I like being alone, mostly, and right now I really needed to be.

All my little alarms and traps said I was. Nobody was waiting for me, nobody had been here, so I drove on down the dirt road to the little house. It was a nice drive, around half a mile, and it let me remember the place a little. It was a good backup for my place in the Ozarks. Just backup, though, because honestly? The mountains are better than the lakefront, and the Ozarks are always better than Ohio. But this place was secure and good enough for now. I'd only been here a couple of times, mostly to check it out and then secure it after I bought it. But it had everything I needed—music, books, Internet, clothes, and food, mostly MREs. I'd drive into town and get fresh food tomorrow, but there was plenty of dried stuff for now. So I had an MRE, cracked open a bottle of twenty-five-year-old Scotch, and sat on the porch looking out at the lake.

It was quiet, I was alone, and my brain stayed empty. At least the mosquitoes were glad to see me. They came at me like they hadn't eaten in months. I got tired of feeding them pretty quick and went inside. I was still restless, cranked up from the drive, so I put on some music, something that might soothe me enough that I could either sleep or think. I picked Keith Jarrett, *The*

Köln Concert. Perfect for what I had in mind. Aside from the fact that the music is totally dope, it helps me drop into kind of an active trance state—sort of zoned out but totally awake and sharper mentally.

And anyway, I love the album, because it's a live recording that should never have happened. It's solo piano, and I have a thing for music made by solo instruments. Bach, Joe Pass, whatever. Something about just having one instrument to think about gets into me and sends me to a good place. Keith Jarrett is one of the best, and *The Köln Concert* is one of *his* best. No distractions, no drums or anything else. Just the man and a truly crappy piano. Seriously—the piano *sucked*. And Jarrett was exhausted when he got to Cologne and was in major pain from a bad back. He took one look at the piece of junk he was supposed to play and said no way and went back to his car. But the promoter was kind of special: a seventeen-year-old girl who thought Jarrett was the absolute greatest thing ever. She actually got him out of his car and back onto the stage with that crappy piano. He sits down, starts playing—and it's maybe one of the greatest improvised concerts ever. A great example of making chicken soup from chicken shit.

I had a top-notch sound system in the cabin, and I was way the fuck out in the middle of the woods, so I cranked it up and just let it rip. That's inspired me before, kicked loose some wicked ideas. That's really the trick to making the gray matter hum. You have to distract it, take it offline, make it think life is a really good idea and full of peace and love and puppies and pink sunsets. For me, music is the way to do that. And I love just about all music, as long as it's done well. I had one great high school teacher who showed me the door in and taught me that all music comes from the same place. You just have to let go of all the labels and listen. I mean, really fucking *listen*. And if you can do that it doesn't matter if it's gamelan or Gershwin or Grateful Dead.

But some of it is better for yelling and throwing stuff, and some of it is better for thinking. This Jarrett recording was absolutely excellent for soothing my unconscious into behaving. It's worked before. This time it didn't do shit. I listened through to the end anyway, sipping the Scotch and feeling tragic. When the music was over and nothing had happened, I gave up and went to bed.

I slept late. I guess all the pain, anxiety, and jet lag finally caught up to me. It was almost noon when I dragged my ass out of bed. I poked around in my supplies for something to eat. It was all stuff with a long shelf life, and just about as appetizing as eating the furniture. But there was some cereal and some canned milk, and I thought I could probably choke it down. I sat down and stared at it for a while, trying to talk myself into eating it.

I was still sitting there feeling like shit when my alarm went off.

It wasn't really loud. I mean, I want to know if somebody's trespassing. But I don't want *them* to know

I know. Like, if there's a gigantic air-raid siren, a klaxon horn, guns firing, signal rockets going up—they're going to know I'm ready, right? And that makes it a lot harder to get the drop on them and decide whether it's going to be a permanent drop.

So this alarm was a muted buzz and a small flashing light, just enough to get my attention inside the house, and it did. I switched it off and checked the panel. Somebody had pulled a car onto my road and parked. I flipped a switch and got a visual. It was just there, not moving. There was one guy leaning on the hood of a rental car, smoking a cigarette.

He didn't look like much; kind of small, wiry, maybe forty years old. His clothes had the tailoring and that scruffy elegance that said he was European and he had a little money. And he was just sitting there, smoking, holding his cigarette like they do in Italy and France.

But just sitting, doing nothing. That could mean a couple of things. He might be waiting for another car or two, filled with storm troopers, before he moved in on me. Or even worse, maybe three or four guys had already jumped out and were sneaking through the bushes toward my house right now, while he sat and waited for them to finish doing horrible things to me and come back to the car.

And sure, I know, maybe he was lost, or just taking a break on a nice country road. But I didn't think so. It doesn't work that way in my world. If he was here, he was here because I was here, and I couldn't think of too many ways that could be good. Besides, the clothes, and the way he smoked the cigarette, said he was from Europe. The way things were shaping up for me right now, that felt like bad news, too. And in any case, better safe than sorry.

I hate sorry, so I'm good at safe. I was ready. I stepped into the kitchen and right through to the back of the pantry. The back wall had a hidden door, and I popped it open. Inside I had a couple of toys I'd stashed away for the idle hours, like this had suddenly turned into. I pulled one out, a cute little Heckler and Koch HK433 assault rifle. I had the longer 18.9-inch barrel on it because it's better at a distance, and there are times when one long shot is a whole lot better than spraying something close up. I fed in a clip, stuck two more in my pocket—I mean, you never know, right?—and slipped out the back door.

I circled away from the driveway and down to the lakeshore. There's a bank that drops down about four feet from the yard to the lake, and a small lip of mud between the bank and the water. I crouched over, letting the bank hide me, and slurped through the mud for about a quarter of a mile, until I was screened by trees and brush and far enough away from the dirt driveway to be invisible. Then I cut up to the main road through the woods and came back toward my driveway. I didn't see anybody, didn't hear anything, didn't notice anything that shouldn't be there.

I kept it stealthy anyway and came up behind the guy on the rental car. Long before I saw him I could smell the smoke from his cigarette. I slid sideways and

snuck up to where I could see his face. He was still
smoking. It had to be his third or fourth since he'd
parked there. Maybe I should just wait a little longer
and he'd die of lung cancer. On the other hand, I kind
of needed to ask him why he was there, was he alone,
all the standard crap. So I worked the action on my
rifle, just one *snick-snick,* so he knew I was there.

He didn't jump. Didn't even flinch. Just took one
last puff on the cigarette and then ground it out with
the pointy toe of his Italian shoes. "That's just the way
how I woulda done it," he said in a thick Brooklyn accent. Like I said, European. I'm never wrong about
that stuff. "Snuck up like that, around the side." He
held his hands up in the air, showing they were empty,
but so casual that I could see he was just being polite
and he wasn't really expecting me to do anything.
"Let's go sit someplace, huh? My ass is killin' me from
sittin' on the fucking hot metal hood. Hey, you got
anything to drink? Fucking hot out here."

"Sure, why not? We'll go have a couple of drinks and
tell jokes," I said. "Except—who the fuck are you, and
why don't I just pop a cap or two in your ass?"

He turned all the way around to face me. "You fucking kiddin' me?" he said. "Who the fuck you think I
am? Santa fucking Claus? I'm your fucking contact."
He gave a lazy wave of his hand. "Benny."

"Contact," I said. My brain spun around the word,
quickly tossing out a bunch of wild stuff and settling
on the most obvious. "Contact from—"

He held up a hand, quickly this time, and said,

"Let's not do the name game, okay? Just in case, you know, somebody might be listening?" He gave me a tiny smile, closer to a smirk. "It can happen—even in all dis rustic splendor." A small snort and then he added, "And seriously, who the fuck you think would give enough of a shit to check up on you in a shit hole in the middle of Tree-Fuck, Ohio?"

It was a question with at least two answers, but the most likely one was Boniface. He'd said he would be in touch. So I played along and asked, "You represent a serious collector?"

"Yeah, that's it," he said. "I like that. Sure, the art collector." He tilted his head down the drive toward my cabin. "Seriously, can we get outa the fucking sun? Huh?"

Yup. Boniface. I put my weapon on safe. "Sure," I said. "Let's do that."

We got outa the fucking sun and went to my fucking cabin.

chapter 19

Benny didn't have a lot to say. Just checking up. The only important thing he did was to give me a phone number to call when I was ready to make a delivery, or if I needed anything special. Then he used the bathroom, lit up again, and left, trailing a cloud of smoke. When he was gone, I opened up the cabin and put the fans on high to get rid of the tobacco smell. Then I just sat and thought for a long time. They were not really any new thoughts, and the old ones were getting depressing as hell.

I knew Boniface could find me eventually, no matter where I went, but he had found me here way too quickly, and it pissed me off—a lot. I felt like I had no secrets left. And I probably didn't. He already knew about Mom. He knew my hideouts. He probably even knew the account numbers and pass codes for my bank accounts. And apparently he knew where I was pretty much all the time.

I really and truly did not like that. In fact, I absolutely hated the shit out of it. Maybe it doesn't seem like such a big deal, like I'm being a whiny dick because some alpha dog knew where I buried all my bones. I mean, just bury them someplace else, right?

It doesn't work that way in my world. My privacy, my secrets—they were the only things keeping me alive and walking around on the outside. If I lost that, I was as good as dead. And I didn't even bother hoping that it would all be over when I did this impossible thing. I would never be free from Boniface. And even if somehow I did bust free, then there was Bailey Stone, and he didn't seem like the kind of sweet, forgiving guy who ever gave up a stranglehold on anybody. He'd hang on just because it made me miserable. So whoever was the last asshat standing would have me by the nut sack, and they'd hold on forever.

I hated that even more. But I wasn't seeing a whole lot of choice from where I was sitting.

And I still hadn't figured out how to steal a wall.

And because the only consistent law of the universe is that things always get worse—forty minutes after Benny left, my alarm went off again.

I switched it off and looked at the monitor. Another rental car. Still moving, but only one guy, the driver, was visible. I reached for my weapon and took a step toward the back door, heading for the lakeshore and the mud again, and then I thought—*Fuck it*. I went out the front door, stepped behind the utility shed, and waited.

In just another minute, the car came barreling down the drive. No subtlety at all to this guy. He slid to a stop and parked next to my truck. The driver jumped out right away, before the dust even started to settle. He was in his thirties, just under six feet, with blond hair and pink cheeks. He looked like a recruiting poster for Aryan Nations, except that he was dressed in beat-to-shit jeans and a faded orange T-shirt that read, "VOLS" in big white letters. He took a couple of steps toward the cabin, then stopped dead, turned in a full circle, and frowned.

"Hey, buddy!" he hollered. "Where you at?"

The voice was pure redneck, like the T-shirt, and the way he stood there like he was waiting for me to bring him a beer, I had a pretty good idea who he was—or, at least, *what*.

Bailey Stone's guy.

Naturally. Stone had already showed he had eyes all over Boniface. And he'd have a few on me, too. So when Benny came a-calling, Stone would follow up right away, to find out what had gone down.

I had to wonder one thing, though. Stone's intel was so good he had a guy here right away, minutes after Benny left. So why wasn't Boniface's network just as good, or better? Bailey Stone was not a subtle guy, and he must have left thumbprints somewhere. Was Boniface so secure, so arrogant, that he didn't feel the need to watch his own back?

I didn't believe it. You don't get to be top dog, and *stay* top dog, by ignoring what the little dogs are doing. Boniface had to know what was going on.

But what the fuck, that didn't matter right now. Dealing with Tennessee T-Shirt was what mattered.

"Buddy?" he called again. "Hey there! Anybody home?" And he stood there with a grin you would probably call "infectious" if you didn't know he worked for a no-class shit-pig like Bailey Stone.

I took a deep breath. No choice but to go through with it. I did the *snick-snick* thing with the bolt action again. That got his attention, and he was facing my way when I stepped out of cover. For just a second he looked unsure. Then he put that big, friendly grin back on his face. "There you are!" he said. "I's afraid you went off on a beer run or somethin'." The grin got bigger. "Since you didn't—that mean you got a couple cold ones in there?"

His name was Garrett Wallace, and like I figured, he was Bailey Stone's guy. He'd sniffed out Benny's visit and followed to see what had happened. There was no reason to lie to him, since the answer was "nothing much." So I told him. He didn't stay very long, maybe because I did not, in fact, offer him a cold one. He just smiled and nodded and gave me a telephone number, telling me I best keep in touch. Then he hopped in his car and took off again like my driveway was the Charlotte Motor Speedway and he was going for the NASCAR championship.

And I went back inside and sat there for a while, staring at my shoes and chewing my teeth. I told myself I'd been in worse spots.

Myself told me I was a lousy liar.

But what the hell. Life goes on. At least for now. And I realized I was hungry. It didn't seem like a really first-rate response to all the shit falling on my head. But I'd skipped breakfast, and with all the jumping around through the woods and pointing my rifle at people, I must have worked up an appetite.

I got up and took two steps toward the kitchen—and my alarm sounded again.

I stepped over and turned it off and started scanning for visual confirmation—because this was really hard to believe. I mean, you lay out cash for a place so you can be alone, and suddenly it's like the entire population of Toledo has come calling. How the hell was this possible? I even had an unlisted number. Was I on a tourist brochure? Things to see in the area—the lake, our wonderful Canadian geese, and Riley Wolfe!

But camera four showed movement. I zoomed in.

For a minute I thought I was seeing a mirage. Maybe a wire got crossed and I was picking up an image from a shopping mall or something. I mean, I know people look like that—but not out in the woods, sneaking through the trees to spy on a true desperado like me.

But no. I was seeing reality. Lunch would have to wait.

I picked up my rifle. At least there were plenty of private spots on my land with nice, soft dirt. Perfect for burying unwanted company.

With that cheery thought, I went outside to wait.

CHAPTER
20

Evelyn had been following Garrett Wallace for quite some time—ever since she picked him out at Hartsfield-Jackson Airport in Atlanta, in fact. It had taken some work to figure out that Wallace was the man she'd been looking for, but Evelyn was patient, and she had her sources. She'd made him right away and followed him when he picked up a rental car. When he climbed in behind the wheel she had casually walked past, as if heading into the rental office, and, when she came to his vehicle, she had "accidentally" dropped her purse. Bending to retrieve it, she placed a magnetic tracker on the undercarriage, picked up her purse, and went back to her own car.

Wallace was easy enough to follow, in spite of his tendency to drive too fast. Evelyn kept well back, stopping for gas, food, and restroom breaks when he did.

No one paid her any notice. Why would they? She was traveling alone, a dumpy middle-aged woman with short hair, some bad tattoos, and too many piercings. Not the kind of woman anyone would want to strike up a friendly conversation with.

No one did. And Evelyn certainly didn't. She stayed on Wallace's tail, making sure he didn't see her at rest stops. She had no idea where they were going, but that was not important. What mattered was that she knew this was Bailey Stone's man, and he was the only lead she had to finding a lever to get Stone off her back. And that had been her top priority, ever since she got the phone call on a number Stone should not have known. It didn't matter that Stone was a regular client who paid well and promptly. What mattered was that he had a grip on her she could not allow anyone to have, and she knew enough about him to know he would never let it go.

So she had done the job for him, sent him pictures he'd asked for of the woman. And then she had killed the "Betty" identity, which she hated to do. Aside from the expense and the hassle of becoming a new person, she *liked* being Betty. But that was over. In her mind, Stone had killed Betty, and he could not be allowed to do that with impunity. All other reasons aside, he would do it again, unless she stopped him.

She didn't underestimate Stone—far from it. He had a vast and powerful organization, and she was one overweight middle-aged woman. But she was a professional, and a good one, and finding out hidden things was one of the things she was very good at. She would find a weakness, a chink in Stone's defenses, something, and she would break his hold.

But she had to do it before Stone discovered her new identity. She knew that was just a matter of time. As soon as he thought about her at all, he would track her down again, just as he had the last time. That was something she couldn't afford. Anonymity was her only real protection. And besides, Evelyn wanted Bailey Stone off the board. She was not particularly vengeful, but he was a threat. It had been a shock to discover he knew her identity, and that knowledge had taken away any illusion of security she'd had.

So Stone had to go. Death or prison, she didn't care. Just as long as she was free of him. Besides, she owed him. She had enjoyed her life in Manhattan, and he had taken that away from her. She would never again get to live as Betty. But she would do what she could to stay Evelyn.

And that would only happen if Stone was gone.

So Evelyn drove northwest, following Garrett Wallace.

A day later, they were in Ohio, and Evelyn was still on Wallace's tail. He took I-75 almost all the way, and she followed. When they got close to Toledo, he turned off the interstate and onto increasingly smaller roads, until they reached a woody, sparsely inhabited area on the lakeshore. Wallace turned down a dirt road toward

the water, and Evelyn drove past, until she found a
place to pull over. About half a mile on she found it, a
pull-off screened by trees and brush. She got out and
sat on a stump with a sandwich and thermos she'd
packed along. If anyone saw her, she was just sitting in
the woods having a nice picnic lunch.

But Evelyn didn't touch the sandwich or the thermos. She was waiting, and while she waited she had
some serious thinking to do. She needed to find out
who Wallace was seeing and why. That was most important. Unknown variables had a way of biting you in
the ass, and Evelyn meant to stay unbitten. Besides, it
was clearly some part of Stone's business, and she
needed to know all she could about that and how it
might affect her. So she should probably wait for Wallace to finish and then ease up as close as possible to the
cabin and find out what she could.

But doing that would take time, and that would risk
losing Wallace. Her tracker had a range of only a couple
of miles, and the way he drove, he'd be out of range in
five minutes. She needed longer than that to find out
why he'd stopped here at the cabin on the lake.

On the other hand, she was reasonably sure she
could find Wallace again. He was using a passport with
his own name, and if he returned to Perth, turned in
his rental car, or almost anything else, she could track
him on her laptop. And she needed to know who or
what was so important, here in the woods, that he'd
come all this way for it. Wallace wouldn't drive all this
way and then out into the wilds if it wasn't crucial to

Bailey Stone's interests. And that made it important to Evelyn.

She made her decision. When Wallace took off in a cloud of dust and burning rubber, Evelyn waited and then carefully made her way through the woods until she saw the cabin he'd visited.

It didn't look like much. Just a small, simple house beside the lake. But Evelyn had not survived in her profession by assuming things. She waited; she watched. When there was no sign of life in the cabin, Evelyn worked her way closer, slowly and carefully. She approached the cabin from the side, so that the small shed beside the place was between her and the cabin. She paused at the back side of the shed. Then she moved stealthily around the side farthest from the cabin, slowly easing up to the corner and then squatting. Just as slowly and carefully, she peeked around the corner toward the cabin—

And found herself looking directly into the barrel of a rifle.

And a voice that was soft and polite but nonetheless sounded very dangerous said, "How can I help you, ma'am?"

CHAPTER
21

I kept her for three days. Stupid, I know. I should have put a slug in her head, right behind the ear, and put her in a nice quiet hole in the woods. I'm not sure why I didn't. I wasn't having any attack of morality or anything. I get that it's not very sporting, but neither am I, so why didn't I plug her and get on with things? I don't know. I guess for a start, it's hard to do that—or at least do it cold—to somebody who looks like everybody's favorite aunt. Which she did, except for the piercings and the tattoos. And those were a fairly new disguise—I could tell that. The skin around the piercings was still red and a little swollen, and I was pretty sure the tattoos were fake, just ink on the outside of the skin.

So I figured she was running from something recent. Or somebody, more likely. The only real question was why she ran to me. Because I knew she had. "Co-incidence" is just a word on a Scrabble board.

But for two days she wouldn't tell me. She didn't talk at all. So I kept her chained up in my safe room, a fire- and bombproof twelve-by-twelve-foot room under the floor of the cabin. I gave her food and water and a bucket to pee in, and that's it. No use getting senti-mental or making friends or anything. Because I was pretty sure that sooner or later I would just have to put her in that hole in the woods.

Something told me not to, not just yet. I mean, sure, I wanted to know how she found me and why. Maybe that was important. But more than that, there was just a naggly little voice in my head telling me to be cool and wait it out for a few days, that it might also be worth it.

So I did. And on day three, that paid off.

I was having breakfast, or trying to. Am I the only guy who ever needed to have breakfast and coffee be-fore he's functional enough to make breakfast and cof-fee? Because I'm one of them, anyway. I wake up most mornings with my head so full of tofu I can barely re-member how to make my legs take me to the kitchen.

This morning was no different. I stumbled to the coffee machine and hit the switch—I always set it up the night before, so all I have to do is remember to turn it on. And then I did something stupid. I tried to make a bowl of cereal before I drank the coffee.

I got out the milk—a brand-new container, so there was a plastic pull tab. You were supposed to just tug on it and it would pop out and you could pour your milk. Great idea. Except when I pulled, it wouldn't come up. I pulled harder. The plastic snapped in my hand. It also cut my finger, deep enough that blood started to pour out.

"Shit," I said. "Fucking plastic."

Everything was made of plastic these days. Oh, they'll tell you it's wonderful stuff—you can do absolutely anything with plastic! Even sculptors and so-called painters use it, to make bright-colored lumps of shit that nobody likes but they stare at it anyway because some dickwad said it was art, and nobody had the nerve to say it was shit—sometimes literally.

I remembered a show I'd gone to in Frankfurt a few years ago—the one in Germany, not Kentucky. I'm not sure they even have art in the Kentucky one. But in Germany, they love it, and this show was a big one. Some brain-damaged geek had taken dozens of dog turds and soaked them in some kind of polymer so they looked fresh. He stuck the preserved shit-lumps on all kinds of items—a dining table, a car seat, even in a gold frame on the wall. And everybody crowded around and stared at it and went, "Wunderbar!" and "Himmel-farb!"

Everybody but me. I had a glass of wine, verified that there were no unattached women worth the effort, and left. It was lousy wine, and I refuse to stare at literal shit. It was just another reason not to like modern art. I mean, seriously, it was nothing but shit soaked in plastic. And another reason to hate plastic. Not just because it was choking the ocean, and little kids stick it in their mouths and choke, and seagulls and turtles and who the fuck knows what else strangle to death on the stuff, but because it was everywhere. And it's not going away anytime soon. Every day some goggle-eyed genius invents a new kind, and suddenly it's taking over everything, doing things you never would've thought a plastic could ever do.

It can even preserve your shit! And now—plastic makes your shit portable! Why leave it where it is? With plastic—you can take your shit anywhere!

Wonderful stuff, plastic. Especially if you have a death wish.

Which I do not. I plan to live forever. And that plan was in danger of getting derailed, because I was about to bleed to death from cutting my finger on a piece of plastic. Fucking plastic.

I threw it in the trash, and just to make a clean sweep, I threw the carton of milk in there, too. That'll teach the bastards.

I guess the pain made me wake up a little, because I had just remembered that there were things called Band-Aids, and even that I had some, when something thumped on the floor. I looked around stupidly for a minute, long enough for a drop of blood to fall from my finger onto the floor. And I woke up some more, because when I looked at the floor I remembered who was underneath it.

I peeled back the cheesy old linoleum and opened up the trapdoor. She was staring up at me with a face that had been pale before I threw her down there. Three days in a dungeon had not given her a tan. She didn't look desperate or scared or anything like that. More like, resigned. Like, okay, fine, if this is how it is, if this is what I got to do—fine.

"I figured out who you are," she said.

"How?"

She shrugged. "A job I had a while ago," she said.

"That doesn't get you out of the hole," I said. Corny, I know, but I was feeling it.

"You let me outa here if I talk?" she asked me.

"Depends what you say," I told her. "I mean, I haven't had coffee yet, so it'd have to be pretty good."

She nodded. "It is," she said. "Better than good."

I looked at her. She looked back.

"All right," I said. "Talk."

She did. And she was right. It was better than good.

After half an hour, with a short pause to get my coffee, she had just about talked her fill. I told her I needed to think about it and sealed her back in again. She didn't whine or complain, just took it. That told me a lot right there. Like, she probably was the pro she said she was. Anyway, it was a pro's attitude.

I got more coffee and took it out on the porch. I sipped and I thought. That helped get my brain back online. One of the first things I thought was that everything she said added up. I believed her.

The second thing I thought was that the cut on my

finger still hurt. I looked at it. I'd forgotten to bandage it, but at least the bleeding had stopped. I went in and got out my first aid kit. I put a bandage on my finger and went to throw away the wrapper. On top of the trash was the milk carton and the stupid fucking plastic thing that had cut me. I decided I hated plastic forever.

I went back out and sat on my porch, looked out at the lake. It didn't look back. Didn't do much at all. Just sat there being all wet and lakey. That was no help. Nothing was. I was stuck like I'd never been stuck before. Too many odd angles and moving parts, and no way to get them all to line up and go to work.

And now this woman I had in my basement. One more moving part, and I didn't know what to do with any of them, let alone something like her that knew who I was and what I looked like and all that terrible stuff. And I didn't even want to think about it, because I couldn't see any way she could help me steal a wall.

I had thought of plenty of ways to steal a wall. I could dig out around the base and blast, then haul it away with a big helicopter. Or I could load it onto a big flatbed truck. Shit, I could just put wheels on the whole damn wall and *push* it all the way up the peninsula, over the Alps, and on to Marseilles. Stealing a wall was not the real problem. It could be done, lots of ways. None of the ways I could think of would work if you wanted to steal a wall without anybody noticing.

And having a dumpy woman with too many fake tattoos in my basement didn't help. Worse than that, it was embarrassing. What's that in your basement, Riley?

Oh, that? Just a woman that, you know. I felt like keeping for a while? Oh, okay—um, why?

Good question. I still wasn't sure why. And on top of everything else, I couldn't help thinking—*What would Mom say?*

Somethin' eatin' at you, J.R.?"

I jumped. I didn't see or hear Mom coming. And I'd been sitting on the crappy, rotting top step of our double-wide, just staring at my shoes, because yeah, something was eating at me.

Mom laughed. She had a truly great laugh, not all kittenish or shy or cover-your-mouth-and-go-tee-hee. When Mom laughed, she really let go, a big, loud, half-wild sound that made you want to laugh along with her. "Oh, my," she said, when she stopped laughing to take a breath. "I guess I gave you a start, J.R. The way you jumped—!" And she was off again, until I almost joined in.

Except I was really in no mood to laugh. And because I was sixteen, the fact that I felt a little bit like doing it anyway pissed me off. "Cut it out," I said. "And don't call me that—I'm *Riley* now. You know that."

She stopped laughing, but she kept a smile on her face. "Yes, I do know that, son," she said. "But you're always going to be J.R. to me." She held up a hand to cut off the snarky remark I was about to make. "I know, it's Riley. I'm not going to call you J.R. where anybody can hear me." She put a hand on me and just smiled for a moment. "And now, I believe there was an open question on the floor? Somethin' eatin' at you . . . *Riley*?"

She gave my name an unnatural emphasis, just so I'd know she was still playing with me, but I let it go. "Yeah," I said. And then I didn't say anything because, like I said, I was sixteen.

Mom waited for me to speak. When I didn't, she finally said, "Well, you want to tell me? Maybe I can help?"

"I don't think so," I said.

"Tell me anyway," she said. "If I can't help you're no worse off than you are now."

I was pretty sure I didn't want to tell her, for a couple of reasons. First, she had a huge collection of old sayings, and she'd trot one out for just about every occasion. The ones that rhymed were the worst, like "Patience is a virtue, possess it if you can—seldom in a woman, *never* in a man." She'd hit the final rhyming syllable with a triumphant smile that made me want to sprint for the horizon.

On top of that, I didn't want to tell her because I was trying to think of a way to do something illegal. Mom had gotten good at looking the other way, but she hadn't actually helped out with anything criminal, except for the one time, forging our new identity. She had always stayed pretty much inside the boundary lines, even though staying inside the lines kept us in a beat-to-shit old double-wide trailer so far from everything you had to order loneliness from a catalog.

But every now and then Mom surprised me. When the chips were down—and that was one of hers—she always came through. I always thought of her as a sort of fragile Southern flower, in danger of wilting because she'd fallen so far from the life she had led before. But she was tough, and she was adaptable. And she was Mom, and I would do just about anything for her. Even listen to her "wisdom" poems when I had to. And every now and then, her old sayings made a lot of sense.

This time, for instance.

But I sure as shit wasn't going to admit that. I just shook my head. "It's nothing," I told her.

She sat on the step next to me. "Well, it's got to be *something*," she said. "It's got you mopin' around like a bear in the winter."

"It's nothing, Mom," I said. "I mean, I can handle it."

She sighed. "*Riley*," she said, and she gave my name that emphasis again. "The first part of solving any problem is admitting you have a problem." She laid a hand on my shoulder. "And once you've done that? The second part is being smart enough to ask for help when you need it."

She'd been right about that. And because I wasn't stupid, even in the middle of an attack of sixteenitis, I had taken her advice. As it turned out, I asked the wrong person for help—not her—which is how I ended up in a cell in Syracuse, New York, until they came down from Jefferson County juvie to get me.

So I thought about that now. She'd been right back then, and she was probably still right. And I was ready to try anything—why not that? But I had nobody to admit to, except myself. So I decided to try it anyway, and talk to myself.

"Hey, Self. I have a problem," I said, in a loud and commanding voice.

Admitting that is the first step, Riley, Self said.

"Yeah, I know that, Self." Still nice and loud and confident sounding.

Okay, good. So what's the problem?

"Well, Self, it's like this," I said. I ticked it off on my fingers. "One badass wants me to do something impossible, or he'll kill me. Another badass wants to help me do it so he can kill the first badass, and then probably kill me. And even if I do the impossible thing, which I can't, one of the badasses will probably kill me anyway. Or best case, he'll own me for the rest of my life. Which is nearly as bad as dead, at least for me." I paused. Self didn't say anything, so I added, "Also, my finger really hurts, and I have someone locked in my basement."

Gee, Riley, Self said. *That sounds like more than one problem.*

"You're right, Self. It's a whole bunch of problems. And I don't know what to do about any of them."

All right, Riley. A bunch of problems. Maybe you should solve them one at a time?

"Sure, Self, that's a great idea," I said. "Um—you got any idea how that might work? I mean, speaking practically for a minute?"

Not really, Self said. *I don't do the practical part.*

"Wow. Okay, so—not all that helpful, then."

Well, Self said. *Sometimes you can't see the forest for the trees.*

"That sounds like Mom again," I said.

Self ignored that. Smart. *Let's look at the trees one at a time, Riley. Which problem is most important?*

"Well, Self," I said, thinking about it, "if I had to pick one tree, I'd say staying alive is most important. Any ideas?"

Nothing very definite, Self said.

"Of course not."

Just this: What would Mom say?

"Mom would probably say, 'Turn your stumbling block into a stepping-stone!'"

Well, Riley, Self said. *That sounds pretty smart. Maybe Mom was right. She usually was right about these things.*

"Okay, Self, sure. And I know this is kind of practical and all, but—you got any idea how to turn my stumbling block into a stepping-stone?"

I expected another Momism, probably something that rhymed this time. Instead, I got a surprise.

Because just like that, Self had an idea.

It was just a whisper at first. Then it got a little louder. It grew, and it kept growing, and little pieces started falling into line behind it. And it got even louder, and more pieces clicked into place, and all of a sudden it was an idea and it was really loud.

I sat up real straight and listened. Then I stood up. I walked down to the dock, thinking about it. I walked back thinking about it some more. Then I went inside and looked at the trapdoor to the basement. Then I went back out and stood on the porch again. Just stood for a minute.

I'd been thinking about the whole thing the wrong way.

I'd been thinking I had to steal the wall, just because the fresco was on it, or *in* it.

Wrong.

And I'd been thinking that even if I did that, whichever asshole survived, he'd have Riley's ass on a platter anyway.

Also wrong.

And I'd been thinking of it as separate problems, and if I didn't solve the first one—stealing the wall—then the second one would eat me, and my finger would still hurt, and I'd have to shoot the woman in the basement and then dig a grave with a hurt finger—and that was wrong, too. Not the part about the finger—the rest of it.

Wrong, wrong, wrong—and wrong had never felt so right. Because Mom was right. I had to look at the trees. And then the forest got clear.

Which it was starting to do. If I thought about this a little bit differently—if I really *did* turn my stumbling blocks into stepping- stones—

Damn. It was actually pretty simple. I could do this.

Dangerous as hell—I had to put everything into the middle of the table if it was going to come off at all, risk things I'd never risked before—but yeah, this could work. It really could. If I could just find the one final key piece, it was going to work.

Now if only my finger would stop hurting. Fucking plastic.

And just like that, the final piece clicked into place. Not the finger—the plastic. Of course.

"Son of a bitch," I said. "That's it."

It really was it. It really could work. No, goddamn it, it *would* work!

It meant shoving everything into the middle of the table, something I'd never done before—but the biggest pot needs the biggest bet. And this was the biggest it had ever been. Not just my life and liberty, which is, let's face it, pretty fucking important. And it was in there this time, too. But this time all the other stuff I cared about was on the chopping block, too. It meant Monique would have to be not just my expert forger but part of the play, which *she* had never done before, and I didn't know if she could pull it off. Even Mom would have to play a part. I would have to move her again, and put her out there where she was visible. I hated like hell to risk her at all, but I was in total endgame this time.

Total risk—total gamble. Because that was the only way. That was the bad news.

The good news? It would work. There was a way to do this.

"There's always a way," I said—and I said it out loud. Because there was a way, and I had found it.

And they'd love it in Frankfurt.

I went inside and opened up the basement trapdoor. "Come on up," I said. "I've got a job for you."

CHAPTER
22

Special Agent Frank Delgado hated working in an office. He had turned down several promotions in his career because they all led to sitting behind a desk. But there were times when it was unavoidable, and this was one of them. He had to put in chair time as a member of the task force. He tried to cheer himself up by reminding himself that he had managed to steer the task force into searching for Riley Wolfe, but even that did not do a lot to relieve his claustrophobic distaste for being cooped up here, with a group of team members he didn't really know. And so far, he hadn't discovered any compelling reasons to know them better.

Right now he was combing through nursing home records from across the country, trying to match up the list of medications he knew Riley Wolfe's mother needed to actual patients taking those meds. It was the only clue he had to finding Riley's mother and thus Riley himself. But there were dozens—hundreds—of matches, and he had no hint about what name she might be registered under. He'd been going through this list for over a week now, and he'd barely made a dent. Since that had also meant over a week of sitting here in the office, Delgado felt like his head was about to explode.

At 2:30 in the afternoon he finally decided he'd had enough. He got up from his desk, stretched, and tucked the list into his jacket pocket. Then he headed out.

"Going for lunch?" a voice called. Delgado paused, then turned. The speaker was Special Agent Helen Rosemond. Delgado had spoken to her twice. She had a voice that grated on his nerves. But they were, after all, on the same task force. So he nodded and said, "Bring you back a sandwich?"

"If they got a wrap?" Rosemond said. "Like, with turkey and a lot of green stuff on it?"

"Sure," Delgado said, and he headed out the door.

"No mayo!" Rosemond called after him, and Delgado waved.

He had really just planned to walk around for a while, but Rosemond's request reminded him that he hadn't eaten since breakfast, and he was suddenly hungry. There were plenty of places nearby where he could get a sandwich, and probably Rosemond's wrap, too. Delgado decided to walk a little first anyway. It was a clear, bright autumn day, and a walk would chase away the claustrophobic grumpiness that had been creeping over him. Maybe it would clear his head a little, too; the tedium of working the list was making him foggy.

Delgado walked briskly but aimlessly for half an hour. He felt better quickly, but he kept walking. And because he was a very good and conscientious agent, in spite of his obsession with Riley Wolfe, he was thinking about the job at hand, and what it would mean if they were truly able to capture—

"Bailey Stone."

The woman's voice spoke softly from behind and to his left. Delgado whipped smoothly sideways and to the right, and before he had turned all the way around his pistol was in his hand.

The woman stood there with a mocking half smile on her face, hands raised only slightly above her hips. "I thought that would get your attention," she said. When Delgado didn't move to holster his weapon, she tilted her head at it. "If you shoot me, you won't get to hear why I said that," she said. She shrugged. "Also, I'd rather not get handcuffed or anything? Can we just talk for a minute?" Delgado still didn't move. "People are staring?" she said.

It was a true. A small knot of people had stopped at the sight of a man pointing a pistol at a woman on the sidewalk, in broad daylight. Most of them were edging away, but a few actually moved closer, to better see whatever the excitement might be.

"Seriously," the woman said. "Just talk. It's worth your while."

Delgado studied her. She was middle-aged, kind of

soft-looking. She had bright orange shoulder-length hair that was almost certainly a wig, and she wore a New Balance logo'd track suit and court shoes. Appearances didn't mean a whole lot, but she seemed about as dangerous as a corgi on a leash. And the crowd was starting to grow.

"All right," he said. He holstered his pistol. "Talk."

The woman nodded and said, "A little more private? Maybe in there?" She pointed across the street to a coffee shop.

"All right," Delgado said again.

He followed her across the street, staying a step behind, and she led the way as if it was the most natural thing in the world. She went into the coffee shop and chose a booth along the wall, where they could both see the door. "This okay?" she asked him, and he nodded, sliding in on one side. The woman slid in opposite.

"Who are you?" Delgado said when they were settled.

She shook her head. "You gotta call me something, call me Betty," she said. "Not my name, not anymore." She raised a hand to cut off the objection he was about to make. "I know, it ain't much. Look, I'm an information professional. Freelance. And I do not exactly work the same side of the street as you? Plus I have just gone to a great deal of work and expense to change my identity again, which is something you Feds don't really approve of, right?"

"So why don't I arrest you?" Delgado said, studying her face. He assumed the way she looked was mostly a disguise, but he was good at reading people, and so far no alarm bells had gone off. Besides, she'd said two magic words, "Bailey Stone," and he definitely wanted to know where that was coming from—and where it was going.

"Because," she said, very serious, "I can give you Bailey Stone."

In spite of himself, Delgado felt his heart jump up to a faster tempo. He pushed it back down with an act of will. He'd heard plenty of promises from people on the "other side of the street," and very few of them panned out. "What do you want in return?" he said.

She looked at him like he'd said something stupid. "I want you to *catch* him, Agent Delgado," she said.

A hassled-looking waitress bumped up against the table. "You all know what you want or you need a minute?" she said in a nearly incoherent jumble of words.

"Two coffees," Betty said.

"That it?" the waitress asked.

"Yeah, that's it," Betty said, and the waitress hurried away.

"Why?" Delgado asked Betty when the waitress was gone. "Why do you want to give up Bailey Stone?" It sounded too good to be true. His experience told him that meant it usually was.

Betty shook her head. "He found out my secret identity," she said with a twist of her mouth that was not quite a smile.

"Is that so bad?"

Betty snorted. "Yeah, terrible," she said. "Listen, I got to stay anonymous, if you know what I mean? People

want to contact me, I got a PO box and a fake name."
She shrugged. "Anonymous. It's all I got for protection.
Bailey Stone found my name. He found *me*."

"You said you changed your name."

She waved that off like it was a pesky fly. "So he'll
find it again," she said. "And I got to change again.
That's who he is, you know that. So . . ." She shrugged.
"He's gotta go. Or else I'm outa business, which means
maybe dead."

Delgado just kept looking at her. In part, he was
trying to get a read on her and whether he could believe her. But he also knew that just looking, silently,
tended to make people nervous, and nervous people
often said things they wouldn't otherwise.

But Betty just looked back. So eventually, Delgado
said, "If you know Stone, you know what might happen to you if he finds out you dropped the dime on
him."

Betty nodded. "So let's make sure he don't find out,"
she said.

He raised an eyebrow. "Are you asking for witness
protection?"

She snorted with amusement. "Shit, no," she said.
"Bailey Stone would pop that bubble in like two seconds. I can do a whole lot better on my own."

Delgado nodded. She was probably right, which was
one indication that she was telling the truth. Someone
who did the work she was claiming would know that
witness protection was no guarantee of safety, not
against a dedicated professional with deep pockets.

Himself, he had no illusions about the security of witness protection. Bailey Stone was completely ruthless and had vast resources. He would find Betty, no matter where they stashed her. Witness protection was only protection against conventional threats. For Bailey Stone, it would barely be a challenge.

"All right," he said. "How are you going to give me Bailey Stone?"

She smiled. "That's the beauty part," she said. "That's why I came to *you*."

He stared at her without expression. What she said could mean anything, and consequently it meant nothing. "Why?" he said flatly.

"Because," she said. "The way you get Bailey Stone is, first you get Riley Wolfe. And I fucking *know* how bad Special Agent Frank Delgado wants Riley Wolfe."

"Who told you that?"

Her smile got bigger. "Riley Wolfe," she said.

Delgado blinked. For him, it was a huge display of emotion. "What's your connection to Riley Wolfe?" he asked.

"Same goddamn thing," she said. "He got the drop on me because he's working for Bailey Stone, and now he's got me by the short and curlies. I want him off the board, too, so's I can get back to making a living." She leaned across the table. "I can give him to you, Agent Delgado. I can give you the both of 'em."

Delgado's expression didn't change, but he forgot to breathe for a minute. He remembered when he saw the expression on Betty's face, a kind of amused pity. He took a breath. "All right," he said. "How do I get to Riley Wolfe?"

She shook her head. "Nuh-uh. Not so fast. I give you this, I walk outa here. No strings, no tricks—I leave, and you let me."

Delgado studied her. "Why do I trust you?"

"You don't," she said, and then she shrugged. "You'd be stupid to trust me. But what are you risking?"

"I'm letting a criminal walk away," he said.

She laughed, a single snort of amusement. "Get the fuck outa here," she said. "You gotta do better than that. Look at what *I'm* risking. You don't believe me, I'm in the crowbar hotel. Stone finds out I'm doing this—*or* Riley Wolfe finds out—the slammer starts to look good. My ass is on the line big-time, sport," she said. She leaned in and looked very serious. "And against that—if I'm playing straight, you get the two major bad guys you want most in the world. I'm a fucking jaywalker compared to those two guys."

"No," he said. "I have to know it's legit before I let you walk."

"So we check it right here, at this table," she said.

"How?"

"You got a phone?" she said, spreading her hands to show she thought it was a stupid question.

Delgado kept his eyes on her and calculated. Trades like this happened all the time. He even knew of cases where the Bureau let a killer walk in return for information deemed more important. And this—Bailey Stone, the target of his task force.

And Riley Wolfe.

Delgado was not actually salivating. But he wanted this to be real, wanted it badly. And because he wanted it so much, he thought it through again. A big risk; he knew nothing about this woman. But the payoff . . . he decided it was worth it. "All right," he said. "You walk."

"Super," she said.

"How do I get Riley Wolfe?"

"Simple," she said. "You find his mother."

Delgado felt a surge of disappointment, but his face didn't move. He'd spent the last few weeks trying to find Wolfe's mother, with no success. But he knew better than to give any information at all away, even by a slight change of expression, if he didn't think it mattered. "Why would I do that?" he said.

She shrugged. "Sooner or later, he turns up to see her," she said. "Always. And he sits there, holds her hand, and he tells her stuff."

"What kind of stuff?"

"Aw, you know. Where he's been, what he's doing, all that shit," she said. "It's like he updates her on his whole life." She snorted. "I mean, she can't hear him, right? She got no brain activity at all for like twenty years now. But what the fuck. He tells her." Delgado said nothing. "Come on, Special Agent. What the fuck, it's a gimme here. You bug the room, you hear Wolfe tell you how to find Stone, and then you grab him on the way out. Huh?"

Delgado's heart was pounding so loudly he was sure she could hear it. But his face stayed impassive. He studied her face for another minute. Finally, he reached into his jacket pocket and pulled out his phone. "All right," he said. "You've got a deal."

Delgado hurried back to the office, more excited than he'd been in a long time. He had a name, and the name of the extended-care facility, and that meant he had Riley Wolfe. And of course, the task force would have Bailey Stone.

There were plenty of reasons to be skeptical, and Delgado would normally lean toward believing them. But this time, he believed Betty. Not that he would ever really trust somebody like Betty. But Delgado trusted his instincts, and this just felt right.

And so he rushed back to the office to get right on it. He hurried in the door, making a beeline for his computer. But three steps in, he was stopped by a shout from the far side of the office.

"Hey! You got my lunch?"

Rosemond. Delgado lurched to a halt. He'd forgotten all about food. But then he smiled and turned to face her.

"No," he said. "But I got dessert."

CHAPTER

23

Benny was not aware that his hands were twisting and untwisting, together and separately. He was fidgeting because he was nervous. That was something he did not have a lot of practice at, so he wasn't very good at it. He was sweating, too, the kind of sweat that has nothing to do with being either hot or physically active. It was being near this woman. She set him on edge. More than that, she scared the shit out of him. Not many things did. Benny was no powder puff. He was a very tough guy, and he had come up in the world a long-ass way by proving it.

But this woman—Benny had seen her in action. It was the scariest thing he'd ever seen. And he had a very strong feeling he was not quite tough enough to survive her. And that made him nervous.

And that was a bad thing. You did not go into face

time with Patrick Boniface nervous. You say the wrong thing because you're off your game, the consequences were severe. In fact, the consequences were this woman. She didn't say anything—not a fucking word so far—and she didn't really *do* anything you could call scary. And she mostly kept the good side of her face toward Benny, which was a relief, because the other side of that face was a fucking nightmare. It looked like it had melted or something.

But that wasn't it, either. Benny had seen plenty of people with faces fucked up by wars and fires and diseases and who the fuck knows what else. With this woman, the face was just a small part of what made her so freaking scary. The rest of it? It was tough to put your finger on what the rest of it was. It was maybe just *her*, something you couldn't name but knew was too much for you. Something on an animal level of awareness, maybe from scent or ESP or who the fuck knows what, whatever it was that makes wild animals know they're in over their head.

Whatever it was, she just looked at you, and you could almost picture the sort of shit she wanted to do to you, and how much she'd enjoy doing it. And since he'd seen her do it, and enjoy it—well, shit. That look put all the reflexes in high gear, got your glands to start squirting adrenaline, made the sweat jump out of your pores.

So being alone with her made Benny very fucking edgy. Even as she led him through this passage carved out of rock, where the temperature was always a steady sixty-two degrees, the sweat had soaked his shirt. She didn't say a word, just led him on. Once he saw her glance briefly at his hands and smile. That's when he became aware that he was fidgeting like a kid caught shoplifting.

He stopped doing the squirmy-wiggly thing with his hands. But he was still a complete mental case by the time they got to the office door. She looked at him, and he froze. But she just put a hand on Benny's chest, pushed him back, and opened the door, closing it in his face without a word after she stepped through.

Benny took the moment to compose himself. Close the eyes, deep breaths, in through the nose, out through the mouth. Three of them and he was a lot calmer. It was a technique he'd learned from an old Green Beanie when they were mercs together in Zaire. It worked. By the time the door opened again, he was a little calmer, ready to face Boniface.

Bernadette tilted her head into the room. She stood a little too close to the doorway, so Benny had to squeeze past her, and she watched as he tried to squirm his way through without touching her. But he made it, and she closed the door with another of those psycho smiles.

But at least she was gone, for now. Benny let out a relieved breath and turned away from the door.

Patrick Boniface sat behind his desk, elbows on the desk and hands steepled in front of him. A fire burned in the fireplace behind him, and soft music played in the background, some classical thing, which Benny knew nothing about. A bunch of violins, and maybe a clarinet, who knew? "Sit down, Benny," Boniface said, giving a slight lean of his head toward one of the chairs opposite his. Benny hurried over and sat.

"Would you like a drink?" Boniface asked politely.

"No, sir. No, thank you," Benny said.

"Are you sure? You look a little out of sorts."

Benny nodded. "I'll be honest with you, Mr. Boniface," he said.

"That's always a good idea," Boniface said with a thin smile.

"That woman. Bernadette. I'm sorry, sir, but—she makes me very damn edgy."

Boniface's smile widened slightly. "She has that effect," he said. "But she is very useful to me. And very loyal."

"Yeah, I'm sure," Benny said. "Still . . ."

Boniface lifted a hand and waved it, dismissing the subject of Bernadette. "You said you've heard from Riley Wolfe," he said.

Benny nodded. "I did, yeah. Yes, sir. As you instructed, I gave him a phone number, a burner, and said to call if he needed to. And so, he did. He called."

"All right," Boniface said. "And what did he have to say?"

"He said he needs to come here. To come and see you," Benny said.

Boniface frowned. He thought for a moment. "Did he say why?"

"No, sir. He did not say why," Benny said. "I asked

him, of course. Several times. He was kinda like—I'd say evasive? Just said he had to talk to you."

"Has he had any more visitors?"

Benny shook his head. "No, sir, not since the day I was there. But after he left that cabin?" He shrugged. "He can be slippery. So anything's possible."

Boniface swiveled his chair away from Benny and stared into the fire. Benny sat and waited patiently. He was good at patience. If Boniface wanted to keep him sitting, fine. Boniface was the thinker, not Benny. And he was the boss, one who paid better than anybody else. There were those consequences, too. So whatever Boniface did was fine with Benny.

After a couple of minutes Boniface turned back to face Benny. "Tell me your impressions of Mr. Wolfe," he said.

"He's very damn smart," Benny said. "Maybe almost as smart as he thinks he is."

"Why almost?" Boniface asked.

Benny snorted. "Nobody could be as smart as he thinks he is," he said. "But he's not far off. And I think, he says he's gonna do something? It gets done. But he don't care about a goddamn thing in the world except himself."

"And his mother," Boniface said.

"Yeah, sure. His mother. Yes, sir. But that's it. I think what makes him tick is, he's got to prove to himself that he's the best, that he can do impossible shit, every time out. But . . ." Benny hesitated.

"But what?" Boniface said.

"I wouldn't trust him as far as I can throw him," Benny said. "Be very careful with this guy, Mr. Boniface. And when you're done with him . . ." Benny shook his head vigorously. "You don't want him loose out there, not knowing what he's gonna know about you. Because he'll see you as a threat. And that makes *him* a threat."

"A threat to me? Really?"

"Yes, sir. Absolutely. Like I said, he always finds a way to do whatever he needs to do. And if you got ahold of him somehow—Yes, sir. He's a threat. Which is why . . . I can't believe I'm sayin' this—but you should maybe give him to Bernadette."

"That thought had already occurred to me," Boniface said. "Why do you think he wants to come all the way out here to see me?"

Benny leaned forward. He had thought about this, a lot. He knew Mr. Boniface would ask him. "I'm pretty sure he's got some plan. You know, for what you asked him to do?"

"Why would that necessitate a visit, all the way out here?"

Benny spread his hands. "It's gotta be somethin' extra, maybe a little nuts. Maybe he needs a big chunk of cash and figured it's better to ask you to your face? But it's somethin' . . . different. I think."

"Something related to what his plan is?"

"Yeah. Definitely. This guy knows the rules. But still . . ."

Boniface waited for a long moment before saying, "Yes? Still?"

Benny hesitated another moment, then shook his head. "Nothing, sir, just a feeling. But don't trust this guy."

Boniface looked at him for a moment, then nodded. "Thank you, Benny. Call Wolfe when you get back and tell him to come to Perth. Ask Bernadette to call the plane, and Étienne, and arrange pickup."

"Yes, sir," Benny said. He got up and gave a nod that was almost a bow of respect, and left.

When he was gone, Boniface sat motionless, a half frown of thought on his face, for a long time.

CHAPTER

24

Étienne did not like this American. To be fair, Étienne did not really like anyone. But Americans in particular rubbed him the wrong way. They all moved through the world with a kind of ignorant arrogance, as if every flower would open for them if they smiled and waved a credit card.

This one was a perfect example. He seemed to have no memory at all of his previous trip in chains, when Étienne had beaten him. No, he came aboard as if he were on holiday, and he wore a stupid blue cap, the kind Americans always wore. It had the crest of some idiot sports team on it. Baseball, almost certainly, a game for cretins. And he was always getting in the way, asking questions, acting like he had a perfect right to do whatever pleased him, always with the same idiot smile. He behaved as if it was a pleasure ride on a hired boat, as if coming here, to Île des Choux, was something he could do whenever he wished.

And this was the man who boasted that he always found a way? He acted like he could not find the way out of a public pissoir. But no, he must put it about that he always found a way. *Eh bien*—Étienne would show him that this time, there was no way but Étienne's. Île des Choux was not one of his stupid amusement parks—there was no mouse, no roller coaster. Île des Choux was so far beyond his naïve American experience that he would be dead in less time than it took to spit. He would never be able to survive here—he could not even get on the *île* alive, without Etienne's help!

Always a way—feh! Did he think he could come here, and without Étienne? There was no way. And so as they approached the island, Étienne took some pleasure in pointing out all the horrible things that would happen to him if he ever tried to cross Étienne or his employer, Monsieur Boniface.

"Look," Étienne said. "You think you find a way, ah? Per'aps in a teeny submarine? Look—" He pointed down below the surface of the water, where a series of dim shadows were just barely visible. "For submarines? Electronic mines. Anything come close—" He waved a hand. "Boom." He smiled happily.

"Really?" the American said, nearly as happy. "Wow, so those are what—mines? Electronic mines? Is that what you said? Hey, they're not gonna go off, are they? I mean, you know, blow *us* up?"

Étienne's smile morphed into a sneer, an expression

he had a great deal more practice with. "You are so stupid you think so?" he said. "You should be glad Étienne is not so stupid as you." He tapped a black electronic box beside the steering wheel. "Thees give a signal so we are not explode. Only Étienne has thees box."

"Wow," the American said. "That's really cool. And that's for all the other stuff, too, right? I mean— missiles and booby traps and all that?"

Étienne snorted. "Again, this is stupid. The other stuff, as you say—it have the sensors, all within an electronic perimeter, yes? And to cross this line, it all shoots at you. Automatic, by computer. Again, BOOM." He smiled. "And so you worry now that when we cross the line, per'aps we, too, shall boom? Hah?"

"Uh, well—yeah, I mean, it's not gonna shoot at us, is it?" He pointed off the bow, where a large red buoy was bobbing closer. "That's your perimeter right there, isn't it?" He peered ahead, then turned to Étienne. "But hey, it didn't blow us up last time. I remember, you did something with a keypad?"

"With thees," Étienne said, tapping the keypad beside the black box. "I put the code. And so it will not shoot at us."

The American leaned over and stared at the box, with its keypad and three red glowing lights across the top. "Huh," he said. "What if—whoops!" His stupid cap slid off his head, and the American grabbed at it. "Damn wind," he said.

"It is a stupid hat to wear on the ocean," Étienne observed.

"Yeah, you got that right. Lemme just set this here for now." He put the cap down on the dashboard-like shelf behind the wheel, with the sports team insignia pointed down, toward the keypad. "So, okay, you got this box to keep you from going BOOM—but what if somebody steals the box?"

Étienne shook his head. Really, the man was too stupid. "The box, it is nothing—unless you 'ave the code! And only Étienne 'ave the code."

"Yeah, well, we're getting kinda close?" the man said, glancing nervously toward the bow. "Maybe you better put in the code now?"

"Eh bien," Étienne said, shrugging. He bent over the keypad, and the American bent with him, leaning down to see. Étienne placed a finger on the man's chest and pushed him back. When he was satisfied that the man was too far away to see, Étienne bent and typed in the twelve-digit security code. There was a *beep,* and the three red lights turned green.

"That's a lot of numbers," the American said.

"Too much of them to hack," Étienne said. "And suppose somehow you do, you get past the perimeter— then you have *les soldats,* eh?"

"The soldiers. Yeah, they looked like a tough bunch."

Étienne grunted. "Oui," he said, and he turned his back. "Maintenant tais-toi," he said. He was tired of this American and his stupidity. And in any case, he needed to concentrate to steer them through the channel.

But as he put his hands on the wheel, he saw the

ridiculous cap perched there. "Feh," he said. He flung the cap over his shoulder without looking.

He did not see the American make a truly remarkable catch, snatching the hat just before it went over the side and then cradling it as if it was something precious. If he had seen it, he would no doubt have assumed that this man had a fetishistic need to preserve the cap. No doubt because it was a good-luck token and he believed his team would lose if anything happened to the cap. Why else would anyone, even an idiot American, care about a stupid cap?

He would have been wrong about that, too. But then, he hadn't seen the tiny hole in the logo patch on the front of the hat. Even if he had, he might not have noticed the tiny, barely visible gleam of *something* hidden inside the patch.

I don't like long boat rides when I'm not driving. Too much can go wrong on a boat, and why should I think anybody else can take care of me better than I can? More than that, I really didn't like long boat rides with an asshole French guy in charge who sneered at me the whole way. And when that long, sneering boat ride ends in a fortified cave where the official greeter was probably going to be Bernadette—it's a perfect trifecta of I-don't-like. But it was the most important part of the plan, the whole reason I had to make this trip. So I kept my smile on and went through with it.

The smile faded a little when we got through the channel, into the tunnel, and tied off at the dock. Because just like I expected, my official greeting committee was a couple of the soldiers in black—and Bernadette.

I wouldn't really say her ruined face lit up with pleasure when she saw me. Her eyes just narrowed a little, like she was being forced to hang out with somebody she didn't like. The feeling was more than mutual. The finger she'd broken started to throb just from me seeing her, and it made me think of a whole bunch of other body parts that would hurt a lot more if she got her way.

But she didn't do a damn thing except watch me while I climbed onto the dock. Then she turned and started toward the main tunnel. The soldiers nodded at me, one said, "Allons-y," and the three of us followed her, me between the two of them.

We wound through the tunnels in Bernadette's wake until we came to the door of Boniface's office. She opened the door and went through. The two soldiers took up station, one on each side of the doorway, and I followed Bernadette into the office.

The office was pretty much like I remembered. There was a nice fire going in the fireplace behind the desk. But the desk itself was deserted. Boniface sat in a beautiful wing chair beside the desk with his hands folded in his lap. There were two straight-backed chairs facing him, and a beautiful coffee table, cut from a huge geode, in between his chair and the two others. A decorator would probably call it a conversation nook.

Whatever you called it, Boniface dominated it. Not just because he had a bigger chair that looked like a throne with him in it. He was just the kind of guy who dominated. And sitting there, watching me plod in behind his goblin, Bernadette, he looked like the major diplomat of a powerful country who was accepting the surrender of a humiliated rival country.

"Sit down, Riley," he said, waving at a straight-backed chair. I took the closest one. Bernadette didn't sit. She moved to her standard position, standing behind Boniface, where she could make faces at me without his seeing. "I hope your trip was pleasant?" he said.

I shrugged. "It was a trip," I said. "A long one."

He nodded as if I made sense. "Would you like a drink?"

"That would be nice," I said. "Maybe some of that Armagnac?"

He smiled approvingly. "Bernadette, if you please?"

I have to admit, one reason I asked for the drink was because I was hoping he would ask Bernadette to fetch it. It's very small-spirited of me, I know that, but it was kind of fun to see her working like a servant, especially working for me. And from the look on her face, she got that. I was pretty sure she wouldn't poison me in front of Boniface, but she looked like she wanted to.

But she handed me a nice big crystal tumbler half filled with Armagnac, which was the other reason I wanted a drink. This stuff was totally yummy. I raised the glass to Bernadette and sipped. If she'd put anything in it, it was the best damn poison I ever tasted.

She watched me sip, then moved back to her spot behind Boniface.

"Benny tells me you need to see me," Boniface said.

"I do," I said. "I've got an idea—but it takes a large chunk of money."

"That's not really a problem," he said dismissively. "Did you really need to come all this way for that?"

"No," I said. "I came all this way because I want to try something wild—and there's a certain amount of risk," I said. I sipped again. That stuff was *good*.

"I assume there usually is?"

"Risk to the *fresco*," I said. Boniface frowned, and I plunged on. "I think this will work, and it's the only way, as far as I can see, but—" I shrugged. "There's a chance it might damage the fresco."

Boniface's frown turned into a scowl. "How much of a chance?"

I sipped again, trying to look thoughtful. "I'd say . . . ten to twenty percent?"

He rubbed his chin. "What is your feeling?" he asked.

"I think it's worth the risk," I said. "I think I can make this work. But I want you to know that there's this chance. Like I said, it's the only way I can see, and I will work my ass off to make it work without any damage. But it's never been done before, it's a little crazy, and I won't know for sure until it's done. And I don't want to end up playing truth or dare with Bernadette if I'm wrong."

He stared at me for a minute, just about as hard as I've ever been stared at. "Tell me," he said at last.

I told him. He focused on me with total intensity, interrupting only once for what was a pretty good question. I laid it all out for him, and yeah, it sounded even crazier saying it out loud in this room. But he listened, and I gave it to him. I showed him some of the research papers I'd gone through. I told him how I thought they would work for this.

He interrupted again. "You have someone specific in mind?"

"I do," I said. I showed him the name, the bio, the list of impressive papers. He nodded and waved me on.

I went on. I gave him all the detail I thought he would need. When I was done, he got up and walked over to the fireplace. He stood there looking into the flames for a long time. Finally, he turned and looked at me and nodded once. "All right," he said. "I'll wire you the money."

"One more thing," I said. He raised an eyebrow. I finished my drink and put the glass down on the coffee table. "I'm going to need a special kind of diversion," I said.

CHAPTER
25

Professor Lakshmi Sabharwal was impressed. Not by the man standing there in her laboratory at Pitt. In spite of what looked like a very nice suit, he was nothing much; in his fifties, a sizable paunch, and a large red nose with a mole on the end. His "hair" was an obvious toupee, too perfect and too dark for someone his age.

And his business card was no big deal, either. She'd never heard of North American Innovation Industries, and the name L. Foster Hargrave was just as meaningless.

But the check . . . *That* was impressive.

He'd come in and introduced himself and said he'd read a couple of her papers. He even quoted one, "The Absorption of Polymer-Based Solutions into Semi-

Porous Surfaces." And he'd put a check down on her worktable.

It was a cashier's check, made out to her personally, in an amount that made her dizzy.

Not that she was motivated by money; she wasn't. If she had been, she probably would have gone to medical school, like her parents had suggested. Like her brother had done; he drove a brand-new Mercedes, a new one every year. Lakshmi herself drove a four-year-old Toyota. She didn't care, and she didn't care that she made an annual salary less than one-quarter of her brother's. No: What motivated Lakshmi Sabharwal was her research. And a check this size . . .

It was enough money to fund her research for at least two years.

The research was what she lived for. It was all that mattered. Since her first science fair project in middle school, Lakshmi had been hooked. Not on the results, although of course it was always nice to come up with something. But the process itself, the long hours in the lab, the dozens of repetitions, each with a small new variable—she found it endlessly fascinating, and far more fulfilling than anything else she knew of.

That included personal relationships; Lakshmi was unmarried. She was extremely smart, she was confident, and she could have made an excellent match anytime. But that would interfere with her work.

That work had led her here, to Pittsburgh, and a tenure-track position at the university. And at first, she'd been able to pursue her research into polymers just as she liked. But the funding dried up, and the pressure grew for her to move on to something else. Polymers were not sexy this year. And so she'd had a great deal of trouble getting anyone else to see how vital it could be to perfect a multiuse plastic solution with a built-in time stamp that could permeate and preserve any surface it could penetrate. Maybe the attention and acclaim—and the all-important funding—were withheld because she was a woman, or because her name didn't sound "American." Well, it was. She was a third-generation citizen and just as American as anybody else—she'd even been a cheerleader in high school. But the way things were nowadays, anybody who looked like her and had a name more complicated than Smith—

Forget it. Not important. This man Hargrave obviously didn't care about anything but results. Those, she could deliver. "Let me understand your parameters," she said. "You want a polymer solution to be applied to a surface—Oh! Very important—what is the composition of this surface?"

Mr. Hargrave nodded affably. "Let's assume it's plaster," he said.

"Aha," she said. "Well then . . . hmp. And when the solution dries, it has to be flexible?"

"That's correct."

"In what sense of the word—that is, just how flexible must it be?"

"Flexible enough so that it can be rolled up like a yoga mat," Mr. Hargrave said.

"Yoga mat," she muttered, wondering if he was making some sort of joke about her ethnicity. She decided it didn't matter. With a check that big, he could make any joke he wanted. "Well then. Plaster is semi-porous, which means that—no, no, that's ridiculous . . . Flexibility is completely—aha! If we add a cross-linking agent? Yes, yes, I think so . . ." Professor Sabharwal was not aware that she was speaking aloud as she rambled through her initial thoughts, until Mr. Hargrave interrupted her.

"You think so?" he demanded. "You think you can do this?"

The professor blinked at him. "It's never been done before," she said. "But it is theoretically possible, yes." And then, seeing the check again, she gave him her best, most dazzling smile. "Some very interesting possibilities," she said. "But very difficult."

"I don't give a shit about interesting," Hargrave said in his gruff and gravelly voice. "Or difficult. Can you do it?"

Professor Sabharwal frowned and pushed the glasses up on her nose. "Well," she said. "If I start with a silicone-based liquid with a low viscosity—as I have already done in small amounts in the laboratory—and as I said, add the cross-linking agent . . ." She frowned harder and pushed a strand of hair off her forehead. "Then when you pour the solution onto the horizontal surface—"

"Horizontal? No," Mr. Hargrave said. "It has to be vertical."

"Oh! Vertical . . . ?" She was silent for a moment, and then her frown faded. "Yes, of course. It's really quite simple," she said. "You would have to construct a holding reservoir of some kind. Over the entire surface, of course. Airtight seal."

"Why is that?" he demanded.

She nodded. "Yes, definitely, reservoir with a seal," she said. "And then—Why? Quite simple—in order for the liquid to fully and *evenly* penetrate the surface. And then it would require enough time to—"

"How *much* time?" the man practically barked at her.

Professor Sabharwal frowned. "Variable. Anywhere from minutes to days. Would that be an important consideration, Mr. Hargrave?"

"It sure would," he growled. "It's gotta set and dry *fast*—minutes, not hours."

"Uh-huh, I see," she said. She frowned and looked off into space. "If I can get an absorption rate that . . . But no, that would mean—Mr. Hargrave, you say that this element of the structure—the *infused* element, once transformed into a malleable form—this must then be extracted from a standing structure and transported, and intact? Without damage?"

"Absolutely essential," Mr. Hargrave said. "If it's damaged, the entire project is a shipwreck. A total disaster," he added, as if uncertain that she would know what "shipwreck" meant.

"Yes, of course," she said, still frowning thoughtfully. "And this is of course the true conundrum. By changing the physical properties of the medium, you naturally also change—but wait a moment . . ."

Professor Sabharwal slumped over her desk for a moment and tapped her fingertips rhythmically. "Uh-huh, yes—which would require . . . Right," she muttered to herself. And then, as if suddenly aware that someone else was present, she snapped her head up and smiled. "Difficult, Mr. Hargrave. Very, very difficult. But with a certain amount of—It would require, ah . . ." She waved a hand, as if dispelling a cloud of noxious fumes. "Yes, I think it could be done."

"You think," he said, and now he was frowning, too.

Professor Sabharwal took a breath. This was not a time for shyness or modesty. It was the opportunity she'd hoped for her entire career. But to promise results, with something this radical—it was risky, and it was not the kind of risk she was comfortable taking. But that check . . . She swallowed and reinforced her smile. "The problem is achieving any flexibility at all," she said. "The plaster itself is rigid, of course. But it is also semipermeable? So the polymer would have to *infuse* the plaster to an extent that would fundamentally modify the—oh! What depth of infusion might be required?"

Mr. Hargrave stared as if he was having trouble following her. "What—depth?"

"Yes, of course, what depth must the polymer penetrate *into* the plaster for best results, in whatever your— Mr. Hargrave, it would all be a great deal easier if you would simply tell me what you're trying to accomplish here."

Hargrave's face lost all of its uncertainty and set in stern lines. "No, absolutely not," he said. "That's entirely confidential—and I must demand that as part of this project, you keep the entire process to yourself, Professor. If any word of this got out to our competitors . . ." He shook his head and looked even more serious. "It all has to stay secret. Or it's no deal."

"Of course, that's not a problem at all," she said. "But I do need to know a number of technical parameters—and the depth of infusion is an extremely important consideration."

"Yes, naturally, I can see that," he said. "Let's say— two to three inches?"

Professor Sabharwal hissed out a breath between her teeth. "Two to three—That would require an extremely fluid solution—very volatile. And then it would have to *set,* rather abruptly, transforming in the drying process to an elastic solid—difficult."

"Just idle curiosity, Professor," Hargrave said. "If I painted your solution over a drawing my daughter made, on, let's say, a plaster wall—would this stuff preserve it?"

Professor Sabarwhal cocked her head at him. "What an odd idea," she said. "Yes, I suppose. Yes, actually it should. But why—"

"So the final product is a fixative as well as a flexible preservative," he said.

"Yes, I think that's accurate," she said. "But a polymer with those properties is entirely unprecedented. I don't know, I'm not sure that—"

She heard a tapping noise and looked at Mr. Hargrave. He was very pointedly tapping his finger on the check and regarding her with a raised eyebrow. Professor Sabharwal got the hint. So she said a quick prayer, crossed her fingers, and plunged ahead. "Yes, I can do it," she said. "Absolutely."

Hargrave looked at her, hard, for what seemed like a long time. He finally nodded, reached out a finger, and pushed the check across the lab table, closer to her. "Good," he said. "I need it in three months."

"Three—that's absurd!" she said, shocked by the idea. It would take her three months just to find a cross-linking agent she could modify to impart flexibility, and—

"Is it really?" Hargrave asked, raising an oversized eyebrow. "Is it still absurd if I double the check?"

Professor Sabharwal gulped, her head spinning. That much money . . . And to create a revolutionary new polymer on top—"I can do it," she said, and she devoutly hoped she could.

Hargrave smiled for the first time. "Of course you can," he said. He held out a hand and took hers, shook it. "It's going to be great doing business with you, Professor Sabanail."

She didn't correct the way he mispronounced her name. She was too busy smiling back and mentally making a list of the equipment she would buy with all that money.

CHAPTER

26

Janice Saberhagen, RN, had not had a moment to herself all day, and she desperately needed to make that phone call. But she needed privacy for that, and there hadn't been any, not since she came in this morning at 7 A.M. First Mrs. Muller had wandered off into the woods surrounding the facility, and then Mr. Gomez had gone into cardiac arrest, and suddenly there were no sterile latex gloves to be had—and it all fell on Janice to make things right, because the administration was so damn cheap they only had one RN on this shift—her. So Janice had been running through the whole facility just about nonstop, and her feet were killing her. It was the new shoes—she knew better, but they'd looked so *cute* when she tried them on.

Janice bought the shoes, and she wore them to work. It was stupid, an impulse buy, just like every other time she bought something stupid. Which, to be honest, was way too often, and the main reason she was in so much trouble right now. If anybody found out about the money she'd taken from petty cash—

But come on, nobody had discovered it so far, and now they never would, because she could replace it. Right after she made this phone call, her money problems were going to be over. At least for now. And she'd promised herself she'd be more careful about money in the future. Really, this time she meant it.

So Janice had been looking to find two seconds without a crisis when she could slip away and make the call—and finally, at almost 10:30, the moment came, and Janice walked briskly toward the staircase, her pace saying she was on another lifesaving errand. She made a hurried stop in the staff room and grabbed her purse. Then she strode off down the hall and took the stairs to the basement. There was nothing down there but some old furniture, the furnace, and the laundry room at one end. As long as nobody was washing sheets or something, it was the perfect place.

Janice stepped out into the basement and looked around cautiously. Nobody else in sight. Good. She took out her phone and then fumbled out the scrap of paper with the number on it. She dialed rapidly, got a digit wrong, and cleared it. She took a breath, steadied herself, and dialed again—carefully this time. It rang four times, and then she heard somebody click on.

"Yes?" The voice sounded weird, alien. It was obviously going through one of those electronic things that change your voice. Janice didn't care. As long as the money came through, it could be Darth Vader on the other end for all she cared.

"It's, um, Janice," she said. "At Creedmore?"

"I know who you are," the voice said. Coming through the voice-disguise thing it sounded really sinister, and Janice shivered.

"You said—you told me—" She paused and took a breath. "Somebody called. About—what you said. They asked about all the meds you named? And then they asked for directions to get here? So I think—"

"When did they call?" It was a demand that she was sure would have sounded harsh even in a natural voice.

"It—they, uh . . . Last night? But I wasn't here, at work, so I just found out this morning and I—"

"All right," the voice growled. "Did they say who they were?"

"FBI," Janice said in an awed whisper, and she shivered again. If she was doing something wrong, and the FBI was involved—but she didn't *know* it was wrong, not really, and there was nothing she could tell anybody about who this person was on the other end of the phone, and she really, truly, swear-to-God needed that money, so—

"Good," the voice said. "You've done well." It sounded kind of like from a movie the way he said it, and with that creepy voice, but it made her feel a little better about the whole thing—like she was part of some story.

"I just, I'm sorry that—thank you," she said. "Um—is it—will, will you . . ."

The voice chuckled, and the sound of it coming through that voice thing was the creepiest thing yet. "I have just wired the money to your account," it said. "Let me know if there's anything else."

"I will, I promise, and I . . ." Janice stopped talking, because the line had gone dead. "Thank you," she said anyway.

Then she put the phone in her purse and trudged back up the stairs to work.

CHAPTER
27

Arthur Kondor was only scary when he wanted to be. It was true that he was well over six feet tall and broad-shouldered; it was also true that beneath his dark unibrow his face showed a number of scars that were almost certainly inflicted by knives and other dangerous weapons. But because Arthur was aware of what he looked like, he had cultivated a very mild neutral expression that he deployed in daily life.

He was showing this mild expression now, to Dr. Hannah Keller, who had been summoned when Arthur and his helpers had arrived at Creedmore Extended Care Facility. Dr. Keller did not like being summoned. She was the only MD on the premises right now, and her purely medical duties were many and vital. But this—Mrs. Cleaver was a special patient, in a persistent vegetative state, and she could not simply be moved around like a sack of potatoes—no matter how much her behavior resembled said sack.

So she scanned the documents Arthur Kondor had presented with a certain amount of care. They seemed in order, but . . . "Where are you taking her?" she said, looking up at the hulking figure who waited patiently in front of her.

Arthur smiled. "I am not permitted to say," he said.

Dr. Keller frowned. "What kind of transport?"

Arthur handed her another document. "A licensed medical transport vehicle," he said. "Fully equipped and custom fitted to care for Mrs. Cleaver."

Dr. Keller, still frowning, looked at this new paper. It stated that the vehicle was indeed equipped with all the vital medical equipment and supplies necessary to maintain Mrs. Cleaver in transit, and that an RN was in attendance. It stated further that the vehicle was the property of Greeley Medical Transport, Inc., which assumed full responsibility for the patient in transit.

"It all seems in order," Dr. Keller said, but she still hesitated. "But . . ."

A large and exceedingly scarred hand plucked the papers from Dr. Keller's grasp. Startled, she looked up. The formerly mild face was no longer so friendly. For the first time, Dr. Keller noticed how cold the blue eyes were. "We need to leave," Arthur said. His voice was neither loud nor threatening, but even so, Dr. Keller felt the hair stand up on the back of her neck. "I have instructions. We need to leave *now*," Arthur said.

Dr. Keller had a very brief impulse to call security.

Then rationality returned; "security" was a fifty-eight-year-old retired cop with a beer belly and a bad back. And this man in front of her . . . Dr. Keller felt a quick shiver run through her. It wasn't worth it. The papers were in order, and she wanted this man to go away as quickly as possible. "All right," she said. "She's in Room 243. Have a safe trip."

Arthur Kondor nodded. "Thank you, Doctor," he said.

It was all going very smoothly, and that made Frank Delgado nervous. He watched from the far corner of the parking lot as Arthur Kondor led his team into the facility. He did not recognize Kondor, but Frank knew what he was. The way he walked, on the balls of his feet, the way he managed to take in the entire area without appearing to really look, and the intangible *something* Kondor radiated; these were as familiar to any agent of the FBI as their own face. This man was violent trouble, a professional who would not hesitate to do whatever he needed to do in order to accomplish his goal. He was exactly the kind of man Riley Wolfe would hire for something like this.

And Delgado watched as, half an hour later, Kondor walked out of the building beside the gurney carrying "Mrs. Cleaver." He watched as they lifted her into the medical transport, labeled "GREELEY MEDICAL TRANSPORT" on the side in large blue letters. And he watched as the attendants closed the back door and climbed in. Kondor took one last look around the area and then climbed into the front passenger's seat. A moment later, the vehicle backed up, turned, and headed out toward the interstate.

Delgado did not follow. There was no need. The trackers he'd put in place would do the job for him. He hadn't really even needed to be there at all. But he had wanted to be there, just to watch. Because with Riley Wolfe, nothing at all was certain. Not ever.

But it had all gone exactly as it should. There was absolutely no reason to think Riley's men had suspected anything.

Delgado switched on the GPS tracker on the seat beside him. It beeped reassuringly, and the screen lit up to show the medical transport, half a mile away and receding, exactly as it should. All perfect.

So why did it all make him uneasy?

No reason at all. It was just nerves, overall paranoia—justified paranoia when dealing with Riley Wolfe. Delgado had been so close, so many times, and every time Wolfe slipped away, usually with some mocking farewell gesture that left Delgado completely deflated. And now, when everything was going smoothly . . .

Of course he was uneasy. Experience demanded that he be a little anxious. But everything indicated that this time would be different. Sooner or later it had to work out. Why not this time?

Delgado looked again at the GPS tracker. It beeped

again. The transport was up onto the interstate now, and two other agents would pick it up there and follow. All according to plan.

He took a deep breath and thought, *Am I really a step ahead this time?*

He was. He had to be. This time, he would get Riley Wolfe.

Delgado let out his breath, put the car in gear, and headed out.

CHAPTER
28

"Goddamn it—no! No way! It's the stupidest goddamn thing I ever heard!" Monique said. "And you come in here and just lay this out like—You're completely insane, you know that?"

And the cocky bastard nodded and smiled. "I thought I might be, yeah," he said.

Monique felt the anger boil up, and she let it spill over. "Fuck you, Riley! Don't you dare smirk at me—not when you're coming at me with this half-assed, crazy bullshit!"

"It's not half-assed," he said calmly. "It's totally got a full ass."

"Fuck you!"

"You said that already."

"I meant it! And I still do! You arrogant, stupid, miserable, rotten smirking prick!"

"Smirking prick—now, there's a disturbing image," he said.

She ignored him. "You self-centered sack of shit! It's bad enough when you risk your own life—"

"Really? So you do care!"

"I care about not getting killed in some idiotic scheme fucking around with some of the most dangerous people in the world!"

Riley looked serious now as he said, "It is dangerous, Monique. I admit that. But it's the only way."

Monique sputtered for a moment, trying to find coherent words when all she really wanted to do was screech, throw things, and kick Riley Wolfe in the head. Instead, she closed her eyes, took a deep breath, and then let it out. When she opened her eyes he was still right there, still watching her soberly. "Jesus. Listen to me. Why is it I'm always mad when you're around?" she said. "I don't like being mad."

"It must mean something," he said, his mouth twitching to indicate exactly what he thought it meant.

"It means I'm going to kill you one of these days," she snapped. Then she sighed and sagged again. "If I live long enough. And if somebody else doesn't kill you first."

"Always possible," Riley said. "Especially right now. But, Monique—this really is the best odds to get out of this whole thing in one piece." She said nothing, just looked down and sighed again. "It's exactly the kind of thing I do—the kind of thing I've been doing for years!" he said, trying to sound confident. Monique just shook her head.

Riley took a step closer and lowered his voice. "I can't do it without you, Monique. And if I don't do it—yeah, they'll kill me. But they'll come after you, too. I don't want that."

"I don't, either," she mumbled. She felt his hand on her shoulder and looked up.

"Monique," he said, and there was a pleading note in his voice. "This is really and truly the only way. And it will work! I know it will!"

"You always say that," she said.

"When was I ever wrong?" he said with a trace of his usual cockiness.

Monique pushed his hand off and sank down onto the battered old couch she kept in her work area. "I don't know if I can do it, Riley," she said. "I'm not like you."

"Thank God for that," he said.

She ignored him again. "I've never done anything like this, and it's—I mean, I make one simple, stupid mistake, and we're dead and fucked, both of us. And it would be on me, because I couldn't—No. No, I can't. I can't do this, Riley. It's just too much . . ."

The old couch shifted under Riley's weight as he sat next to her and took her hand. "You *can* do this, Monique. All you have to do is what you always do—"

"But with the whole fucking world watching me!" she said, pulling her hand away. "And I'm not even *me* anymore!"

"You can do this, Monique," he said. "I know you can, or I wouldn't ask you."

"Shit," she said. "What choice have I got?"

He picked up both her hands from where she'd dropped them in her lap, and this time she didn't pull away. "None at all," he said.

"Shit," she said again.

CHAPTER
29

Arthur Kondor stood in the dark at a pull-off on an old state road. The wind whipped at his jacket and he smelled rain coming. He didn't care. Weather meant nothing to him, except in how it might affect a schedule. This time, there could be a tropical cloudburst, and it wouldn't matter. This was the last changeover, and it would be done before the rain came, before it could possibly affect his plans.

The last changeover. There had been a lot of them over the last two days and nights. Each time, the comatose woman was transferred from one vehicle to another under Kondor's watchful eyes. Each time, the transfer was made with no problem, and when it was complete, Kondor would climb into the front seat and nod to the driver. None of the drivers knew where they were going, of course. Kondor gave them step-by-step instructions until they reached the next transfer point, and then the process repeated. The same each time.

Until this final changeover. This time, Kondor's instructions were a little different. That didn't matter to Kondor. He didn't care if he was told to enter a Walmart and paint every clerk red. It would not occur to him to ask why anyone wanted the clerks painted, why at Walmart, why it had to be red—he didn't care. None of his business. He did exactly what he was told without thinking too much, and he did it very, very well. That's why people like Riley Wolfe hired him, and why they paid him so much.

Kondor saw a glow on the horizon. His hand went inside his jacket, where a Heckler and Koch MP7 snuggled up against his belt. It was just automatic caution. He didn't expect any trouble. He didn't get any, either. As he expected, the glow turned into headlights, and a minute later a medical transport van turned into the pull-off, followed immediately by a second.

The driver's window of the first van rolled down and a man stuck his head out. "Seen any coyotes?" the driver asked.

It was the pass phrase. Kondor stepped forward and gave the counter. "No, but I heard them howl," he said.

The driver nodded. He gave three short beeps on the horn and climbed out of his vehicle. The driver of the second vehicle joined him a moment later. "Okay," the first driver said. "Let's get 'er done."

It took only a few minutes to transfer the comatose woman to the new van. When it was done, Kondor paid off the driver of the vehicle he'd arrived in and sent him on his way. Then he did a final electronic sweep. He'd done one already, several times. But the Feds thought they were clever. And they had some new tracers that stayed dormant, turning on several days later, precisely to avoid sweeps like Kondor was doing.

He found only the three tracers he'd found earlier. As instructed, he removed two of them and tossed them into a ditch beside the road. The third tracer, the one that had been hidden extra carefully, he put into his pocket. He walked back to the second van and opened the back door. He stepped up into the interior and looked down at the woman lying there. The life support machinery beeped and whispered softly.

Kondor took the tracer from his pocket. He leaned over and placed it exactly as it had been when he removed it from the other woman. Same location, same position. Then he climbed out and closed the door.

The rain had started at last. Kondor turned up the collar of his jacket and walked back to the two drivers. To one of them, he handed an envelope. "Take her to this address," he said. "She's preregistered. You get paid when she arrives safely."

The driver looked into the envelope, nodded, looked up at Kondor.

"Go," Kondor said.

He watched as the van turned back out onto the country road and disappeared over the next hill. Then he turned to the other driver and nodded. "Let's go," he said.

Two minutes later, they were gone, in the opposite direction, and the pull-off was dark and quiet again.

Professor Sabharwal was nervous. In part that was understandable. She had not had a full night's sleep in three months. Almost all of her waking hours had been spent here, in her lab, working on the new polymer. Aside from the fact that the money from this project would fund her research for at least two years, the work itself had become all consuming. As she got closer to achieving the polymer that Hargrave had ordered, her excitement with the project had blossomed into something so exhilarating that it sustained her.

But now, with the work ended and Hargrave arriving, the accumulated strain and fatigue had hit her like a bag of bricks, and she was physically, mentally, and emotionally worn out, completely tattered. Perhaps more worrying, she was facing her great benefactor with a finished product that she feared he would find far from finished. So her hands shook, and so did her voice, as she greeted him.

"As I told you on the phone, Mr. Hargrave, I've made up a very large supply for you—there it is, right over there," she said, leading him into the laboratory and waving at a row of neatly stacked five-gallon plastic buckets, all carefully sealed and labeled, "SAB-151."

"Now I need to tell you, that is—I hope you can understand what the—I mean, um—that I have had to make one small sacrifice in order to meet your deadline? I'm sorry—I'm so sorry, I did all that I—But you see, it's just the time element? And I was completely— In any case, I was unable to satisfactorily achieve *all* the desired results? Most of it, nearly all of it, yes, certainly. Everything except one small—I was forced to make a decision to give up just a little in the one small area involving the speed at which the solution dries?" she said, all in one breath as she ushered him over to the desk and chair at one end of her laboratory. "I do apologize, Mr. Hargrave, I hope it doesn't—If only I'd had a little more time I'm sure—"

"How long will it take to dry?" Hargrave demanded.

She sucked in air through her teeth. In her anxious condition, the hissing sound startled her. "Oh!" she said. "I have not totally completed testing but—I am reasonably sure that twenty-four hours, perhaps a little longer—I believe that would suffice."

"You *believe*?"

She sucked in air again and clamped down her jaw. "There is always an element of uncertainty, Mr. Hargrave," she said, hating the way her voice shook. "There are variables—humidity and temperature in the environment, the presence or absence of sunlight—it's impossible to say for sure, which is of course why extensive testing is—" She lurched to a halt as she saw his face.

"So it could take longer than twenty-four hours?" he said, scowling.

"Potentially, yes," she admitted.

"Well, how the hell will I know when it is dry and ready?"

"By examining the surface elasticity," she said. "That should allow you to ascertain the, uh . . ."

Hargrave frowned, and she stumbled to a stop, her heart hammering. And she couldn't help thinking, *What if he wants the money back?*

But after what seemed an eternity to Professor Sabharwal, Hargrave shrugged. "Well, hell," he said. "If it will do what it should in all the other parameters—"

"Oh, yes, sir, I assure you, it will, absolutely," Professor Sabharwal interjected.

"Well then . . . all right," he said.

"It will perform exactly as specified, I can guarantee that," she said. And then, feeling a little ashamed of her one small failure and her neurotic performance defending it, she attempted to recoup her cool by demonstrating that she was, after all, extremely intelligent, and she had deduced the purpose behind Hargrave's odd commission. "So, Mr. Hargrave—where exactly is this fresco located?"

If Hargrave's frown had caused her heart to hammer, the look he gave her now stopped it dead. "Who told you *fresco*?" he said, in a soft voice that was absolutely terrifying.

"It, it, I—nobody—I didn't," she stammered weakly.

He took a step toward her, and she wanted to run but she could not move. "I didn't say anything about a fresco, did I?"

"I just assumed—because everything about the, the—and lime plaster, you said that—no damage to the—I mean," she blathered.

Hargrave took another step toward her.

"It was a perfectly natural—I just figured that everything you said—and with climate change, perhaps an old church somewhere and it needed to be moved before perhaps flooding was—oh my God . . ." The words came sputtering out at a breakneck pace, but they did not slow Hargrave down, and suddenly he was right in front of her, so close she could feel his breath on her face.

"So, so, so, it is a fresco?" she said, nearly in a whimper. "Did I, did I—was I right?"

"Yes," Hargrave said. "You *were* right." He shook his head. "I'm very sorry."

Professor Sabharwal just barely had time to think, *Oh, good, I was right.* And then she felt his hands on her neck and the world went dark.

It was just luck that Special Agent Frank Delgado was on duty when it happened. Afterward, he was never sure if it was good luck or bad. But one way or the other, Delgado was there for the whole thing, start to finish.

They'd been watching Gentle Rest Extended Care for five weeks, around the clock. For once, Delgado was glad to be part of a large and well-funded task force. He never could have covered the place for five weeks, 24/7, by himself. Three teams of two agents took turns, with a mobile squad standing ready nearby. There were cameras covering all angles of the building, the room was bugged, and everything that happened, audio and video, was recorded. It was a huge expenditure, and it would never have been authorized for any target who wasn't a top priority like Bailey Stone.

And for five weeks, three teams of agents, a mobile squad, and a team of tech support agents had seen and heard nothing except nurses' gossip and routine medical chat.

And then.

There had been a bustle of staff in and out of the room, changing sheets on the bed, fluffing up pillows, bringing in fresh flowers—all kinds of signs that company was expected. And then, at long last, Delgado heard a new voice, one he had not heard before in the five weeks of waiting. And with a burst of adrenaline that was so intense it was close to nausea, Delgado realized whom he was hearing.

Riley Wolfe.

Delgado heard a nurse chatting, then her footsteps receding, and then the scrape of a chair moving across the floor. And then—

"Hello, Mom, it's me. How they treating you?" the voice said, and there was no longer any doubt. It was him.

Delgado clicked on his radio and spoke the prearranged signal to the rest of the team. "Alpha team, this is team leader. Red, Red, we have Red. He's here," he said. Then he put down the radio and leaned forward, listening intently.

"Well, I do hope you like it here," the voice went on.

"It seems like a good place—those flowers, they're fresh—are those gardenias? That's your favorite, isn't it? Well, that surely is nice."

Delgado was fascinated. This was Wolfe's voice, at last. He'd never heard it before, and although he was not surprised to hear the distinctly Southern lilt to the words, the tenderness in those words was unexpected.

"Well, so, I do hope you like it here, Mom," Riley went on. "You just may have to stay here a little while. I might be gone for a while, and, uh—I don't want you to worry or anything, it's just business. But . . ." He was quiet for a moment before he continued. "It's kinda funny, Mom. Remember you used to talk about 'the far side of the world' like it was, you know, all romantic and interesting? Well, that's just exactly where I'm going. The far side of the world. To the most isolated spot on earth. I got to do a favor for a man who lives there. And you should see this place, Mom! This man who lives there has tunneled out a big old solid rock island in the middle of absolutely nowhere! He's got all kinds of things to keep people away—exploding mines in the water, missiles on top, mercenary soldiers patrolling—But inside? Down in this great big cave he's made? He's got some of the most amazing art I ever saw! Great stuff, Mom, truly great! And I got to go through it, and, uh . . ." There was a rustling on the audio as Wolfe adjusted his position in the chair. "I won't lie to you 'bout this, Mom. This is a very dangerous man. Now, he likes me, so I should be okay, but . . ."

Another, smaller, rustling, and Wolfe lowered his

voice. "There's this other man, Mom. Just as dangerous. And he, uh—he got me in a kind of bind? And
he's using me to get at this other man, so . . . I think
there's gonna be a big fight. But I don't want you to
fret about that, because I'm not gonna get in on that,
Mom, don't you worry. I'll get out of there before the
shooting starts, I promise."

There was silence for a while, and Delgado was
afraid that somehow Riley Wolfe had slipped away. But
finally, the voice came back. "Anyway," he said at last,
"I guess you'll be okay here? And I'll come see you the
moment I get back, I promise." The sound of a light
kiss, then: "I got to go now, Mom, but like I said, I'll
come see you and tell you all about it just as soon as I
get back. Love you, Mom."

A final chair scrape. Delgado picked up the radio,
ready to order the team to move in and take Riley
Wolfe. This was it, the payoff to an obsession of many
years. And as his finger closed on the microphone, he
paused.

He thought over what he had heard Wolfe tell his
mother. He was not sure what all of it meant. But he
was certain it was important. He was also sure that, if
it was true, Wolfe would never give up Bailey Stone. It
would mean his certain death. That led to a conclusion
he couldn't refute.

If he took Riley Wolfe now, they would never get
Bailey Stone. The whole operation would be a huge
waste of time and resources.

Frank Delgado was willing to make that sacrifice.

But Special Agent Delgado could not. Stone was the whole focus of the task force, their number one target. Riley Wolfe was certainly a wanted man, but he was not in the same league. And taking him now meant losing Stone. It was one or the other. He was in position to make the call. The choice was all his. One or the other. Stone or Wolfe.

The decision was incredibly painful, but it was not difficult. Delgado was a good agent, and he knew his duty.

So when he spoke into the microphone, it was only to say, "This is team leader. Stand down. Let him go."

There was a pause, and then a disbelieving voice came back over the radio, "Say again, team leader?"

Delgado sighed. It was bad enough to have to say it once. Nonetheless, he repeated it. "Let him go, repeat, let. Him. Go."

Delgado put the microphone down. No one looking at his face would have guessed it, but he was churning inside with a maelstrom of bleak thoughts and emotions. The moment he'd waited so many years for had come and gone. As if to rub his nose in it, he had been the one forced to let it go.

He waited patiently for the tide of misery to ebb. He had some small hope that he might see Wolfe exit the building and get a glimpse—perhaps even a photograph. But although he watched for half an hour, the only people who came out—three old women, a young female nurse, and a white-haired couple—couldn't possibly have been Riley Wolfe.

Delgado just sat there for a while longer anyway; he told himself that Wolfe would be back, that he always came back to his mother. They would be waiting for him when he did. The thought did nothing to cheer him. It was driven out of his head by another thought repeating on an endless loop.

I had him and I let him go. I let Riley Wolfe go.

CHAPTER
30

I t was time.

All the prep work was done. Everything I could do to get my machine in gear and on the trail had been done. Now I had to put all the planning and worrying and setting up out of my head and just *do* it.

The first step for me is always the same. I turn myself into somebody else.

It starts like this: I sit in front of the full-length mirror and stare hard at *my* face for the last time. Pretty soon it wouldn't be my face. It would be somebody else's, somebody no one had ever seen before, including me. Because I was playing God and making a brand-new person, and that takes careful preparation.

For me, it takes a ritual, too. Not like prayers and incense and whining to some imaginary superbeing. This is a little more serious than that kind of oogabooga crap. This is the ritual that turns Riley into Not Riley. No chanting, no incense—it's only a ritual because I've repeated it so many times. At some point it turned into a list of things I had to do in exactly the same order every time. And the more I did it, the more mojo it gave me to do it exactly that way, the same every time. Sooner or later, you realize it's turned into a ritual.

But it started as just good practice. Just doing the stuff that was practical and effective to turn Me into Somebody Else. If it sounds a little freaky that it's always the same thing every time, like some kind of obsessive-compulsive fit—too bad. Maybe it is. But there's a really good reason for that. Why? Simple: It works. Every time I do it, the New Me I make is successful. And because it works every time I do it the same way, I do it the same way every time so it will work. Yeah, sure, circular logic. Stupid. Except for one thing.

Like I said. It works.

So I stare into the mirror. And then, as I start seeing the change, I put on my music. Same playlist every time. First, while I'm still staring at Old Me, it's Tupac—"All Eyez on Me." That was playing now, as I concentrated on the area around my eyes. I would add a couple of lines, and—

"Riley, are you sure about my hair like this? Because I never—Oh! That's Tupac, isn't it? I love this song!"

Monique. Tearing into the room, breaking my concentration. And for what? Because we had decided her hair should be cornrowed. I mean, it was different from her normal hair, it was different from the 'fro she wore when we were scouting the Museo—it gave her a whole new profile, which is important. And we'd given her a couple of big patches of vitiligo on her face, those patches some people have where the pigment disappears. She looked very different, not at all Moniquey, and that was a very good thing.

And it had been her idea to do cornrows. She said she hadn't done it since she was a kid, and oh what fun.

And now she wasn't sure?

I paused the music. "Monique, it's fine," I said. "It's even necessary."

"I don't know," she said, looking very dubious.

"Well, I know," I said. "Trust me here—you need a totally different look, and this is it. Unless you want to go with a shaved head?"

"Oh, Jesus, no, Riley, don't even," she said. "It's just I don't know," she said, putting a hand to her hair and then bending in to look in my mirror over my shoulder. "It doesn't feel like—you know. It doesn't feel like *me.*"

I mean, really. Didn't feel like *her?* I know Monique is way smarter than anybody else I know and probably smarter even than me—but come on. "Monique," I said, with a really powerful grip on my temper, "it *isn't* you! That's the whole fucking idea!"

"Don't get snappish, Riley," she said, with a kind of scolding tone of voice. "I'm just saying it doesn't feel right. I'm not comfortable being this person."

"Well, relax," I said. "You've got plenty of time getting comfortable. Our flight doesn't leave for six hours."

"Oh, God," she moaned. "Oh, my fucking God, when you say that it just—it's terrifying, Riley, just to think of what we're doing—and one small mistake and Jesus Christ . . ."

"Monique," I said. "Would you get a grip? We've been over this a hundred times."

"But all of a sudden it's so fucking *real*," she moaned.

"Yes, it is real," I said. I heard a snarly tone in my voice and took a deep breath. "It's very, very real, Monique. With even realer consequences. But here's the thing—so are we." She looked at me with a what-the-fuck expression. "We are just as real as you can get, Monique. What we do, how good we are at doing it— that is just about the most real thing in the whole fucking world. This is all part of that," I said, waving a hand at all the stuff lying around to change us, "and we are going to be amazingly good at it."

"But, Riley," she said, getting kind of whiny.

"*And*, Monique," I said, riding over the top of her voice, "and if we don't totally fuck up, everybody will take our new real for the *real* real—because people see what you want them to see."

"But what if I do fuck up?" she said.

"You probably will," I said, and she looked like I'd slapped her. "But it doesn't matter. You can fuck up once or twice, and nobody notices. Because they don't know you. A fuckup is just a glitch. And like I said, they see what you tell them to see. All you have to do is pretend you didn't fuck up and go back to being yourself. Your *new* self," I said.

"I just don't know," she said.

"You don't have to," I said. "I know. And what I know is you'll be fine."

"But that's—you can't just—"

"Yes, I can," I said. "All you have to do is that art part. Leave the talking and all the other shit to me. Anybody says something to you, use your German on them." She spoke nearly perfect German, with a Bavarian accent. I never got that, but she said German went with doing art history, which is what she did back when she was legit, so okay.

"Yeah, I know, but still," she said.

I sighed. "What do you want, a hug? Want me to hold your hand and say 'there, there'?"

"Hell, no," she said.

"It is dangerous. We know that. But I've done shit that was twice as dangerous a hundred times." Kind of a lie; it had never been this dangerous before. But she needed to hear a pep talk. "We got a plan, Monique. We know who we are and what we're doing and all we got to do is *do* it."

She sighed. "Yeah, I guess. Okay," she said. She took a last look in the mirror, straightened up, and said, "I better finish packing."

She went out of the room a little happier, and I turned back to the mirror and tried to get my concentration back. I put the music back on, starting Tupac from the beginning.

Five minutes later it was Iron Maiden, "Hallowed Be Thy Name," and I was working on my hair. I'd grown it out, dyed it, and I was going for that carefully styled shaggy look. Just exactly the way New Me would want his hair—*my* hair. First, get the bangs carefully but casually off to the side, and then—

"Riley, do you like this top? I mean, with this jacket? I'm not sure it says *Me*. Yes, I know, I mean *New* Me— but just the same, I don't know—the colors? Or maybe the cut?"

Monique again, of course. Costume question this time—and that was something *she* was always in charge of, even when I went solo, so why ask me? I know she was nervous—shit, I was nervous, too, and this was what I did. But I'd thought it was all settled. And I needed to do Me, without interruptions, without ruining the ritual. Maybe it sounds goofy, but that's how it is. I have to have the ritual, because I've always done it, and I've always won.

And this time, when it mattered more than ever, Monique was breaking the magic.

We settled the shirt thing. A few minutes later it was the shoes. And then should she bring something super dressy, in case we went back to that fancy restaurant. It went like that until it was time to go to the airport, and I never did get to finish up the Ritual. I had to hurry through the change like I'd never done before, not sure if it was going to work. I mean, I got all the pieces on,

I looked different, I knew I could talk different, but it all felt phony, unnatural, because I hadn't done the Ritual.

And as we hustled into a cab and headed for the airport, I couldn't shake a really horrible feeling that because I hadn't done it, the whole thing was going to turn to shit.

CHAPTER
31

Father Matteo loved his job. It is true that it was not, strictly speaking, an exalted position, especially for someone with his background and education. Like many Jesuits, he was highly educated and accomplished in his field. But unlike some in his order, and many more in the secular population, he had never really cared about the measuring sticks that others might apply to life. He had his own priorities, and they were God, art, and humanity, in that order. And so he was very happy to be here, in the Vatican, in his current position. As assistant curator in charge of murals and frescoes, he could serve all three concerns simultaneously.

He was happy enough, in fact, that he often found himself humming quietly as he went on his daily rounds. He was humming now; not an "Agnus Dei" or any other religious tune. He was humming Ed Sheeran's "Thinking Out Loud," a song he'd heard his niece singing. He had thought it was a nice song, the lyrics showed a laudable sentiment, and in any case the melody had become permanently lodged in his head—what he'd heard his niece call an earworm.

So he was quite happy as he strolled through the Stanze di Raffaello, and if anyone thought it was unusual to see a priest humming Ed Sheeran, they didn't say so

His contentment continued as he walked through the first and second of the Raphael rooms, pausing now and then to gaze in awe at the magnificent frescoes, as he always did, or to answer some tourist's questions in one of the five languages he spoke. He loved the Raphael rooms; they were really quite overwhelmingly beautiful. Even now, even to Father Matteo, who saw them every day. The astonishing, glorious images on all the walls, the ceiling, virtually everywhere, the superb work of a great artist in his prime, covering every surface in an unbelievable blaze of splendor. And still, after five years in this job, Father Matteo marveled at the beauty of Raphael's work.

And so he was, perhaps, a little light-headed when he crossed the black-and-white marble floor toward the Stanza di Eliodoro and saw the usually animated flock of gawkers flooding back toward him—all of them.

In a very great hurry.

For only a moment, Father Matteo gaped, wondering why anyone would flee from Raphael—and then he smelled smoke.

Smoke—from the very next one of the Raphael rooms. And smoke meant fire. Unthinkable—not here, in the heart of the great *museo*—and only one floor below the Pope's apartments! With a crowd of people in the room!

All three of Father Matteo's loves were threatened at the same time, and he was galvanized into immediate action. Instantly, a meek, middle-aged priest was transformed into a superhero, and Father Matteo charged into the Room of Heliodorus.

And skidded to a stop just as quickly.

Two men stood on the white marble bench that framed one of the room's two windows. At their feet squatted some kind of dark metal pot. From the pot, a thick and greasy plume of black smoke was pouring upward, coiling toward the ceiling—and toward the wonderful fresco above the window, as well. Already Father Matteo could see dark smudges forming on that fresco.

"No," the priest moaned.

The two men snapped their heads around and glared at him. "Yes, Father!" one of them snarled in Spanish. He was a swarthy, heavyset man with an intimidating scowl. His partner was thin, smaller, but just as ferocious-looking. "And unless we get an immediate audience with the Holy Father—we will destroy all the paintings in this room!"

"I beg you to do no such thing!" Father Matteo said. "In the name of God, gentlemen—"

"Yes, the name of God!" the second man cried. "And for the liberation of Catalonia!"

"Viva Catalonia!" the first man echoed.

"Please, the Holy Father is in South America," Father Matteo pleaded. "I beg you, do not desecrate this room—"

"South America?!" the smaller man said, looking confused.

"Idiot!" the heavyset man said. He slapped his partner. "You said you had checked the schedule!"

"I—I must have looked at the wrong page," the other man said woefully.

"Idiot!" the larger man repeated. "Now we will have to—" He paused and cocked his head—and Father Matteo heard it, too.

Rapid footsteps—coming *toward* them.

A flicker of hope came to life in Father Matteo's breast. It had to be the gendarmes—perhaps even the Swiss Guard! There was still a hope to save the frescoes! "They are coming for you now," he called to the two men. They looked at him. "Please, let us have peace in this holy place. Do not resist with violence."

The two looked at each other. The larger man said something urgent and rapid in a language Matteo did not understand—Catalan? The other man nodded agreement, and the first man glared at Matteo. "Tell the Holy Father that unless he gives his blessing to the independence of Catalonia, we will return!" and he turned to the window, kicked it open—and the two men disappeared outside.

Father Matteo lunged to the window and grabbed the smoking black pot. It was hot, and it burned his hands. But he carried it to the center of the room anyway, placed it down on the floor, and immediately undid the cincture around his waist and whipped off his cassock, flinging it on top to extinguish the fire.

He was standing there in his underwear a moment later when the gendarmes pounded into the room. "Hands up!" the young man in the lead called, aiming a pistol at Father Matteo.

The second gendarme was older and recognized the father. He pushed his companion's weapon down and said, "No, Fredo." He looked at Father Matteo. "What happened, Father?"

"Two men," Matteo said. "They demanded an audience with the Holy Father. They had this, this thing—" He kicked at the black pot, now hidden by his cassock. "And the smoke—a great stream of oily smoke—as you see, it has damaged the fresco!"

"The two men, Father," the older gendarme said. "Where did they go?"

Father Matteo hadn't even considered the two men—not when the frescoes were threatened. "They went out the window," he said dismissively. And staring upward, he tried to assess the damage they had done. He followed his gaze and walked toward the window, barely aware that the gendarmes were speaking to him.

"Out the window, Father? Are you sure? We are on the third floor, you know—Father?"

"Oh, dear—oh, no, look at that," Father Matteo said as he saw that a black smudge was indeed spread across the front of the fresco. "And that smoke—so *oily*—it will soak into the paint and—no, no. No, we cannot allow it!"

The two gendarmes watched the priest as he stood there in his underwear, gaping upward at the smudged painting. They exchanged a significant look.

"Father?" the older gendarme called. "Did you mean these men went out *this* window?"

"This *third-floor* window?" the younger man added.

"Yes, of course. Right out the window," Father Matteo said. "I can only hope that—I must call Berzetti immediately. If we hurry, perhaps it can be saved—Berzetti can save it!" And he strode rapidly toward the door.

"Father!" the older gendarme called urgently. Happily, his tone was compelling enough to cause Father Matteo to pause and look back.

"What is it? Really, if Berzetti is to save the fresco, I must hurry—"

The gendarme nodded understandingly. "Of course, Father—but perhaps you should put on your clothes first . . . ?"

Father Matteo moved his mouth like a fish out of water and then, with a start, glanced down at himself, clad only in his underwear. "Oh!" he exclaimed. "Oh, my . . ."

He rushed back and recovered his cassock. The fire in the black pot was out now, but the cassock had several large holes burned into it, and it stank. Still, it was better than nothing—much better. As he struggled into the reeking, still-smoldering garment, the gendarmes looked out the window for any sign of the two men. There was nothing to see, of course. But had they been able to look up on the roof, they would have seen both of the "Catalans" doubled over with laughter and clutching their sides as they hurried away.

In the meantime, Father Matteo finished tying his cincture. "Now then!" he said. He nodded at the gendarmes and hurried from the room. If he and Berzetti were quick enough, perhaps they could save the fresco.

Father Matteo devoutly hoped so. *The Liberation of St. Peter* was one of his favorites.

I do my homework. It's important. You miss some small nothing of a factoid and it turns out to be the crucial piece, and your whole brilliant scheme turns into a flaming shit heap, with you smoldering underneath it. So I do research. I poke around, I find out how things work—and I find out who pulls which strings and why.

I had four good candidates when I went back to Rome. I checked them all out completely, down to knowing their shoe size. And I found one who ticked off every single item on my list. He was absolutely perfect. His name was Rodolfo Berzetti.

By the time I was done looking him over, I knew

everything about Rodolfo Berzetti. I probably knew more about him than his mother knew. I knew why he wasn't married yet at the age of forty-three. I knew what he did on his long vacations to Thailand. And I knew why he was my perfect candidate.

For starters, his job; Rodolfo was an expert at restoring damaged artwork. And he was a full-time employee of the Vatican.

It's not a job that you would think of all by yourself, not right away. I mean, full-time work in art restoration? Isn't the Vatican supposed to be all praying and priests and that kind of thing? And it is—but like I said, the Vatican also has a huge collection of some of the greatest artwork in the world. And you can sure as shit argue with how they got some of it—"confiscating," which means stealing, and blackmailing people with threats of Hell, and terrifying people into "donating" when they die—but you cannot argue with the fact that they take care of it.

Caring for great art is a whole lot more complicated than dusting the frames once a week. So the Vatican has a big staff of very expert people to take care of this collection. Rodolfo Berzetti was one of them. If a painting or a mural—or a fresco—suffers damage from aging, or if it takes a hit of some kind, or if it was in storage so long the paint began to crack, Rodolfo was the guy on staff to fix it. Pretty it up so it was good as new. He was good at what he did, too—not the best in the world, not by a long shot, but he was good.

And why didn't the Vatican, with its tons of money

and incredible collection, have the guy who *was* the best? Why did they have Rodolfo Berzetti the just okay?

Come on, take a guess. I'll give you a hint: It rhymes with "honey." Except it starts with an *m*.

Rodolfo Berzetti had honey with an *m*. Lots of it. He came from a family of old money, and in Italy that means *really* old. His ancestors in the fifteenth century ran a successful bank in Venice, in the days when Venetian banks were the best. Usually the *only*, and naturally that means bigger profits. The family's fortune had grown through the years, jumping up into the stratosphere during World War II. They had a patent on a key piece of tech that had to go into every single round of ammunition any Italian artillery fired during the war. That's a lot of artillery. That translates to a lot of money, even if it's only a penny or two per round. And the really funny thing? The government *paid* them! Can you believe it? They paid! Even toward the end of the war, when people were starving and the soldiers had no food, no shoes, the Berzettis collected their royalty for that little piece of tech.

They got paid. And their really rich turned into *stupid* rich.

Rodolfo was the only son in the current generation. That meant whatever he wanted, he got. When he wanted this job at the Vatican, discreet inquiries were made, a cardinal got a new and glorious altarpiece for his home cathedral—and Rodolfo got a job.

So Rodolfo Berzetti didn't *need* a job. And he didn't

do jack shit to earn it. Unless you think buying gold altarpieces is a legit tough job. He just wanted the job, like it was a shiny new toy. And like every rich kid, he got it. Because Rodolfo was *stupid* rich. Rich enough to fly in sushi from Edo twice a week on a special chartered flight. So rich he could actually afford to own a bunch of art that should have been in the Louvre—or in the Vatican. Plenty rich enough for those long vacations in Thailand, where he was not, strictly speaking, getting a tan at a beach resort.

And all this stupid rich just fell into his fat lap because it was inherited money. The only thing he did to earn it was get born. That meant he spent his whole life getting everything he ever wanted with no real effort. It meant that whenever he wanted anything—*anything*— he just naturally assumed he had the right to take it. It meant one thing more, too. Something that was a little more important.

It meant I didn't like him. And that meant he was just what I was looking for.

That turned out to be a fatal flaw.

I found him in the basement of the *museo,* in his workshop. He had a large canvas stretched onto an easel and he was bent over it, frowning at something in the lower-right-hand corner. His great big ass stuck out into the room, butt crack showing, and the fat that hung over the collar of his shirt jiggled slightly as he moved a small paintbrush.

He had earbuds in, and he was humming tunelessly

along to something, so when I slipped through the door and into a pool of shadow beside the door, he didn't hear me.

Good for me. Not so good for him.

I watched him for a minute from the shadows by the door. And then I stepped into the room and the shadow came with me.

I was in the Darkness.

It comes over me at these times for most of my life, since that bad day at the old quarry when I turned into Me. It's like everything gets dark around me until I'm not really driving anymore, just watching, like I'm sitting in a theater with the lights out watching an old movie.

The Darkness came over me now, and it kept me quiet and hidden as I came up behind Berzetti. I reached into my pocket and took out a small syringe. I took the safety guard off the needle and held it up, and—

He must have sensed something at the very last second. He turned his head to one side, saw me, and—

Too late.

I jammed the needle into his fat, stuck-out ass and squeezed the plunger down. Berzetti jerked upright and turned, flailing his arms so wildly that his hand hit his glasses so they flew off his face and went up in the air. As the glasses hit the floor he turned all the way around until he was gaping at me with a look of horror on his fat face.

That's the expression he died with.

It would take a microscopic autopsy to make anybody guess he died of anything but a natural heart attack. Nobody was going to do that. There was no reason, and there would be no sign of foul play. And an autopsy desecrates the body. Anyway, fat people have heart attacks all the time.

Rodolfo Berzetti was having one now—just not a natural one. He had a good two seconds to gape at me and wonder what was happening. And then it had already happened. And then he slumped to the floor. And then it was over.

I watched as everything that was Rodolfo Berzetti trickled away back to the recycle bin. Then he was gone. His eyes glazed over, and his bowels emptied, and I decided that was my cue to leave.

I did.

Y our credentials are impeccable," Enzo Minutti said. He raised his eyes from the beautifully printed CV and put them on the man to whom the pages belonged. As a senior member of the Vatican Personnel Office, Minutti interviewed many people seeking employment, and even so, this man impressed. He was pleasant, carried himself well, and seemed very well qualified. "The testimonials and the photographs of your work are quite compelling, Signor Campinelli."

"Grazie," Campinelli said. "Mille grazie, Signor Minutti." Beautifully dressed, average height, shaggy brown hair, Campinelli was a man in his thirties, a little young to be applying for such a prestigious position but clearly quite gifted.

Minutti shrugged. His qualifications would do him no good this time. "Unfortunately, we already have on staff a very good restorer. I cannot offer you employment at this time. Very sorry, Signor Campinelli."

"Oh," said Campinelli, quite clearly crestfallen. "That's—I had so hoped. It was, if I may say, the dream of a lifetime—to be here, at the center of God's Holy City—and with one of the greatest collections in the world!"

"Yes, I'm sure, I completely understand," Minutti said. "But unfortunately—" He lifted a hand to indicate that he was helpless in this matter. "I will certainly keep your résumé on file, Signor Campinelli. And if anything should ever—"

He was interrupted by the harsh braying of the telephone on his desk. Somewhat annoyed to be interrupted, he frowned and picked up the receiver. "Pronto, Minutti," he said.

What he heard must have surprised him, for he blinked rapidly several times. "What? . . . But that is terrible! When did that happen? . . . I see . . . Yes, I see . . . What's that? . . . Yes, I understand, but—Well, of course, but these skills are not found at the market—No, I don't see—Well, normally it can take several weeks—"

Minutti lifted his eyes to Campinelli, still sitting across from him in a dejected slump. "But actually, as it happens, I believe I can promise an immediate solution. Yes, immediate. Ciao, Father."

He hung up the phone and looked at Campinelli, who was still looking like a boy whose puppy had died. "Signor Campinelli?" he said.

Campinelli lifted his eyes to see Minutti regarding him with a broad smile. "Yes, Signor Minutti?"

Minutti's smile got wider. "Buona fortuna," he said.

Captain Christian Koelliker was unhappy. Not merely because he had a dead body to deal with—that had happened before, and, the captain assumed, it would probably happen again. At least this body was neat, except for the *Scheisse,* the result of the customary loosened bowels. And it was quite apparent what had caused the death. A simple heart attack, no reason to suspect foul play, no art treasures missing—nothing at all out of the ordinary.

And yet . . .

Captain Koelliker was an officer of the Pontifical Swiss Guard, and like all police officers he was always suspicious. Also like most police officers, he trusted his instincts. Right now, his instincts were telling him that all was not as it seemed. If this was true—if this apparently accidental death was not accidental—it could mean a threat to the Pope, however peripheral, and this he would never permit.

And so even though there was no factual reason to do so, he bent over to examine the body again. It lay where it had fallen, on its side. The man's glasses lay a few feet away, one lens shattered. The corpse had that unsettling expression of surprise and horror on the face. That didn't affect Captain Koelliker. He'd seen it before. Most people were surprised, and horrified, when death came for them.

Koelliker squatted by the body. A tiny paintbrush was on the floor three inches from the outstretched hand. He touched the bristles; still wet. Glancing up at the painting, the captain could see the spot where the brush had been plied—there, at the bottom of the canvas.

So Berzetti had been working on that small spot at the bottom of the painting. A heart attack hit, and he fell, dead nearly instantly. All very logical; Berzetti had been bent nearly double to get at that particular spot on the canvas. He was a fat man. The extra strain from the pressure of bending over could easily trigger a heart attack. It all made perfect sense.

Except . . .

Koelliker frowned. Something tugged at his subconscious, a nagging little thing he couldn't quite grasp. He stood again and took a step back, looking over the scene. Bent over, heart attack, boom—Berzetti falls and dies. Perfectly natural and sensible.

But then why hadn't he fallen face forward? Perhaps even into the canvas he was working on? Why had he instead fallen almost *backward*, away from the canvas? And the glasses—the frames said they were quite expensive. Would a high-quality lens shatter if dropped from only a couple of feet up?

There was almost certainly an explanation. Perhaps

a number of them. And nothing about it truly screamed "foul." But it bothered Captain Koelliker nonetheless.

"Has the family been notified?" he said over his shoulder.

"No, Captain," Corporal Schmidt said. "Not without your order."

Koelliker made up his mind. "Good. You may notify them now. But tell them we must hold the body for a few days."

"Hold the body, Captain?" Schmidt said, clearly puzzled.

"Yes, of course," Koelliker replied. "For the autopsy."

He took one last look, then turned and strode out of the basement.

CHAPTER

32

That's about all we know for sure," Special Agent Rosemond said. She nodded once at the display at the far end of the conference table, where a full-screen picture leered down at the assembled agents of the task force. In large block letters, it was labeled, "BAILEY STONE." "Now here's the guesswork." She tapped her computer, and the next PowerPoint slide came up on the screen. A map of the Indian Ocean filled the display. Even accounting for scale, it was huge, and mostly empty, except for the edges of three landmasses.

"That's South Africa on the left, Australia on the right, and Antarctica below. In the middle, that tiny little dot right there—"

She clicked the next slide; same picture but with a small dot in the center of the screen circled in red.

"The Kerguelen Islands. If it looks like they're sort

of isolated, out in the middle of nowhere—that is not an optical illusion. The Kerguelen Islands are the ass-end of nowhere.

"You say to yourself, 'Gosh, Helen, I love geography and that's really interesting—but why do we give a shit?'" There were a couple of amused snorts from the assembled agents—not from Frank Delgado, and not from Special Agent in Charge Dellmore Finn.

Rosemond didn't seem to notice. She smirked and said, "We care an entire fucking shitload. Want to guess why?"

She looked around the room, holding her smirk. There were no takers. Special Agent in Charge Finn rotated his hand in a get-on-with-it gesture. Rosemond nodded. "Because," she said, "the Kerguelen Islands are, by pure scientific measurement, *the* most isolated spot on planet Earth."

There was a low mutter of surprise around the table. Rosemond nodded and said, "The nickel drops, right? That's where Riley Wolfe said he was going—the most isolated spot on earth. On the far side of the world. And that's right here." She pointed at the image on the screen. "Kerguelen Islands."

Special Agent Hillman, the IT specialist, raised a hand. "Bailey Stone is in Australia," he said. "I mean, we're still targeting him, right?"

"Bailey Stone is still our primary target," Finn said firmly.

"Right, okay, so," Hillman said, "couldn't Wolfe have been saying that, you know, like, metaphorically?

The far-side-of-the-earth thing? I mean, Australia is on the far side, too, so—why do you think it's this Kergle-whatever Islands?"

Rosemond's smirk grew into a broad smile, the kind generally referred to as a cat-that-ate-the-canary smile. "Because," she said, "according to our best information, the Kerguelen Islands is where this guy lives." She hit a key and a new picture came up on-screen, a mug shot of a man. "Anybody recognize that beautiful, suave face?" Rosemond asked mockingly.

"Jesus fuck," Special Agent Berkowitz said. "Patrick Boniface?!"

"Got it in one," Rosemond said happily. "Patrick Boniface. King of arms dealers, and not coincidentally the most ruthless sonofabitch on the planet."

The room buzzed with talk for a few seconds before SAC Finn raised his hand for quiet. "Why do we think Wolfe is going to see Boniface?" he asked.

Rosemond shrugged. "It's guesswork," she said. "But I think it's right. Wolfe said another dangerous man, somebody that Bailey Stone was trying to kill, right?" She paused and looked around the table. "Bailey Stone has had a hard-on for Boniface for like ten years now. He's made several attempts, and they've all blown up in his face. Disastrously." Rosemond looked serious. "The profilers say that Bailey Stone wants to be number one—*needs* to be. And they also say that his personality would react to being beat down by trying even harder, again and again, until he succeeds. And on top of that—Wolfe mentioned great art. We know Boniface collects art. A lot of works that have gone missing are supposed to be in his collection now."

She glanced at Delgado, raising an eyebrow. Delgado nodded once.

"So, do the math, guys. We did—and it adds up to this."

Rosemond put up her last slide. It showed three frames next to each other, two photographs and one blank square with a question mark in the center. The two pictures were again labeled, "BONIFACE" and "STONE." The question mark read "WOLFE" underneath. "We still don't know what Riley Wolfe looks like," she said. "But we know this: Bailey Stone is using Riley Wolfe to get at Patrick Boniface," she said.

Agent Berkowitz raised her hand. "Hold on," she said. "*If* Riley Wolfe is getting in between Boniface and Stone—doesn't that drop him in a world of trouble?"

"Two worlds," Rosemond said. "More and deeper shit than you can imagine."

"So why would he do that?" Berkowitz said.

Rosemond shrugged. "Pure guesswork? But I think one of them—probably Boniface?—grabbed him by the balls, and the other one, Stone, found out and decided to take advantage."

"And if Boniface finds out?" Agent Hillman asked.

Rosemond shook her head. "If that happens, you can bury what's left of Riley Wolfe in a Band-Aid box," she said. "Which would break your heart, right, Frank?"

They all turned to look at Delgado. He didn't appear to have heard. He was looking at the table in front of him, frowning, deep in thought. Because what the two other agents had just said had jolted a new thought into his head. If Riley was truly caught between the two arms dealers, he would know the situation was untenable. He would absolutely *hate* being forced to do anything for anybody else. The threat of death would be minor compared to his resentment at being *used*. And being Riley Wolfe, he would find a way out of it. Which meant—

"Okay, Frank, never mind, go back to sleep," Rosemond said. Delgado didn't look up, and she shrugged and went on.

"Anyway," Rosemond said. "That's the situation, as far as our intel can take us." She looked around the table again. For a long moment, no one said a thing. Then SAC Finn stood up. "It's my opinion that this assessment is spot on. The AD agrees, and she gave us the green light to act on it." He took a moment to look at each agent individually. "If we could take even one of these guys into custody, it would justify this task force's budget for ten years. If there's a chance to get *both* of them—people, that is nothing short of historic. And if we scoop up Riley Wolfe in the bargain—that would mean that Special Agent Delgado could retire happy."

Everyone chuckled—except Delgado. He was still frowning at the tabletop.

"All right, team. I want this planned, prepped, and ready to go ASAP. Let's make history!"

Finn nodded once and then strode out of the room.

The rest of the agents stood up, stretched, and began to leave in twos and threes.

All but Delgado. He kept sitting there, thinking. And he didn't like where his thoughts were leading him.

Ten minutes later he was still sitting at the table when SAC Finn went by the room to get a cup of coffee. Finn paused in the doorway and looked in. Delgado didn't look up. His eyes were fixed on the table in front of him and it was clear his mind was far away. Finn watched for a moment and then moved on.

A few minutes later Finn came back—with two cups of coffee. He entered the conference room and sat beside Delgado. Delgado didn't look up. Finn pushed a cup of coffee onto the table in front of him.

Delgado looked up. His eyeballs clicked into focus on Finn, then on the coffee. He picked up the cup and took a sip.

"Something bothering you, Frank?" Finn said.

Delgado nodded, took another sip.

"Like to share it?"

Delgado said nothing. Finn let the silence grow, sipping his own coffee. Finally, Delgado looked at the SAC. "I think we're being played," he said.

Finn blinked. "Played. By whom?"

Delgado gave Finn a small, strange smile. "Riley Wolfe," he said, as if it was painful but obvious.

Finn nodded, sipped. "Okay. How?"

"I don't know," Delgado said.

Finn sipped again, remembering what his grand-mother had said about patience being a virtue. "Then why do you think we're being played, Frank?"

Delgado frowned. "Something Rosemond said," he said. "He knows he's in a world of trouble. Two worlds."

Finn was clear that Delgado had not suffered from gender confusion and that "he" meant Riley Wolfe, not Rosemond. "Okay," he said. "He's not an idiot; he'd know that. These are two very bad dudes. So?"

Delgado put down his coffee cup, a little too hard. A small splash flowed over the rim and onto the table. "He would *do* something about it," he said.

"That's crazy," Finn said.

"Maybe."

"These are two of the most dangerous men in the world—what could he even *think* he could do?"

Delgado shrugged.

That wasn't good enough for Finn. He pushed a little. "Wouldn't it be a hell of a lot easier to do what they want him to do? And then be done with it?"

Delgado gave Finn a skeptical look. "If it was you," he said, "would you trust either Boniface or Stone to let you go? Once you'd been inside their heads?"

Finn smiled. "No. I would not. I would be very damn certain that they would either kill me or keep me on a string forever."

Delgado nodded and picked up his coffee again.

"So you think Riley Wolfe will . . . do something?" Finn said.

"He has to," Delgado said.

"*Has* to, Frank? Why?"

Delgado shrugged. "Because he's Riley Wolfe."

Finn looked at Delgado. When Delgado stayed silent, Finn looked into his own coffee cup. There was no secret message in the Styrofoam cup. He thought about what Delgado had said. On the surface, it was absurd to think of one man taking on either Boniface or Stone. Even if that one man was Riley Wolfe. But Finn knew that Frank Delgado knew Riley Wolfe better than anyone else in the world. And he trusted that a good agent has good instincts. Delgado, for all his tendencies to chase Riley, was a very damn good agent. "All right," he said at last. "What will he do, Frank?"

Delgado shook his head, a single slow shake. "I don't know," he said.

"Will it be something that keeps us from taking down Stone and Boniface?"

"No," Delgado said without hesitation.

"You're sure?"

Delgado nodded. "I think—I think that's what he wants," Delgado said.

Finn shook his head, somewhat puzzled. "He *wants* us to take down Boniface and Stone."

"Of course," Delgado said. It was obvious to him. "He gets us to do the heavy lifting—take out one, or both, of his big problems."

"And that bothers you?"

"No," Delgado said firmly. "It's what he does after that—that's what bothers me."

Finn sipped his coffee. He wasn't quite sure where Delgado was going with this. He was willing to follow along, but he needed an answer to one supremely important question. "Just because Riley Wolfe wants us to do it," he said, "is there a reason why that should stop us from doing it anyway?" Finn said.

Delgado frowned, then slowly shook his head. "I don't know," he said. "I don't think so, but . . ."

"You don't think so?"

Delgado hesitated, then said, "No. No reason."

Finn waited. Delgado stayed silent. After two minutes, Finn finished the last sip of his coffee and stood up. "Well then," he said. "Let's do it." He turned to go.

"Dellmore?" Delgado said.

Finn turned.

"I'd like to keep the surveillance on Wolfe's mother," he said. "Just in case."

Finn thought about it. It was a hassle, but it made sense. There had been absolutely no way to tail or track Wolfe. But he would definitely be back for his mother. Finn nodded. "I'll start the paperwork," he said. He pointed at Delgado. "But *you* gotta finish it."

Delgado nodded. And he almost smiled.

CHAPTER
33

"Buongiorno!" Father Matteo said, a bright and cheerful greeting based partly on his basic kindness—but mostly on his hope that this new man truly could restore *The Liberation of St. Peter* to its pristine glory.

The new man looked up. He stood amid a pile of boxes, several large buckets, and a stack of metal pipes clearly intended to be the scaffolding needed to reach the tainted fresco. He was dressed in paint-stained working clothes, but somehow he made them look stylish. He had round, gold-framed spectacles, and he brushed a shaggy lock of brown hair from his forehead. He smiled. "Buongiorno, Father," he said.

The priest held out a hand. "I am Father Matteo, assistant curator," he said.

"Ah!" the new man said. He took Father Matteo's hand in a firm grip and shook it. "Carlo Campinelli! A pleasure to meet you, Father!" He beamed and waved a hand around the Stanza di Eliodoro. "And what an amazing, truly gratifying pleasure to be here—a thrill! To work amid such glory! Raphael is absolutely one of the greatest geniuses—his composition, his use of color—the way he commands this entire space! It's just . . . ahhh." He turned shining eyes back to Father Matteo. "All my life I've dreamed of something like this. And to be here at last, using the gifts God gave me, to make some small contribution to His glory—I am a happy man, Father."

"I am very pleased to hear it, Signor Campinelli," Father Matteo said. He hesitated to ask, but he was just slightly concerned. Not actually worried, but aside from the scaffolding, he did not recognize some of the equipment—much of it!—that Campinelli was deploying. And as a curator, a man well versed in the fundamentals of restoration, he felt he should know what all these odd things were intended to do. "But tell me— what are all these boxes, the buckets and the machines? I am not familiar with any technique that, that—I can't imagine what all this is for!"

"Ah, Father, you will *love* this!" Campinelli said. He dove into one of the boxes with the eagerness of a true enthusiast. "See here—this is the latest—from Germany! A brand-new technique! You see, this special fluid is used to carefully steam the surface—*But!*" he said, raising a hand to forestall an objection that had, indeed, been on the tip of Father Matteo's tongue. "Here is the beautiful thing, Father—this special liquid turns to steam at a much lower temperature, so there is no damage from the heat—and at the same time, the condensed fluid actually protects the fresco while we work!"

"I have never heard of such a thing!" Father Matteo said, bewildered.

"You would not have," Campinelli said. "The factory has been keeping it completely secret—I don't know why. Perhaps only because Germans love secrets, eh? But as an Italian—I love *finding* secrets. I heard of this, tracked it down, and here we are!"

He beamed like a proud parent, and Father Matteo felt compelled to say, "Wonderful."

"It is! It is indeed wonderful, Father, and because it is a German invention—well, you know what they're like, eh? I had to sign papers, pull strings, and make promises to get it, Father, believe me—practically had to give them my firstborn child! This is the first time they've permitted its use outside Germany!"

"What kind of promises did you make?" Father Matteo asked. And to show he, too, was human, and appreciated a joke, he added, "Aside from the firstborn child, of course."

Campinelli smiled. "I will only say that, first, if I allow anyone else to get near this, I am quite certain I will disappear and my body will never be found. Aside from that, Father—" Campinelli bent and pulled a thick pile of paper from the box and waved it at Father Matteo. "Instructions!" he said. "And all in German! I must follow them to the letter, and I do not speak German, more than a few words. And so—I had to promise to let their expert come along and supervise, so that—Aha! Here she is now! Direct from the factory in Frankfurt!" He nodded at the doorway. A young black woman was just entering the room, carrying a large wooden artist's case, the kind that held dozens of tubes of paint, a number of brushes, and so on. She had large lavender-framed glasses and wore coveralls and a scarf over her carefully plaited hair.

"Katrina!" Campinelli called. The woman looked up, startled. She had a very pretty face—except that it was marked with several pale patches where the natural pigment had vanished. Father Matteo was not terribly familiar with people of African ancestry, but he had seen the condition before.

The woman hesitated in the doorway, then took a deep breath and came forward. "Herr Campinelli?" she said uncertainly.

Campinelli waved at Matteo. "Das ist Pfarrer Matteo," he said in bad, heavily accented German. "Verstehen?" He turned to Father Matteo. "She speaks no Italian," he said with a shrug. Then, to Katrina, he repeated, "Matteo—*curator*. Verstehen, Katrina?"

Katrina shifted her weight uncomfortably. "Ja, ich verstehe," she said. She nodded at Father Matteo. "Freut mich, Sie kennenzulernen," she said. She hesitated again, then nodded and stepped past them and began to set up her materials.

Campinelli winked at Father Matteo. "All work and no play, these Germans," he said. "Still, at a time like this—it doesn't hurt, eh, Father?"

"No, certainly not," Father Matteo said. Raising his voice slightly, he called, "Wilkommen, Fräulein." He did not really speak German, but he knew a few basic words, and these seemed appropriate.

Without looking up, Katrina muttered, "Danke," and continued her work.

"Well, Father," Campinelli said, "perhaps Katrina has the right of it. I should get right to work."

"Then you are optimistic?" Father Matteo asked eagerly. "You can save the fresco?"

"I think so, Father—especially with this new technique," Campinelli said. Once more he pushed the hair away from his forehead. "It is a complicated process, and as I said, a new one. But with the help of God—and Katrina—I think we can perform a small miracle. A secular miracle, Father," he said, smiling.

"I will settle for any kind of miracle," Father Matteo said. "As long as the fresco can be saved."

They spoke a few more words, but Campinelli was clearly anxious to get to his work, and so Father Matteo left shortly. And as he walked away, he allowed himself to feel a little bit of hope. Campinelli seemed quite confident, and his optimism was contagious.

Good, Father Matteo thought, *Very, very good.*

Jesus *fuck,* that was terrifying!" Monique said. "No fucking way I can keep this up!"

"For shame, Katrina! To use such language here, in the Holy See!"

"Aw, come on, Riley, fuck that—"

Before she could finish her sentence, Monique was surprised to feel his hand clamp over her mouth. "No," he said softly. "Stop right now. I mean it." He looked into her eyes with intensity. He waited a moment, until she nodded, before removing his hand. "Listen," he said, lowering his voice even further. "You have to be Katrina *all the time*. Our lives depend on it." He put both hands on her shoulders and squeezed, just short of painfully. "Seriously. You don't need to talk to anyone, do any tricks, nothing but the job—but you *absolutely have to stay in character* or we are dead."

"But, damn it, Riley—"

"No. No more Riley. I'm Carlo. I mean it, Katrina." She bit her lip and turned her head to the side. He put a finger to her chin and turned her face back toward his. "Don't forget again. *Capisce?*"

She blinked at him for a moment, not sure if she should laugh or cry. Then she took a deep breath and nodded. "Ich verstehe," she said.

He held her shoulders a moment longer, before giving a final squeeze and stepping back. "Bene," he said. And he bent to unpacking their equipment.

Shit, Monique—no, damn it, Katrina! she thought as she watched him work. *What the fuck have we got ourselves into?* she thought for the nine thousandth time.

But she knew the answer to that. They had gotten themselves into the deepest possible shit, and they were swimming against a very powerful tide trying to get out. Odds were, they wouldn't make it. So much stacked against them, and on their side—what? This ridiculous scheme that depended on her impersonating a German technical restoration expert? She couldn't. She just couldn't. There was no way she could maintain any fictional character for what, two weeks? Three? Let alone a character as unlikely as this one. A factory representative of a German chemical company? Just plain stupid! She didn't look like it, she didn't *feel* like it, and she had no idea how to act like it. Someone would find her out—it was a near certainty. And then—the whole flimsy scheme would collapse, Riley would be killed— *she* would probably be killed, too, just for good measure. It was hopeless, idiotic, a truly stupid idea for coping with something beyond hope, and she was going to die trying to do something she knew couldn't be done.

But she also knew she had to try. It truly was her only chance to survive. And she could not do the job if she was whining and moaning and picturing her own gooey death. That would ensure that her fears would be a self-fulfilling prophecy.

So she shook her head and took a deep breath. *Gemütlich es ist alles gut,* she thought to herself, and bent to her work.

You are absolutely certain, Doctor?" Captain Koelliker asked. "There can be no possible doubt?"

"There is always doubt, Capitano," the doctor said

with a shrug. "But see for yourself—look here—" He pulled back the sheet, revealing the buttocks area of the body on his autopsy table. "This is it, right here." He put a fingertip, secure in its latex glove, next to something invisible on the buttock.

"I see nothing," Koelliker said.

The doctor nodded. "Exactly the point. And even I would have seen nothing, except that you asked for a microscopic examination." The doctor slapped the exposed butt cheek playfully. "Your exact words, Capitano. 'Microscopic examination.'"

Koelliker found himself growing annoyed and bit down on an impulse to say something rude. "Show me, please, Doctor?"

The doctor opened his mouth, then closed it, and turned away from the table. "A moment," he said. He took a step to his right, to an adjacent table, and pulled open a drawer. From inside, he withdrew a magnifying glass and handed it to Koelliker. "Here," he said. "Look again, with this."

Koelliker held the glass over the corpse's butt and bent over.

"Here. Right here," the doctor said, indicating a spot.

Koelliker moved the glass over it and stared. For a moment, he saw nothing but pale and flabby flesh. But then—"A pimple?" he asked.

"No, not a pimple, not at all," the doctor said. "A puncture wound. Because it occurred right before the heart stopped, there is no bruising. And it's a very small

puncture, almost certainly from a thirty-gauge needle."
Koelliker looked up at him. "That's very small," the
doctor added.

Koelliker bent back down again. He could see a little more clearly now—it was definitely a puncture
wound. "What would such a needle be used for, typi-
cally?" he asked.

"Injection, of course," the doctor said.

"Of?"

"Something liquid enough to flow easily through
such a small hole," the doctor said.

Koelliker looked again, to see if the doctor was being funny, something Koelliker disliked immensely.
"Such as?" he asked. "Particularly in the present case?"

The doctor shrugged. "In this case, I would guess a
solution of potassium."

Koelliker straightened and put down the magnifying glass. "Potassium is not lethal," he said.

"Ordinarily, no," the doctor said. "But a large
enough shot of it, that is very fatal. And"—he raised a
finger—"it causes a heart attack."

"You found a large amount of potassium in Berzetti's blood?"

"I found almost none at all," the doctor said. "That
is why I suspect it."

"Doctor," Koelliker said warningly.

"I am quite serious," the doctor said. "Potassium
largely dissipates in a few hours, leaving no trace, except
possibly—*possibly*—a slightly elevated level in the blood.
Ideal for murder, really. I'm astonished it isn't used more

often." He smiled. "Of course, perhaps it is! Who would know?"

Captain Koelliker was suddenly tired. Very, very tired. "So your proof is that there is no real proof," he said.

"Yes, exactly," the doctor said. "But look at it as a problem in logic. First, we suspect foul play. Second, we find this small puncture wound. So perhaps there *was* foul play." He tapped the tiny spot again with his gloved finger. "But third, we find no trace of anything in the blood that shouldn't be there. If our suspicion is correct, what does this mean?"

"Tell me," Koelliker said, fighting his impatience.

The doctor raised a hand and waved it, and spoke in a lower, confiding tone. "Very briefly, I considered that perhaps he was using heroin. But there is no trace, not of any narcotic—and to think of this large man, contorting to inject himself here—No, Capitano, I think not." He spread his arms. "Logically, we must conclude that someone else caused the wound, that something in the wound caused death, and that, because there is no trace, that something is most likely potassium. You see?"

Koelliker nodded. He saw. He just wasn't sure what to do about what he was seeing. "But you are convinced that this injection was the cause of death?"

The doctor shrugged. "In a court of law, I would be a fool to say so. But only for your ears, Capitano—just for *your* ears—I believe the death was caused by an injection of potassium."

Koelliker looked at the doctor for a long moment. The doctor began to look uncomfortable, and the captain realized he was letting his fatigue and irritation get the best of him. He straightened, looked at the body one last time. "Thank you, Doctor," he said. He turned from the table and its contents and quickly left the room.

CHAPTER
34

Three days into the restoration of the fresco, the project seemed to be going well, at least as far as Father Matteo could tell. While it was true that Campinelli had asked that he be left alone as much as possible—the Stanza di Eliodoro was temporarily blocked off from public view—Father Matteo had hoped that the blockade would not include him. Not merely because, as curator, he felt he had a duty to inspect now and then but additionally because he was fascinated by this strange new technique and longed to see it in operation.

But Signor Campinelli had very respectfully requested that Father Matteo, too, keep his distance. "The fumes," Campinelli told Father Matteo. "From the chemicals we must use, the special steam solution—they can be toxic."

In order to keep these fumes from spreading

through the *museo*—and even upstairs to the Holy Father's apartments—and possibly causing harm, Campinelli and his assistant had constructed a heavy plastic curtain around their work area. Additionally, they put a large fan in the window to suck out the fumes. It screened their work, and it was very noisy, but it was effective. And so, somewhat frustratingly, the work of restoration was hidden from Father Matteo and anyone else who happened to pass by. It was possible to see only the very top of the scaffolding that had been constructed—necessary, since the fresco was over the top of the arch that held the window, high above the floor.

Father Matteo accepted with good grace and stayed away, for the most part. But he could not help pausing by the doorway and sticking his head inside for a peek, no more than three or four times a day. And if Campinelli was not completely engrossed in his work, he would often come and chat with Father Matteo for a few minutes. The strange and sullen German woman stayed with the work, avoiding Father Matteo as if afraid she might catch some disease from exposure to a Jesuit.

Other than that, the restoration appeared to be going smoothly. Campinelli and Katrina worked long hours, made no disturbance, and said or did nothing that might hint that there were any problems with the work. They kept to themselves, showing up early each morning and working until well after dark, and neither Campinelli nor the woman was ever seen anywhere else in Vatican City, except right there at work in the Stanza di Eliodoro.

Father Matteo was quite surprised therefore, when, on the afternoon of the third day, Captain Koelliker came to see him and inquired what he might have noticed about Signor Campinelli. "Noticed, Capitano? What on earth do you mean?"

"I mean, has he betrayed any signs, however small, that seemed out of place?"

Astonished, Father Matteo simply blinked for a moment. "I—I cannot imagine what you might mean," he said at last. "What kind of thing would I have noticed?"

"Anything unusual," Koelliker said with absolutely no expression on his face. "Anything that seems inconsistent or unusual. Anything at all."

Father Matteo shook his head, still baffled.

Koelliker sighed. He did not want to give away any hint of what he was looking for, certainly not to someone as innocent and unworldly as Father Matteo. So he merely made his words more precise and said, "Perhaps some hint that Signor Campinelli might not be what he claims to be."

Father Matteo was dumbfounded. "He—Signor Campinelli? You ask if he, he might be . . . what. Something else?"

"I do ask."

"But that's—I have never even . . . He seems to be extremely clever, very competent, and a rather nice person as well."

Koelliker just looked at him, clearly expecting something more substantial.

Father Matteo spread his hands in bewilderment.

"But that's it, that's all of it, Capitano," he said. "What else might there be? Because—exactly what are you suggesting? That Signor Campinelli might be . . . what?"

"I'm sure it's nothing at all, Father," Koelliker said. "I have reason to suspect that we may have a small problem. It seems possible that Signor Campinelli might be involved."

"But why, Capitano? Merely because he is new here?"

Koelliker nodded. "Yes, exactly so," he said. "It is probably nothing at all. But because Campinelli is a new arrival, I feel I must be certain of him. Otherwise I am not doing my job."

"Yes, of course, but—what kind of small problem are we speaking of?" Father Matteo asked.

"I'm sure it is nothing," Koelliker said. "Perhaps I am being overcautious. And normally, I would speak to the man myself. But in this case—as I said, it's probably nothing. And I don't want to disturb his work—you know how people react when a policeman starts asking questions, hm? And you seem to get along with the man."

"Yes, he is quite pleasant," Father Matteo said. "And of course, extremely knowledgeable about art. I enjoy his conversation a great deal—I cannot imagine that he could be involved in anything that, that—What kind of thing, exactly, Capitano?"

Koelliker gave him a small and polite smile, the kind that only a Swiss policeman can produce. It said nothing, expressed nothing except observance of a social formality, and hinted at nothing except that the captain would say nothing at all in answer to the question. "In any case," Koelliker said, "I would appreciate it very much if you would let me know of any small thing that seems out of place?"

"Of course," Father Matteo said. "But—"

"Thank you, Father," Koelliker said, rising abruptly, giving the father a small bow and leaving.

Father Matteo watched him go, sighing and wondering what on earth he was supposed to watch for.

Something was not right.

Somebody somewhere nearby had hit one of my mental tripwires. A small and silent alarm was ringing in my head. I didn't know what caused it, or who or why, but I knew. My inner alarm is right more often than it's wrong. Even if it's wrong I pay attention. Because the one time I laugh it off will be the time the hammer comes down on my head.

So I paid attention when the alarm went off. It was going off now. It was a small alarm, but it was persistent. Something had fallen off the tracks. Somebody was on to me, and that was not a good thing.

I went over my back trail. I replayed and rethought every single step I'd made since I got here. Nothing stuck up out of the dirt. As far as I could tell I'd done everything perfectly. And I'd kept a close eye on Monique, just to be safe. She'd been fine, too. Probably gotten a reputation for being aloof, and that could hurt her social life in the long run. I couldn't work up a lot of feeling about that possibility.

I rethought it all again. And again. And I came up with nothing, no mistake, no flaw. And I knew that didn't matter. Because somehow, some toss of the dice had come up snake eyes, and somebody else was grabbing for my ante.

I hadn't been doing a whole lot outside of working on the fresco. I said hello to all the gendarmes on guard—it never hurts to be on good terms with the cops. But other than that, nothing but grinding away. Really the only contact I'd had was with the priest, Father Matteo. He seemed like the least suspicious person in the world. And I couldn't believe his innocent talk was a front for a devious mind. But there was nobody else. It had to be him. If not him in person—then was it possible that somebody was using him to stalk me?

My alarm had gone off this morning, when Father Matteo stopped by for his usual chat. He'd been coming around a lot, practically begging for stories about gallery openings, parties with artists, all that stuff. Sort of pathetic, really. He was like a little kid who couldn't go out to play because of his bad allergies, so he wanted to hear all about what the other, healthy kids got to do.

This morning he'd been different. His chatter had been slow, unnatural, kind of forced, like he was trying to act like nothing was wrong when he knew something was. And I had to think that meant somebody was on to me and using him to find an opening.

It really seemed unlikely. Father Matteo was open, honest, sincere—exactly the kind of person who made a really bad cat's-paw. But something was wrong, and there was nothing else I could think of that might be even a remote possibility. So I assumed just for a minute that I was right. And never mind who was using him; somebody was. I didn't believe he'd try this on his own. So it had to be a cop of whatever flavor, and not Boniface or Stone.

All right: a cop. On the surface that didn't make sense. Why? Because normally any cop with more than a hunch would just haul me in and smack me around until I confessed.

This approach, if that's what it was, was a lot more subtle, and that meant two things. First, whoever it was didn't have anything but a suspicion. Probably based on me being new and unknown. Second, and a little more troubling, it meant they were very damn sharp, and they were looking at me. And sooner or later, they would find out that Carlo Campinelli was a kid from Bologna who had died fifteen years ago in a Vespa accident, and the guy using his name was up to no good. When they figured that out, the game was over. And all future games with it.

So right, obviously I couldn't let that happen.

On the other hand—how the hell did I stop it? Especially since I didn't know who it was or what they might have on me. I needed more time to finish, and if I had to spend some of that time taking care of this problem, that would just leave me vulnerable longer—

and probably create new problems at the same time. Particularly if I solved this problem by finding out who the cop was and taking him out. A second "accidental" death would be too much for anybody to swallow.

I had to throw suspicion away from myself, and at the same time give myself time to get finished and get out of here alive. Which sounds simple—but how?

I pondered that for two more days and didn't come up with anything. Like everything else in this crappy game, it was a blank wall.

And that, in a weird way, was what gave me my answer.

Because I remembered feeling exactly like this just before I'd come up with this plan. And that made me remember what had pushed me over the edge into figuring it out: my imaginary talk with Mom. Remembering how she'd always had a proverb for every situation. And she had one for right now, too.

Good old Mom. She came through for me again. It was even the same old saying.

Stumbling blocks into stepping-stones.

Before his talk with the captain, Father Matteo had truly looked forward to spending his few minutes each day with Carlo Campinelli. And he had chatted freely, without inhibition of any kind. Never about anything of real consequence, of course. Just about art, artists, and the art world itself—Father Matteo loved it. Of course, the world of high-profile gallery openings and the social swirl of the accompanying scene were things he knew about only secondhand, mostly from the art periodicals he read. It had been very pleasant to speak with someone who came from that world, knew those people, and their conversations had been open and agreeable.

But now that he was *supposed* to be chatting freely in order to uncover some unnamed something sinister, the father found that he was completely constrained, awkward, unnatural, uncertain. Every remark he made seemed forced, stupid, completely out of sync. All the joy he'd taken in Campinelli's company fled, and Father Matteo felt like doing exactly the same thing.

But he did not flee. As a Jesuit, he believed that he should be clever and wise enough to do such a simple thing, and that his order had always excelled at justifying small political deceptions for a greater and more important end. He persisted, out of a sense of duty and a growing conviction that there was absolutely nothing abnormal about Campinelli and that his mission from the captain was ruining what had promised to be a very enjoyable friendship.

With increasing reluctance, he had his chats with Campinelli, seeking to draw him into some indiscretion, which, Father Matteo was quite sure, he would not recognize as such even if it ever came. And with even more reluctance, he duly reported the details of the conversations to Captain Koelliker. He was morally certain that nothing would come of it.

Until Captain Koelliker proved him wrong.

They were sitting in the captain's office, sipping espresso, thoughtfully provided by the captain's assistant. Koelliker was taking notes, looking up occasionally. And suddenly he frowned, flipped back a page in his notebook, and looked up again.

"This is not the first time he has mentioned the Urbino Bible," Koelliker said.

"What? Isn't it? I didn't notice," Father Matteo said. "Is that significant?"

"Possibly," Koelliker said.

"I believe he simply asked where it is at the moment, and perhaps how easy it would be to look at it, or—I really don't recall what else, but . . ."

He stopped speaking because Koelliker was clearly no longer listening. He was whipping through all the pages of his notes, and when he was done he stared fixedly at the wall behind Father Matteo's head. "Hmp, *three* times, each time asking for a little more information," he said—clearly speaking to himself, so Father Matteo said nothing until the silence had gone on long enough to be uncomfortable.

"Capitano . . . ?" he said hesitantly.

Koelliker flicked his eyes to the priest with an almost audible *click*. "Tell me, Father," he said. "If you wanted to steal one of the holy relics we have here, how would you go about it?"

"What? Why would I ever—that's preposterous, Capitano—!"

"Indulge me," Koelliker said. He laced his hands behind his head and leaned back in his chair. "Suppose you are not a priest but a thief. What would be the best approach? Some plausible reason that would get you close to your target without the need for stealth, breaking in, attempting to get past all of our security. Which I believe is excellent? Some way to get in and grab something without all that bother. How would you go about it. Hm?"

"Well," Father Matteo said. He frowned, thought for a moment. "I suppose I would fabricate some legitimate reason for being inside the *museo*. Not too close to my target, since that would be too obvious, but close enough to move quickly. Oh—and once inside, I would wait for a certain period of time, so everyone was accustomed to my presence."

Koelliker applauded. "Very good, Father! You would make a fine thief!"

"I am sure I hope not."

Koelliker leaned forward and looked very serious again. "Let us assume further that you will do whatever you must to lay your hands on this treasure," he said.

"Certainly," Father Matteo said mildly, "I can assure you that, as a Jesuit, I am familiar with the idea that the end can sometimes justify the means."

"Just so," Koelliker said. "And so, if some person discovered your true purpose—if they found that you were not at all what you claimed to be but instead you were our hypothetical thief—what would you do then, Father?"

"I believe I would probably flee," Father Matteo said.

"Ah! But you cannot!" Koelliker said. "You *must* obtain this treasure! But you are discovered—and this person will expose you to the authorities unless you stop them. How do you do that?"

"I suppose persuasion would be rather a long shot," Father Matteo said.

"Indeed it would. And what does that leave?"

"Well," the priest said, "if I am the unscrupulous rogue you postulate, I suppose I would have to—"

Father Matteo paused and gaped at Koelliker. Because Father Matteo was not a worldly man, but he was a smart one. And although he would certainly phrase it differently, the nickel had just dropped. "Capitano," he said, and the shock showed in his voice, "are you suggesting . . . ?" He could not bring himself to say it. "Do you mean Berzetti . . . ?"

"That is exactly what I mean," Koelliker said.

"Dear God," Father Matteo said. "You can't be serious."

"But I can," Koelliker said. "And in fact, I am."

"But that's—I can't believe—"

"You will agree with me that thieves have made attempts on our artifacts in the past? Sometimes even successfully?"

"Yes, certainly, but—"

"And how much would you say the Urbino Bible is worth, Father?"

Father Matteo made a disgusted noise and waved his hand. "That's an absurd question. It is a great work of art, one of the most beautiful illuminated manuscripts in the world, as well as a monument to faith and—"

"And absolutely encrusted with jewels," Koelliker said. "Every page adorned with gold leaf. And to a collector, it would be a true prize, wouldn't you say?"

Father Matteo did not say. There was no need.

Captain Koelliker nodded. "A true prize indeed," he said.

CHAPTER 35

An autumn wind was blowing through Paris, picking lightweight trash from the streets and flinging it along the Champs-Élysées. The front page of yesterday's *Le Figaro* whipped past, followed by a handful of leaves, a paper napkin, and a piece of cellophane from a cigarette packet. Flocks of people seemed to blow along, too, as if propelled by the same brisk wind. The wind still had an aftertaste of summer, though, and the natives wore jackets that they did not yet need to button up.

Other flocks strolled slowly—tour groups, families, and couples of all ages holding hands. These people stopped to stare at the things that all their lives they had seen only in books and movies. Most of these people seemed happy—and why not? Paris has a magic that is all its own, and it has some small enchantment for everyone. And Paris never disappoints.

But not all who come to Paris are there to stroll the Champs-Élysées and drink espresso and pastis in the cafés. Because Paris is also a place where very serious business is conducted. There are grim, almost Germanic buildings in outer arrondissements, where vast sums of money are manipulated and matters of life and death are decided.

One such forbidding edifice lies east of the grand and beautiful Champs-Élysées, on the Boulevard Mortier. Its appearance is even more grim because even a casual glance reveals security provisions that are only seen at the top tier of government buildings, usually headquarters of military or intelligence organizations.

They are necessary here, because this building is the home of a very serious organization, the DGSE, Direction Générale de la Sécurité Extérieure—the French intelligence agency assigned to deal with external threats to the republic of France and its interests. And in a conference room on the second floor, a group of very serious people was gathered around a table.

At the head of the table was a man with graying hair, a broken nose, and a short and scruffy beard. His name was Bertrand Bouchard, and he was the director of DGSE's Action Division. This is the section that performs black ops, clandestine missions, and small paramilitary operations where regular troops would be inappropriate or politically embarrassing. Several of Bouchard's subordinates sat along the side of the table to his left. Without exception, they looked like very hard individuals.

Sitting to Bouchard's right was FBI SAC Dellmore Finn, flanked by Special Agent Frank Delgado. Next to Delgado was Howard Fleming, who commanded a team from the FBI's Critical Incident Response Group, which was more or less the FBI equivalent of a SWAT team.

"We know of this man, of course," Bouchard said. "Patrick Boniface is in theory a French citizen. And we know of his, what—his fortress, eh?" He spoke English with the kind of musical French accent that Maurice Chevalier made sound romantic. It did not sound romantic in Bouchard's speech, however, because his voice was as rough as his face. "This place, Île des Choux, it is guarded by missiles, electronics, mines, and other weapon systems you cannot imagine." He shrugged. "And so we leave him alone, because he does no great harm to France, and the price is too high."

Delgado felt a knot forming in his stomach. Not from eating French food; because he wanted this to happen very badly, and Bouchard's words were not encouraging. In fact, Delgado had been nursing a bad feeling about the whole operation, ever since he had realized that their target, Île des Choux, was nominally a French possession. That meant they could not simply pull the CIRG team together and attack. They had to have French permission and cooperation.

That was usually a tricky thing to procure. France was, of course, an old and valued ally, and a member of NATO as well. But the French can be extremely prickly when it comes to matters of national sovereignty and pride, and it was often difficult to know where they would draw the line.

But they had to try. And so they were here, in Paris, which did not make Delgado happy. The magic of Paris was wasted on him; any magic would be, because he was closer to grabbing Riley Wolfe than he had been before, and he had run into an invisible barrier, a wall of diplomatic, legalistic obstacles that were more prohibitive than barbed wire and land mines. He wanted to stand on the table and shout, knock down all the hurdles and hitches, and leap across the barrier to grab Riley Wolfe.

But he said nothing. He was experienced and smart enough to know that the situation called for diplomacy and tact. He was well aware, too, that neither of these was his strongest suit. Finn was quite good at it when he wanted to be, however. That was one of the reasons he was SAC of a task force that regularly dealt with foreign governments.

So Delgado simply clamped his jaw shut and waited.

"We believe the situation has now changed," SAC Finn said. Bouchard's face did not change. It might have been carved out of desert rock, the features etched in by harsh winds over the years. "We have credible information that an attack will be made on Boniface, at Île des Choux."

"French territory," Bouchard said. "How is this your affair?"

Finn nodded. "The attack will be made by an American citizen," he said. "Bailey Stone."

"Ah," Bouchard said. His face moved into a small fraction of expression, halfway between interest and indifference. "And so you propose, what? A joint operation?"

"Yes," Finn said. "Exactly. A joint operation, between your team and our FBI force, led by Agent Fleming." Fleming nodded, as stone-faced as Bouchard. He was an ex-Marine, a former lieutenant of Force Recon, and clearly did not feel he had to yield anything in toughness.

"Mmm," Bouchard said. "My team would of course have the lead."

Finn shrugged. "Of course," he said. "It's French territory."

"But here we come to the, comment dit-on l'essentiel—" He glanced to his left, at one of his men who had a dark and battered face and a shaved head. The man's mouth lifted slightly into the ghost of a smile, and he intoned in a heavy French accent, "The neety-greety."

"Yes, exactly, nitty-gritty," Bouchard said. "To be honest, these formidable fortifications must take their toll. And I do not like the idea of the high casualties," he said. "You must understand, Île des Choux, it is a true casse-tête—the defenses, they are remarkably complete."

"We think we can surprise them," Finn said.

Bouchard spread his hands. "But no, but you must see—It is surrounded by an electronic perimeter that makes surprise impossible, eh? You cannot approach without alerting Boniface, activating missile batteries, artillery—even I do not know the full extent of what Monsieur Boniface can throw at us. But I do know it will be too much."

Delgado couldn't hold back any longer. "The perimeter defenses will be offline," he said. "Turned off."

Bouchard looked at him and raised an eyebrow. "And you know this how?"

Delgado glanced at Finn, who nodded, although a little reluctantly. "Bailey Stone knows about Boniface's defenses," he said. "He knows he can't get past them. Unless he has a way to take them out."

Bouchard's mouth twitched. "My friend," he said, "you use logic on a Frenchman?" He shook his head. "This is never a good idea. You have no more than that?"

Delgado shrugged. "There is also a confidential informant," he admitted.

"Ah," Bouchard said. "And this informant tells you what? The perimeter defense will go down, when, at a certain time?"

"We don't have a specific time, merely a time frame," Finn put in. "Our idea was that our combined force will wait nearby, at, uh—" He glanced down at a notebook that lay open before him. "At Port-aux-Français?"

Bouchard moved his shoulders in a fractional shrug. "Mostly a research station. But yes, this is at least possible," he admitted.

"Right," Finn said. "So the strike force trickles in, a few at a time, because I am pretty sure Boniface will notice a large force coming in all at once."

Bouchard nodded. "Certainement," he murmured.

"We get everybody there, and we wait," Finn continued. "With four attack helicopters and our two teams. Boniface's perimeter network has a distinctive electronic signature. We can monitor from there, and when we hear it go dark, we mount up. We can be there in about half an hour."

Bouchard sighed and tapped his fingers on the table. "It is a great deal less certain than I would like," he said.

"To get both Stone and Boniface? We think the risk is worth it," Finn said.

"Perhaps you do not value the lives of your men as we do," Bouchard said. Then he quickly raised a hand to cut off Finn's response. "No, I should not have said this. Apologies. But you must acknowledge, this is not so certain a thing. The peril is very real."

"It is," Finn said.

"In any case, it is not my decision," Bouchard said. "I must speak with my minister."

"Of course," Finn said.

"And I must also say, mes amis, that in the current political climate? There is very little enthusiasm for doing anything at all with our American friends, hm?"

"Some things rise above politics," Finn said.

Bouchard gave a single snort of laughter. "Not in France," he said.

CHAPTER
36

He's taking too long," Bailey Stone said. He slurped from his glass of bourbon. "Haven't heard from him in what, six, seven weeks? No more—It's like three months? It's too damn long."

"Oh, now, come on," Garrett Wallace said. "Gonna take some time."

"You should've told him to check in, let us know what he's doing," Stone said. "Why didn't you tell him that? Huh?"

"You told me not to."

"He's gonna fuck us over," Stone went on, as if he hadn't heard. "You know damn well he will—he's gonna take the first chance he gets and fuck us over."

"Bailey, you got this guy by the balls," Wallace said. "He don't come through for you, we scrag that girlfriend."

"And where is she, Garrett?" Stone demanded. "Tell me that one. Where did that girl get to? Huh?"

"I don't know."

"Well, I don't know, either," Stone said. "Hasn't been in her apartment for weeks, nobody's seen her—where'd she get to, Garrett?"

"She'll turn up, Bailey," Garrett said soothingly.

"Yeah, well, you just better hope she does," Stone said, scowling. He chugged the rest of his drink and slammed the glass down on the side table. "God-*damn* it! We shoulda heard something by now."

"Come on, now, Bailey," Wallace said. "The man's stealin' a damn *wall*. That's gotta take some time, right?"

Stone stood abruptly and threw his empty glass into the fireplace. It shattered. Stone glared at the fragments for a minute. Then he sat back down.

"Feel a little better now?" Wallace asked him.

"Yes, I do," Stone admitted. "But god-*damn* it, Garrett."

"I know," Wallace said. He got up and poured a fresh glassful, handed it to Stone. "Just got to wait a bit longer, Bailey. You can do that."

Stone snorted and took the glass. "You know damn well I can't," he said. "Never could just set on my ass and do nothing, waiting."

"Just a little bit longer," Wallace said soothingly.

Stone sighed and sipped. "Yeah, all right," he said. He brightened. "But then we gon' kick some ass, god-damn it!"

"Yes, we will, Bailey," Wallace said. "Abso-fuckin'-lutely kick some ass."

He took out the cameras in the room," Benny said. "So's we can't see what he's doin' in there? But we know whatever it is, he's doin' it."

"How do we know this?" Patrick Boniface asked. He sat behind his desk, and Bernadette stood behind him and to one side.

Benny turned one hand palm up. "We got people in there," he said. "The room is closed, sealed off right now, but our people all say he's in there. And we know he took delivery of that plastic stuff, and it's in there with him? So most likely thing, he's putting it onto the fresco, just like he said. And he has this helper, which is—it's some German girl? A black German girl?"

Boniface nodded. "That would be Monique, of course."

"Yeah, has to be," Benny said.

"Why would he want her there with him?" Boniface asked.

"Keep an eye on her?" Benny said tentatively. Boniface frowned. "And anyways," Benny added, "she knows all the technical stuff, about painting and all that?"

"I suppose so," Boniface said.

"You think he's up to somethin'?" Benny asked.

Boniface shook his head. "No, Benny. I *know* he is,"

Boniface said. "He is most definitely up to *something*—but I need to know what."

Benny nodded and waited, while Boniface frowned at nothing, then stood up, walked over to the bookshelf, and pulled out an old and worn book. Benny had seen him take out this same book a few times before, generally when he was lost in thought about some difficult problem. As he had done the other times, Boniface flipped through the book slowly, stopped at one page, and looked at it for several minutes.

Then, abruptly, Boniface slammed the book shut, so sudden and loud that Benny jumped a little. Boniface put the book back in its place and resumed his seat behind the desk. "We do nothing for now," he said. "Tell your people to keep watching and to report immediately if anything unusual happens. *Unusual*, hm?" he said, raising one eyebrow.

Benny nodded. "You got it," he said.

Monique was coming apart at the edges. I could almost see the little strands of her poise peeling apart like string cheese and flopping to the floor. She wasn't used to this kind of thing, and the strain of pretending to be somebody else, surrounded by people who would imprison or even kill her if they knew the truth, was picking off little pieces of her and spitting them back in her face. It wasn't like that for me—this was what I lived for; the adrenaline rush of swimming out into the deep water with no life preserver, knowing that all you've got between you and a quick lights-out is your brain and your balls.

Monique wasn't built that way. She was kind of academic, and in spite of making her living on the dark side of the street, she never had to do it in a way that made her aware that she was actually living a life of crime and staring at prison if she got caught. Out here in the field with me, she got her nose rubbed in it every second of every day. And on top of that, the fate that awaited her if we failed was a lot worse than prison. It also didn't help that this whole piece of the plan depended on her to do some of her best work.

That would have been crazy-hard under the best of circumstances. But to do it here, in what amounted to enemy territory—no. It was way the hell out of her comfort zone, and it was getting to her. I watched her carefully, and I could see that a dozen times every day she reached the point where she absolutely had to scream, throw her paintbrush out the window, and run for high ground. And the only thing that stopped her was me reminding her that if she did, she was signing her own death warrant.

So far, she had managed to pull it together and keep going. But I knew the time was coming when she couldn't do that again, and then she really would scream and run away. She knew it, too. She tried hard, but it wasn't going to last forever. I don't even think she knew she was doing it, but I could see her muttering under her breath, "I'm Katrina," over and over in and endless mantra. "Katrina Katrina Katrina." I knew the signs. She was cracking.

But Katrina soldiered on. Sprawled on top of the rickety scaffolding, surrounded by all her paints and brushes, she labored away at making a cartoon of *The Liberation of St. Peter.* Not the kind of cartoon that might feature SpongeBob or Bugs Bunny, of course. This was the kind of cartoon that Raphael himself would have made in preparation for painting a fresco such as this one.

For Raphael, and for anyone creating a fresco, there's this basic problem. The image has to be painted onto the wall while the plaster is wet. And plaster dries quickly; there is no time for anything but to slap on a finished image fast, without standing around and scratching your ass and wondering if maybe the pineapple ought to go over *there*.

But a fresco is a permanent work of art. It will last as long as the wall it's painted on lasts. The artist wants it to be perfect—and the cartoon solves this problem. You work all that stuff out ahead of time, on paper, exactly to scale, so you can see it before you make it forever. And then, from this full-size full-color picture, you copy right onto the wet plaster.

That picture is called the cartoon. And if you think they should call it something else so you don't get it confused with Looney Tunes, tough luck. Raphael was there way before Chuck Jones.

A cartoon of *The Liberation of St. Peter* was an absolutely vital part of my plan. We were dead and fucked without it.

It was one of the big reasons I insisted on having Monique come along. And it had to be a totally perfect copy. One tiny screw-up and we might as well have stayed home.

So Monique—"Katrina Katrina Katrina!"—was laboring away to make the cartoon. This was the sort of thing she was normally very good at—better than good. She was one of the very best ever. But normally, she could do her work in the safety and privacy of her studio. Here she felt exposed and threatened, in constant danger. And although the plaster was not wet, she faced a time limit just as definite, and the consequences of going over were a lot more serious than having to face dry plaster.

And that put one more time limit on me. Besides getting it done and getting out before I got caught, now I had to do it before Monique flipped out.

I could feel the breath on the back of my neck, too. It wasn't just Father Matteo's stumble-ass attempts to be "normal," or his I-am-not-hiding-anything attitude. Whoever had put the good father up to it was getting close. It was all coming to a head, and soon.

Normally this part gets my adrenaline going, my brain working full speed, and I feel totally alive and ready to kick ass on anything and everything that comes at me. That's normally. This was not. Nothing about this whole thing had been normal. Ever since I woke up on Étienne's boat it had all gone sideways, and for the first time in my career I knew I wasn't driving and I fucking *hated* that.

But as a very wise man once said—I think it was Lincoln, or maybe Shakespeare—"It is what it is." And this was. So the sooner I got it done and got back to being Me again, the better.

Something was going to pop, and soon. I just had to make my move sooner.

CHAPTER
37

t finally came, the moment Monique had been waiting
for—the moment when she absolutely *had* to throw
her paintbrush across the room and yell, "Motherfucker!" And she actually *did* throw the brush—but
she caught herself just in time, and instead yelled, "Ar-
schloch Scheisskerl Saftsack!!" which was nearly the
same thing, except in character, and that sent a tiny
trickle of pride sliding through her veins.

It also had exactly the desired effect. Riley came racing over to her, a look of extreme anxiety on his face.
"Katrina?" he said. "Che cos'è?"

And because of the mood she was in—the mood
that had caused her outburst—Monique looked at him
for a long moment and then, weirdly, giggled. "I kind
of like your hair like that," she said in English.

It was very gratifying to see the look that came over his face. "Ssst!" he whispered. "Someone could hear you!"

"Oh, okay," she whispered back. "Then let's get the fuck out of here, okay?"

His mouth moved like he was a giant fish trying to breathe, and he obviously thought she had either snapped under the pressure or totally flipped out, and so Monique giggled again.

And then he got it. "You're finished?" he whispered.

"I am!" she whispered back. And totally caving to the feeling of exhilaration, she darted her head forward and gave him a huge sloppy kiss. Before he could react, she backed off again and said again, "Let's get the fuck out of here!"

"Let me see!" Riley said, and she led him behind the plastic curtain to where she had laid out the finished cartoon. He got down on all fours and examined it closely, going over every inch, twice. When he was done, he stood up, grabbed her, and returned the sloppy kiss. "It's magnificent!" he said. And still speaking in a whisper, he said, "You know what to do now?"

She nodded. "Take the cartoon to Frankfurt, lose the disguise, wait for you."

"I'll be right behind," he said. "As fast as possible. And then—"

"And then I am *gone*," Monique said triumphantly. "Totally, completely out of it and gone!"

Riley nodded. "I'll give you directions to a safe

place," he said. "It's in a wilderness area, in the Adirondacks. Very important, Monique—you go directly there and wait for me!"

"Don't be too long," she said. "I fucking *hate* trees."

"Stroll out of here like you're just going for lunch, and don't look back," he said. "Don't stop for anything until you're in Frankfurt. I'll be there as soon as I can." He held her shoulders for a long moment, looking into her eyes. "Be careful, Monique. This isn't over yet."

She looked back at him just as intensely. Then she smiled. "It is for me," she said.

Ever since Captain Koelliker had convinced him that Signor Campinelli was, in all likelihood, attempting to steal the Urbino Bible, Father Matteo had been nervous, uneasy, and reluctant when he stopped for a chat with the man. Today was different. Today a wave of excitement had washed away all his discomfort. Because today—

"You see, Father?" Campinelli said, and his voice betrayed that he, too, felt the excitement. "The vacuum seal is now in place!"

The two of them stood side by side, craning their necks upward to where a shallow black plastic tray had been fitted precisely over *The Liberation of St. Peter*. "It is held in place by six vacuum clamps," Campinelli said. "There—at the corners, and in the middle of each side."

Father Matteo stared, forgetting for the moment

that this man was a criminal, that he wanted to steal a priceless relic—forgetting everything except that he was witnessing the pinnacle moment of a wonderful new restoration process.

"The vacuum clamps . . . ?" Father Matteo said.

Even though the sentence was incomplete, Campinelli understood him. "Do not concern yourself, Father," he said reassuringly. "The pad of the clamp that touches the fresco is a very soft, nonabrasive material. It cannot possibly harm the fresco."

"Of course not," Father Matteo said softly. "And when the seal is removed—the process is complete? The fresco is fully restored?"

"Absolutely," Campinelli said. "Nothing left to do but clean up."

"Wonderful," Father Matteo said. "And when will—how long must the seal remain in place?"

"Ah!" Campinelli said. "An excellent question, Father! It is vitally important—absolutely crucial, Father!—that the seal remains completely untouched for at least three weeks! At *least*. Otherwise . . ." Campinelli shuddered and shook his head.

"What?" Father Matteo said. "What would happen?"

"The process that is occurring absolutely has to take place under the seal," he said. "In a lightless vacuum. Exposure to the atmosphere would cause a chemical reaction that would actually *melt* the plaster, Father. The fresco would literally liquefy and drip off the wall."

"Dear Lord," Father Matteo said.

"Yes, it's unthinkable. Absolutely dreadful. So," Campinelli said, "whatever else happens, the seal *must* remain in place for a minimum of three weeks—four would be better, but three at the very least. Remember this, Father," Campinelli said, placing a familiar hand on Matteo's shoulder, "if I should die, or if I am kidnapped by gypsies—whatever happens, Father!" He lowered his voice and spoke even more urgently. "The seal *must not be removed* for at least three weeks!"

Father Matteo stared at Campinelli, somewhat stunned by what he'd said, and by his urgency in saying it. But all he said was, "I will remember."

And why do you think he said that, Father?" Captain Koelliker said, raising one eyebrow.

"I am sure I don't know," Father Matteo confessed. "At the time, it did not strike me as . . . suspicious?"

"No? Really?

Father Matteo spread his hands helplessly. "Capitano, you will have to forgive me," he said. "I know that you must always be on guard, suspect everyone, watch every shadow in case it is hiding something—"

"True enough," Koelliker murmured.

"But this is not the world I live in!" Father Matteo protested. "And to me, Signor Campinelli seemed very much to be an eager, hardworking, charming man, doing his best to save a great work of art! And I would very much like to believe that is who he is."

"So would I, Father," Koelliker said.

"So, please," Father Matteo said. "Is it not possible that you are mistaken?"

Koelliker shook his head. "I'm sorry, Father," he said. "It is quite impossible."

"But how can you be certain? Without any evidence, or—"

Captain Koelliker pushed a piece of paper across the desk. Father Matteo looked at it, then raised his eyes to Koelliker. "Please, take a look," Koelliker said.

Father Matteo picked up the paper and began to read. He looked up, startled; Koelliker motioned for him to read on, and he did.

When he finished, he slowly placed the paper back on the desk. "I see," he said. "And there is no possibility that, that—perhaps there were *two* Carlo Campinellis from Bologna?"

"I checked the Codice Fiscale," Koelliker said. "Our Carlo Campinelli is using the same number as the Carlo Campinelli here—" He flicked the paper with a finger. "The Carlo Campinelli who was killed in a Vespa accident fifteen years ago."

"I see," Father Matteo said. He had truly hoped that Signor Campinelli was legitimate, but this was quite final. The Codice Fiscale, the Italian equivalent of a Social Security number, would not be in error.

"It is a common practice," Koelliker said. "Criminals buy and sell these numbers to other criminals, who use them to establish a fraudulent identity. Exactly," he went on relentlessly, "as this man has done."

"I see," Father Matteo said again. He was aware that

he was repeating himself, but he could think of nothing else to say. His last hope was crushed, and his face showed it.

Captain Koelliker let him have a few moments of silence, and finally Father Matteo looked up and nodded. "All right, then," he said. "And so now, we will go and arrest him?"

"I think not," Koelliker said.

Father Matteo looked surprised. "Why on earth not?"

"It will be a much tighter case, and a very much stiffer penalty, if we catch him in the act," Koelliker said. "We know what he plans to steal, after all."

"The Urbino Bible," Father Matteo said.

"And so we will simply put a very careful, and *very* inconspicuous, guard on the Urbino Bible. And wait for our thief to try to steal it. When he has it in his hands—we take him."

He looked at Father Matteo, and he was unable to hide a small, and very Swiss, smile of satisfaction.

After a moment, Father Matteo nodded. "Very well," he said.

Captain Koelliker was having lunch at his desk when the alarm went off. His immediate thought was that it had to be the attempt on the Urbino Bible, and for a moment he was too startled to move—the alarm? Their plan had been to keep careful watch and then move in silently, without any loud noises or movements that might panic the throng of tourists.

But then his instincts took over. An alarm was an alarm, after all. He dropped his sandwich and was out the door.

Koelliker hurried out and across the plaza to the Vatican Library. Although it was not open to the general public, qualified scholars and researchers were welcome to use the unique resources of the library, and that of course meant a staff of librarians. So there was a small crowd of people milling about in confusion when Koelliker came in.

"Captain!" Koelliker recognized the voice and quickly found the face that went with it—Corporal Amacker, assigned to the squad watching the Urbino Bible. He beckoned, and Koelliker hurried over.

"What is it?" Koelliker demanded. "The Bible—is it . . . ?"

"It's fine, sir," Amacker said. "Completely untouched. We've had it in our sight every moment."

"Then what is it? Why did the alarm go off?"

"Captain, we're not sure," Amacker said. "Something triggered the alarm on one of the upper windows." He pointed to the large arched window at the far end of the room. "We checked it out, sir, and there's nothing. It might have been a malfunction."

Koelliker frowned. It was possible for the alarm to misbehave, of course. But it was so rare that he could not recall the last time it had happened. "Send someone onto the roof to check from the outside," he said. Amacker nodded, and Koelliker began a cautious inspection of the area surrounding the Urbino Bible, and then the rest of the area. Something was wrong, and he didn't know what it was. But it tugged at his subconscious, and he very carefully examined the entire room.

He was standing beside the case that held the precious book, staring down at it without really seeing it, when a breathless Father Matteo found him. "Capitano!" the priest called. Koelliker looked up, and one glance was more than enough to see that Father Matteo was very upset about something.

"Father?" Koelliker said. "What is it?"

Father Matteo waved a piece of paper frantically. "This!" he said. "This note was on my—I don't know what to think at all, it can't be—Here, see for yourself," he said, and thrust the paper at Koelliker.

Dear Father Matteo, it read.

I regret to inform you that I am not a very good person. And please do not offer to hear my sins; there are far too many, and I am sure that confession would not help.

But it has been such a pleasure chatting with you, I could not leave without a few small words of explanation. And perhaps an apology, for the small and nearly harmless deception.

Very important—it was not ALL deception. I really did a great deal of work on the fresco. I think you will be very surprised when you see what I've done! And MOST important—What I told you about leaving the seal in place is true. It is vitally important that you do not remove it for a mini-

mum of three weeks—four would be better! Please,
Father, I beg you—do NOT remove the seal!!

Other than that? I am already far away as you
read this. As I said, I am not a very good person.
But I am very good at what I do. And now it is
done.

It was all about the fresco, and it always was.
Ciao, Father.

> *Very best wishes,*
> *"Carlo Campinelli"*

And under that were scrawled two letters: *R.W.*

Koelliker looked up. "What does this mean, it was all about the fresco?"

"I don't know," Father Matteo said. "I haven't any idea at all, just—"

"But the fresco is completely covered over by this seal?"

"Yes, of course."

Koelliker looked again at the note, but it still made no sense to him. What could it possibly mean? He thought of how the whole episode had begun, with the two men—Catalan separatists, apparently—damaging the painting and making such odd threats. How could that possibly fit? And then Berzetti dead—all so this man could gain access to the fresco? For what purpose? Something to do with the fresco—*The Liberation of St. Peter*. It was all about that? How? And what was the real "all" if not stealing the Urbino Bible? And then the letters beneath the fraudulent signature: *R.W.* Were those the initials of the real person behind this imposture? If so, why would he risk leaving such an important clue to his identity? And what did the letters stand for—or who? It would take solid-steel testicles to do something so brazen. Only an idiot would do so—an idiot or a man so overwhelmingly confident of his abilities that . . .

Time stopped for Captain Koelliker.

Like most in the international law enforcement community—and particularly those involved in security for precious artifacts—Koelliker knew the name of a man who fit that description. And his initials were, in fact, *R.W.*

Riley Wolfe.

Riley Wolfe would certainly be capable of an attempt on the Urbino Bible. He was known to be an expert at disguise, and at parkour—the alarm on the roof! And Riley Wolfe would not hesitate to tell the world what he had done. Far from it; he would trumpet it to the world. Riley Wolfe stole the Urbino Bible!

Except the Bible was right here in its place, in front of him. So if it truly had been Riley Wolfe, then why, or what—

Captain Koelliker had a wild, stupid, ridiculous thought. *It was all about the fresco,* the note read. Was it even conceivable—

"Father Matteo," he said. "Would it be possible to somehow steal a fresco? Perhaps peel it off the wall?"

Father Matteo looked pityingly at Koelliker. "Capitano," he said. "I beg you, put the thought out of your mind."

"But the note said—"

But Father Matteo was shaking his head quite vigorously. "No, absolutely not," he said. "A fresco is actually part of the wall, Capitano. It is embedded in the actual plaster of the wall! And to steal it—you would have to remove the wall itself!"

"I see," Koelliker said. "But then . . ." And he went silent. For there was no "but then." He looked at the note. Then he looked at the Urbino Bible. "However," he said, "if your Campinelli is, in reality, the man I think he is . . . Father, I think we must remove the seal on the fresco."

"No, absolutely not," Father Matteo said.

"If there is even the most remote chance that anyone in the world could steal a fresco—"

"But I tell you, Capitano, that's absurd!"

"—then this man would find the way to do it. And," Koelliker said, raising his voice slightly to override the priest, "placing a seal over it—telling you to leave it for three weeks—this gives him time to escape—*with* the stolen fresco!"

"Capitano, please, disabuse yourself of this mad notion," Father Matteo said. "To steal a fresco—No, absolutely not. It can't be done."

Koelliker sighed. "Then I suppose you will insist on leaving this seal in place over the fresco?"

Father Matteo spread his hands helplessly. "But, Capitano, please—what choice do I have?" he said. "If there is even the slightest chance that he is telling the truth . . . ?" He shook his head. "Yes, certainly. We must leave it in place."

"For three weeks," Koelliker said.

"Or even four," Father Matteo said.

Koelliker nodded. He knew well the limits of his authority, and he was there. "Amacker!" he called, and the corporal trotted over. "You are familiar with this Carlo Campinelli?"

"I have seen him, Captain," Amacker said. "I know his face."

"Take your men," Koelliker said. "Do not make a fuss. We don't want to alarm our visitors. But find him. Find Campinelli."

"Yes, sir," Amacker said. He hurried away and began dispersing the rest of the squad. Koelliker noted that one man stayed behind to guard the Urbino Bible. This man, a stocky man with a red beard, took up position beside the book, and Koelliker nodded his approval.

"What will you do if you find him, Capitano?" Father Matteo asked hesitatingly.

Koelliker snorted. "No need to worry about that, Father," he said. "I'm sure he's long gone by now. And equally sure that he's not even Carlo Campinelli anymore. If this man is who I suspect, he had a disguise ready. You could walk past him now and not know it was the same man."

"I see," Father Matteo said.

They stood there in silence, side by side, for what

seemed a very long time. Then abruptly, Captain Koelliker spun on his heel and headed out.

"Capitano!" Father Matteo called after him. Koelliker paused and looked back. "What are you going to do?"

"I'm going to finish my sandwich," Koelliker said. And he marched out.

Father Matteo watched him go but made no move to leave himself. He was completely at a loss for where he should go, or what he should do. He scarcely even knew what to think. As hard as it had been to accept the notion that Campinelli was a thief, he had accepted it. In the face of Koelliker's evidence—and now the note that was essentially a confession—he had to admit that it was true.

But now Campinelli was gone—and apparently without taking anything. And he claimed that he had actually restored the fresco—*you will be very surprised when you see what I've done!* he had written. So he had come to steal the Urbino Bible, pretending to restore the fresco—and now he had left—*without* the Bible, but after really restoring the fresco?

Father Matteo could only wonder what it all meant.

Still, life went on. He had duties to attend to. And after all, no real harm had been done, had it? So he must put the whole thing out of his mind and carry on.

So be it, Father Matteo thought. He took a deep breath and straightened up, and headed out, with a brief stop to look once more at the Urbino Bible. It was still there. Of course it was. Perhaps the security measures had persuaded the thief to leave without it. It had been very well guarded, as it was even now. And with a friendly nod at the burly guard with the red beard, Father Matteo left the library.

C aptain Koelliker did, at least, get to finish his lunch. He even got halfway through a cup of good Swiss coffee before Corporal Amacker came into his office.

Koelliker could tell by the corporal's bearing that they had not found Campinelli. He had not really expected that they would. Due diligence had required that he order the search, and he had.

But Amacker stood in front of the desk and said nothing, and Koelliker knew that something else was bothering the corporal, other than a search with no results.

Koelliker sighed and put down his coffee cup. "You didn't find Campinelli," he said.

"No, sir," Amacker said.

"I did not expect that you would," Koelliker said. But that statement did not appear to make Amacker any easier. "Well, what, then?" he asked.

"I'm not sure, Captain," Amacker said. "Just—we found this? Um, just outside the library?" He carefully placed an object on the desk in front of Koelliker.

At first, it was impossible to tell what the thing was. It was some kind of reddish material, wadded up and

shapeless. Koelliker picked it up, turned it over, straightened it out. After a moment, he could tell that it was a
false beard, the kind you might glue onto your face for
a part in a movie. And that made no sense; who would
wear a fake beard to the Vatican Library? And then
discard it?

But wait—he had seen a red beard recently. Where
had it been . . . ?

And then he remembered.

"Scheisse," Koelliker said. He stood up and beckoned to Amacker. "Come with me," he said. He had to
check, but he knew what he would find when he got
back to the library.

He was right.

The Urbino Bible was gone.

PART 3

CHAPTER
38

Monique was most definitely a city girl. Aside from the fact that she had been born and raised and educated in cities, and that she knew very little about the countryside except that that's where food came from, she just didn't like peace and quiet and bucolic scenery. She needed the adrenaline that only a great city can provide, the sense that exciting things were happening all around you, all the time, and that you were part of a smart, fast-moving culture. She could not be happy without the sound of crowds, the smell of traffic, and the promise of galleries and shops and the theater.

That said, Monique had never been so glad to see a view that held nothing but trees, bushes, and chipmunks. The past few weeks had told her that cities, crowds, people, all meant danger. She had fled Rome as if her life depended on it—and of course, she was quite sure it did. Her brief stay in Frankfurt had been just as bad. She could feel the lethal pursuers breathing down her neck. Even when Riley arrived, he had not been able to reassure her, and she had hurried to finish the work—as much as you could hurry when you are doing something that has to be absolutely perfect or you will die horribly.

And when they finished, Monique had fled Frankfurt in just as much of a cold sweat. Everybody in the airport seemed to be staring at her with sinister intentions, and every passenger on the flight to New York appeared to be watching her, waiting for her to lower her guard.

So in spite of being completely exhausted, Monique stayed awake, all the way across the Atlantic. And when she landed in New York at around midnight, she didn't wait for daylight. She just grabbed a rental car and drove north as fast as she could, straight up I-87 to the Adirondacks and the place Riley had told her to find. She drove straight through the night, arriving at her destination as the sun was just starting to color the sky in the east.

Riley's directions were very good; otherwise, she would never have found the place. That was a comforting thought. It meant nobody else could find it, either. She came off I-87 onto a much smaller state road, and from that onto a county road plagued with potholes. And from there the directions led her onto even smaller and bumpier roads as she drove farther up into the mountains, until she found herself on a series of dirt roads, the last one not much more than a slightly widened trail.

And then, finally, the big steel gate Riley had described. It was set into a barbed-wire fence hung with signs warning of an electric shock for anybody who touched it. Beside the gate was a box, secured with a combination lock. Monique opened it with the combination Riley had given her and turned off the security systems. She drove through the gate, turned it all back on, closed the box, and shut the gate behind her.

It was another mile or so down the smallest and bumpiest dirt road yet, and then she drove into a little clearing. Set at the far edge was a small and battered-looking log cabin. Safety. Monique parked, turned off the engine, and collapsed against the steering wheel with her forehead pressed to the back of her hands. She stayed like that for several minutes, just breathing. She felt suddenly empty, drained of all emotion, all energy, all possibility of moving and doing anything. It surprised her to realize how totally spent she was. But she'd been living in fear for weeks. Now it was over, and she was as safe as she could be.

Monique did not exactly fall asleep. It was more like tumbling into a trance, a kind of numb haze. She knew where she was, and that she needed to get out of the car. She just couldn't summon up the energy to do that, or anything else. And the front door of the cabin suddenly seemed so far away. So she just sat, breathed, let her mind go blank.

Eventually, the sound of birds registered on her

overworked senses. She sat up, blinked at the suddenly bright morning around her, and stumbled out of the car and into the cabin. She made it all the way inside and to the battered couch that slouched in front of the big stone fireplace. She flopped facedown onto the couch and was asleep in under three minutes.

The sun was setting when Monique opened her eyes. She lay on her back, looking up at a wooden ceiling crossed with large wooden beams. That made absolutely no sense. The ceiling in her apartment was acoustic tiles, not wood. She blinked, and it came back to her: Rome, Frankfurt, New York, the drive north—she was in Riley's mountain hideout. And weirdly enough, that felt good.

Monique stretched, got up, and explored the cabin. One entire wall was a floor-to-ceiling bookshelf, and it was packed with books. Beside it was a rolling cabinet with a stereo amplifier and a CD player. A large rack of music CDs stood beside it.

A short hallway led to two small bedrooms. The area opposite the fireplace was the kitchen. It held a heavy wooden table and three chairs, a battered refrigerator, and a sink with a hand pump—Riley had told her the water came from a well and was fresh, clean, and delicious. Next to the fridge was a large pantry filled with freeze-dried food. At the back of the pantry she found a carefully disguised panel. She pulled it open and found the compartment Riley had described. He had said it had a small selection of weapons.

But to Monique it looked like an entire arsenal. She

stared at the assortment of pistols, rifles, boxes of ammunition, and other things that she did not really want to know about. Monique did not like guns, and her experience with them was extremely limited. Under the circumstances, however, she was very glad they were there.

She selected a pistol that didn't seem too ridiculous, a simple revolver with a duct-taped grip. She examined it carefully, figured out how to pop open the cylinder; it was not loaded. Although it was a simple matter to see that the bullets went right into those six little holes in the cylinder, there was nothing that indicated which bullets to use.

Monique sorted through the many boxes of bullets. Each one had a bunch of numbers printed on the side—but the pistol did not. How was she supposed to know which ones to use? So she tried a bullet from each box until she found some that fit, in a box that read ".357" on the side. She was relieved that the number was small—she was pretty sure that meant the pistol was not as lethal as one with a bigger number. She loaded the pistol and, feeling a little foolish, stuck it into the waistband of her slacks.

Monique kept the pistol with her for the next three days. She even got used to the weight of it on her hip. And surprisingly enough, she relaxed. She pulled books from the shelf and read. She listened to music. And she found a couple of notebooks and some pencils, and she spent much of her time drawing. Sometimes she sat outside and sketched trees, birds, and flowers. And sometimes she sat at the heavy wooden table inside and just drew shapes, letting her pencil go wherever her subconscious told it to go. It was therapeutic. Monique slowly began to unwind and put the constant terror that had haunted her immediate past out of her mind. To her enormous surprise, she *liked* it here in the woods. The quiet, the loneliness, the isolation—all the things that should have driven her crazy—were soothing instead. She was alive, she was safe, it was over.

On the evening of her third day at the cabin, Monique sat at the table sketching. She was drawing from memory the faces of old friends from school and enjoying herself a lot. Each face carried so many memories, most of them good, and it was a bit like going through a yearbook.

She had almost finished a portrait of the boy who had taken her to the senior prom, when she heard a noise, a kind of tapping sound, just outside the door.

Monique froze. The tapping was too regular to be a windblown branch. Could it be a bird, or a small animal? Slowly and silently, she stood up and pulled the pistol from her waistband. Holding it in the two-handed grip she'd seen people on TV use, she stepped to the door. She stood there for a moment, waiting for the sound to repeat. It didn't. Very carefully, she unlatched the door, turned the handle, and then, very fast, flung open the door.

Out of the corner of her eye, Monique saw a bright flash of light—and then nothing at all.

CHAPTER
39

I f you have never tried to lug around a large piece of plaster that's been soaked in plastic and rolled up, take my advice and don't start now. It's too heavy for one person, or even three, and too big to stuff into anything except a custom-made shipping crate, and then it's packed away where you can't really keep an eye on it to make sure that there's no damage, which bothered me more than it should, and—

Just take my word for it; don't try it. It's a nightmare.

But I did it. It took time, and it was time I couldn't afford. I knew all kinds of BOLOs had gone out for me, everything from the Vatican cops to Interpol. And I'd already spent too much time in Frankfurt getting the thing ready, and then packed, and sending Monique off to safety. I could feel hot breath on the back of my neck. But finally I got the crate to a small airport on Sicily. I made one quick stop to mail a package, heavily insured, and then I called Stone's redneck associate, Garrett Wallace. "I'm on my way," I told him.

"Outstanding," he said.

"You got the flash drive?"

"Oh, hell, yes," he said.

"And the picture was clear? You could see the code?" I mean, it was kind of important, and the asshole was not being real communicative.

Wallace gave a kind of laid-back, good ole boy chuckle. "That big ole Frog got fingers like sausages," he said. "We kinda had to squint to see around them."

"But you did?" I said. "You got the code?"

He chuckled again. "I think you'da heard from us by now if we didn't get it."

He sounded so cheerful and friendly that for just a second I almost wanted to like him—almost. I stopped myself in time. The job was hard enough. I didn't need to make friends with a sociopathic hillbilly. So I just went over the plan with him one more time, stressing the timing.

"Yeah, sure, we got all that, don't you worry," he said. "It's gonna be just fine, Riley, we got this."

I didn't have much choice, so I believed him and hung up. Then I called the number Benny gave me. I told him where I was, and that I had the Thing for the Guy. Either he hadn't seen *Goodfellas,* or he just didn't think that was funny, and he didn't seem like he wanted

to chat, so I hung up and sat on the crate by the runway, waiting. I figured it would take some time, and I
was a little worried about hanging out in one place for
too long. Sicily was too close to Rome for comfort.

But Boniface must have had his jet standing by
someplace nearby, because it was there in just under
two hours. I heard the engines, watched the plane approach, and recognized Boniface's Cessna Citation X as
it touched down and taxied over. The door opened, the
stairs rolled up, and my old flame Danielle stepped out
with her robotic corporate smile already set in place.
We got a few hardy Sicilian peasants from the baggage
claim area to help. They loaded the big crate into the
plane and we were in the air in under an hour.

The plane circled climbed up to altitude, and I could
finally relax. I mean, not really *relax*, if that has to
mean having five or six fruity drinks with paper umbrellas in them and then singing karaoke. This was not
the time to get sloppy, not yet. There were still a couple
of very tense moments ahead, and getting through
them with all my body parts intact was going to be
very, very iffy. Besides, I was pretty sure I did not want
to witness Danielle singing karaoke. She'd probably
pick a Plastic Bertrand song like "Jet Boy, Jet Girl." Or
worse, some Jacques Brel. The thought of her letting
her hair down and singing "Les Coeurs Tendres" at
thirty thousand feet was not a happy one.

But I could relax a little without paper umbrellas or
karaoke. And I had a long flight ahead of me, the

length of the whole continent of Africa, and then a big chunk of ocean, so there was no point in spending the whole time biting my nails and trembling in fear. I kicked back a little and let Danielle bring me things. Just little things; a very nice lobster thermidor with braised asparagus and a half bottle of Pouilly-Fuissé. And of course some more of that excellent coffee so I wouldn't get too comfortable. When I was full, I leaned back and pondered.

It had all gone about as well as I could have hoped, and that was nice. And Monique was away, out of it, safely tucked away in one of my hidey-holes, which was a bigger relief than maybe it should have been. And she was at a place I had paid for in cash, so there was no record of it that Stone or Boniface could find, as far as I could tell. She was as safe as I could make her. So I figured it was okay if I enjoyed the comforts Danielle could provide, and kicked back just a little for the duration of the flight. But I didn't kid myself. It wasn't over, not by a mile and a half. The hard part hadn't even begun yet.

It seems funny to think of it that way, but it was true. I'd gone into this thinking stealing a fresco was going to be the hardest thing I'd ever done. But it was this next part that was making me lose sleep. For one thing, if I had gotten caught at the Vatican, all they'd have done was lock me up. If anything went wrong from here on, the best I could hope for was a quick and easy death, without any attention from Boniface's girlfriend, Bernadette.

Thinking about that made relaxing a real challenge. But I managed somehow. Mostly because it was a truly long-ass flight, around seven thousand miles, with a stop at Cape Town to refuel. Maybe you can stay scared shitless that long. I can't do it. After only an hour or so, I tilted the chair back and put away all the bad thoughts.

I slept a little, I had a couple more light snacks, and I went over what had to happen next if I was going to get out of it alive. I broke that up with a couple more minor treats from Danielle's kitchen. A beef Wellington with a Château Margaux, a fettuccini with black truffles and some truly exceptional pinot grigio I'd never heard of—just a few simple, hearty peasant dishes like that, just to help wile away the long hours of the flight.

By the time we landed in the Kerguelen Islands I had gained a couple of pounds. Other than that, not much had changed. I was still worried, and I was still pretty sure I ought to be. This next step was maybe the most dangerous. And it was totally out of my control, which I hate like cancer. But there was no choice. I had to keep moving forward with my noble smile stitched to my rugged masculine face.

So I did. I supervised the guys who wrestled the crate off the jet and onto a trailer towed by a waiting ATV. They were the same uniformed guys I'd seen last time through, or at least it looked like them. When we had the crate loaded, I bade a fond farewell to Danielle, and we rode across the island to the wharf, where Étienne was waiting, with his familiar friendly sneer in place.

We got the crate on board, without any help from Étienne. He stood on the bridge, right next to the duplicate controls for the cargo hook, and did nothing. Just stood with his arms folded. But there was a set of controls for the hook on the gunwale, right next to the crane. So I attached the hook, we hoisted the crate on board, and forty minutes or so after landing I was headed out to sea.

Étienne kept up his usual stream of lighthearted chatter, which is to say sneering silence. Twenty minutes after casting off we were out of sight of land. I remembered a phrase I'd read in an old book about the British Navy: We had "sunk the land." I thought that was right on the money, because the odds were pretty good that I was sunk. But there was still the endgame. It had to play out, and this was the last quiet time before it started. So I decided to put a little space between me and Étienne's endless good cheer.

I stepped back to the rear end of the boat and watched the waves. They were a whole lot more fun than chatting with Étienne, but aside from that they were not the most interesting scenery I'd ever seen. In fact, they were pretty damn dull. They didn't have any tricks, they didn't change color—nothing. They just sort of rolled around. Under other circumstances it might have been dreary.

Not this time. Even dull scenery gets a little more interesting when you think it might be the last time you see it.

*   *   *

Benny was nervous. This was not a usual condition for him. A hard life, filled with hard deeds, had cured him of feeling antsy most of the time. This was different.

In the first place, he had been here, inside the rock, for too long. As much as he liked working for Mr. Boniface, he just as much did not like his employer's choice of residence. If Benny was there longer than a few days, he could feel the walls closing in. Not claustrophobia exactly; it just started getting to him. Stuck inside a big fucking rock, for Christ's sake. In the middle of the ocean, two thousand miles from everything.

On top of that, there was Bernadette. Being around that fucking horror show was definitely hard on the nerves. Not just the face, which was bad enough. It looked like it had caught on fire and somebody tried to put it out with a chain saw. But the eyes were a hell of a lot worse than the face. Those eyes of hers looked like she could see inside you, and like she thought she might like to rearrange you so everybody else could see your insides, too. If it was up to him, Bernadette would be chained to a fucking wall in the goddamn basement and fed chunks of raw meat. Or better yet, tie an anchor to her neck and chuck her into the fucking ocean.

Of course, it wasn't up to him. It was up to Mr. Boniface, and Mr. Boniface fucking *liked* Bernadette, so that was that.

All that was enough to make anybody a little antsy.

But now, all kinds of shit was about to hit the fan. Mr. Boniface said it was all under control, and Mr. Boniface was always right, but what the fuck, this was complicated. And Benny did not at all trust this Riley Wolfe character. From what Benny knew, and from what he'd seen, the guy was way too fucking slick for his own good, and he always had some kind of bullshit move coming at you from out of nowhere, and Benny was pretty sure this time was no exception.

But what the hell, it wasn't up to him. Mr. Boniface did the thinking, and he said this part would be smooth and easy. And Mr. Boniface gave the orders, and his orders were to meet the boat and make sure everything happened the way it should. That's what he would do.

The boat came chugging into the tunnel right when it should. It was kind of dark in there, before the tunnel opened up into the area by the dock, but Benny could see Étienne sitting there at the wheel. So far, so good. All perfectly normal.

The boat slid into place at the dock, and two of the mercs waiting with him grabbed the lines and tied up. Then Riley Wolfe stepped out on deck and Benny tensed up. No matter what Mr. Boniface said, this guy was just too damn slick, and Benny had thought that if something funny was going to happen, it would be now, while they were unloading. But Riley just nodded at him and said, "It's heavy as hell," and Benny motioned to the other waiting mercs to help out. Benny stepped to the side and watched, his hand resting near the Glock he had tucked into his waistband.

Nothing happened, except that they got the crate up onto the dock and onto a big handcart, and then Éti-enne cast off and chugged away while Benny, Riley, and the mercs wheeled the crate down the corridor.

I could feel it coming. I didn't know what it was, but I knew it was bad, and it had my name on it, and it was coming. No reason to think so, but that didn't matter. I *knew*.

I don't claim it's a superpower, and I am not the only guy in the world who feels like this sometimes. If you talk to professional soldiers, or anybody who lives on the edge of adrenaline, they'll tell you the same thing. Sometimes you just know. It's a kind of a mental radar system. And like I've said before, I've got it, too. It tells me when somebody's loading up shit and aim-ing for the fan, and it's usually right. You can call it ESP, or gut feeling, or instinct, whatever you want. The name doesn't matter. It's real. And if you want to keep breathing, you listen to it when it talks to you.

It was screaming at me now.

Why? Who the fuck knows. Everything looked fine and dandy. We were just a couple of happy guys and six heavily armed professional killers out for a stroll along a stone corridor with a big crate. What could be more innocent? All we needed was a puppy and a kite and it would've been a perfect picture of a happy day at the park.

But it was wrong. It was all dead wrong, and about

to go wronger, and I knew it. This was not one of those times when my gut was whispering, *Careful, watch it, something just might happen.* Nope; this was a two-hundred-decibel full-throat screaming chorus screeching out a warning that a full-bore, flat-out no-kidding-run-for-your-fucking-life-as-fast-as-you-can-right-now-or-you-are-totally-fucking-dead was right around the corner.

I didn't know what set it off. Maybe it was Benny, who seemed a little nervous. Maybe it was just being here, in a truly awful and dangerous place with no way out. And maybe it was being on the edge of a series of events that would leave a big pile of dead bodies behind, with no guarantee I wouldn't be one of them.

Usually that slippery turf on the edge of death gives me a lift, makes me feel more alive, right at home.

Not this time. This was something else, something sticking up just ahead, poking up out of the darkness like a tombstone with my name on it. It was right there, just out of sight, and it was pouring out a warning. It flooded over me, this great big wave of dread and nausea, and it made me break out in a cold sweat. I felt my heart start to hammer and my hands get greasy and I was breathing too hard and there was not a single goddamn thing I could do except keep walking toward whatever it was and get ready for something I just knew was going to be final.

And all I could do was go straight at it.

It got worse.

We got to the end of the corridor, to Boniface's

huge art gallery. Benny opened the big double door, the mercs rolled the crate in, and Benny motioned me to follow. I stepped through the doorway, and Boniface was waiting. And right behind him, with a look on her face like a rabid leopard that hasn't been fed, was Bernadette.

This was it. This was what my radar had been screaming about. I knew that as sure as if it was written on a big white banner in red letters and hung from the ceiling. Her face said it all, just as if she was hung with a sign saying, "HERE I AM! RILEY'S HORRIBLE DEATH!"

I looked around for some way out, which was pretty stupid. There wasn't any way out and I knew it. I was in a fortress hollowed out of a rock on an island that was the most isolated spot on the planet. I was here until Boniface wanted to let me go. And he didn't say anything about that, but I knew he was not going to say it. He was going to give me to Bernadette.

I knew that, too, the second I saw her. She locked her eyes on to me and it nearly knocked me back a step.

I tried to look back. Then I tried to look away. It didn't matter to Bernadette. She just kept watching me. She didn't even blink. By the time I pulled my eyes off her, the crate was open. Boniface was hopping like a kid on Christmas, telling his guys careful, easy, *merde*, watch it, and then they had it out of the crate.

It didn't look like much, just a big, heavy roll of some kind of off-white something. The plastic solution had soaked in, set, and dried, and I had rolled it up for shipping with the painting side facing in. When it had been carefully unrolled, Boniface stood over it and looked it over. He walked around it, gazing intently, pausing to admire a detail here and there, before he finally nodded. "You did it," he said.

"Yes, I did," I said. "Surprised?"

"No," he said. "Astonished." He looked at me with the first real smile I'd seen on his face. "You are a truly remarkable man, Riley. A genius."

"Thanks," I said. I mean, what else would I say?

He was looking at the fresco again, with an expression somewhere between a man in love seeing his sweetheart and a fourteen-year-old kid seeing his first strip show. "It's truly amazing," he said. "So beautiful . . ." He just stared at it for a minute, and when he looked up again there was actually a tear at the corner of one eye. No, really—a tear. "It's wonderful," he said. "Thank you."

"You're welcome," I said. And because I was still feeling that rising sense of dread—feeling it stronger than ever now that I was facing Boniface and Bernadette—I added, "So I'd like to go home now . . . ?"

Bernadette made a noise in her throat that I can't describe. It was the kind of sound an apex predator makes when they see dinner standing in front of them, and if I hadn't known for sure before, I did now.

"I'm afraid not," Boniface said.

"Not?" I said. "I mean, I'd known it was coming, but—"What do you mean, 'not'?"

He shook his head. "I mean," he said, "that even

though I am incredibly grateful for what you have done, betrayal has a price. And even if I could forgive you—Bernadette could not." He smiled at her, and she practically purred at him. "And so, however much I might regret it—" He turned to the mercs and said, "Lock him up."

For a second I thought maybe I could talk him out of it. Just for a second; that's how long it took for his men to grab my arms, twist them behind my back, and start to march me away.

"Wait a goddamn minute!" I yelled. "I stole the fucking fresco for you—I even fucking delivered it! What the fuck is this?!"

"You did," Boniface said, and he was back to being all ice. He walked around the guards and stood in front of me. "And please note that I am very grateful and that I respect you, Riley. Because of this, I will not even ask you when Bailey Stone will arrive. You would not tell me, would you?"

I couldn't think of a single word to say. I didn't even stammer. He knew. He had probably known all along.

"I didn't think so," Boniface said. He nodded to the guards. "Take him."

CHAPTER

40

I knew I was in deep shit. I had accepted that, and I was already working on ways to get myself into the shallow end. That was before it all got worse—almost as worse as I could imagine, and believe me, I can imagine some very bad shit.

The first was this:

Benny had come along with the mercs who marched me to my cell. It turns out that wasn't so I'd have somebody to talk to. He came along to show me the sights.

The first tourist attraction was a real showstopper. About halfway down the last corridor that led to the cells, Benny called a halt in front of a door. It wasn't locked, barred, or even closed. It was just a door, and it was open. Benny turned to me and smirked. "This here is Bernadette's hobby room," he said. "It's gonna get real familiar for you." Still smiling, he peeked in the door. "Oh, jeez, I hope you don't mind company," he said. "She got somebody in there already."

He looked at me with a pretend-surprised face and gestured. "Take a look," he said.

I really didn't want to look. I had some kind of idea what I would see, and what it meant for me, and I didn't need to see it to be scared shitless. Besides that, I could hear sounds from inside—a kind of gurgling, mewling sound that wasn't like anything I'd ever heard before, or ever wanted to hear again. Just this weird, mindless rising and falling sound that was as far from human as it could be. I wasn't going to look. But one of the mercs gave me a shove, and I stumbled forward into the open doorway.

The first thing I saw was a worktable. There were a couple of big scoop lights hanging over it. They weren't turned on, so it was a little dim in there. I didn't see anybody, but the sound didn't stop, and something was strapped to the table. It was about the size of a large sofa cushion. There was a stainless steel table on the side. It had what looked like hedge clippers on it, and a couple of other tools I couldn't quite make out. I didn't see what was making the noise.

Benny reached around me, flipped a switch, and the lights came on, and I could see what was on the table. It was the thing making the strangled cat noise, and it was a nightmare.

I'm pretty sure it had started out as a human being. It was nothing like now. Arms, legs, nose, ears— everything had been snipped off. All that was left of it was the torso. It wriggled, helpless to do anything else. And the final touch? Its eyes were wide open, because the eyelids had been cut away. And hanging directly above the table, where the permanently open eyes could see everything—*had* to see everything—there was a large mirror.

A mirror. Sure. So every hideous, agonizing, permanent thing Bernadette does to you is right there in front of you in living color, and you can't look away. After all, where's the fun if you can't see what's going on?

I heard a kind of gagging, choking sound, followed by a weird high-pitched giggle. The gagging turned out to be me. The giggle was Benny. I turned away from the thing on the table, and he was right there in my face, showing teeth. "She likes to take it real slow," he said. "Cuts off one little piece at a time, cauterizes it. The fingers, one joint at a time—like I said, slow. So it lasts a long fucking time."

I couldn't think of a whole lot to say.

"That guy in there, he's the one was feeding info to Bailey Stone," Benny said with a snort. "Like we wouldn't find out? Fucking stupid, huh? Oh, hey, I don't mean nothing personal, you know, 'cuz that's kinda what you did?" He snickered. "Naw, this guy? He shoulda known better. But . . ." He shrugged. "What the fuck. He betrayed Mr. Boniface, we find out—of course we find the fuck out." He shook his head. "She fucking *hates* that." He nodded, still smiling. "Bernadette, I mean. She's real loyal, and if somebody betrays Mr. Boniface? Oooh." He gave a fake shiver, like he was overcome with horror. "So I gotta tell you?" He jerked his head at the wiggly thing on the table. "That's you in a couple of weeks." He winked. "Maybe she makes it last even longer if she really likes you."

He let me think about that for a minute before we moved on. It was still very much on my mind when Benny halted us in front of another cell and slid open the observation panel. "Mr. Boniface thought you'd like to see this, too," he said. And before I could decide if I was going to take a look, one of the mercs grabbed the back of my head and shoved my face up against the peek hole, hard enough that for a few seconds the only thing I saw was stars. When my head cleared and I could see again, I really wished I could go back to just seeing the stars. Because sitting inside the cell was something that dropped everything off the scale of awful into a whole new arithmetic.

The thing in Bernadette's playroom was about the worst thing I'd ever seen. Knowing they wanted to turn me into its twin kicked it way past that. But what I saw in this second room? It was even worse than that. Which sounds impossible, I know, but it was.

It was Monique.

Her face was bruised—puffy eyes, a big lump on one cheek—and she was holding one arm like it might be hurting a lot. Other than that, she just sat there on the stone shelf, chained to the wall, knees up to her chin.

Just sat there. Face empty of everything human. Didn't even look up to see what the thumping sound was when my head hit her door.

They had Monique.

Behind me I heard Benny laughing, and I lost it. I turned around and grabbed him by the throat. I lifted him off the ground and slammed his head against the wall, and I have to say I was fast, I hit hard, and he didn't expect it.

And of course, the reason he didn't expect it was pretty clear. It was because only an idiot would try anything with a bunch of hard-ass mercenaries standing by. Two seconds after I grabbed Benny they slammed their rifle stocks against my head and my kidneys and had me on the floor before I could really get going. Then they started kicking, probably so they wouldn't have to bend over. They were clearly very experienced at this whole kicking-the-shit-out-of-somebody move, because I stayed conscious for a good long time before one of them kicked me in the temple and it all went dark.

I have to say, it's almost always nice to know you're dealing with real professionals. It saves so much worry and so much time. You need the confidence of knowing that the people around you are good at what they do, experienced at doing it, and put everything into their work. And the guys working for Boniface fit the bill. They were so good that when I woke up, I didn't know where I was, and I couldn't figure it out because I was seeing double. My head was pounding like I had a *taiko* drummer on each temple, I couldn't breathe without pain, and my legs hurt like hell and pounded with a counterbeat to my skull. I didn't recognize either of the rooms my double vision showed me. For that matter, I wasn't really sure what my name was. I decided I should try to find out why these things were so, and I sat up.

It was one of the worst mistakes I ever made.

The first thing I did was to throw up, all over myself, my bed, everything within a five-foot radius. After that I sat there just hoping something would kill me quickly. I would have done it myself, but I couldn't move. Everything that merely hurt before was agony now—agony with a disco beat. I closed my eyes, which took every bit of strength I had.

It takes some time. If you have ever really and truly had the shit kicked out of you by people who know what they're doing and like doing it, you know what I mean. Nothing works for a while. Things won't come into focus—not objects, thoughts, memories . . . nothing. And you don't really give a rat's ass that they don't, because you are devoting all your willpower to trying to breathe, trying to make at least one of the pains go away.

Of course that doesn't work. The pain gets stronger. But eventually a little life comes back into you, just enough so you can whimper. When I got to that point, I opened my eyes.

The good news was that I wasn't seeing double anymore. The bad news was that I knew where I was, and

I remembered how I got here. I was on a nice firm stone mattress, chained to the wall, like I had been on my first visit to Île des Choux. Worse, Monique was in a room just like it.

I did a quick survey of damage. My right shoulder was sore as hell, but I could move it. Probably I'd fallen on it. No biggie, but there was no strength in it. I felt my head with both hands. It was mess. Both hands came away wet. There was bleeding on both sides, but on the left it was swollen up like a pumpkin, too. I probably had a concussion, and maybe there was some little interior bleeding thing that would knock me dead sometime in the next twenty-four hours. No way to know. But at least that would keep me off Bernadette's hobby shop table.

Breathing still hurt, so I prodded with my fingers. Three ribs definitely broken, one or two more maybe.

My left leg was stiff and hurt like hell, but my right was worse. I couldn't bend it at all. The knee was swollen so big it was threatening to bloat out and rip the pants leg.

I added it up: I could barely stand, and if I tried I might get so dizzy I'd fall on my face. If I did make it to my feet, I could only limp, and not fast. One arm, my right, was probably no good for anything more energetic than turning the pages of a comic book. All that aside, I was chained to a stone wall in the dungeon of an impregnable fortress surrounded by well-armed, well-trained people who wouldn't mind killing me. And somehow, I had to get out of my chains, get Monique, and get away, before a psychotic bitch from a bad 1950s horror movie chopped at me until I looked like a Thanksgiving turkey.

Sure. No problem. I would have laughed, except if I did I'd probably start bleeding internally.

I looked for something I'd missed, some small thing that might give me a tiny edge, a little bitty door, some slim possibility. Because I have lived my life by Riley's Golden Rule, the one that says there's always a way. And there was a way here, too. It was just really well hidden, and I was running out of time.

So things were about as bad as they could be, but I still had one tiny little hope. It wasn't much, but it was all I had. Bailey Stone was coming with his gang of professionals, who, I had to believe, were every bit as good as the psychopaths who worked for Boniface. And he would bring a lot of them, because he was attacking. Maybe even enough of them to win, even though Boniface knew they were coming. Probably not, but what the hell, that was all I had.

And I was pretty sure Stone hadn't come yet, because I could hear, just dimly, all the normal sounds of Île des Choux out in the hall. I couldn't tell how long it had been since I got beat and kicked into a different time zone. But unless I had been unconscious for ten or twelve hours, which I didn't believe, it was night outside. Nobody with enough sense to tie their own shoes would attack this place at night. That would multiply the odds against you, turn Not Likely into Forget It, Slim.

Bailey Stone couldn't possibly do that. He'd do the smart thing, the thing that everybody from Geronimo to Stormin' Norman believed in. He'd attack at dawn, when there was enough light to see but your enemy was still only half awake. He'd come in with the rising sun, guns blazing, ready to kick some serious ass.

So I had one very small flicker of hope that maybe, somehow, Stone might win and get me out of here. I mean, miracles happen, right?

Sure they do. But only in fairy tales.

I knew the odds against Stone were long. But there was a chance. I mean, unless he did something so stupid that it killed that tiny chance, too.

And guess what? That's exactly what Stone did.

Bailey Stone attacked at night. That should tell you everything right there—he attacked at *night*.

Lord knows I am no von Clausewitz. But I sure as shit knew better than that. Why is it so stupid? Think about it for a second. Stone's guys are outside, on the ocean, trying to take a hostile rock armed with every defensive weapon a top-dog arms dealer can think of. And the force they're attacking is where? *Underground.* Inside that rock. Where it is *always fucking dark*! So in the dark, they're going up against guys fucking *used* to the dark, top-notch pros who are on their home turf. Bailey Stone's guys, on the other hand, have never been here, don't really know what it looks like or where things are—things like weapons systems, for instance— and they attack in the *dark*.

Get the picture? Sure you do. Because you're not in

the dark in hostile, unfamiliar territory, like Bailey Stone.

I mean, seriously, why? All they had to do was pop Étienne, grab his boat, enter the code from the flash drive I gave them to turn off the security perimeter—come on. How hard do you have to make it? I love a challenge myself, but this? Even if they had surprise, which they thought they did, there were enough obstacles. So they made one more big one?

And Boniface knew they were coming. Maybe not when—I mean, he was probably just as surprised that they came at night. But then, Boniface was not stupid. He wouldn't guess that somebody who got big enough to challenge him was dumb enough to attack at night, because *he* wouldn't do it. But when it came? What the hell, batter up. Boniface was ready, and he was at home. He had all the advantages already. And Bailey Stone gave him the last big one by attacking in the dark.

It can't have been pretty. The sound of it was awful, and not just because it made my poor damaged head hurt even more. Shooting and explosions, followed by a whole lot of screaming. But you know what's worse than screams of pain? When the wounded suddenly stop screaming, and you know enough about the people involved to know why. Here's a hint: They didn't stop screaming because Boniface's mercs gave them a nice shot of morphine for the pain.

And when it was over, just in case I still had one tiny, practically invisible little flicker of hope, I heard a couple of guys go by, laughing and talking. I listened hard, praying I might hear a Southern accent. That would mean Stone had won, I was saved, I could get Monique out of here—

When everything is at its darkest and you catch yourself hoping—don't. Seriously, just don't. Bad idea, always. It just makes things darker when whatever stupid miracle you were hoping for doesn't happen. Because it doesn't. It never does. And it didn't this time.

The voices I heard were speaking French. Boniface's guys. Stone got his ass handed to him. Duh.

Riley's Seventeenth Law: Miracles don't happen.

Just to make sure I didn't miss this important and obvious law of nature, a face appeared in the little barred window set in my cell door. I looked up and saw the face and I did not find it comforting that somebody was checking up on me. Because the face belonged to Bernadette. She was looking at me with the nightmare side of her face, and I was pretty sure that was on purpose. She pushed it right up against the bars, and she started to whisper at me in French. Nothing much; just tender little endearments, words like you might say to your lover when you have a hot evening planned.

They always say that French is the language of love, or at least of sex. And to be perfectly fair, the things Bernadette whispered at me really did sound sexy. I mean, if you just heard the words and didn't see the face. Maybe you could even stretch it a little and say yeah, she really was talking about sex.

Except I always thought of sex as involving pleasure, and what she was actually saying was about as far from

pleasure as I could imagine. At least for me; the look
on that half-melted face told me she was going to have
one major orgasm after another when she got around
to me.

It went on for a couple of minutes. I mean, she was
enjoying the hell out of it. It was her foreplay, I guess.
I couldn't do anything but sit and listen and wish I
didn't speak French. But finally, she left, and I could go
back to being completely overwhelmed by misery, pain,
and terror—which, to be honest, was kind of a relief
after Bernadette.

It was over. All of it. It had been a pretty good run,
but I was at the finish line. We all have to go sometime,
but it seemed way too bad that it was so soon. And
even worse that I had to drag Monique down with me.
I mean, who knows? Maybe we would've finally gotten
something together. It didn't have to be permanent.
Who needs kids, house in the suburbs, PTA meetings,
all that shit? I had just been hoping for somebody to
hold on to now and then.

Maybe I could've found some miracle new treatment for Mom, too. Something that would make her
sit up, blink, and say, "Well now, what on *earth*?" That
would've been nice.

And maybe one last big score. I had my eye on a
couple of very cool things that would look really good
on my score sheet.

But fuck it, that was all over, everything. All dead,
because I was. Or I would be pretty soon. I mean, not
that soon, apparently. There was the formality of a cou-

ple of weeks of unbelievable agony first. After that, though; boom. Lights out. Everything all gone forever and ever. That was all of it, all that was left. Bye, Riley. Exit stage down and out. This time, there was no way.

And then I heard shots.

CHAPTER
41

Frank Delgado was tired.

He was tired of the weather; it was supposed to be summer here, but the wind that seemed to blow over them constantly had a sharp edge to it that reminded him of Chicago. Storms came up out of nowhere, and although their violence was familiar to Delgado, who had grown up in South Florida, these storms also seemed to have that same cold edge to them, and that made them feel wrong.

He was also tired of the unchanging blankness of their surroundings at this most remote outpost. There was nothing but rock, a couple of buildings—including a hangar—and the unending roll of the waves. It was all *French* blankness, too, which made it seem even more alien, more like the landscape of a different planet.

And connected to that, he was tired of hearing

French spoken. That seemed petty and un-woke even to him, but it was true. As someone who grew up hearing Spanish spoken at home, he found French a special torment. He could almost recognize some of the words—*merde* was *mierda,* for example. But how was *eau* any relation at all to *agua?* And even with words that were close, the pronunciation was off just enough to tease him without actually delivering meaning.

Frank Delgado was just as tired of the members of his own task force. He'd been cooped up with them for three weeks. He was not, at the best of times, a social man. In this situation, crammed together with the others, trying to stay out of sight as much as possible, his minimal social skills were pushed beyond their limits; all the standard jokes had become tired, annoying; and all the daily routines of eating, sleeping, and so on were so tiresome and repetitive they made his teeth hurt. Living in close quarters with these people, and with the French team, on a knife-edge of tension, waiting endlessly for something with no way of knowing when, or even if, it was coming—it had all become an exhausting chore just to get by every day.

But most of all, Frank Delgado was *physically* tired, for the simple reason that he was not sleeping more than two or three hours a night, because he did not want to miss it when the signal came. It had been his confidential informant who said the perimeter defense on Île des Choux would go down. If it did not—if this whole trip was no more than a colossal waste of time and money for *two* different governments—it was all on him. As time stretched on and nothing happened, the weight of that responsibility became crushing. This, too, added another level of exhaustion.

So Delgado waited and watched, with fading hope, sometimes dozing in the metal chair. And because he was so tired, on so many levels, he almost missed it when it finally came.

It was night. Delgado had dozed briefly once or twice and had lost track of the time, but it was dark outside and had been for a while. He was in his usual place, in a corner of the hangar that had been walled off into a small room. There was always some activity there, because the room held all the team's electronic monitoring equipment. Several technicians from both teams sat there 24/7, watching the monitors to sound the signal when the defensive perimeter of Île des Choux went down.

They also watched the radar screen for any signs of traffic in the vicinity. They had been told that Bailey Stone was coming, but there was no way to know when. There had been a couple of false alarms—a cargo ship once, and then a tanker—but it was not a well-traveled area. Boredom was a problem, fatigue from being on high alert and from watching for something that would not come.

Delgado tried to keep his confidence alive. Sooner or later, he had to believe that Stone's strike force would hit Boniface. As the days turned into weeks, he was less sure, but he stayed here in the nerve center, sitting in a battered metal chair. He was not on duty, not watching the screens and dials. He was, rather, slumped over at the back of the room. It had become his post, the place where he waited and watched. And he was falling asleep. He had just decided to get up and stretch his legs when one of the French techs jerked forward and held up a hand. Before Delgado could really register what that meant, the Frenchman tore off his headset and said, "Le périmètre est ouvert!"

Delgado blinked, once more feeling resentment at the French language. *Périmètre* was obviously *perimeter*. And *ouvert*—it was over? What did that mean? Perimeters can't be over. No, that had to be wrong. *Ouvert* had to mean something else, like—

Wait.

The French troopers were jumping up. Was it possible? Delgado fought through the fog of sleep that had been settling over him and tried to think. *Ouvert*—could it be? Did it mean—

Yes, it did. The Frenchmen on duty were all on their feet, obviously excited. One of them, a man Delgado knew as Mercier, looked at Delgado, jerked his head toward the door, and said, "It is now, Frank! We go now!" and then hurried out the door. *Open*, Delgado thought. Ouvert *means open. The perimeter is open.*

And before Frank knew what he was doing, he was on his feet and out the door, too.

The inside of the hangar quickly turned from an uninhabited dead zone to a beehive of activity. The two teams, FBI and French, came in at a run, some of them still pulling on clothing or finishing sandwiches as they ran. Men scrambled in all directions to find equipment. Delgado managed to locate his assault rifle, pull on his flak jacket, and get to his place on the lead chopper. And ten minutes after the alert, the four helicopters of the joint team were in the air and headed for Île des Choux.

They flew low, just above the waves. The half-hour trip over the dark ocean seemed much longer. But finally, there it was ahead of them. Île des Choux. The choppers circled once as they descended, and Delgado could see wreckage in the surf, bobbing wildly in the rough waters; chunks of material that had come from boats, and here and there something that had to be all or part of a human being. It was obviously the detritus of a failed assault, and also obvious that Stone's attack was already over.

That was troubling. A surprise assault should have lasted a lot longer. No matter how well armed and well prepared Boniface's force might be, if they'd been caught unaware, the attackers should have gained a foothold, moved forward, and the fighting should still be going on. There were no signs that this was the case.

If it was over—who had won? If Boniface, would the defenders be back on guard, all their lethal systems ready for more? Delgado glanced up front to the cockpit. SAC Finn was there, conferring with Bertrand Bouchard and one of the French technicians. After a quick and heated discussion, they separated. Bouchard spoke to the pilot, and the chopper began its final approach. Finn came back, and raising his voice to be heard over the engine noise, he called, "It's a go! Lock and load!"

Delgado breathed a sigh of relief. They must have determined that the perimeter was still *ouvert*. Most likely the defenders, relaxing after their victory, had simply not turned it back on yet. They were going in— he would finally come face-to-face with Riley Wolfe. And, of course, Bailey Stone and Boniface.

The helicopters came in on the island's central plateau, picking out the best landing zone with their spotlights. The plateau was flat, and they found a good spot quickly. It was close to their target—American infrared satellite imaging and French intelligence had determined that there were several hatches there, for service access to the weapons systems on top, and possibly for emergency exit.

All four choppers came down quickly and the members of the joint team leapt out. The FBI's CIRG strike force leader, Fleming, ran forward with his French counterpart, a dark and wiry man named Delacroix. They sprinted to the nearby access hatch and knelt, dropping two large packs to the ground beside them. Working quickly and efficiently, they pulled explosive charges from the packs, wired them to the hatch, and ran back, waving for everyone to take cover. The rest of the team crouched down in what cover they could find, and a moment later the charges blew.

From his secure spot behind a boulder, Delgado watched as a large metal hatch cover shot straight up into the air. It came down on the far side of the plateau, which Delgado thought was either outstanding skill by Fleming and Delacroix or, more likely, really good luck. The two demolition men ran forward to look, waved an all clear, and SAC Finn jumped up. "Let's do it!" he called.

With the rest of the team, Delgado jumped up. His ears were still ringing, but that didn't matter. He ran forward to the opening where the access hatch had been moments before and looked in. It was even darker than the night around him. Dimly he could see a ladder leading down into the interior. But vision ended only about ten feet down, and the ladder vanished into complete darkness.

A French trooper jostled him from behind, whispering urgently, "Allons-y!" Delgado didn't need a translation; he slung his assault rifle around to his back and went down into darkness.

Monique had given up hope days ago. Maybe weeks; she had no idea how long she had been here. There was no way to measure time in this unchanging damp, dim stone cell, and she had stopped trying. What was the point? She was here, she would die here, and how long she waited for that certainty didn't really matter.

When she first got here she had made one brief, very stupid attempt to get away. It had lasted only a few seconds, but the beating it brought on lasted for what seemed like hours. She didn't try again.

There was no reason for hope. No one knew she was

here, and no one was coming to save her. So she sat. She waited. Out of boredom more than hunger, she ate the green slop they brought her. Other than that, nothing changed. The monotony became just another layer of pain for Monique to shut out. Gradually, she fell into a hopeless slump, in which she would simply stare at her hands. When they brought her meals, she no longer even looked up. What did it matter?

And then one day—one night? no way to tell—she heard gunfire, shouting, explosions.

It took a few minutes for the sounds to break through the choking cloud of hopelessness and indifference Monique had built. But finally, the sounds registered. There was fighting going on. Could it mean rescue?

She tried to clamp down on the hope that flickered inside her, but she couldn't stop a small flame from glowing. Fighting meant change. Any change at all had to be better, didn't it?

Monique raised her eyes to the small barred window in the door and waited. The shooting stopped. Soon after, she heard voices. They sounded happy, triumphant. And they were the same voices she'd been hearing all along.

Nothing had changed. She was still locked up here, waiting to die.

And then she heard more shooting, more shouts and screams and explosions. This time, she didn't bother to look up. It was just more of the same. There was no reason to think it meant anything to her. She slumped back into the gray ache of despair. She didn't even look up later when the cell door opened. Not even when she heard the slow footsteps of someone coming in.

Not until she heard the voice.

"Come with me if you want to live," it said.

B enny was no longer nervous. Now he was scared shitless.

He'd been riding high, along with all the other guys who worked for Mr. Boniface. Big bad Bailey Stone had come with a small army, and they'd been waiting, ready. It hadn't even been a contest. They'd come pouring into the tunnel from their boats, and they'd walked right into Mr. Boniface's traps. It had been a turkey shoot. Bang, bang, bang, all fall down. It was almost mean, to knock off those poor bastards. They never had a chance.

Mercenaries are human, too, and when it was over, when they realized what an easy win it was, well, shit. Of course they wanted to celebrate a little. Most of the guys broke open a bottle or two, and Benny joined them. He even made a joke out of it, saying that he needed a drink or two—his trigger finger was sore from popping so many of Stone's clowns.

So nobody was expecting it, and nobody was ready, when the Feds came pouring down from up top.

And it had been a turkey shoot again—but this time Benny and Mr. Boniface's guys were on the wrong end of it. The guys started giving up, throwing down their weapons, flinging their hands up and shouting, "Ne tirez pas! Je me rends!" *Don't shoot! I surrender!*

The mercs were professional soldiers. They knew when it was over, and they knew what kind of treatment they could expect as hired guns; nothing like as serious as what Mr. Boniface would get. Most of them had been in this situation before. All of them knew that a few years in the slammer was better than a nine millimeter between the eyes.

For Benny, it was a different story. He was right up there close to the top, one of Mr. Boniface's top guys. Besides that, he had a rap sheet a mile long, and it included some very heavy shit. If Benny was captured, he had a real simple choice: do the stand-up thing and spend the rest of his life in prison, or rat out Mr. Boniface and die a whole lot sooner.

So he did what anybody in his position would have done. He panicked.

There were two possible escape routes out of this place. One was the shaft that led up top, to the island's central plateau. But that was the way the Feds had come in, so that was out. The other way was down the tunnel to the docks, maybe grab a boat—but two steps down that way and he ran into a crowd of Feds. He ducked back before they saw him, but it didn't matter. That way was out, too.

Which left nothing but give up or go down fighting.

There had to be another way. Thinking furiously, Benny retreated. But one passage after another was flooded with Feds. Slowly, step by step, he moved backward, deeper into the heart of the island, scrabbling for some kind of break, or an idea for how to make one. But finally, he was at the last tunnel, the one that led to the cells, and there was no way out of there.

And it hit him. Maybe there was.

He turned down this last passage and ran toward the end.

Giving up completely is not as easy as it sounds. Some dim-witted, thoughtless asshole always seems to come along and try to give you one more hope. I'd been sitting there trying to give up for hours, and it kept happening.

First, Bailey Stone's stupid attack. I knew it would fail, but I hoped anyway. And when it was over and I tried to give up again, the second attack came. This one sounded different, and when it was over I thought maybe it had succeeded, so I hoped again. I mean, if it was who I thought it was, it meant I was only going to get stuck in another cell somewhere. But at least it would have better food, and a complete lack of Bernadette. And I'd found a way out of some pretty tough prisons in the past.

So I hoped again. I really didn't want to, but that stupid little spark jumped up and I couldn't snuff it out. I hoped, and when I heard somebody fumbling to open my cell, I was still hoping.

And then Benny slipped in. He closed the door behind him and turned toward me, a Glock 17 in his hand. I was pleased to see he had some purple marks on his neck from where I'd grabbed him. But it didn't slow him down. He stepped right over and held it to my head. "You're coming with me," he said. "So shut the fuck up and don't try any stupid shit." For emphasis, he poked me with the pistol, hard, right on the great big goose egg I'd gotten from my beating the last time I saw him.

I shut up, and I didn't try stupid shit, as he unlocked my shackles. He pulled me up to my feet, the pistol always right on the same tender spot. Even if I felt like trying stupid shit, he was a pro. He didn't give me any openings.

"Hands on top of yer head," he said. "Out the fuckin' door."

I did what he said. I mean, there wasn't a lot of choice. But I knew that whatever he had in mind, somewhere along the way there would be a chance. Hope again. So I went along down the corridor, Benny right behind me, Glock on my head. With my knee swollen up, my right leg was almost useless, so walking was painful, and hard to do convincingly. So I didn't move too fast. Benny didn't like that, and he kept prodding me with the Glock, urging me to go faster. I did what I could, and we moved along in silence until we came to the main passageway, and there Benny stopped.

"How this works," he said. "You're my ticket outa here, awright?"

"Jesus, seriously?" I said. "Nobody gives a shit about me."

Benny chuckled and jabbed my goose egg at the same time. "No, they don't," he said. "But I seen a coupla guys with FBI on their vests. And I got a hunch they want you alive."

"More like dead or alive," I said.

He poked me again. "We're gonna give it a shot, so shut the fuck up," he said.

Riley's Brand-New Law: Better to give it a shot than to get shot. I shrugged and took another painful step forward. Benny stayed behind me, poking me forward with the Glock.

And then there was a soft, strange noise behind me, kind of a wet crunch. Something red shot past me and went *shplat!* on the floor.

And Benny fell face forward. I mean, literally right on his face. *Thump.*

And you know what? This is really stupid, and I have no defense. But it's true. It happened again. I saw Benny lying there in a puddle of blood, absolutely dead, and—

I felt hope.

Really; it jumped up in me one more time. I mean, seriously—was I just too stupid to live? Hope? Come on, Riley. In any case, at least it didn't last very long. Only until I turned around to see what had snuffed Benny. That's when all the hope died.

Bernadette.

Smiling that let's-see-what's-inside-you smile.

See you later, hope.

She stood there holding a small dagger, still dripping Benny's blood and totally ready to put some of mine on there with it. I took a step backward, away from her, and my bad knee made me stumble and wave my arms like an idiot to keep from falling over.

Bernadette's smile just got bigger, like she was a half-melted Cheshire cat—if you can picture a Cheshire cat that wants to cut you open and strangle you with your own intestines. "Tu es blessé, mon petit amour," she whispered. *You are hurt, my little love.* And she seemed to salivate at the thought that there was no way I could run and no way I could fight her except really feebly. She took a small step toward me. "Viens à moi, mon chéri." Another small step. She raised her knife. "Je vais—"

"Laissez tomber le couteau!" The voice was loud, commanding, and no more than ten feet behind me. I didn't even have time to think about looking. But quicker than thought, Bernadette threw her knife. Almost as quickly, there was a loud gunshot that took Bernadette in the shoulder and spun her around and to the floor.

I turned now. A large man wearing a flak jacket that read "DGSE" on it in big gold letters was on one knee. He held an assault rifle in one hand. His other hand was at his throat, plucking feebly at the handle of Bernadette's knife. I turned back to Bernadette. She was still on the floor, unmoving. It looked like my luck had just come in. Maybe I should have reconsidered my attitude toward hope. Because all of a sudden it looked like I had a chance to get out of here in one piece.

I didn't check either one of them for a pulse, and I didn't even think about calling for help. I just grabbed the French trooper's rifle, pulled off his flak vest, and turned back down the corridor to the cells and hobbled away as fast as I could, stopping for just two seconds to grab the keys from Benny's body. Then two seconds more, because the keys were lying in the puddle of blood and I had to wipe them off on his shirt.

Limping as fast as I could, I went to the door of Monique's cell and opened it. She looked like she was in rough shape. I mean, not physically, except for the bruises I'd seen before. I mean mentally. Monique didn't have my experience with this kind of crap. She had given up already. She didn't even look up when I came in.

So I couldn't help myself. "Come with me if you want to live," I said. And I did it in my best Arnold Schwarzenegger imitation, which I know is wrong, but what the hell.

Monique looked up. For a minute she just stared at me with dead eyes in a dead face. And then she blinked. "Idiot," she said. "Kyle Reese says that, not the Terminator."

Just like that, Monique had come back to life.

CHAPTER

42

The sun was coming up over the Indian Ocean. Mercier, one of the French troopers, had said that New Zealand was over that way, around 7,700 kilometers east of Île des Choux. Delgado blinked into the rising sun and tried to convert that to miles in his head. Over three thousand—almost four? A long way. He was too tired to remember whether a mile was 2.2 kilometers, or the other way around.

It didn't matter. What mattered was that the operation had been a huge success. They'd swept into the fortress inside Île des Choux and caught the defenders completely by surprise, overwhelming them quickly and with very light casualties. Boniface was in French custody, and Bertrand Bouchard and the men of his DGSE strike force were extremely pleased.

And Bailey Stone was in the hands of the FBI's

CIRG medics. He had two serious wounds, but he would probably live to face prosecution. All the surviving mercenaries from both sides, about half of them wounded, had been rounded up, sorted out, and bound with plastic zip ties. So SAC Finn was just as happy as his French counterpart. It was over, all wrapped up neatly, and they could go home knowing they'd done a very good job against long odds. A complete success.

Except . . .

Delgado had found no sign of Riley Wolfe.

He had definitely been here. Delgado had interviewed several of the captured mercenaries, and they all said, yes, Wolfe had been here, down in the cells. Delgado had gone to the cells and found them all empty. He had carefully examined all the captured mercenaries, looking for any sign that one of them was Wolfe in disguise. None of them were. He had just as carefully looked at all the dead and wounded. And again, he found nothing.

And so Delgado had gone through the entire interior of Île des Choux, searched all the rooms as carefully as he could, and still he found no trace of Riley Wolfe.

As a last forlorn hope he had come here, to the plateau on top of the island. There was a great deal of activity at the landing area—the makeshift field hospital was there, as well as a roped-off holding area for the prisoners. All he had found was a sunrise over the ocean.

Riley Wolfe had slipped away. Again. But how?

The answer didn't come until an hour and a half later. Delgado was with SAC Finn preparing to transport Bailey Stone back to the French base and then to Cape Town for transport back to the States. Special Agent Rosemond was with them, since she would accompany Stone all the way home. SAC Finn asked Delgado to talk to Bouchard about using one of their choppers, and Delgado half turned to comply—

"Choppers are expensive," Rosemond said. "We should have sent the bastard back on that boat."

Delgado froze.

"What boat?" Finn said.

"It went back about an hour ago? For medical supplies?"

Delgado turned around. "Who was on that boat?" he said in a fierce whisper.

Rosemond actually took a step back, a look of surprise on her face. "A French guy, and a woman with him. A black woman?" she said.

"You saw this?" Delgado demanded.

"Yeah, sure I saw it," she said, sounding a little defensive. "Agent Benito and I were down there, making sure the boats were all secure? And this guy and the woman came out on the dock—he was limping, so—"

"How do you know he was French?"

"He, uh, he had the accent. And he was wearing the DGSE flak jacket," she said.

Delgado turned away, feeling sick. Of course he had a French accent. Riley Wolfe was fluent in French. Getting the DGSE jacket would be a simple matter of stripping it from one of the casualties. And then on to the boat and Riley Wolfe slipped away from him *again*.

For a moment Frank Delgado closed his eyes and let the despair wash over him. He wanted to sit down and cry himself to sleep. But then the thought came back to him, the thing that could keep him going, calm his pain, and sustain him all the way home. He took a deep breath and opened his eyes.

We still have his mother, he thought. *And he will come for her.*

And something very close to a smile came onto his face.

I have always believed that when your luck is in you should ride it until it runs out. And my luck was in— all the way in. I thought it might have come back when Benny had taken me out of the cell. Because once I was unchained I had a chance. And when Bernadette got shot—and at the same time took out the DGSE guy who would have put me right back in chains—then I was sure. My luck was in.

And I rode it. All the way to Monique. I kept riding it all the way down the long corridor to the docks. There were Feds everywhere, FBI and French. But they were busy rounding up the mercs, disarming them, herding them away, and nobody had any idea of stopping a limping guy in a DGSE vest who spoke perfect French.

I had already figured that the only way out would be

by boat. We got all the way to the dock with no problem, and my luck gave me one more gift. Étienne's boat was there, tied off sloppily where Stone's guys had left it. They'd had to lead the way with it, since it had the electronics to get them in. I can handle just about anything that floats, but it was always nice to have a familiar boat when you were in a hurry.

There were a couple of FBI pogues on the dock who gave me a look. One of them, a woman, wanted to know what we were doing. In a really convincing French accent, I told her we were going back for more medical supplies and would return soon. She let us go.

And finally, my luck rode with us out the channel into the open ocean with no problem at all.

And then we were on our own.

Monique had been having a hard time keeping up with her own life. In the first place, it felt like it hadn't actually been *hers* for way too long. Ever since Riley had showed up with his I-have-a-problem-and-you're-in-it speech, and then talked her into the craziest *bullshit* she'd ever heard of. She hadn't felt like it was even *her* through all the wildly dangerous and completely insane crap that happened after that—the trip to Rome, the terrifying disguise and trip back, and then escaping to Frankfurt, the Adirondacks, and then *boom!* right back into the sewer. It had all been totally out of her control. For way too long she'd been spinning around in somebody else's crazy circles, hit by wild, random shots that sent her careening off in another unknown direction.

So once Riley had steered them out of the tunnel and away onto the ocean, Monique let herself relax. For the first time in weeks, she could take a deep breath of free air as *herself*. She did, and it felt wonderful. Staring out off the back of the boat at the rough waves of the Indian Ocean, she could believe that she was out of danger at last. Oh, she was well aware that there was another leg to run, and she had no doubt that Riley would somehow manage to make it a lot wilder and more hazardous than it had to be. But it would be normal hazards, and not wearing somebody else's face while running from gangs of psychotic killers with automatic weapons, or being chained to the wall in the dungeon of fortified secret underground hideouts—that crazy shit was over at last. And whatever misadventures might come on this last part of the long, strange trip, Monique had an illogical confidence that somehow Riley would steer them through it and get them home.

There was a distant rumble of thunder, and Monique turned her head to the front, where the sound was coming from. A low line of black clouds was gathering on the horizon. But it was just a storm; it didn't seem threatening, not after the last few weeks of hell. So she sat and enjoyed her return to her own life for a while. The sound and movement of the boat, the rolling waves, it all felt soothing and sane. It reminded her of the time she'd gone with Riley to his private island.

That trip hadn't been all sunshine, lollipops, and rainbows, but it had been a mostly good time—and she had been *her* every second; Monique, herself, a strong and capable woman who didn't need anybody else and didn't take shit from anybody. Now, at long last, she could go back to being that person again. She could make her own choices again—do nothing if she wanted, and even decide when to eat, when to go to the bathroom.

And come to think of it, now would be a good time for that.

Monique stood up, stretched, took one last deep breath of the fresh salt air, and looked at Riley. He was hunched over the wheel, his glance flicking from the water ahead of them to what she supposed was the GPS screen. "Can I assume there's some kind of restroom downstairs?" she asked him.

"Downstairs is *below,* and the restroom is a *head,*" he said.

Monique shook her head. "Isn't it nice? Things are getting back to normal."

"What? What does that mean?" he said without looking.

"I feel like killing you again," she said. "Since you know what I mean, why the *fuck* does it matter what I call the bathroom?" she said.

"It's hallowed naval tradition," he told her.

"Well, unless peeing on the deck is also hallowed tradition—is there a restroom downstairs?"

"First door on the right," he said.

"Door?" she said. "It doesn't have some sort of arcane name like hatch, or porthole?"

"It's all right," he said. "Since I know what you mean."

Monique flipped him the finger and climbed down the ladder from the cockpit. The door, or whatever it was called, to the downstairs part of the boat, or *below,* was to the right of the ladder. Monique stepped off the ladder and pulled the latch. Nothing; the door was stuck. She pulled harder. Still nothing.

Monique took a step back and tilted her head up toward the cockpit. "Riley?" she called. "This door is—"

The door leapt open and from inside a figure jumped at her so fast she had time only to register that it had a nightmare mask for a face—and then something moved in a blur and slammed into her head, and—

CHAPTER

43

I like to think I am good with boats. I've put in my time on everything from canoes to square-rigged sailboats, and a boat like this one didn't really throw anything at me I couldn't handle. It was big, and it tended to wallow a little, but it was built for these waters, and that's what mattered. And under ordinary circumstances, I could have handled it with absolutely no problem.

But if you've spent time on any body of water bigger than a duck pond, you know that there's always a problem. Something that comes at you out of nowhere and knocks you for a loop. When you're in unknown waters—and a totally unknown ocean—then the WTF factor is multiplied.

On top of that, we were headed right into a squall line. It was dead ahead, no way to avoid it. Or anyway, it would have been a squall line in waters I knew about.

I didn't have a clue what kind of storm might blow up here, but I didn't think it would be gentle spring rain. I had thousands of miles of open ocean on all sides, and that makes the wind stronger, the waves bigger, and the uh-ohs a whole lot scarier. And I could already feel the wind picking up and the rollers getting higher.

So I was staying totally busy doing nothing more than keeping us on course without hitting a wave wrong and taking on water. It took concentration, and that was harder than it should have been right now. I mean, I was just a few hours past getting the crap kicked out of me. My head was still throbbing, and every now and then things would swim out of focus and get far away for a few seconds.

So I admit that I wasn't paying as much attention to Monique as I should have. I heard her shout something, but I figured it had to be "Where's the toilet paper?" or "How do I flush?" Something like that. Maybe I should have listened. But what the hell, if she couldn't find the bathroom and pee by herself, she needed more help than I could give her. And she must have found everything okay, because I heard her coming back up the ladder again pretty soon.

Maybe *too* soon . . . ?

Like I said, my brain was still not all the way back online. It was moving a little slow. Too slow to figure out that, yeah, Monique *was* back again too soon, so that must mean—

I half turned away from the wheel, but way too late. She was on me before I could even blink.

I caught a half glimpse of the melted face, and below that a blood-soaked shirt that made her seem even scarier. She smashed into me, jamming me back against the wheel. And then she had her knife at my throat, bending me backward. I could feel the edge of her blade against my throat and the small tickle of blood running down my neck, and I waited for the savage slash that would open my artery and bleed me out.

It didn't come.

Instead, Bernadette held the knife edge tight against my throat for several long seconds. Then she hissed and leaned her face closer to mine. "J'ai besoin de toi vivant, petit prince," she whispered. "Pour l'instant . . ."

It was wonderful to hear that she needed me alive, even if only for now. But I had a pretty good hunch it wouldn't last too long. As soon as I did whatever she needed me for, it would be lights-out for Riley.

And Monique! Was she still in the head? Bernadette probably wouldn't "need" her. Would she come back up and—or had Bernadette already—

I didn't get more than a few seconds to wonder before Bernadette was chaining me to the wheel—the same chain Étienne had used on me my first trip to Île des Choux. I could still spin the wheel, awkwardly, but I wasn't going anywhere.

Bernadette thought so, too. She stepped back away from me, gave me the once-over, and put the knife away. She leaned for a moment against the bulkhead, and I got my first good look at her. She was a mess. Even through the savage scarring of her face, I could

see the exhaustion lines, around her eyes and on the
unscarred part of her forehead. She looked like she
needed a couple of days of sleep. But I had seen her get
shot. She should have been dead. And she had definitely lost a lot of blood. That makes anybody weak,
dizzy, sleepy.

But Bernadette was on her feet, and she was still fast
and strong enough to handle me with no problem.
How was that possible? I had seen the shot hit her, spin
her around, and drop her.

I took a couple of quick looks, and when I added
them up I could see why. I thought the shot had taken
her in the shoulder, but Bernadette had been moving
when it hit. She'd torn the sleeve away on that side, and
I could see where the bullet had clipped her on the
outside of the shoulder instead. Hard enough to knock
her over and soak through the shirt. Unfortunately, not
hard enough to finish her off.

Bernadette straightened up and took a Glock from
her waistband, probably taken from Benny, judging by
the dried blood on it. She gestured at me with the pistol. "Où est la radio?" she said.

I tipped my head to the right. The VHF radio was
in easy reach, even for somebody chained to the wheel.

"Bien," she said. She gestured again. "Soyez un bon
garçon et faites ce que je dis." She gave me a frequency
and told me what to say—and I thought about calling
out a Mayday instead. I gave that up in under two seconds. There was nobody to answer it out here, except
the FBI and DGSE, and I was not eager to talk to

them. Anyway, it would take them maybe an hour to get here—if they could find me at all. It's not as easy as you might think to find a small boat on a big ocean, even when you know approximately where it is. As far as I could see it, my only chance was to do exactly what Bernadette said and hope for some small opening. She scared the hell out of me, but she was beat to shit, and I thought I could take her out if I got half a chance. Until then, it seemed like a good idea to be a good boy. I picked up the microphone.

She had me call Boniface's guys at the little hangar where he kept his jet. Repeating her word for word, I told them to get the plane ready and meet us at the dock. They wanted to know why. Bernadette snatched the microphone from me and told them why: Because she said so. They didn't argue anymore after that.

And then she sat on the bench, just out of my reach. Her back was to the open deck below, and her eyes were on me. Behind her and just to the side I could see the big cargo hook Étienne had used to load and unload the boat. It was run all the way up now, of course, so it wouldn't swing. Beyond that, the boat's wake churned and burbled. I couldn't see any of the deck below us. If Monique was there, living or dead, I would have to step back until I was just about in Bernadette's lap before I could see. I wasn't eager to try that.

And anyway, Bernadette caught me looking. She half stood, waved the gun at me, and said, "Allons-y!" in a tone of voice that could scare the stink out of a skunk. I went.

I watched her for the next half hour, quick glances out of the corner of my eye. Not because I admired her profile. Like I said, she'd lost a lot of blood. On top of that, she'd just done a few things that would make anybody tired, even if they were in the peak of health. She'd been running on adrenaline, and even though it had gotten her here, alive and in charge, there had to be a letdown now. All the adrenaline would be burned off. The excitement of her escape and jumping me—that was all over. She was safe for the time being. She had to be feeling a major letdown, right? A little nap would start to look like a really good idea about now, wouldn't it?

So I watched her, looking for any small sign that she wasn't all aboard mentally. At first, nothing. She kept her eyes open and the Glock pointed at me. Once or twice it wavered and she nodded forward a little and I thought maybe she would fall asleep or black out. No such luck. Each time she jerked upright again.

But it had to come. She had to reach the point when she nodded, dozed just for a second, didn't she? I mean, any human being who had gone through what Bernadette had gone through would just absolutely have to nod off now, and she was, after all, human—wasn't she? Underneath there somewhere, maybe?

Maybe not. Over the next hour she sagged a few more times, but she always snapped right back up again. I kept watching, but it started to matter less. Because over that same hour, something else was happening, and it had given me an idea. With just one little break, that idea could turn into a plan.

Remember that storm I was worried about? The one headed straight for our boat? It was coming closer, and it was looking like it might be a rough one. And that was a very, very good thing—for me. With a little luck, it might not be quite as good for Bernadette. I just needed one small favor from the storm god. I tried to remember who that was in these waters, so I could ask politely. All I could come up with was Freyr, the Norse god of rain. I wasn't sure it would be a good idea to ask anybody from that group, not after what I'd done to Arvid on that statue of Njord. Njord couldn't have been happy about me getting all that gooey crap on his spear. Besides, Freyr was Njord's son, and gods hold a grudge a really long time. And anyway I was in the Indian Ocean—so was it the Hindu deity I should try for? Not Vishnu. Was it Indra? That felt right. How did I pray to Indra?

And why the hell was I thinking about that kind of crazy shit? I was about to get ripped apart by a psychotic monster, if the boat didn't go under in the coming storm. I pulled my focus back.

The storm was much closer. The boat had started to roll a lot more in the increasing swell. Normally, that would have worried me a little. Right now it was just what I wanted. If only Indra would step in and swing that roll just a few degrees to the right . . .

No such luck. Ten more minutes and it hadn't happened, and it looked like it wasn't going to. Maybe Indra had been talking to Njord. I was going to have to make this happen myself.

I glanced quickly at Bernadette. She was still doing her weird little dance—slump for a second, then jerk back upright. I looked back to the front, but I turned my body to a slight angle, so that every time she sagged I could see it out of the corner of my eye. And every time she did that, I slipped a hand down and toggled a little switch that was right there on the right side of the wheel. The one that controlled the cargo hook. You know, the hook on the end of that nice steel arm? The one that let down a cable so they could hoist big boxes on and off Étienne's boat?

Yeah, that was my idea. And if the hook started to swing just right, it might help me do something a lot more interesting than lifting boxes.

I let out the cable, two seconds at a time, five or six times. But I couldn't tell how much cable I'd unspooled. So the next time Bernadette slumped forward and closed her eyes, I risked a quick glance straight back. Just for a half second, but long enough.

The cargo hook was about halfway down, and the roll of the storm swell had it swinging. But right now it was swinging out over the right side of the boat, which did me no good at all. I'd been hoping that Indra or Freyr or somebody would turn the storm just a couple of degrees. They'd let me down. Or paid me back, whatever. Either way, I was going to have to make my own luck.

I looked at the GPS. If there hadn't been a storm in the way, we would be seeing our destination in a little while. It had to be now.

Slowly, just a tiny bit at a time, I started to ease the wheel to the left. It had to be so gradual Bernadette wouldn't see what I was doing—but quick enough to make it happen before our boat ride was over. And with it my life. And almost certainly Monique's, if that hadn't happened already.

I turned us as slowly as I could with my heart thumping like a Ginger Baker solo. Slowly, unnoticeably at first, the boat swung further into the wind . . .

Bernadette slumped again, and I took another look. The cargo hook was swinging faster, bigger arcs, and only a little bit off the line I needed it to take. I snapped my head forward again and eased us one more degree to the left. And the next time Bernadette sagged, I let out a little more cable. Then a little more . . .

I looked at the GPS. We were noticeably off course now but close enough so any break in the clouds would show the island, off to the side instead of straight ahead. The clouds were not breaking—they were getting bigger, darker, and closer. Storms on the open ocean can get worse faster than you can turn the wheel—but they can disappear just as fast, and if that happened and Bernadette saw how far off course we were, my guess was she would be unhappy. I had to do this soon—very soon.

Bernadette slumped. I let out a little more cable. Then I jerked around for a quick look—perfect. The cable was swinging the hook just right. And now if I could only—

I flicked my eyes down. Bernadette's eyes were open.

And she was looking right at me and watching me look backward.

She snarled and stood up and I thought she would come for me—but instead she whipped around, gun raised, to see what I had been looking at, and—

It was really rotten timing on her part.

The cargo hook—the nice, big, heavy, beautiful steel cargo hook—swung back with perfect timing and hit her dead between the eyes.

And Bernadette—superhuman, unstoppable, shoot-me-and-I-keep-coming Bernadette—dropped to the deck like a bag of cement.

I watched her for a few seconds, almost as stunned as she was. I couldn't believe something as simple as getting clobbered with a heavy steel hook could stop her. But it could. It did. She wasn't moving. She lay there on the deck and I couldn't tell if she was dead or alive, but she was definitely out of it, and that was all that mattered. The key to the chain that bound me to the wheel had to be right there in her pocket. And that raised a small problem.

Bernadette was right there—but "right there" was six feet away.

Stretched out as far as I could go, my chains only went about three feet.

I looked around, which I knew was useless. There was nothing in sight that could help me. I cursed Éti-enne. What kind of shitty sailor puts out to sea with no boat hook at hand? I mean, I know not to speak ill of the dead, and I was pretty sure he was, but seriously.

Everybody knows how important boat hooks are. Especially to me, right now.

But there wasn't one. Maybe Étienne would still be alive if he'd thought to have one handy. Served him right, the cheap-ass bastard.

Okay, deep breath; no boat hook. No nothing except me. Beat-up, half-broken Riley. It would have to be enough. Considering where I'd been over the last day, I was pretty proud of myself for saying it: There's always a way.

And there was. I dropped down onto the deck, which was harder than it should have been because my right leg wouldn't bend at all. I eased all the way down onto my stomach, so my whole body weight was hanging from the chain on my hands, yanking my arms half out of their sockets, and right away I learned something important. My left shoulder was in bad shape, too. For a minute the pain was so intense I thought I'd burst into tears. But instead, I stretched out on my stomach and worked my good leg toward Bernadette.

For once, something went right. I could get my leg over just far enough that I could lift it and drop the foot onto the center of her back, right between her shoulders. I raised the leg—and froze. If I dropped it onto Bernadette and it woke her . . .

But if I didn't do it, I was chained to the wheel and it was all over anyway. I had to do this.

Very slowly and carefully, and even gently, I laid my foot down on Bernadette's back. She didn't even twitch. Slowly, carefully, I flexed my foot, hooked it over her, and pulled.

It was slow, and it was hard work. Bernadette was a lot heavier than she looked, and the extra strain on my hurt shoulder was something special. But an inch or two at a time, I pulled her closer, closer—and finally close enough. I got a hand on her, dragged her all the way over, and stuck a hand in the pocket of her pants. There it was—the key. I pulled it out, stood up, and in a few more seconds I was free.

The storm had been getting stronger around us, and the boat was pitching a whole lot more than it should. Especially if I wanted to live a little longer. I did, so I had to get the boat back on course. Aside from stopping the severe motion of the boat, we needed to get safely into the dock that was just about a mile and a half away now. Because if I missed the island, the next stop was Antarctica, and I hadn't brought my long johns. I grabbed the wheel and swung us back on course.

And now, almost as important—I had to know about Monique.

I'd had no idea what happened to her and no way to find out until now, and this whole time it had been chewing at me. I mean, I cared about her more than I should. I needed her for my work. And goddamn it, we had unfinished personal business, too.

So I hobbled over to the ladder—

And I saw Monique.

She lay there on the deck in an unnatural position,

one arm twisted under her and the other flung out to the side. Her body was totally limp and rolled slightly with the motion of the boat, and she looked just about as dead as you can look.

My stomach shrank to a small ball of acid and I lunged for the ladder down—and almost did a swan dive to the lower deck, right onto my head, because of course my bad leg collapsed on me. I caught myself, slid down, and hobbled to Monique. I clumsied myself down to the deck beside her and felt for a pulse; nothing.

I bent over and put my head onto her chest. For an endless moment I couldn't hear a thing except the rising wind and the waves smashing into us. And then I heard it, faint and slow, but it was there—

Lub-dub.

Lub-dub.

Monique was alive.

I straightened up and examined her. There was a huge swelling on the side of her head that hadn't been there before. I peeled back her eyelids. The pupil of her right eye was dilated; the left one was not. I tried to remember what that meant—concussion? Or worse?

No way to know—and nothing I could do about it either way, except tuck her into a bunk and get her to a hospital ASAP. No problem—there was a bunk in the cabin, and a hospital only about . . . oh, three thousand miles away?

We do what we can. We do what we have to do. Even when our hearts are pounding and pumping pain out into our brains, and our stomachs are churning knots of broken glass. We do what we can.

I scooped up Monique. She was totally limp, a rag doll with more deadweight than seemed possible. And almost more than I could handle right now. I had to get my bad leg straight out, bend the good one, and drape her over my shoulder. Then I pulled myself up to my feet using the gunwale. It took forever, and I thought I would black out when I finally got up. But I didn't. Somehow I got up and managed a step toward the door that led below—and was almost beheaded by the cargo hook. It was swinging crazily in the storm wind and it whipped past my ear fast enough to leave a vapor trail.

But it missed me, and I got Monique below without dropping either one of us onto the deck. I pulled back the covers on the bunk. They were pretty far from clean, but there were bigger issues right now. I laid her down and pulled the covers up. She still looked more dead than anything else, and I checked her pulse again. Still going, very faintly.

I straightened up and looked at her lying there on the filthy bunk. That beautiful face battered and slack, all that talent and smartness and ornery independence locked up inside a brain that might be checking out already. Maybe a slow leak in some small blood vessel that would kill her anytime in the next twelve hours. Maybe something in there damaged and straining, stretching, ready to burst and kill her quickly. And maybe she'd wake up and be physically just fine—but it wouldn't be Monique any more, just a dull stranger with her face.

"Live, goddamn it," I told her. She'd never been good at taking orders. I really hoped she'd listen this time.

I took another few seconds to tuck her in tight, so the covers would hold her in place when the boat pitched and rolled.

Which it was doing right now, a lot rougher than it had a few minutes ago. I hadn't paid any attention to the boat or the weather, and it was reminding me just how freaking stupid that was. As I straightened from securing Monique, there was a massive thunderclap, and with one great gust of wind the rain began to slam into the hull. The boat heeled over a little too far for my liking, and I didn't need to tune in the Weather Channel to know the storm had arrived. And that meant I had get up to the wheel pretty quick.

I put a hand on the door to the deck and at the last second remembered the hook, still swinging out on deck, so I ducked low as I pushed it open.

That saved my life.

The knife slashed a half inch over my head and came for me again on the back stroke. I twisted back and it missed me by a quarter inch this time, and almost as close I heard a hiss that was half animal and half something from a bad movie.

Bernadette stood there in the doorway in a blinding spray of rain and wind, and she looked twice as wild as the storm. Her hair was plastered to her head, and one eye was swollen shut from the thump she'd taken from the cargo hook. But the other eye, the one in the melted part of her face, was wide open, bloodshot, and filled with hate. As I stared and wondered what the hell it took to kill her, or if it was even possible, she stepped at me with her knife up for another try.

Before she could gut me I pulled the door toward me as hard as I could. It caught her on the wrist and I heard something crack—I couldn't tell if it was the door or her wrist, but all that mattered was that the knife clattered to the floor. I heard her grunt, and I pushed on the door as hard as I'd pulled. It caught her in the chest and pushed her back out onto the deck, and I stumbled out after her.

I had no idea what I was going to try to do, but I knew if I didn't stay on her and do something, she would have me, even without her knife. It was one of the hardest things I've ever done, and I don't mean because I was so beat-up I could hardly stand. It was her. In my mind, Bernadette had turned into some kind of undead monster, an immortal thing that would just keep coming at me until it got me and shredded me into a heap of red ribbons.

But I had to try, even though I was half sure she couldn't be killed. I went at her as fast as I could, and she was faster. She swung a kick at my head, and I blocked it—but my arm went numb. I took a feeble step forward to get inside the arc of her kick and threw a punch. It hit her as she sidestepped, so the impact was much less, and as the punch pulled me past her she swung an elbow that caught me on the jaw and knocked me off my feet.

I scrabbled away across the rain-slick deck toward the stern of the boat, and she came right after, stomping on my bad leg. I wanted to scream with the pain, but before I could she landed a kick on my good knee that took the breath out of me. I was pretty sure that if she got me with another one like that I'd break into small pieces, but I was halfway to shattered already, and on a slippery deck already, so what could I do?

Really stupid, I know, but one more time I heard Mom: *Turn your stumbling blocks into stepping-stones!* And this time I knew right away what that meant.

As Bernadette was raising her foot to crash it down and finish me, I whipped around on the slippery deck, like a fidget spinner. Her foot was already up, and with my bad leg I crashed into her plant foot, the one still on the deck. It probably hurt me more than it did her. The shock of it went through me and took the pain of my leg into another dimension—but Bernadette went down and I hauled myself to the gunwale and onto my feet.

I got up just in time to see her scramble to her feet, too. She stood there panting a little, staring at me with that one red eye in the monster face, and then she smiled, because she knew, just as sure as I did, that I was out of moves and backed against the gunwale with no room to do anything but let her come and kill me.

So she stood there for a second enjoying it, and all I

could do was watch her. And then I caught sight of the hook, still swinging in its crazy arc behind her. My eyes flicked to it, hoping for a repeat miracle—and she saw me look. She turned and dodged, and the hook sailed harmlessly past her. It came straight at me, and now it was my turn to dodge and I couldn't.

So I caught the hook, grabbing the steel cable with one hand and the hook with the other. It stung but I got it, and I wasted a second staring at it, dangling from my hands by the steel cable. I looked up at Bernadette, sure she was slithering at me, coming for the kill.

She wasn't. She was staring at the hook hanging from my hands and she wasn't smirking anymore, and I couldn't figure out why.

I'd like to say it was just all the beating up I'd taken, the blows on the head, the swollen and damaged leg, all the extra pain that seemed to fill every nook and cranny of my body, but let's face it. It was just plain good old-fashioned stupid. I was so completely convinced I had to run from her I just couldn't think about attacking Bernadette. I was so used to her having all the weapons and the supernatural mojo, and me just trying to get away from her, that it took me a couple of seconds before I remembered what I had in my hands.

A weapon. The cargo hook was a weapon.

And just as I realized that, Bernadette figured out that I was slow to catch on and she came at me. I had just enough time to swing the hook and let it fly sidearm.

And it missed her.

Because I threw sidearm, though, the hook curled

as it went past her, and just as it began to swing back I got both hands on the cable and yanked. Hard. As hard as I have ever yanked on anything. To be honest, I just wanted to hit her with the hook, slam her to her knees, hurt her since she couldn't be killed, at least slow her, and I screwed that up, too.

But.

I said I yanked hard. Looking back, maybe too hard. What can I say? I definitely had a lot of adrenaline happening. And I admit I didn't like her, and she scared me, and I half believed she couldn't be killed. So I put everything I had into that yank—but I swear I never thought it would happen like this.

When I pulled the cable, the hook bit into Bernadette's back, just below the ribs. It went into her. And it stuck. When I yanked it was like setting the hook in a really big bass. That hook went deep into her side and stuck there. Bernadette said, "Aaaaggghuh," or words to that effect, and for a moment the two of us froze like that. I mean, she had that hook in her, and I was in a kind of a freaked-out funk, and I'm not sure which of us was more shocked.

Well, okay, to be fair, I'm pretty sure Bernadette was more shocked. She put a hand down to the hook, not like pulling it out, just sort of caressing it, which looked so damn wrong it kept me staring, unable to move. And then she looked at me and this expression came onto her face that made it seem like all that melted scar tissue on one side had taken over her whole face and she was bringing it all to me—

She took a step forward. At me. With a steel hook stabbed into her.

I was right. She couldn't be killed. I know that sounds stupid when you are far away and it's happening to somebody else—but it was happening to *me*. I was on a boat getting hammered by a storm, and something that looked like a movie monster was coming at me, and I had seen the creature hit with enough to kill four or five superheroes, and it was still coming at me. None of us are really very far away from being half-monkey savages hiding from the dark in a cave. At a certain point, that monkey-man takes over, and ghosts are real, and the darkness is filled with things that cannot die—and I was there now, with one of the things from the darkness coming at me.

She took another step forward.

I couldn't move. I could just watch her, feeling the hair stand up all over my body. Another step—and I was filled with a blind, unthinking terror—but suddenly I *had* to move. I was jammed against the gunwale and couldn't retreat any farther—I needed to find a weapon. Without taking my eyes off Bernadette, I scrabbled blindly behind me for something, anything—a rock, a big stick, anything at all to hit her with. All I found was some kind of metal lever sticking up from the gunwale. It felt like it was only a few inches long, but it was metal and it was all there was. I pulled at it. It stuck. I pulled harder, pulled in another direction—

And Bernadette jerked to a stop.

I was so sure she couldn't be stopped that it took me

a moment to see it. But the cable attached to the hook had gone tight—so tight she could no longer move forward. And as I blinked at this miracle, and she tried to take another step forward, she went backward.

Just a little. And she struggled against it and the tiny part of me that could think at all through the cloud of caveman terror was sure she would break away and keep coming forward. But she didn't. She stayed stopped. And then . . .

Bernadette began to rise up into the air.

It's hard to explain this, but at the time it made perfect sense.

I mean, in my mind she had already turned into some kind of supernatural *thing,* so yeah—of course she could fly. And I just stood and watched for a couple of seconds before it occurred to me that—wait a minute; really? I turned around and looked at the gunwale. The piece of metal I'd grabbed was the dual controls for the cargo hook. Bernadette wasn't really flying back to Oz. I had jammed the control lever down to wind in the cable; that was all.

I turned back and took another couple of seconds to watch Bernadette fly anyway. Seriously, why wouldn't I? It was partly fear that she'd jump down and come after me again—but the other part was just pure old-fashioned fun. She had a big hook stuck in her gut, and it was hauling her up into the air—yay! At last, right in front of my eyes, somebody truly bad was getting what they deserved. That almost never happens.

I finally snapped out of it and reached for the cargo

hook's controls. I'm not sure what I meant to do, and I never got to figure it out, because just when I got my hand on the lever again, a truly big wave came over the transom and knocked me off my feet. I held on to the lever as I fell, until my fall yanked it out of my hand. The boat rolled horribly, the water sloshed over me, the cargo arm swung wildly out over the side of the boat, with Bernadette dangling on the end, and another giant crash of thunder nearly deafened me.

I spit salt water and wiped my eyes clear, but I didn't need to look too hard to know. We were in danger of broaching to, filling with water, and sinking. All of a sudden, that seemed more interesting than watching Bernadette fly away.

I pulled myself to my feet on a deck now ankle-deep in water, and more pouring on board every second. So I forgot about Bernadette and floundered up to the bridge. Even harder now; my injuries were worse, I was wading through water, and the boat was rolling like a hog in mud. I pulled myself up the ladder as another giant wave slopped over the transom. But we were still floating, and I got to the controls. I turned us back on course, turned on the pumps, and prayed.

It was a very busy forty minutes later that the island came in sight. The storm had not let up, but we were no longer taking on water, and the pumps had done their job. We were going to make it to the dock. The crew Bernadette had summoned would be waiting for us, and then—

Bernadette.

I jerked around and looked back, and she was gone. For just a second I was scared witless—and then I saw the steel cable of the cargo crane. It hung over the side, half slack. When the wave knocked me over I must have jammed the control lever forward, unspooling all the cable and dumping Bernadette into the ocean. I thought it might be a good idea to leave her there. I was pretty sure there were things in these waters that would eat just about anything—great white sharks especially. That made me smile. I felt sorry for the shark that tried to take a bite out of Bernadette.

The crew was waiting on the pier. I didn't think they'd heard what had happened on Île des Choux; it was too soon. And anyway, they weren't about to argue with anything Bernadette had told them to do. They gave me a couple of odd looks—I mean, they must have wondered where she had gone. I thought it might be a bad idea to show them. Instead, I just took over her role and ordered them around. We got Monique onto the little cart and across the island to the jet, and half an hour later we were in the air.

The flight to Cape Town took forever. I sat beside Monique the whole time, just watching her. Nothing changed. She was breathing, her heart was beating, and that was it.

An ambulance was waiting when we landed. It took us straight to what was supposed to be the best hospital in South Africa. The doctors took one look at Monique and got very serious looks on their faces. They put her on a gurney and rolled her quickly away, and I followed, up until we got to surgery. They wouldn't let me in, wouldn't even start to operate until I agreed to go sit in the waiting room.

I did. I sat in the waiting room and waited. The magazines were lousy, the coffee from the vending machine was worse, and the smell of medicine and anguish was overwhelming.

I just fucking *hate* hospitals. I hoped this was a good one.

I waited.

CHAPTER
44

In the three and a half weeks since the raid on Île des Choux, Frank Delgado had really had time for only three things: paperwork, interviewing prisoners, and more paperwork. Normally, this was exactly the sort of bureaucratic routine BS that made Delgado crazy. But this time, he didn't really mind. He had a clear and simple happy thought that kept him going as he waded through endless heaps of official forms, prisoner transfers, interview transcripts, and itemized expense forms.

Riley Wolfe's mother.

The thought was never far from his consciousness. The first telephone call he'd made when they returned from the Kerguelen Islands was to the surveillance team around Wolfe's mother. She was still there, the team was ready and waiting, and everything was as it should be. Yes, Riley Wolfe himself had slipped away—again—and was now at large. But Delgado had his mother under constant watch. And Riley Wolfe always came back to her. *Always.* When he did, he would find the FBI waiting for him.

So Frank Delgado waded manfully through three and a half weeks of soul-crushing tedium, and for the first ten days he had done so with something very close to a smile on his face. But as time passed and Riley Wolfe did not turn up at his mother's bedside, the almost-smile faded. It was replaced by a worried frown.

It had been too long. Wolfe should have returned by now.

When he did not, Delgado speculated that perhaps he had been injured, or even killed. The only reason to believe he was alive and had escaped Île des Choux during the raid was Rosemond's sketchy description of the man who had limped down to the dock and taken a boat. Delgado had, of course, done his due diligence and checked the story. All members of the French team were accounted for. None of them had gone back for "medical supplies."

The story fit Riley Wolfe perfectly. It *had* to have been him. That meant he had left alive and well, except for the limp. So why hadn't he hurried back to check on his mother?

Delgado worried at that for a few days. There were plenty of possible reasons, but none of them felt right. Delgado knew only a very little about Wolfe, but he knew that Riley would have made a beeline to his mother as soon as he returned. If he was alive and at liberty, he would head there as soon as possible. That was his pattern. But he hadn't.

One of the things that made Frank Delgado a successful investigator was his ability to think outside the box. He had solved many puzzling cases in his career by turning assumptions on their heads and looking at things from a different angle. And when he finally did that with this puzzle, he came up with a very troubling thought.

Assume Wolfe was alive and free. No point to the surveillance otherwise. He would have been to see his mother by now.

Assume further that he would stick to his habitual pattern and visit his mother ASAP. He would have been there already.

He had not been there. His mother was under tight surveillance 24/7, and she'd had no visitors. Period. That ruled out one of his ingenious disguises.

Therefore . . .

There was really only one answer. And it was an answer Delgado hated. Usually, he got a feeling of satisfaction when he came up with a creative answer. This time, he just felt sick.

But it was not certain, not yet. Delgado put the stack of paperwork aside and leaned back in his desk chair. If he was wrong, Riley Wolfe was in jail, injured, or even dead. Jail was out—Delgado would have heard. Injured? He had been limping when last seen, but beyond that? It was possible but seemed unlikely. He had escaped two elite teams, neutralized Stone and Boniface—who was left to injure him? And dead? Of course, accidents happen. But again, it was long odds. Delgado was convinced that Wolfe had escaped, relatively unhurt. And he had not visited his mother.

He was back to his painful conclusion. But how could he prove it was right? Or maybe wrong, although Delgado held little hope of that. He was, sadly, quite sure he had found the answer. But proof?

Delgado got up, walked to the coffee machine, poured a cup, and thought as he walked back to his desk, sipping. By the time he sat down again he had an answer. One simple phone call should do it. But he didn't make the call. He sat and finished his coffee, delaying as long as he could. When the coffee was gone, he waited a few minutes more. And then, with a sigh, he made the phone call.

One of the agents on the surveillance team was Special Agent Martha Chen, posing as one of the nursing home's staff. She had nurse's credentials, which had come in handy for other undercover jobs in the past. Delgado called her and told her what he wanted. She understood immediately and promised to call back quickly.

"Quickly" turned out to be a day and a half. Delgado spent the time taking Tums and trying to concentrate on prisoner interview transcripts. When Chen finally called back, he was ready to bite somebody.

"You were right," Special Agent Chen told him.

Delgado nodded and reached for the Tums. "There's no doubt?"

"No doubt at all," Chen said. "I compared the medical records from the first place, Creedmore? That's where she was when we initiated surveillance?"

"I remember," Delgado said.

"So I got the file from Creedmore," Chen said. "I looked over her charts, bio data, everything. The meds all match. Otherwise we would have known right away. But the rest of it? Height, weight, vitals—they just plain do not match with this woman," Chen said. "She's an inch and a half taller. Body weight has increased by more than fifteen pounds. That's a hell of a lot of weight to gain on an IV diet. Also," she said, "vital signs are way off, brain wave patterns different—It's two different women. No doubt at all."

Delgado thanked her and hung up.

The outside-the-box answer had been right. Riley Wolfe had not changed his pattern. He had changed his mother. Somewhere along the way, when his real mother was being moved, she had been swapped out for some other comatose woman. They had even found the GPS trackers planted on the mother's body and switched them. Which meant, of course, that Riley Wolfe had been on to them from the very first. He had even *used* the FBI, just as Delgado had feared, to break him out of his impossible situation. He had sent that woman, "Betty," with a baited hook he knew Delgado could not ignore.

And Frank Delgado had not ignored it. He had snapped it up eagerly, swallowed the hook, and done exactly what Riley Wolfe wanted him to do. Worse,

Delgado had done it knowingly, thinking he was one step ahead this time. He had not been. Just like always, he had been a step behind. Riley Wolfe had played him perfectly. And Frank Delgado had lost again.

For a few minutes he just sat. He really wished he hadn't asked Chen to check. At least for a few more days. It had been very pleasant to think that for once, finally, he had a handle on Riley Wolfe. He should have known better.

Riley Wolfe had slipped away again.

Delgado allowed himself a couple of moments of quiet misery. Then he swallowed a handful of Tums, reached for the next transcript, and went back to work.

Father Matteo stared upward, to the space above the scaffolding. The airtight plastic sealer installed by Campinelli—or whatever his name really was—was firmly in place. And Father Matteo had been staring up at it for four weeks, for hours at a time, tilting his head up until the pain in his neck from craning it upward became intolerable. There was no conceivable reason for this. It couldn't help in any way. Father Matteo knew that. He recognized that the behavior was irrational and even foolish. He stared anyway. And when his neck grew too sore to continue, he would walk away, go back to his other duties. And he would keep wondering, until he couldn't stand it any longer. Then he would go back and stare again.

What if Captain Koelliker had been right?

What if somehow, impossibly, this thief had found a way to steal *The Liberation of St. Peter*? The very idea was too fantastic to consider—and yet . . . Koelliker was not a fool. Even after Father Matteo had explained what a fresco was, that it was part of the actual wall— even then, Koelliker apparently believed that this particular thief could find a way to steal it. If so . . . if he had really done the impossible and stolen the fresco . . .

The hole in his heart would be far bigger than the one in the Stanza di Eliodoro.

But what could he do? He prayed, of course. But other than that? There was no possible action that could help in any way. He had to wait, had to follow the urgent instructions to leave the seal in place, because there was no way to know if the thief had told the truth—no way short of removing the seal, and that he could not do, even if Koelliker was correct that this would give the thief time to escape safely. The choice between letting a thief escape and even the smallest chance of damage to the fresco—it was no choice at all. Father Matteo would gladly liberate every thief in Europe to protect such a great work of art.

And so he had waited. And he had stared upward and then walked away with a sore neck, every single day.

Until today.

Today Father Matteo would take off the seal and see for himself if—

In his mind, it always stopped at "if." A stolen fresco was impossible—but all kinds of other damage was not. If damage had been done, left untouched beneath the seal for all this time so that it became permanent mutilation—no. He could not accept that. A ruined fresco was unthinkable. Of course it was possible, but no, he refused to believe it. As a man of faith—of *reasoned* faith, he believed—he had to believe that God, in this holy place, would not permit such a desecration.

And so Father Matteo had waited a full four weeks to remove the seal, even though every day, every moment, was torture. But he refused to weaken. He had fixed his mind firmly on the longer period. Not the minimal three weeks, but the full four. Again, there was no logical reason for this. But there was a compelling *illogical* reason, and Father Matteo embraced it. He had waited the extra week for what he told himself was a very Catholic motive. This fourth week was penance, punishment and atonement for a sin Father Matteo could not name and had not committed. And he was quite unreasonably convinced that it would ensure the fresco's safety.

Pure superstition, and he knew it. But it had felt right, and the extra week of suffering gave him a certain amount of peace.

And so today, now, with the help of two junior members of the *museo*'s staff, he would remove the seal. He would finally see.

One last time he craned his neck up to the place where the wonderful fresco had been—where it would be again, when the seal came off! And this time, he looked up, not for any bootless attempt to see *through* the seal but to see what lay beneath. The two junior assistants, chosen for their strength, were up there now, on a scaffolding, one on each corner, carefully loosening the vacuum clamps that held the seal in place.

Father Matteo concentrated fiercely on the two young men, willing them to be cautious, precise in their movements. He focused on them so intently that he was quite unaware that Captain Koelliker had come up to stand behind him and watch.

One corner of the seal lurched—but the two young men steadied it, paused, and continued.

"Carefully, carefully," Father Matteo muttered. He was covered with sweat, his heart was pounding wildly, and he held his breath as the assistants loosened the clamps that held the seal in place. And then with agonizing slowness, the clamps came off, the two assistants lowered the seal, and Father Matteo began to pray, scarcely daring to look—

It was done.

The two assistants lowered the seal to the floor of the scaffolding. "Finito," one of the young men said triumphantly. The other called down to Father Matteo.

"Signor? Lavoro finito!" He pointed at the spot where the seal had been.

"Well," Captain Koelliker said, so close behind Father Matteo that the priest jumped, startled.

"Oh!" Father Matteo said. "Capitano, I did not see you!"

"No," Koelliker said. He pointed upward. "But you see this, hm?"

Father Matteo nodded, and both men looked at

what the two assistants had just revealed. "I see," he said. "I am not sure I believe it, but I see."

Captain Koelliker nodded. "Yes," he said. "I am quite sure I don't believe it."

Father Matteo sighed. "But there it is," he said.

And they stood together and looked.

Doctors are all assholes. They're usually the same guys you knew in high school who you wouldn't lend your pen to, because they might hurt themselves. But they spend a ton of money learning to say "elbow" in Latin, and they think that somehow makes them total hot shit, and they take revenge on you for not lending them the pen. They talk down to you, try to make you feel stupid, like you can't possibly understand what they're really saying, like you damn well better do just exactly what they tell you to do because they are always right and you're just a dumb lump of dog meat because you don't have an MD after your name.

I have seen doctors all over the world, and they're all the same. Oh, sure, they come in handy. I mean, when you got shot or get some horrible disease, I'm not saying you should go to an astrologer. You go to a doctor, and usually they make a good stab at fixing you up. They can even be heroic now and then—like Doctors Without Borders? Or the ones who risk their own lives during a plague like Ebola. Those doctors are the real deal, authentic heroes.

But you take your normal, everyday doctor, and give

them a chance to show off, do something spectacular that you couldn't do in a million years—they won't let you forget that they are in charge and you're only fit to sit somewhere and drink horrible vending machine coffee.

These doctors were true to type. They went into surgery all cheerful and optimistic, and came out looking sober and gloomy. Of course they had done everything possible, and done it incredibly well, but—? They gave me a whole long list of bullshit reasons why Monique would probably not recover. Too many hours lying around untreated, while the little vein in her head continued to leak and the pressure on her brain grew—and they made it sound like my fault. I mean, seriously, why hadn't I gotten her to them sooner? What was wrong with me? And then they went on with how this type of head injury is always chancy. Impossible to tell how much damage was already done. So much depended on the individual. Blah blah blah.

And they said that I should expect either no recovery or incomplete recovery. Best case? Impaired cognitive function, slurred speech, some loss of motor control—and most likely was that she would not recover at all and I would now have two women on my hands in persistent vegetative states.

Bullshit, bullshit, bullshit.

Monique would recover. I knew it. And not just the kind of recover where she opens her eyes, makes baby sounds, drools, and needs a diaper for the rest of her life. Monique was going to recover all the way, return to being *Monique*. She would wake up, look at me, and snarl, *What the fuck have you done now?* And she would go back to her studio, back to being the greatest art forger in the world, and someday, she would give in and we would hook up again. No way all that was over. No. Monique would get better. I never doubted that for even a second.

The doctors shook their heads and told me not to expect too much. They told me a complete recovery was highly unlikely.

I told them to go fuck themselves. Then I got Monique into a quiet and clean place to recover, just outside of Cape Town, and I got her the best around-the-clock nursing care I could find, and I watched them as they laid her on the bed, hooked her up to all the machines, and then tucked her in.

I stood over her and looked down at her face. It wasn't quite the same face I knew so well. The swelling had gone down, but the bruises had darkened and gotten bigger. And of course, her head was shaved, for the surgery, and there were bandages over the incisions. But it was still her face. It was Monique, and someday soon she would open her eyes and she would *be* Monique again. I knew she would. She had to.

I mean, I wasn't in love with her or anything stupid like that. And I didn't feel like it was my fault she was here. I didn't ask for any of the crap Boniface and Stone had poured onto the two of us. But I had handled it, for both of us. I got the two of them out of action, and I got us both out alive. Me. It was totally impossible, but I did it, and if Monique got banged up, I'm really and truly sorry, absolutely—but it wasn't my fault.

I had to say, though, that I couldn't have done it without her help. I knew she'd been freaking out the whole time, but she got it done. She held on to her character, and she did the job, and we got away with it. I was grateful for that. Hell, I would tell her so to her face, just as soon as she woke up. She did an amazingly great job. When I delivered the fresco to Boniface, it was such a perfect copy that he really and truly thought it was the original.

Of course it wasn't. It was Monique's absolutely perfect copy, made from her perfect cartoon. Because come on: You can't steal a fucking wall from the fucking Vatican.

But you *can* smuggle out that perfect cartoon. And you *can* take it to Frankfurt and transfer the image to plaster, pour on Dr. Sabharwal's amazing polymer goo, and then cart the thing all the way to Boniface, the lying bastard. Served him right to get fooled by a fake. Because it was a fake. It had to be, and he should have known it. You can't fucking steal a fucking wall from the fucking Vatican.

But guess what? You *can* steal the Urbino Bible. And I did. By the time Monique woke up, I would have the cash for it, and she would have her share, like always. Maybe with a bonus for all the doctor time. Yeah, she'd yell for a while, and call me names, just like always. But I'd get her laughing again. I always did. And someday, when we were back to normal, she would finally give in and give me a replay of that one amazing night we'd had together. Maybe more than one night this time. She would get better, and it would happen. I knew it would. It was just a matter of time.

I sat down beside her bed to wait.

ACKNOWLEDGMENTS

Special thanks to Dr. Alexander D. Schwab, associate professor of chemistry at Appalachian State University, who willingly embraced the concept of "plausible even if not necessarily likely," and provided background information on polymers. Thanks also to Stephanie and Kurt McClung, who helped me with the French dialogue—and more important, taught me that yes, indeed, Paris never disappoints. And thanks to Greg Parker, who suggested the title for this book when I couldn't think of one.